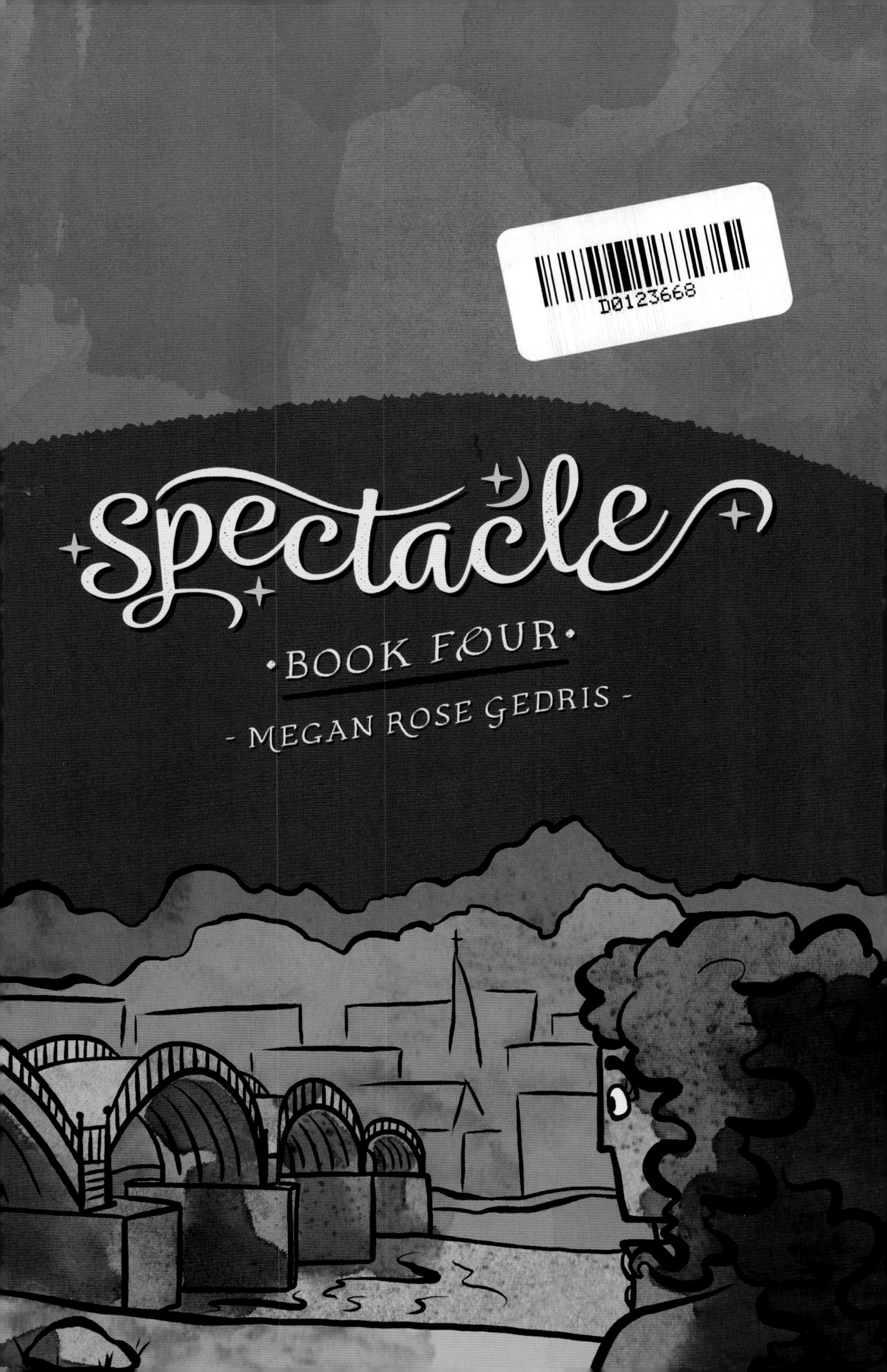
Spectacle
BOOK FOUR
- MEGAN ROSE GEDRIS -

Designed by Sarah Rockwell
Edited by Sarah Gaydos

PUBLISHED BY ONI-LION FORGE PUBLISHING GROUP, LLC

James Lucas Jones, president & publisher
Sarah Gaydos, editor in chief
Charlie Chu, e.v.p. of creative & business development
Alex Segura, s.v.p of marketing & sales
Brad Rooks, director of operations
Amber O'Neill, special projects manager
Margot Wood, director of marketing & sales
Katie Sainz, marketing manager
Tara Lehmann, publicist
Holly Aitchison, consumer marketing manager
Troy Look, director of design & production
Kate Z. Stone, senior graphic designer
Carey Hall, graphic designer
Sarah Rockwell, graphic designer
Hilary Thompson, graphic designer
Angie Knowles, digital prepress lead
Vincent Kukua, digital prepress technician
Jasmine Amiri, senior editor
Shawna Gore, senior editor
Amanda Meadows, senior editor
Robert Meyers, senior editor, licensing
Desiree Rodriguez, editor
Grace Scheipeter, editor
Zack Soto, editor
Chris Cerasi, editorial coordinator
Steve Ellis, vice president of games
Ben Eisner, game developer
Michelle Nguyen, executive assistant
Jung Lee, logistics coordinator
Joe Nozemack, publisher emeritus

onipress.com /lionforge.com

rosalarian.com
/rosalarian

First Edition: December 2021

ISBN 978-1-62010-981-6
eISBN 978-1-63715-034-4

1 2 3 4 5 6 7 8 9 10

Originally published as *Spectacle* #16-20.

Library of Congress Control Number: 2021939363

Printed in China.

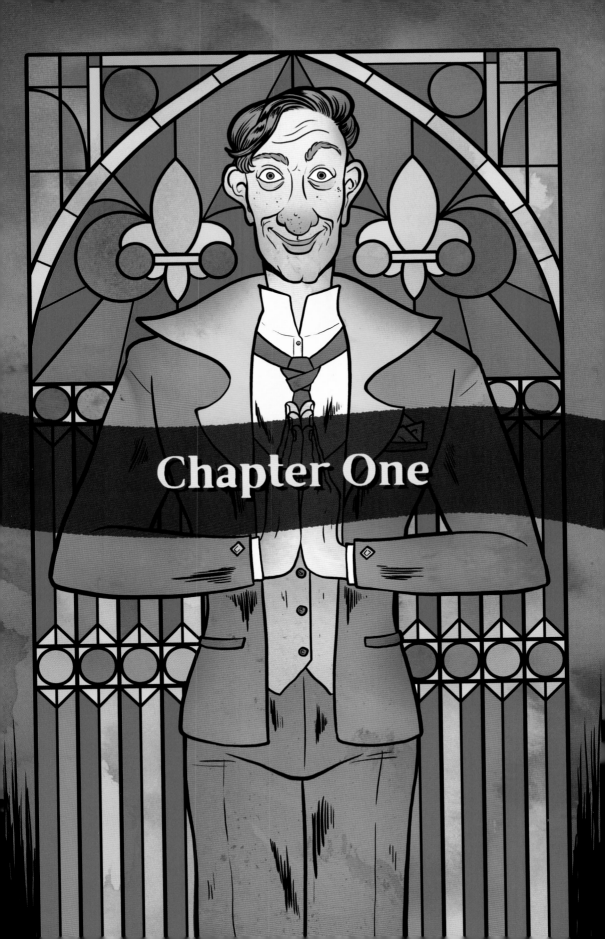

Chapter One

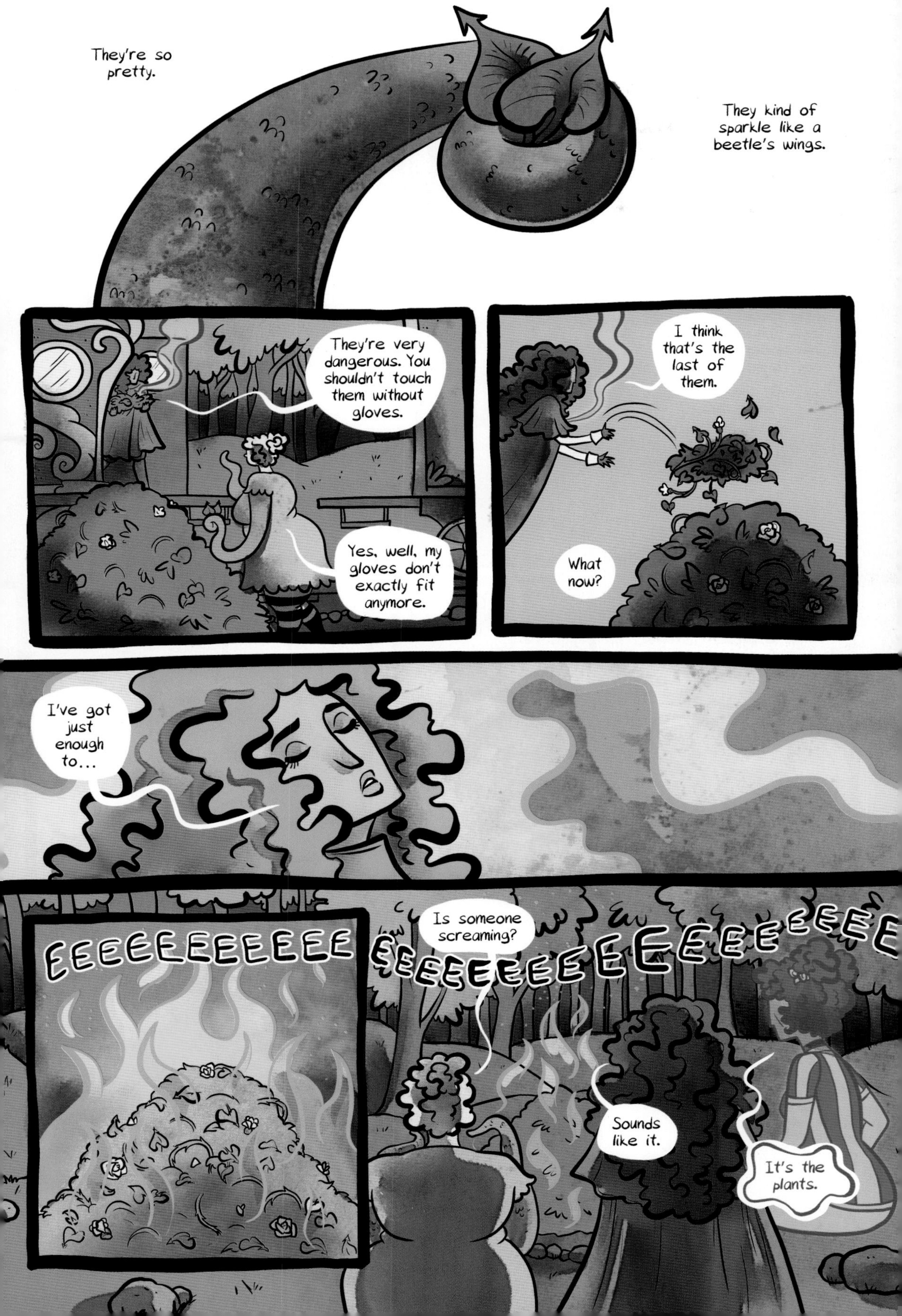
They're so pretty.
They kind of sparkle like a beetle's wings.
They're very dangerous. You shouldn't touch them without gloves.
Yes, well, my gloves don't exactly fit anymore.
I think that's the last of them.
What now?
I've got just enough to...
EEEEEEEEEEEE EEEEEEEEEEEEEEEEEEEE
Is someone screaming?
Sounds like it.
It's the plants.

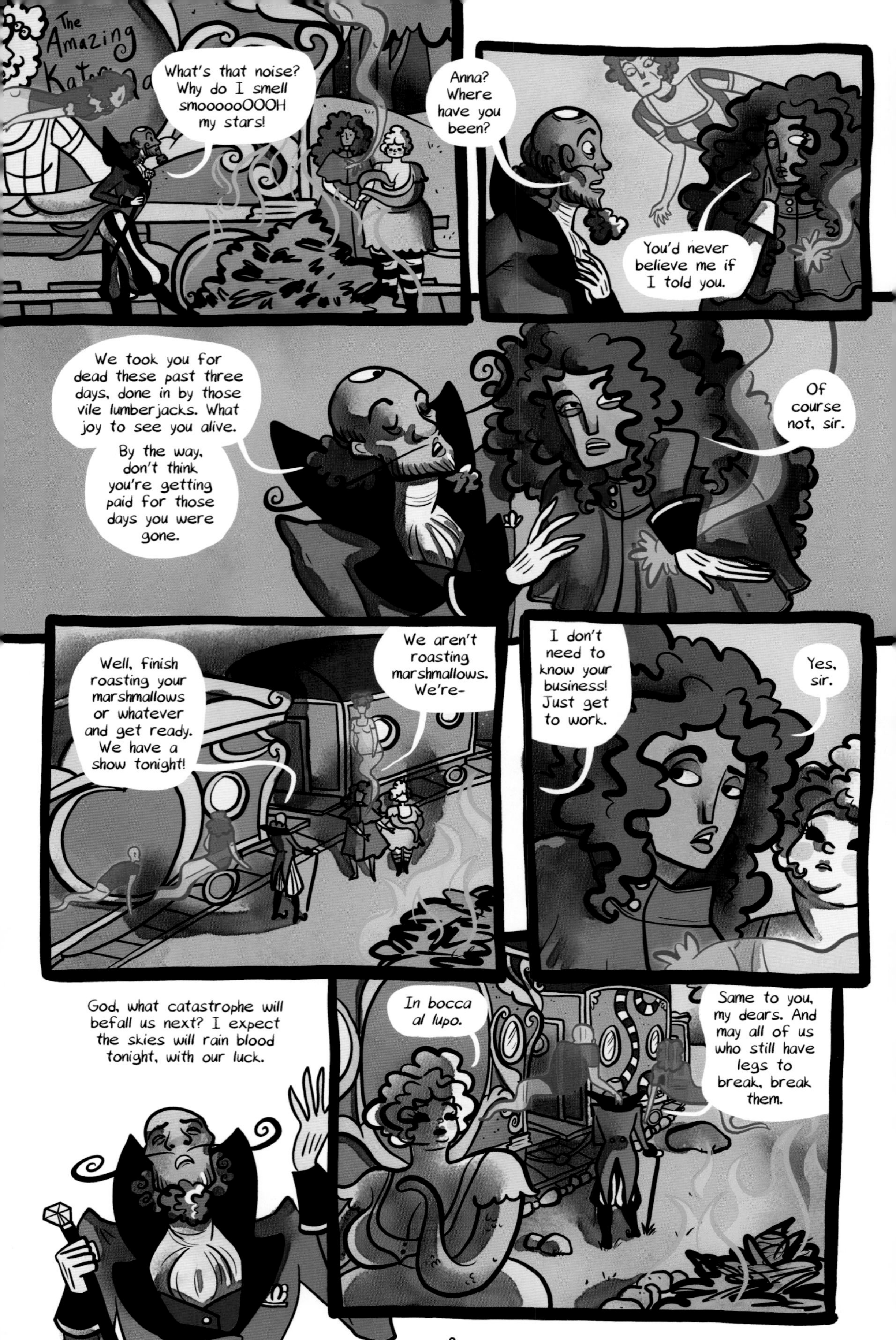
The Amazing
What's that noise? Why do I smell smooooo000H my stars!
Anna? Where have you been?
You'd never believe me if I told you.
We took you for dead these past three days, done in by those vile lumberjacks. What joy to see you alive.
By the way, don't think you're getting paid for those days you were gone.
Of course not, sir.
Well, finish roasting your marshmallows or whatever and get ready. We have a show tonight!
We aren't roasting marshmallows. We're-
I don't need to know your business! Just get to work.
Yes, sir.
God, what catastrophe will befall us next? I expect the skies will rain blood tonight, with our luck.
In bocca al lupo.
Same to you, my dears. And may all of us who still have legs to break, break them.

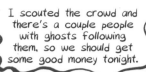

I scouted the crowd and there's a couple people with ghosts following them, so we should get some good money tonight.

Good. I'd like one stop on this tour to go smoothly.

Give me just a second. I think my crystal ball rolled under the table.

Hi.

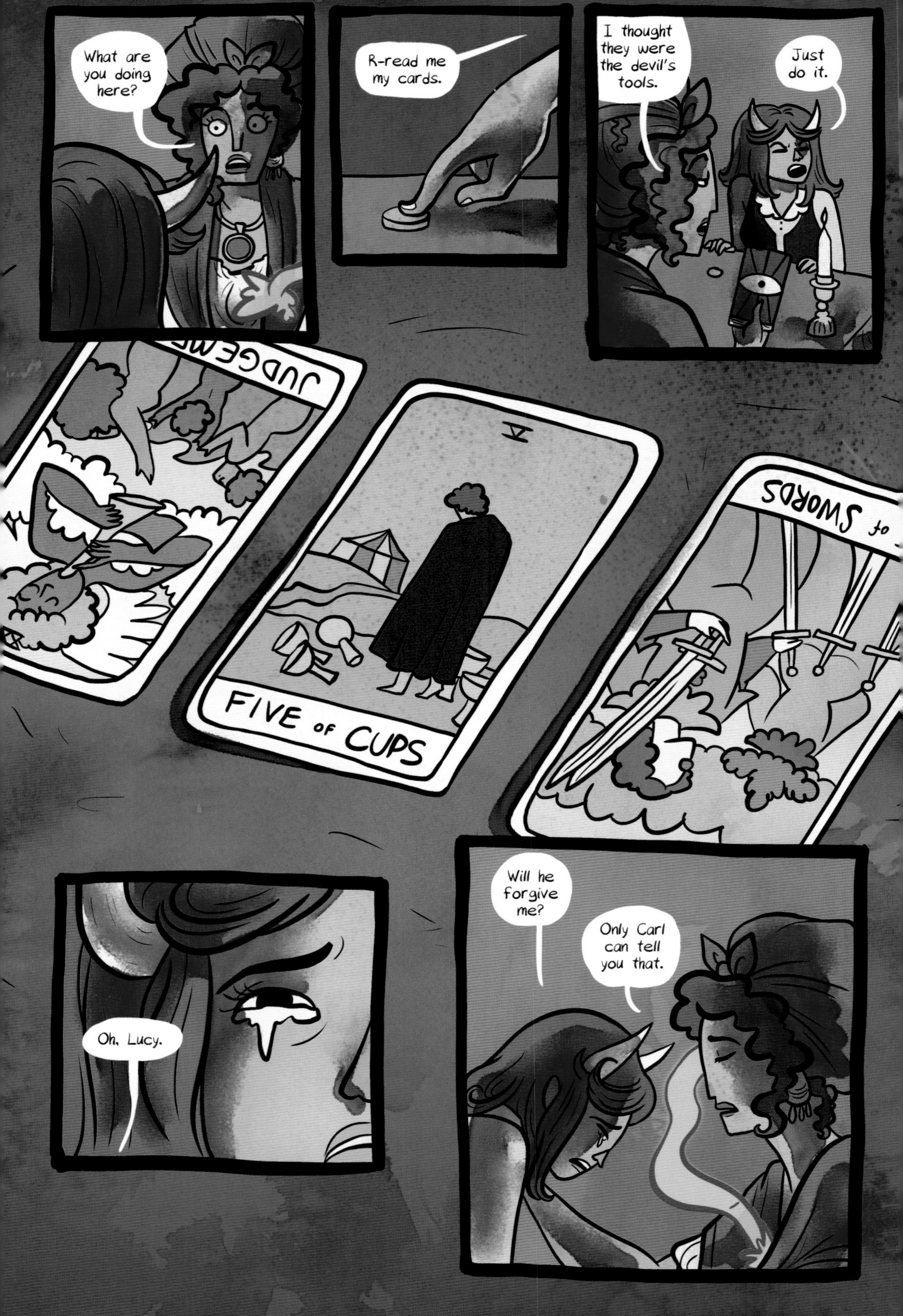
What are you doing here?
R-read me my cards.
I thought they were the devil's tools.
Just do it.
JUDGEMENT
FIVE of CUPS
SWORDS
Will he forgive me?
Only Carl can tell you that.
Oh, Lucy.

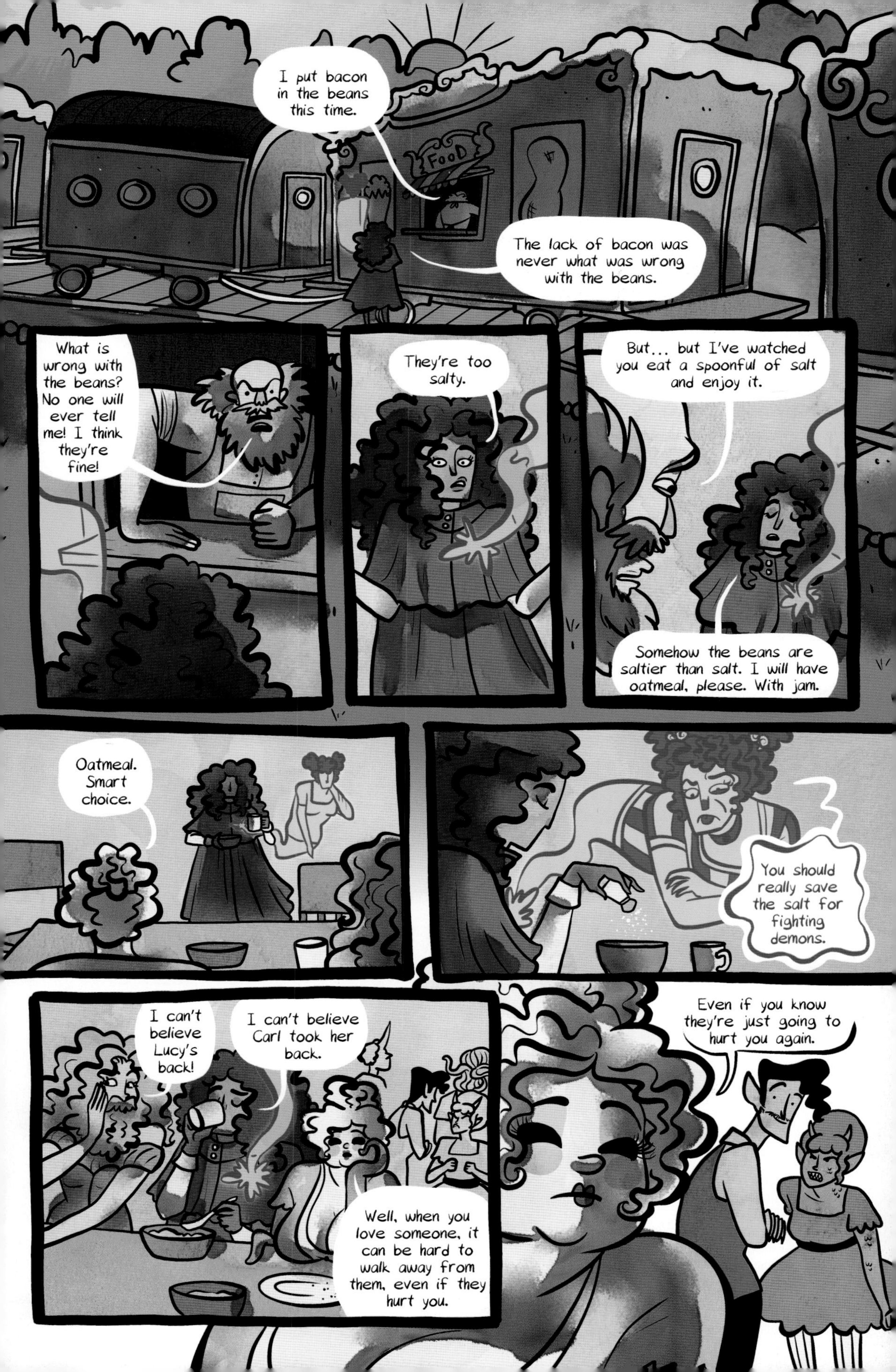

I put bacon in the beans this time.
The lack of bacon was never what was wrong with the beans.
What is wrong with the beans? No one will ever tell me! I think they're fine!
They're too salty.
But... but I've watched you eat a spoonful of salt and enjoy it.
Somehow the beans are saltier than salt. I will have oatmeal, please. With jam.
Oatmeal. Smart choice.
You should really save the salt for fighting demons.
I can't believe Lucy's back!
I can't believe Carl took her back.
Well, when you love someone, it can be hard to walk away from them, even if they hurt you.
Even if you know they're just going to hurt you again.
FOOD

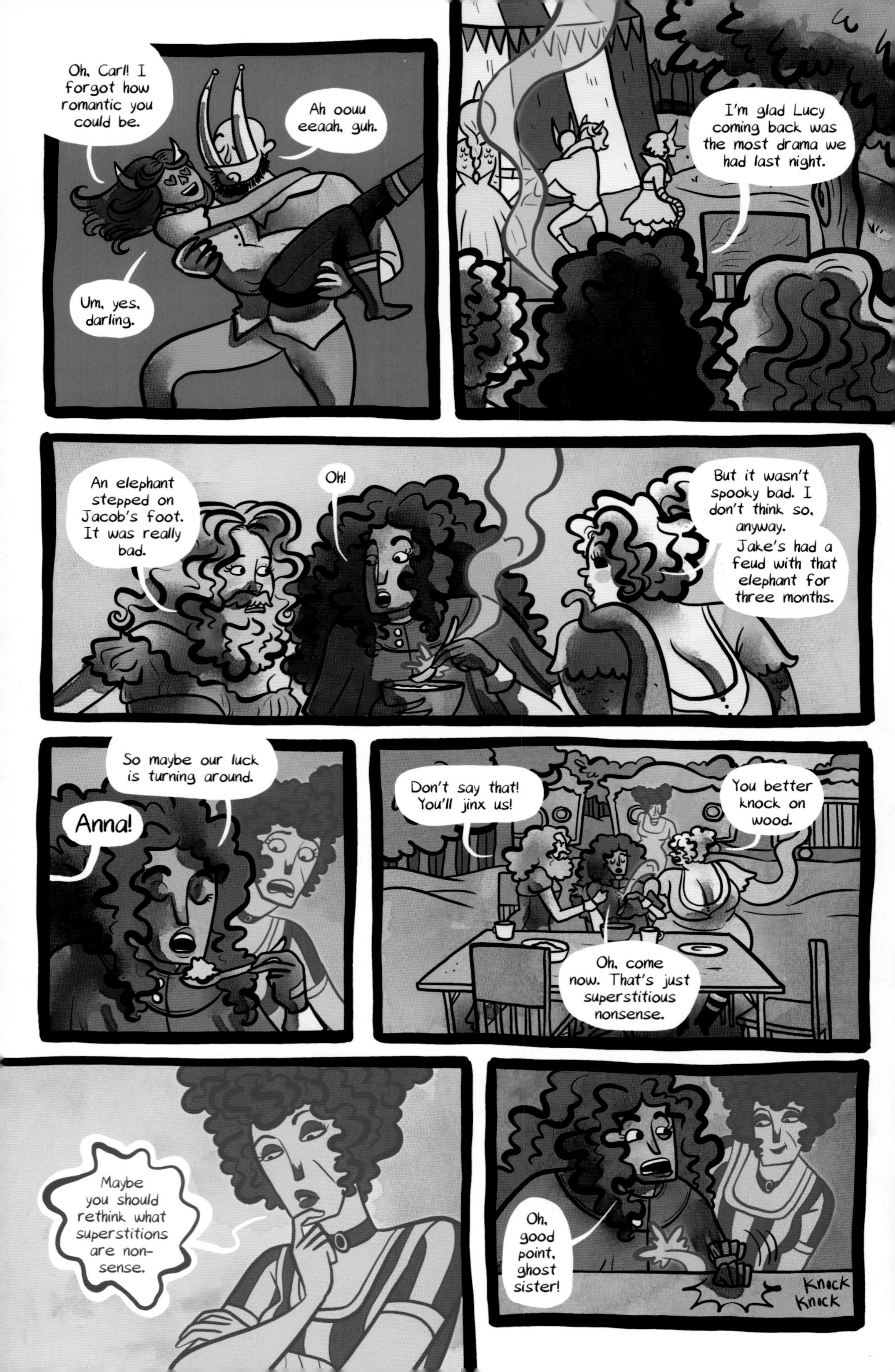

Oh, Carl! I forgot how romantic you could be.
Ah oouu eeaah, guh.
Um, yes, darling.
I'm glad Lucy coming back was the most drama we had last night.
An elephant stepped on Jacob's foot. It was really bad.
Oh!
But it wasn't spooky bad. I don't think so, anyway.
Jake's had a feud with that elephant for three months.
So maybe our luck is turning around.
Anna!
Don't say that! You'll jinx us!
You better knock on wood.
Oh, come now. That's just superstitious nonsense.
Maybe you should rethink what superstitions are non-sense.
Oh, good point, ghost sister!
Knock Knock

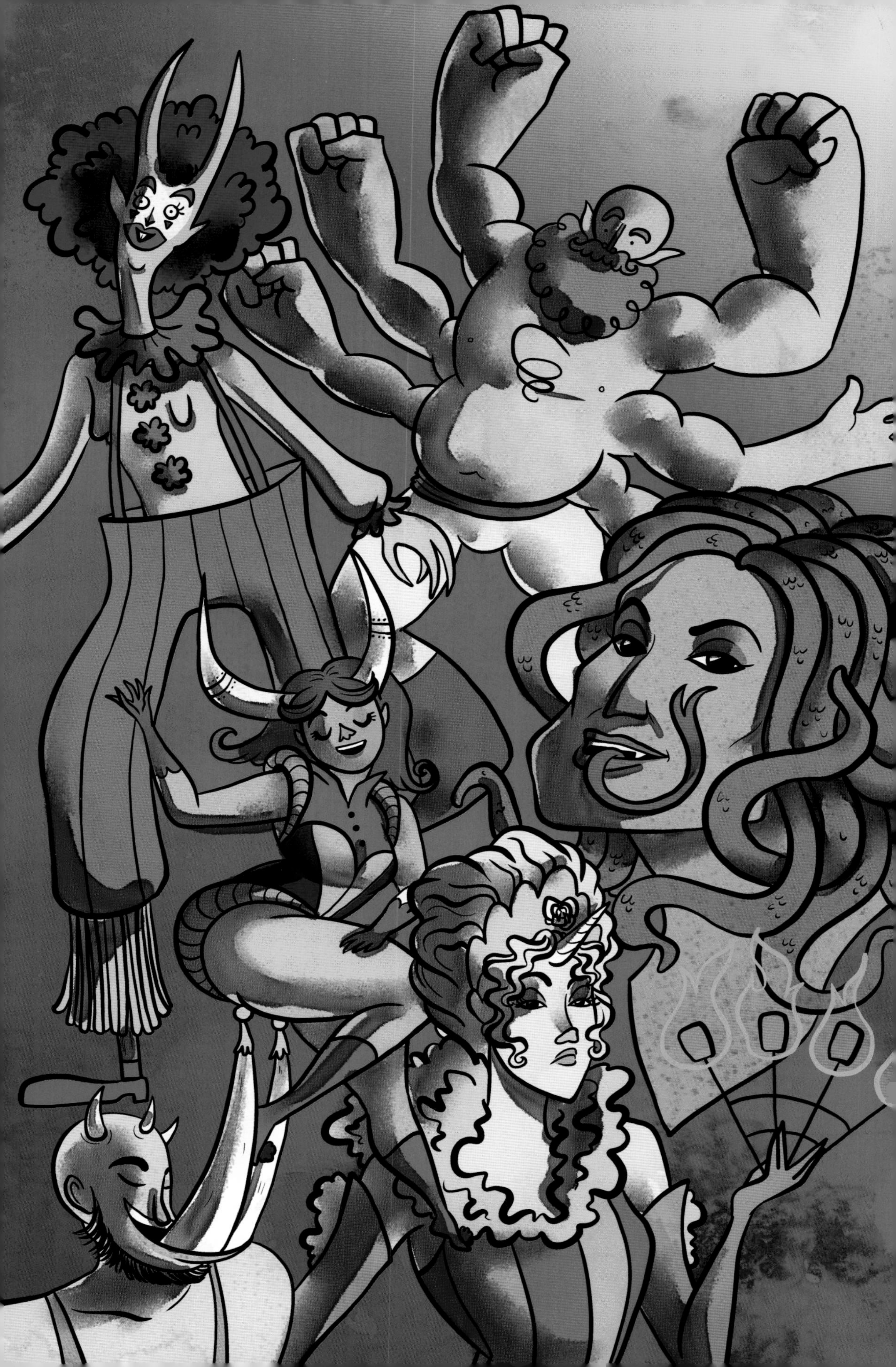

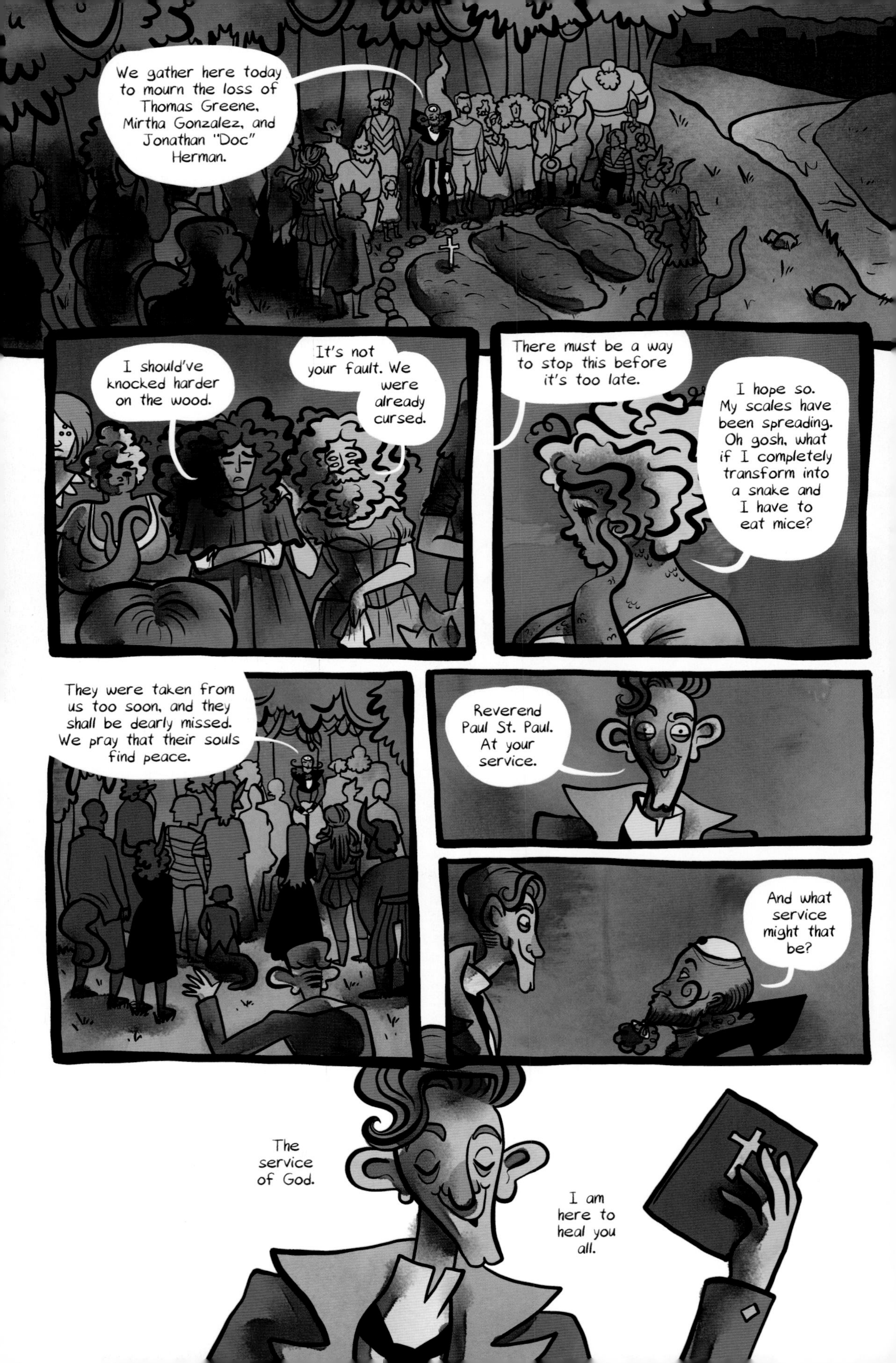
We gather here today to mourn the loss of Thomas Greene, Mirtha Gonzalez, and Jonathan "Doc" Herman.
I should've knocked harder on the wood.
It's not your fault. We were already cursed.
There must be a way to stop this before it's too late.
I hope so. My scales have been spreading. Oh gosh, what if I completely transform into a snake and I have to eat mice?
They were taken from us too soon, and they shall be dearly missed. We pray that their souls find peace.
Reverend Paul St. Paul. At your service.
And what service might that be?
The service of God.
I am here to heal you all.

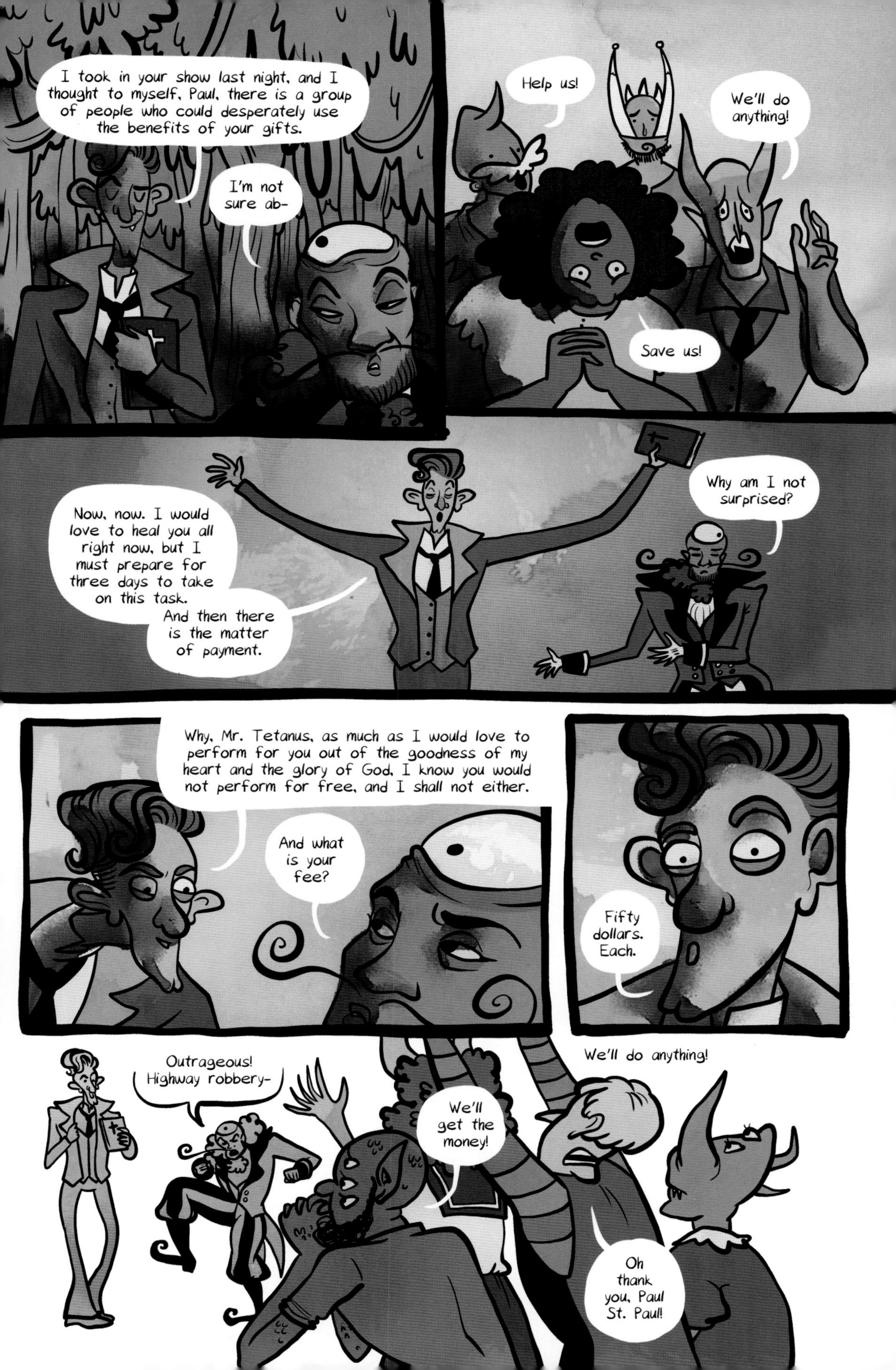
I took in your show last night, and I thought to myself, Paul, there is a group of people who could desperately use the benefits of your gifts.
I'm not sure ab-
Help us!
We'll do anything!
Save us!
Now, now. I would love to heal you all right now, but I must prepare for three days to take on this task.
And then there is the matter of payment.
Why am I not surprised?
Why, Mr. Tetanus, as much as I would love to perform for you out of the goodness of my heart and the glory of God, I know you would not perform for free, and I shall not either.
And what is your fee?
Fifty dollars. Each.
Outrageous! Highway robbery-
We'll get the money!
We'll do anything!
Oh thank you, Paul St. Paul!

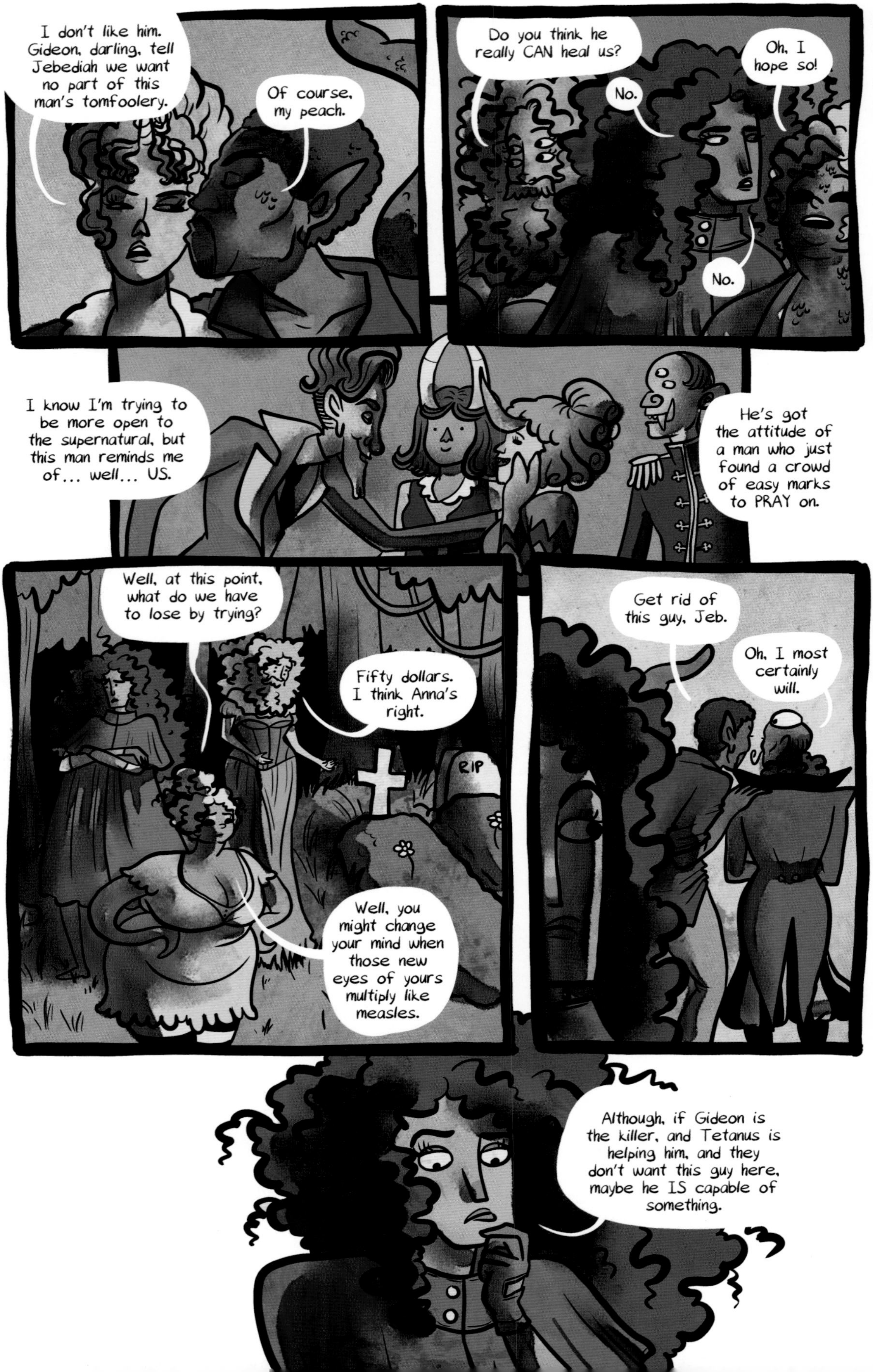

I don't like him. Gideon, darling, tell Jebediah we want no part of this man's tomfoolery.
Of course, my peach.
Do you think he really CAN heal us?
No.
Oh, I hope so!
No.
I know I'm trying to be more open to the supernatural, but this man reminds me of... well... US.
He's got the attitude of a man who just found a crowd of easy marks to PRAY on.
Well, at this point, what do we have to lose by trying?
Fifty dollars. I think Anna's right.
RIP
Well, you might change your mind when those new eyes of yours multiply like measles.
Get rid of this guy, Jeb.
Oh, I most certainly will.
Although, if Gideon is the killer, and Tetanus is helping him, and they don't want this guy here, maybe he IS capable of something.

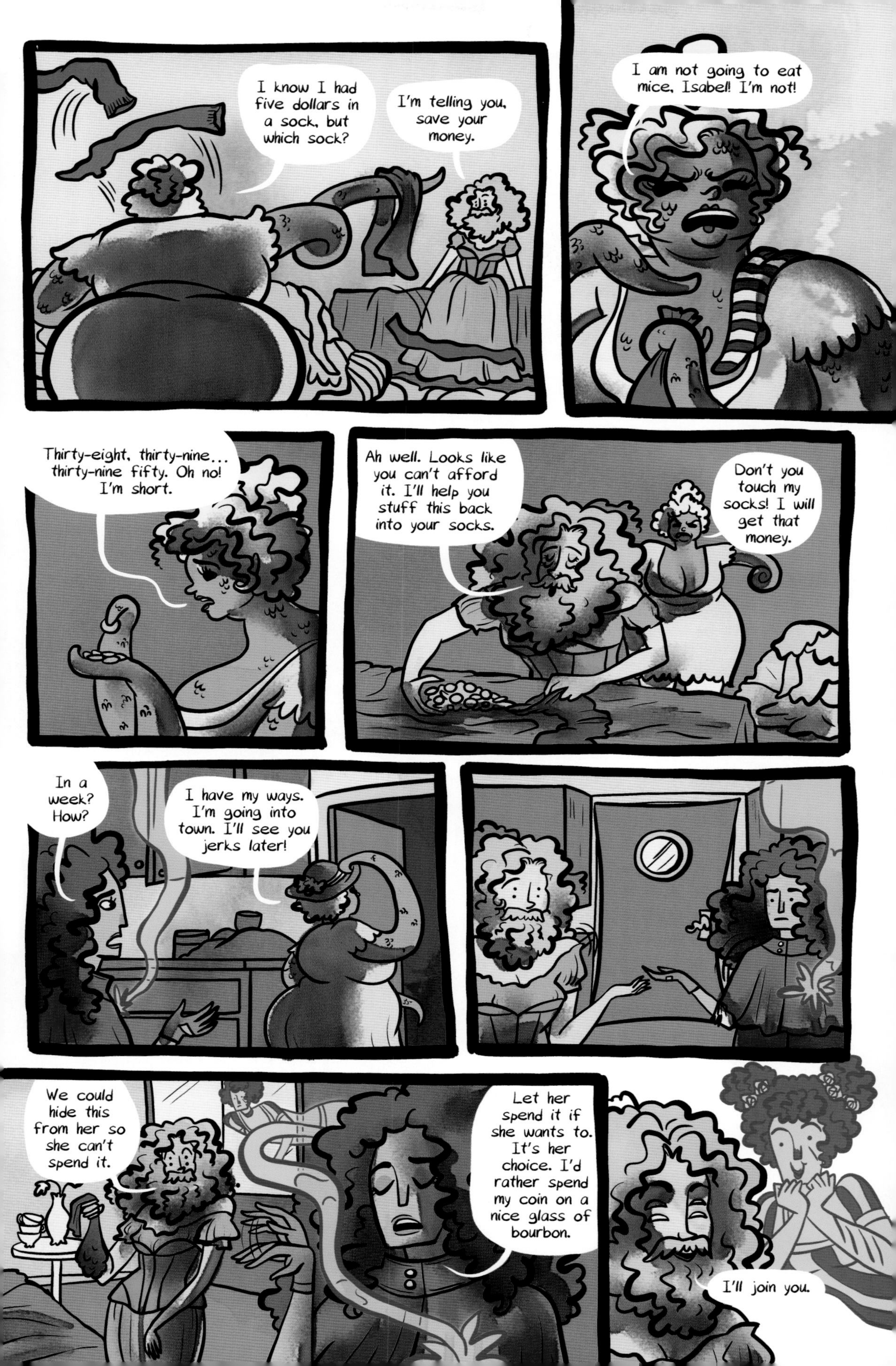
I know I had five dollars in a sock, but which sock?
I'm telling you, save your money.
I am not going to eat mice, Isabel! I'm not!
Thirty-eight, thirty-nine... thirty-nine fifty. Oh no! I'm short.
Ah well. Looks like you can't afford it. I'll help you stuff this back into your socks.
Don't you touch my socks! I will get that money.
In a week? How?
I have my ways. I'm going into town. I'll see you jerks later!
We could hide this from her so she can't spend it.
Let her spend it if she wants to. It's her choice. I'd rather spend my coin on a nice glass of bourbon.
I'll join you.

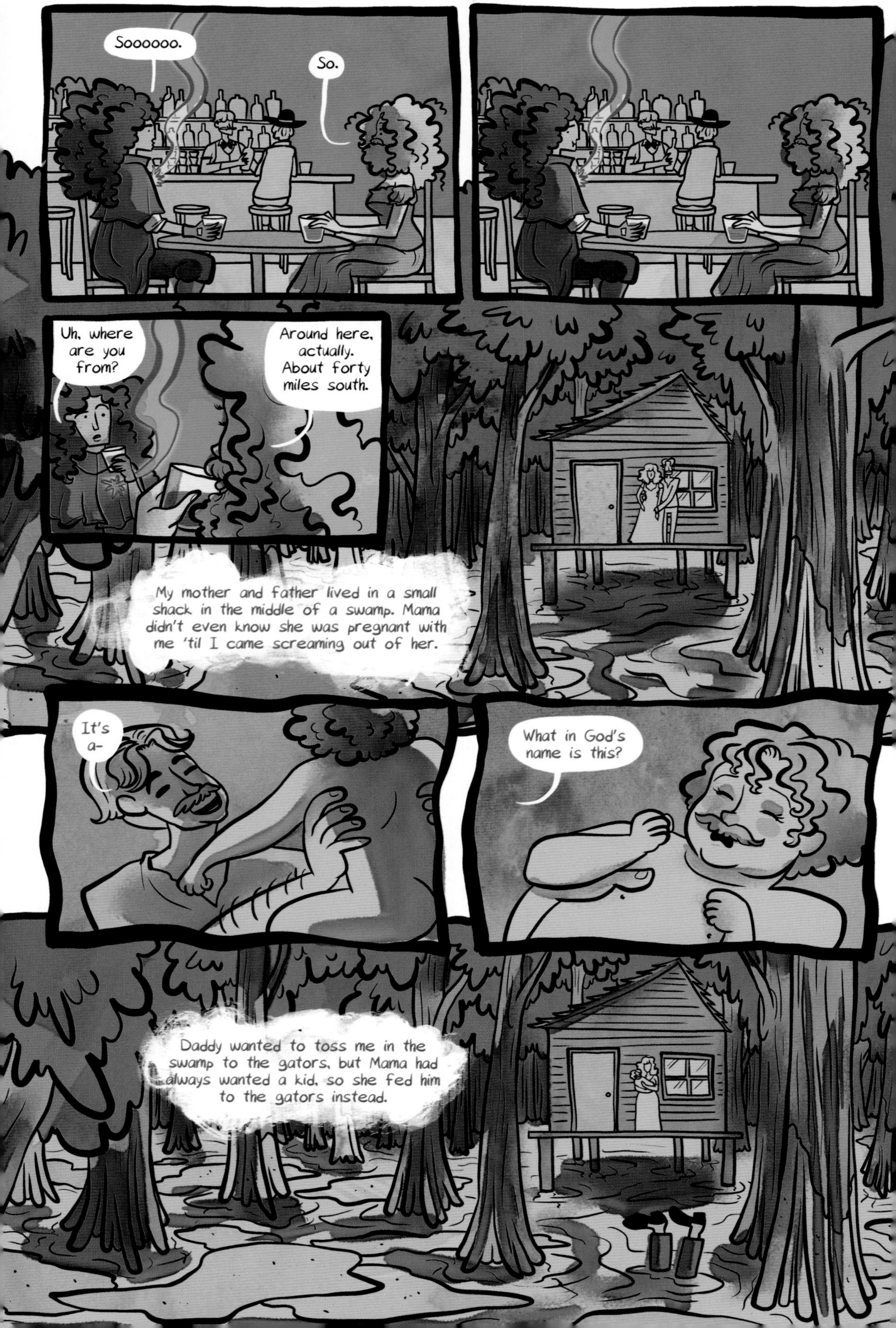
Soooooo.
So.
Uh, where are you from?
Around here, actually. About forty miles south.
My mother and father lived in a small shack in the middle of a swamp. Mama didn't even know she was pregnant with me 'til I came screaming out of her.
It's a-
What in God's name is this?
Daddy wanted to toss me in the swamp to the gators, but Mama had always wanted a kid, so she fed him to the gators instead.

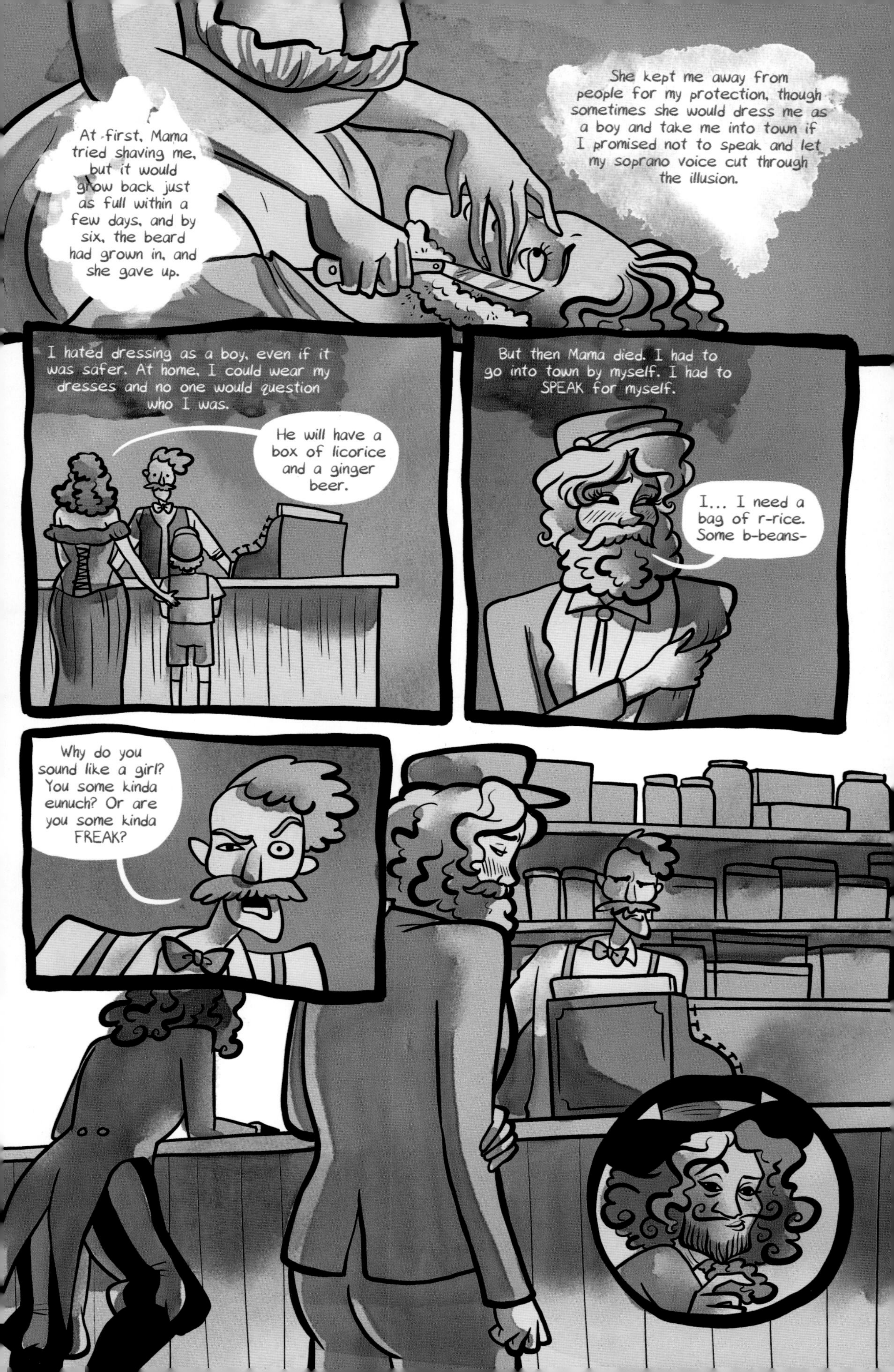
At first, Mama tried shaving me, but it would grow back just as full within a few days, and by six, the beard had grown in, and she gave up.
She kept me away from people for my protection, though sometimes she would dress me as a boy and take me into town if I promised not to speak and let my soprano voice cut through the illusion.
I hated dressing as a boy, even if it was safer. At home, I could wear my dresses and no one would question who I was.
He will have a box of licorice and a ginger beer.
But then Mama died. I had to go into town by myself. I had to SPEAK for myself.
I... I need a bag of r-rice. Some b-beans-
Why do you sound like a girl? You some kinda eunuch? Or are you some kinda FREAK?

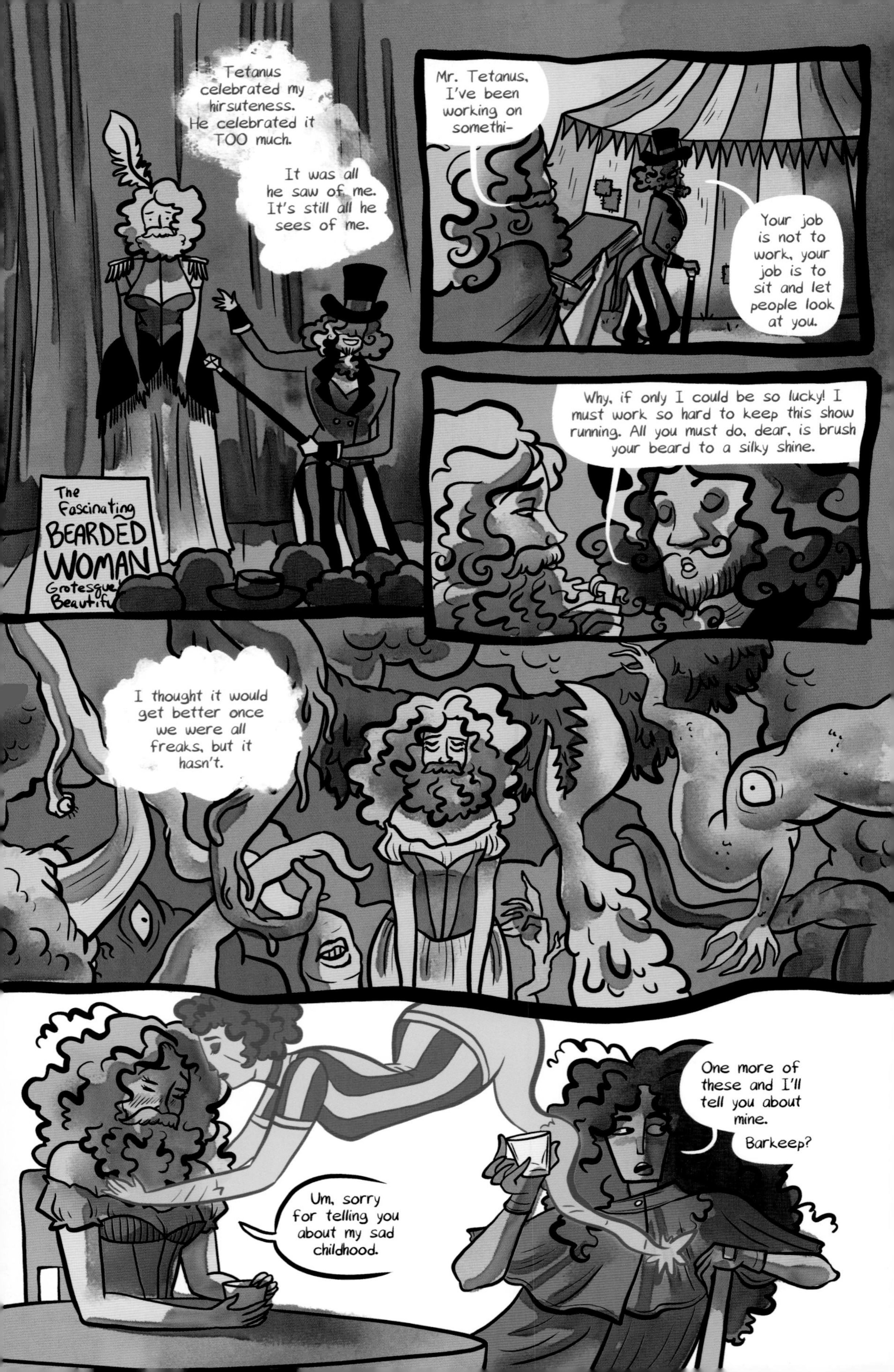
Tetanus celebrated my hirsuteness. He celebrated it TOO much.
It was all he saw of me. It's still all he sees of me.
The Fascinating BEARDED WOMAN Grotesque Beautifu
Mr. Tetanus, I've been working on somethi-
Your job is not to work, your job is to sit and let people look at you.
Why, if only I could be so lucky! I must work so hard to keep this show running. All you must do, dear, is brush your beard to a silky shine.
I thought it would get better once we were all freaks, but it hasn't.
Um, sorry for telling you about my sad childhood.
One more of these and I'll tell you about mine.
Barkeep?

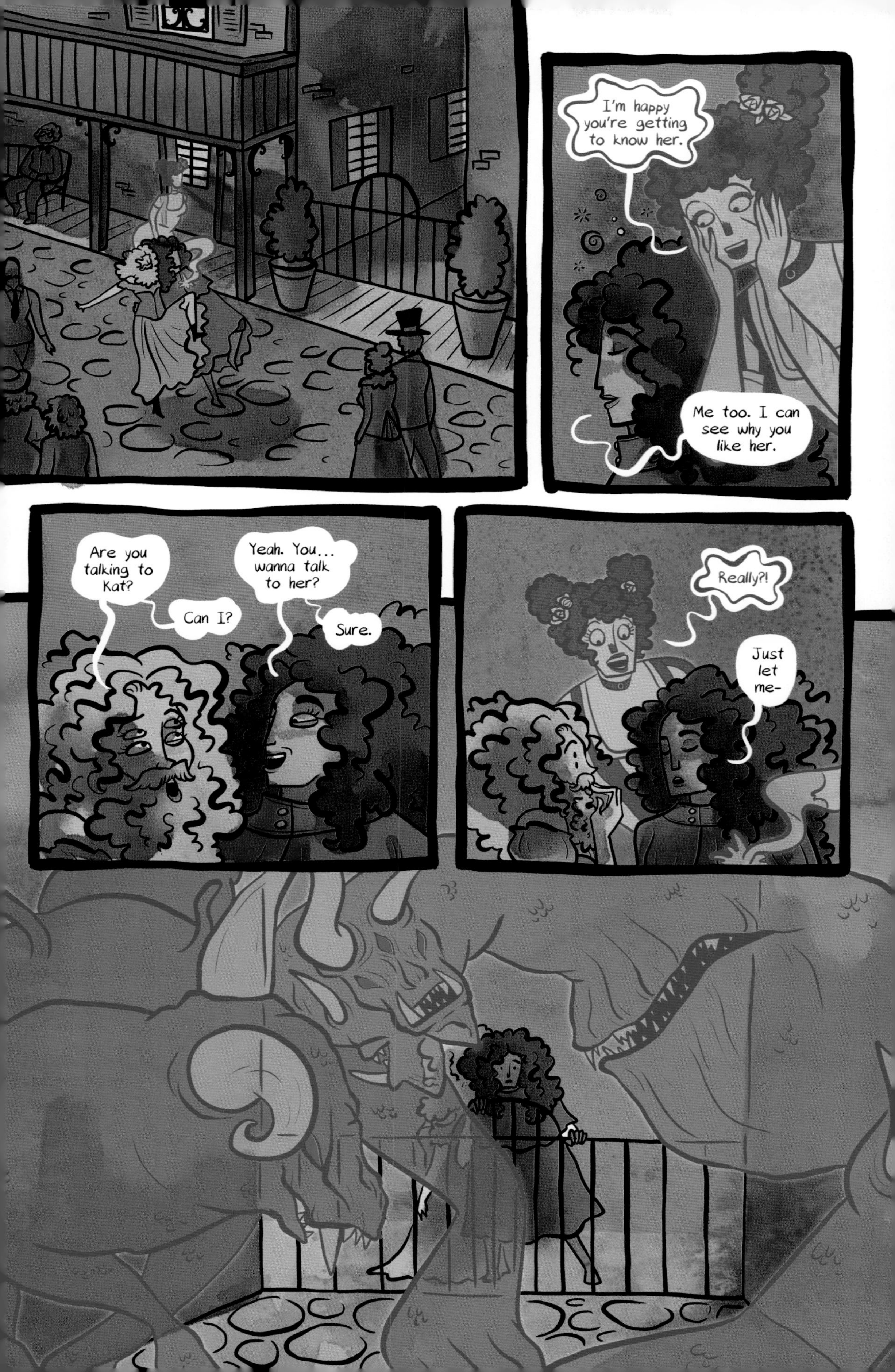
I'm happy you're getting to know her.
Me too. I can see why you like her.
Are you talking to Kat?
Can I?
Yeah. You... wanna talk to her?
Sure.
Really?!
Just let me-

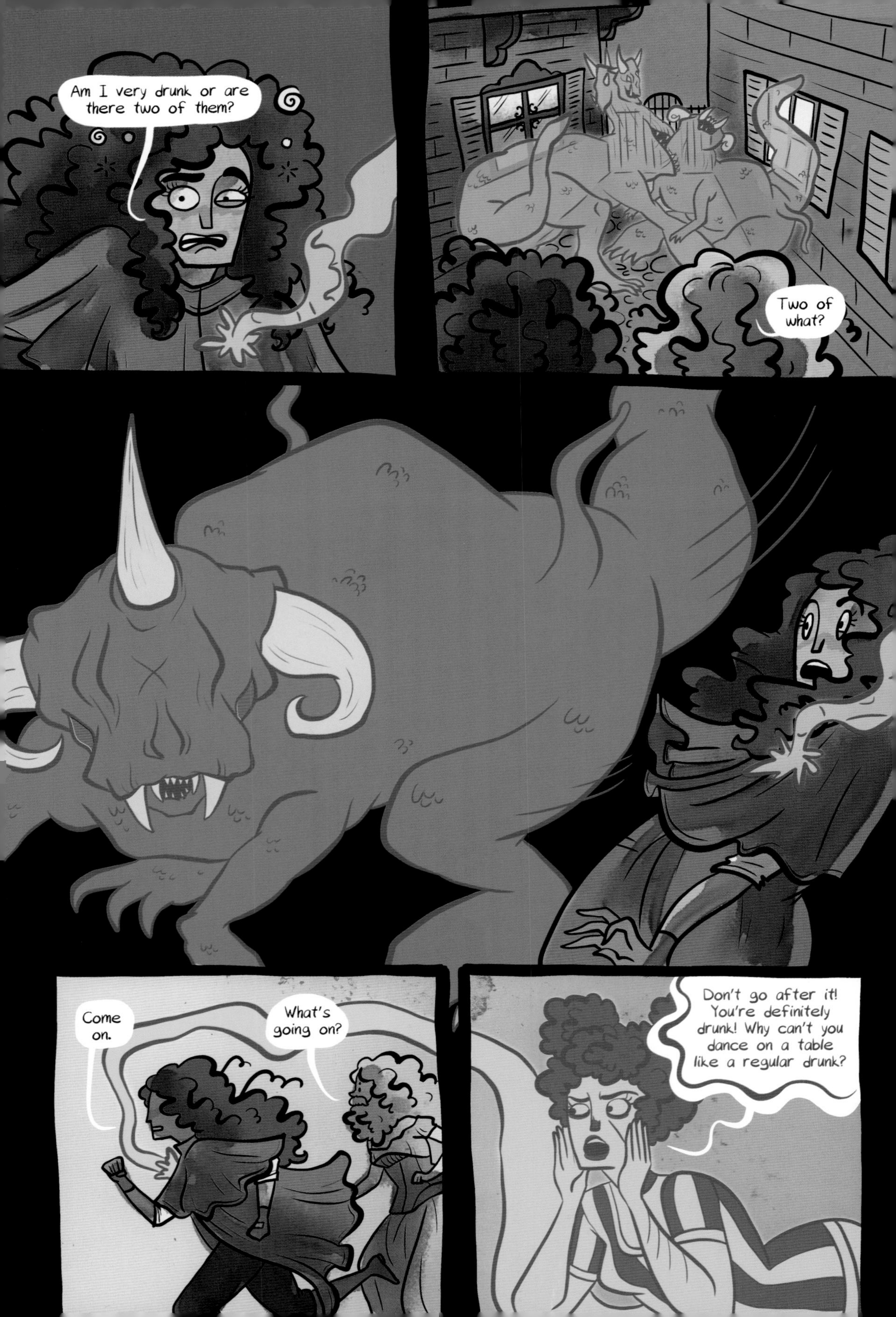
Am I very drunk or are there two of them?
Two of what?
Come on.
What's going on?
Don't go after it! You're definitely drunk! Why can't you dance on a table like a regular drunk?

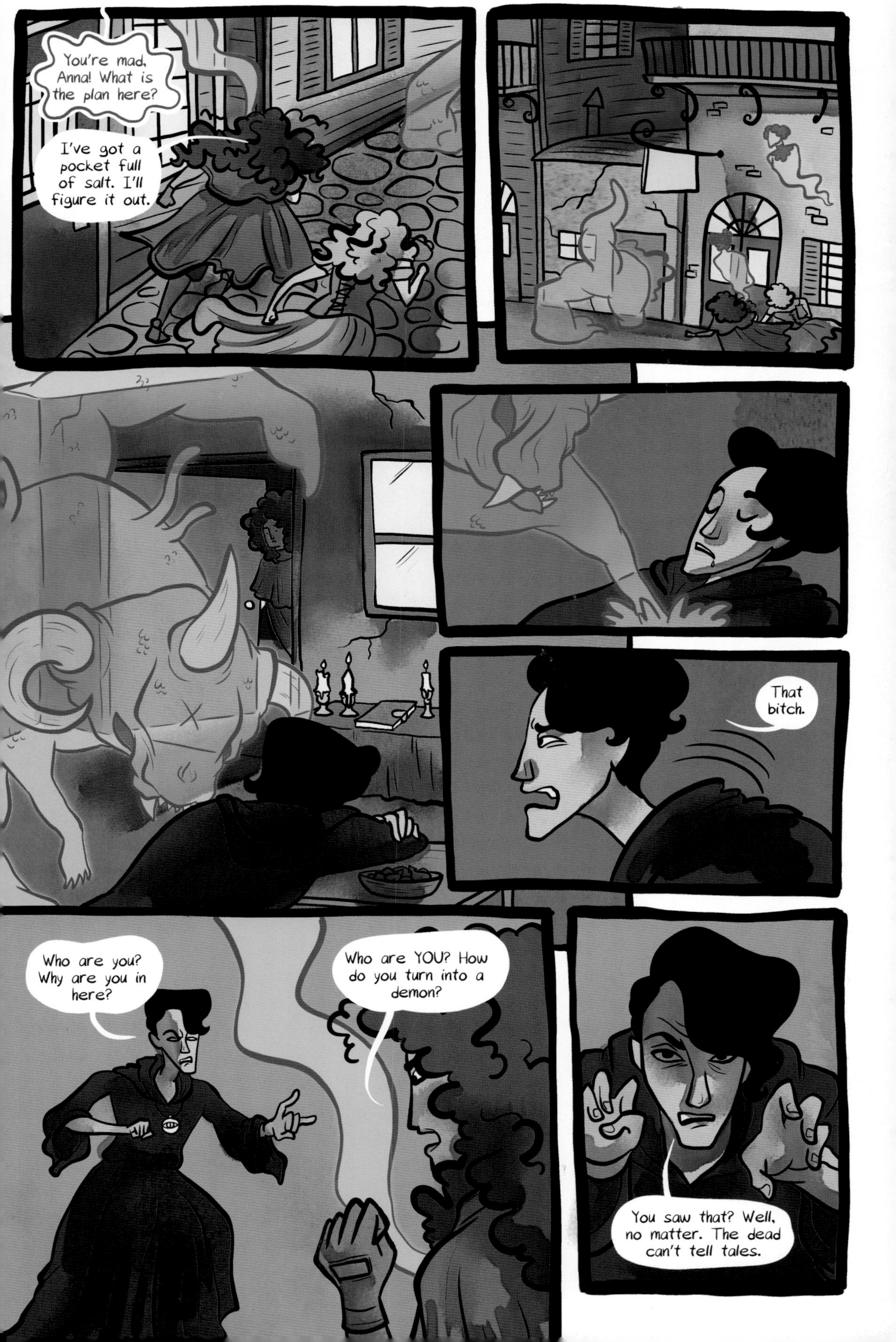
You're mad, Anna! What is the plan here?
I've got a pocket full of salt. I'll figure it out.
That bitch.
Who are you? Why are you in here?
Who are YOU? How do you turn into a demon?
You saw that? Well, no matter. The dead can't tell tales.

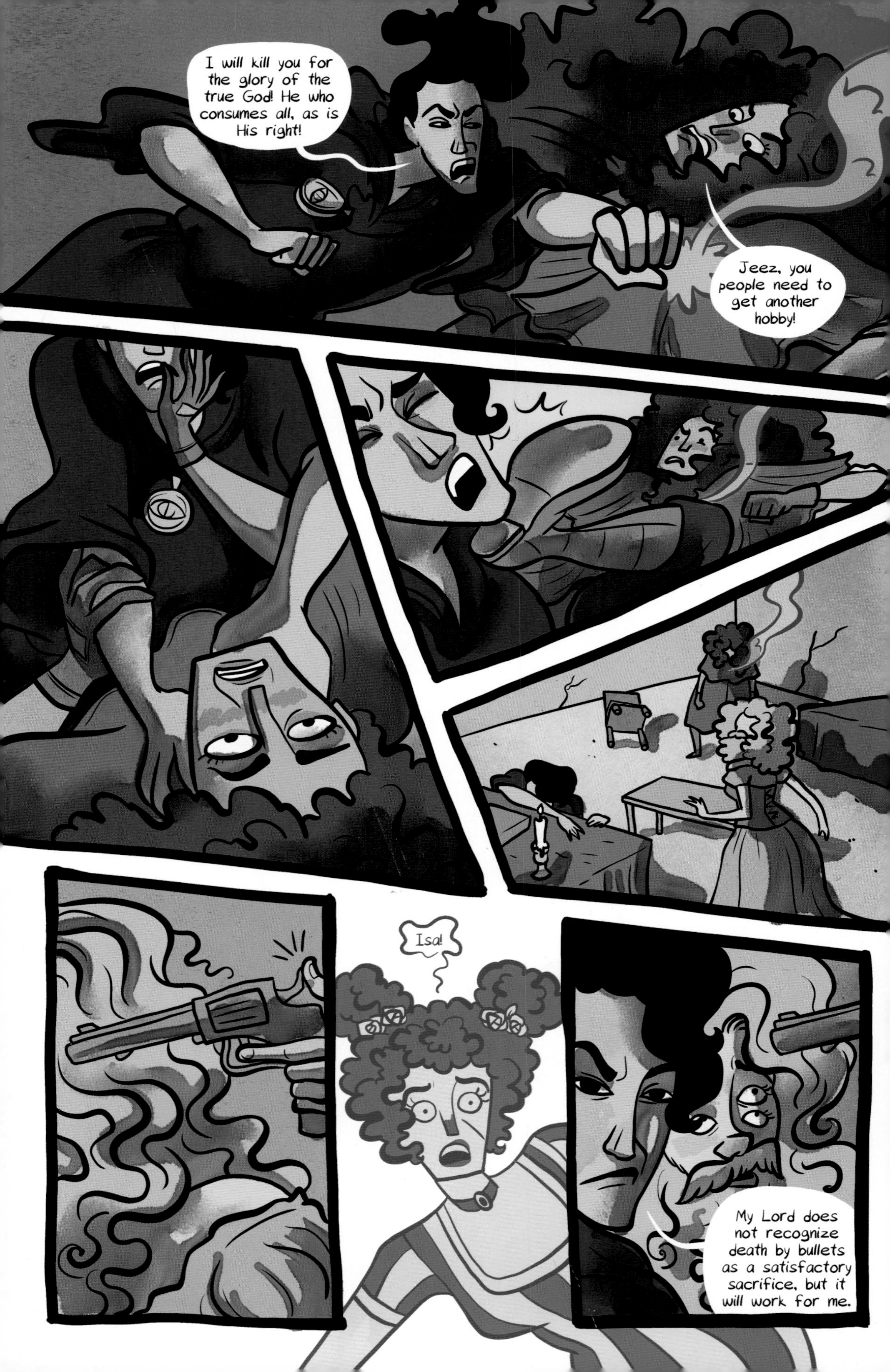
I will kill you for the glory of the true God! He who consumes all, as is His right!
Jeez, you people need to get another hobby!
Isa!
My Lord does not recognize death by bullets as a satisfactory sacrifice, but it will work for me.

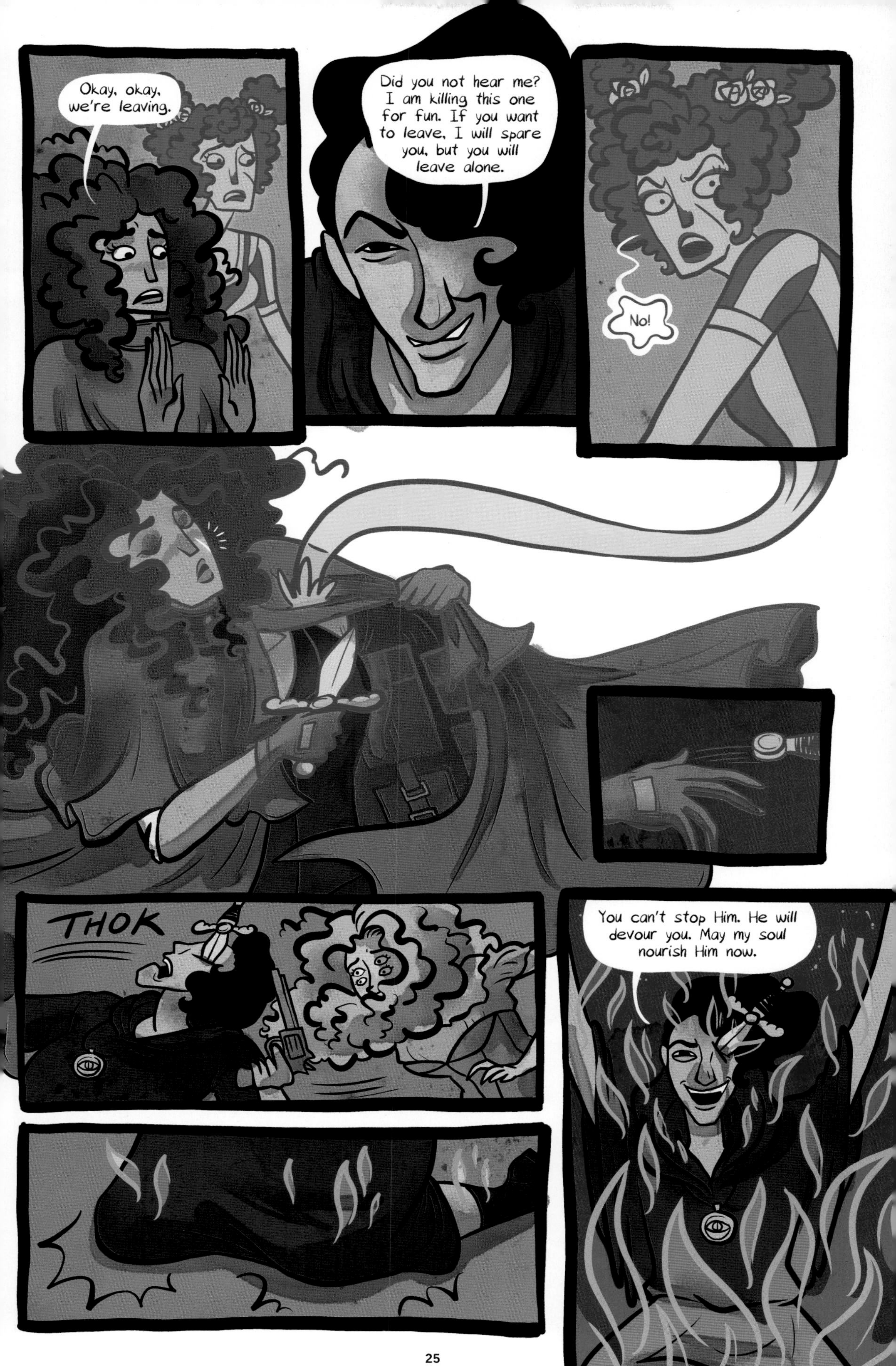
Okay, okay, we're leaving.
Did you not hear me? I am killing this one for fun. If you want to leave, I will spare you, but you will leave alone.
No!
THOK
You can't stop Him. He will devour you. May my soul nourish Him now.

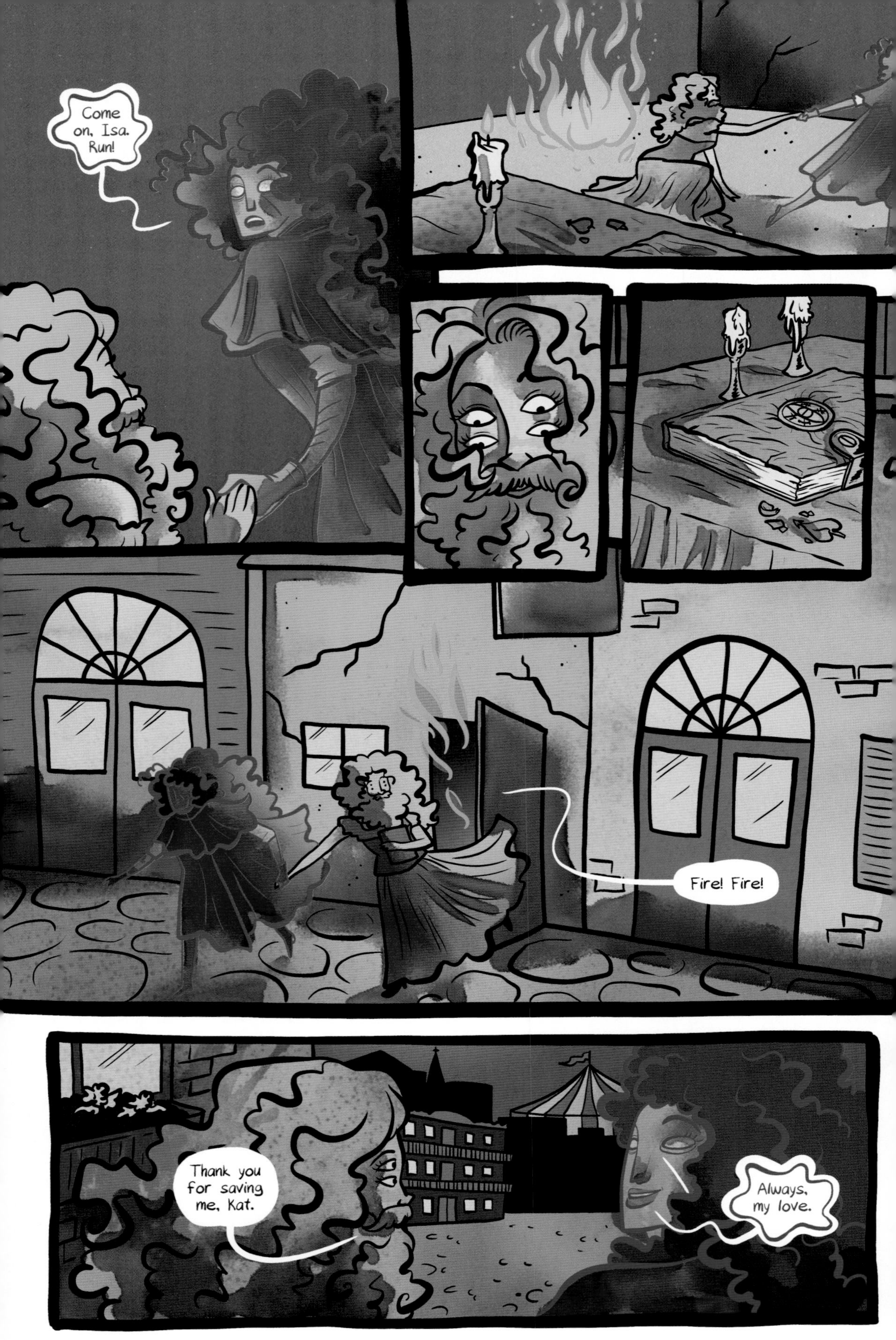
Come on, Isa. Run!
Fire! Fire!
Thank you for saving me, Kat.
Always, my love.

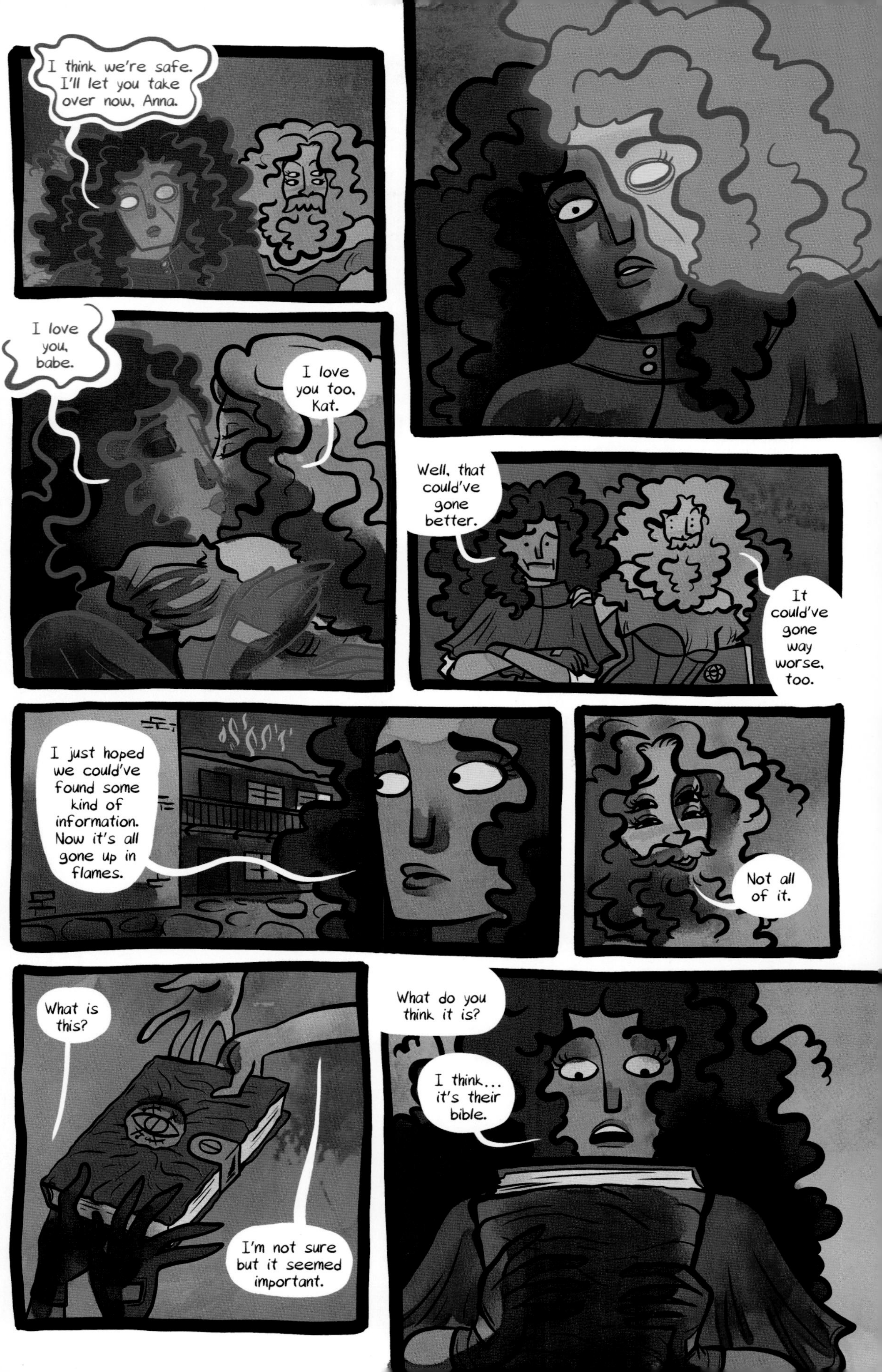
I think we're safe. I'll let you take over now, Anna.
I love you, babe.
I love you too, Kat.
Well, that could've gone better.
It could've gone way worse, too.
I just hoped we could've found some kind of information. Now it's all gone up in flames.
Not all of it.
What is this?
I'm not sure but it seemed important.
What do you think it is?
I think... it's their bible.

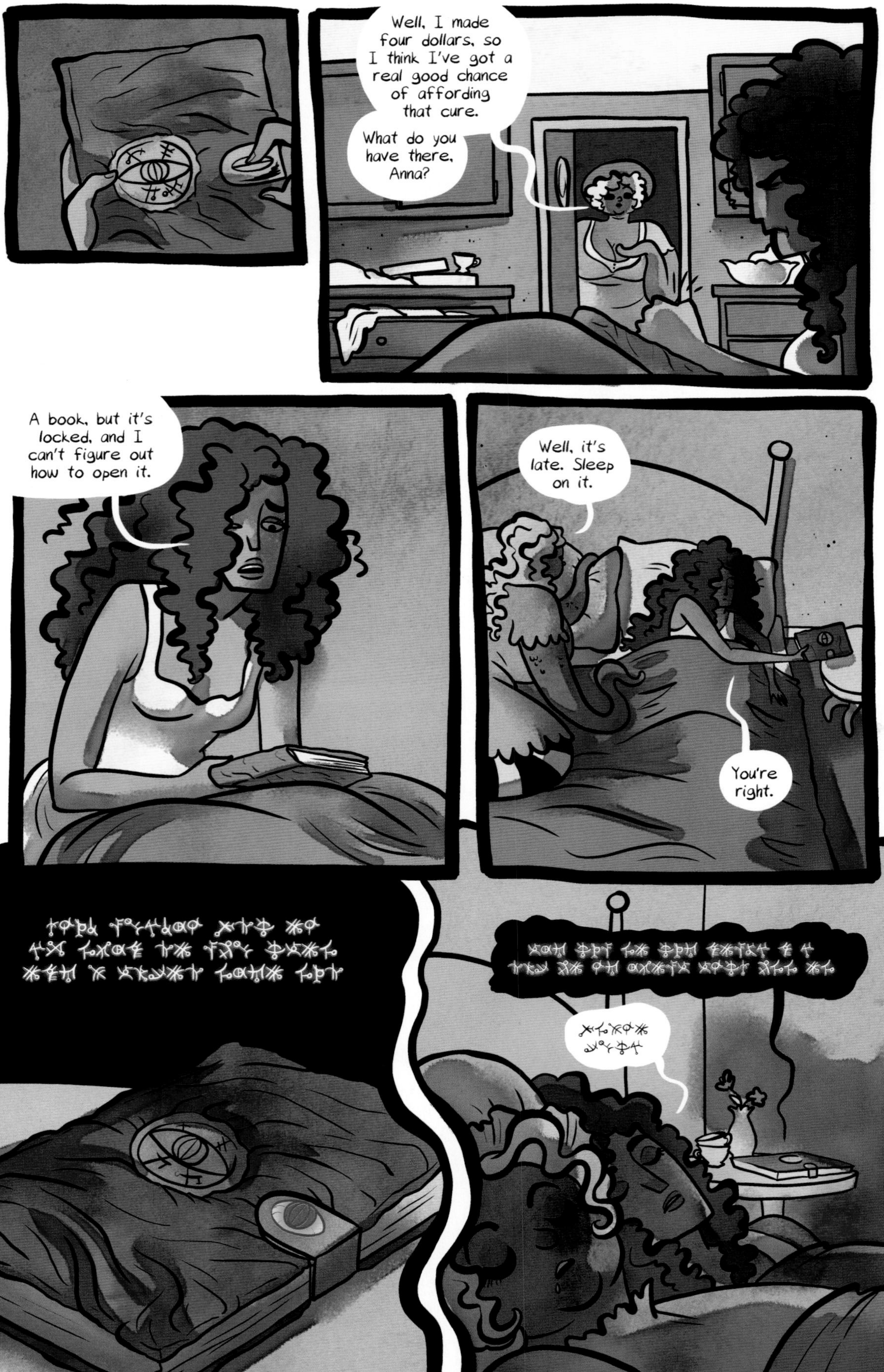
Well, I made four dollars, so I think I've got a real good chance of affording that cure.
What do you have there, Anna?
A book, but it's locked, and I can't figure out how to open it.
Well, it's late. Sleep on it.
You're right.

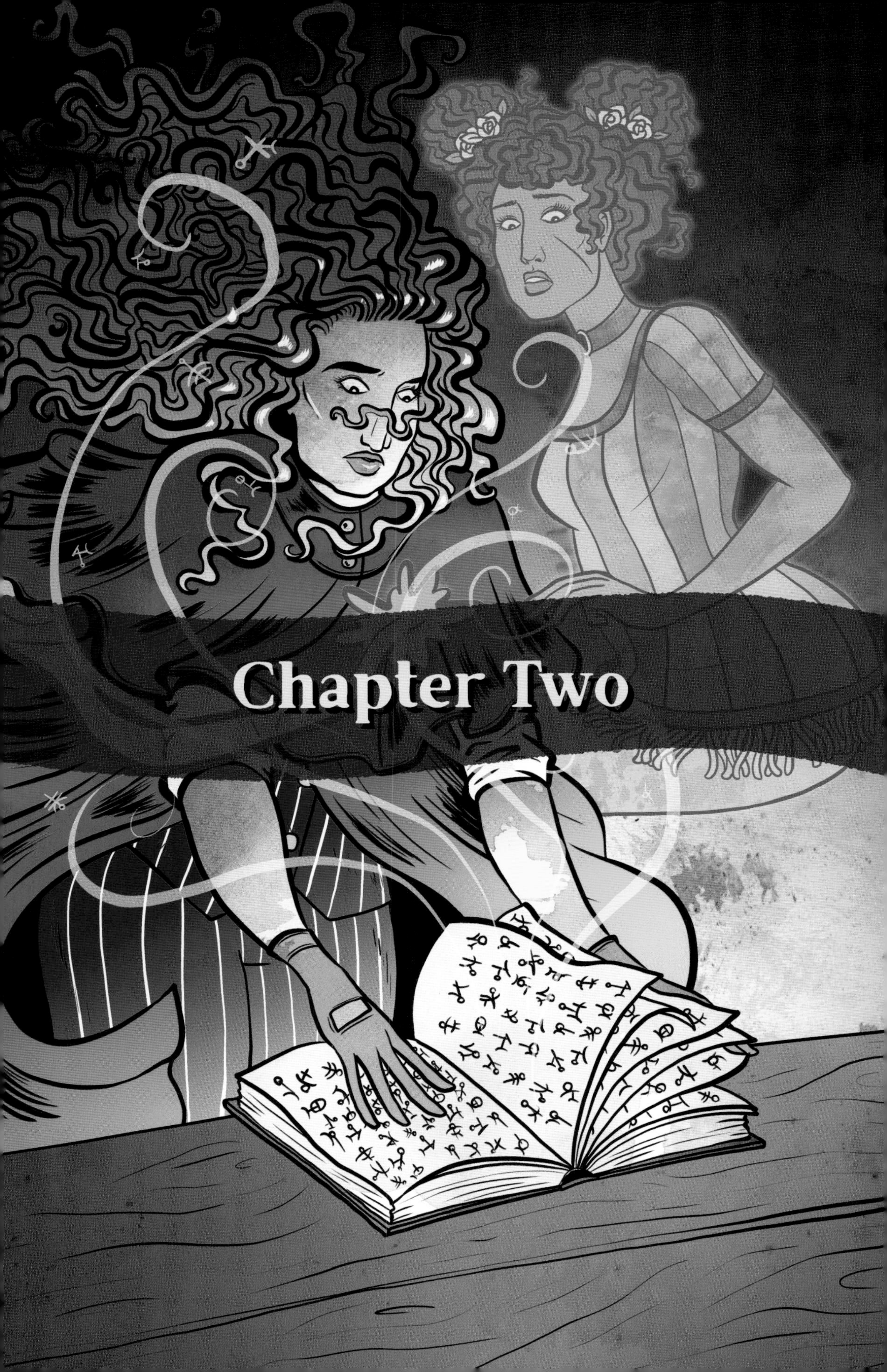
Chapter Two

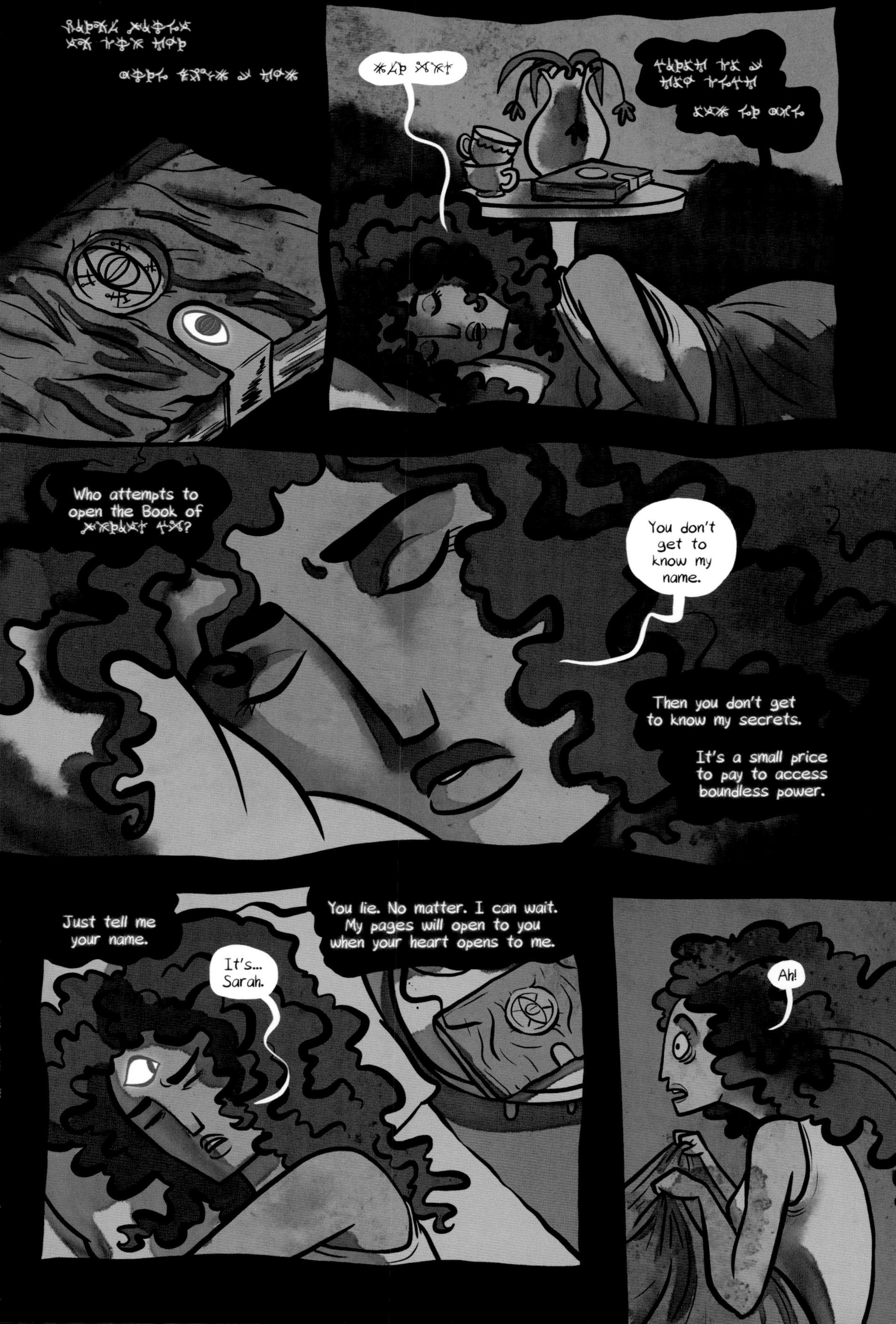

Who attempts to open the Book of ?
You don't get to know my name.
Then you don't get to know my secrets.
It's a small price to pay to access boundless power.
Just tell me your name.
It's... Sarah.
You lie. No matter. I can wait. My pages will open to you when your heart opens to me.
Ah!

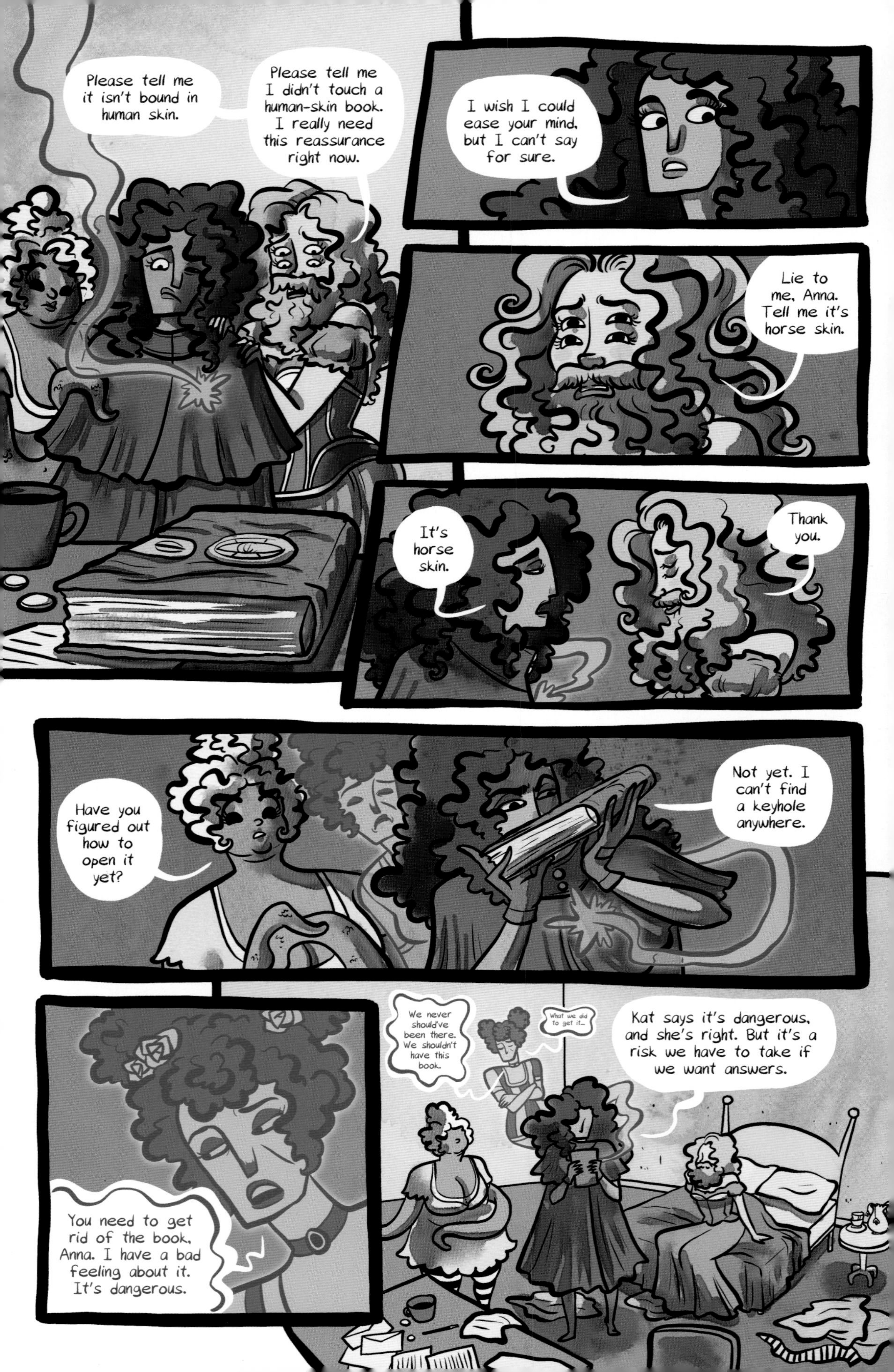
Please tell me it isn't bound in human skin.
Please tell me I didn't touch a human-skin book. I really need this reassurance right now.
I wish I could ease your mind, but I can't say for sure.
Lie to me, Anna. Tell me it's horse skin.
It's horse skin.
Thank you.
Have you figured out how to open it yet?
Not yet. I can't find a keyhole anywhere.
You need to get rid of the book, Anna. I have a bad feeling about it. It's dangerous.
We never should've been there. We shouldn't have this book.
What we did to get it...
Kat says it's dangerous, and she's right. But it's a risk we have to take if we want answers.

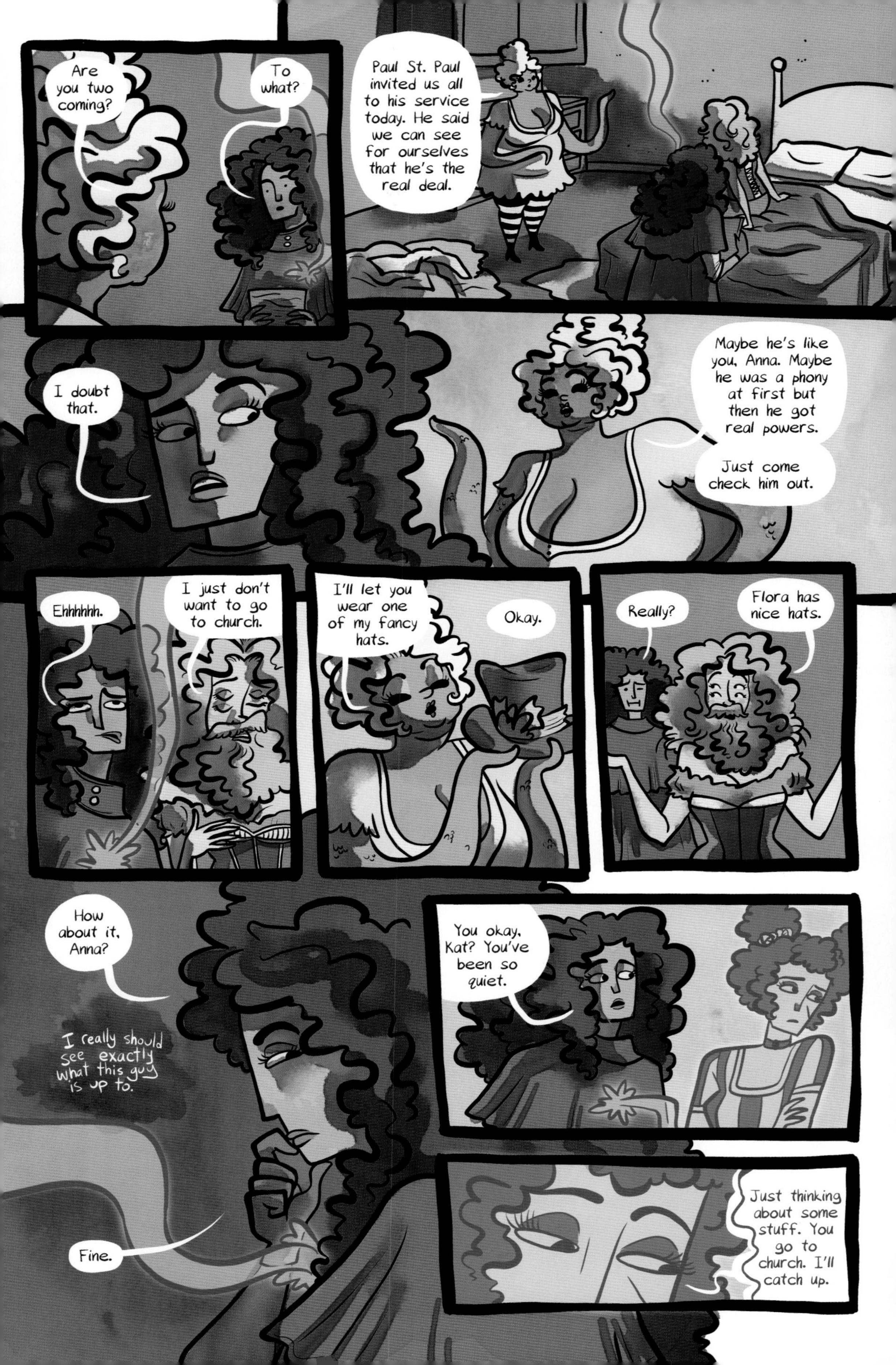

Are you two coming?
To what?
Paul St. Paul invited us all to his service today. He said we can see for ourselves that he's the real deal.
I doubt that.
Maybe he's like you, Anna. Maybe he was a phony at first but then he got real powers.
Just come check him out.
Ehhhhhh.
I just don't want to go to church.
I'll let you wear one of my fancy hats.
Okay.
Really?
Flora has nice hats.
How about it, Anna?
I really should see exactly what this guy is up to.
Fine.
You okay, Kat? You've been so quiet.
Just thinking about some stuff. You go to church. I'll catch up.

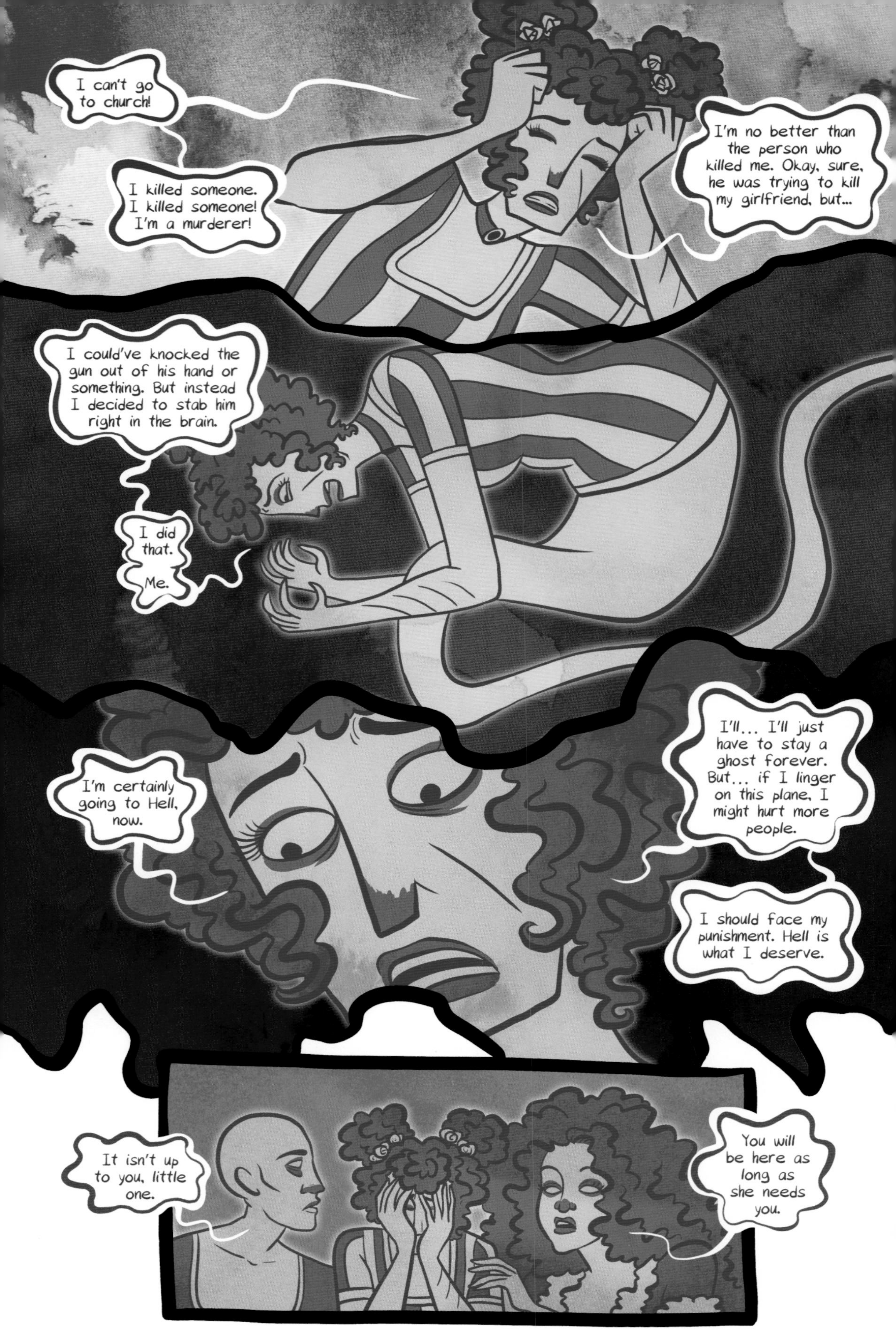

I can't go to church!
I killed someone. I killed someone! I'm a murderer!
I'm no better than the person who killed me. Okay, sure, he was trying to kill my girlfriend, but...
I could've knocked the gun out of his hand or something. But instead I decided to stab him right in the brain.
I did that.
Me.
I'm certainly going to Hell, now.
I'll... I'll just have to stay a ghost forever. But... if I linger on this plane, I might hurt more people.
I should face my punishment. Hell is what I deserve.
It isn't up to you, little one.
You will be here as long as she needs you.

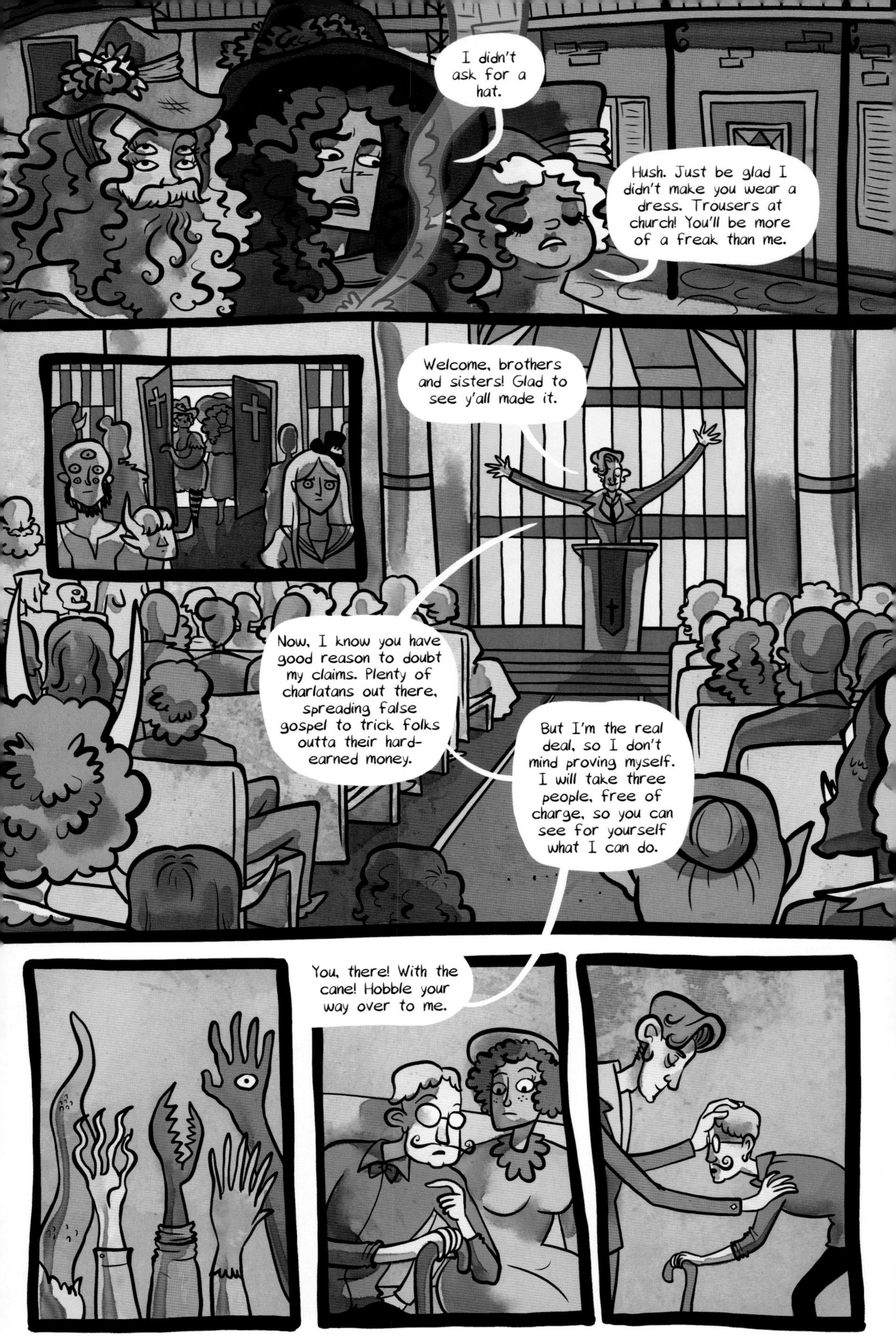
I didn't ask for a hat.
Hush. Just be glad I didn't make you wear a dress. Trousers at church! You'll be more of a freak than me.
Welcome, brothers and sisters! Glad to see y'all made it.
Now, I know you have good reason to doubt my claims. Plenty of charlatans out there, spreading false gospel to trick folks outta their hard-earned money.
But I'm the real deal, so I don't mind proving myself. I will take three people, free of charge, so you can see for yourself what I can do.
You, there! With the cane! Hobble your way over to me.

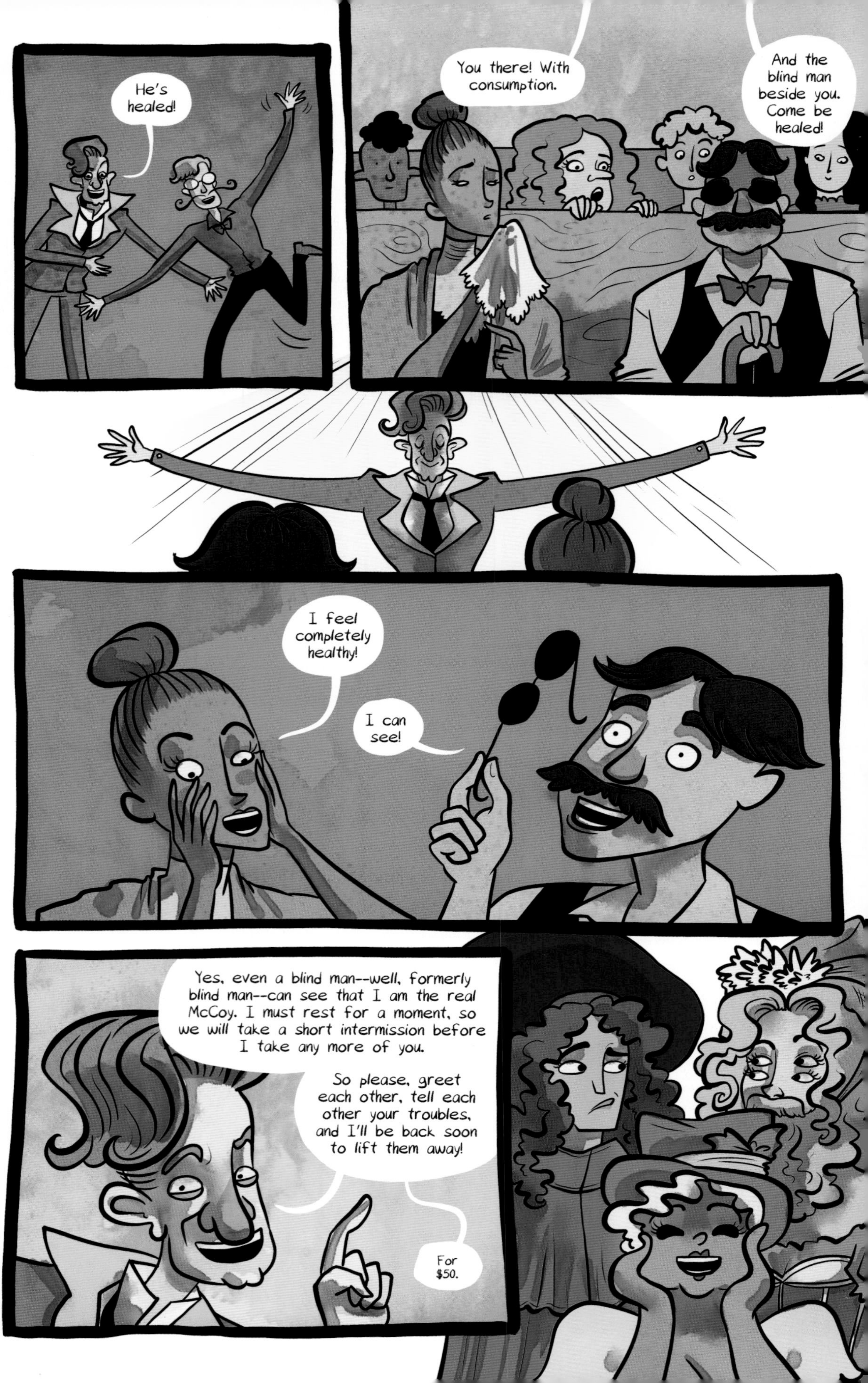
He's healed!
You there! With consumption.
And the blind man beside you. Come be healed!
I feel completely healthy!
I can see!
Yes, even a blind man--well, formerly blind man--can see that I am the real McCoy. I must rest for a moment, so we will take a short intermission before I take any more of you.
So please, greet each other, tell each other your troubles, and I'll be back soon to lift them away!
For $50.

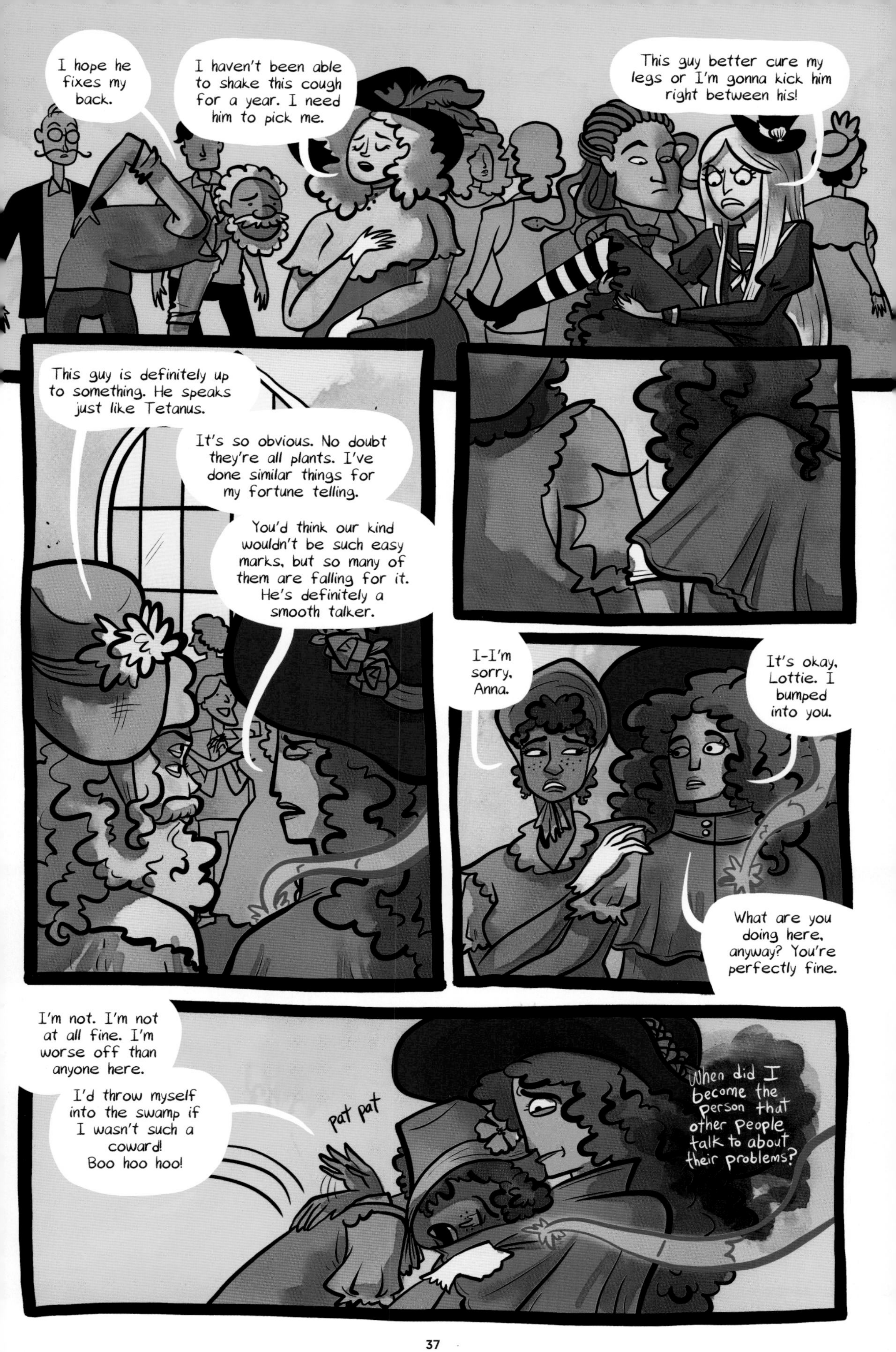

I hope he fixes my back.
I haven't been able to shake this cough for a year. I need him to pick me.
This guy better cure my legs or I'm gonna kick him right between his!
This guy is definitely up to something. He speaks just like Tetanus.
It's so obvious. No doubt they're all plants. I've done similar things for my fortune telling.
You'd think our kind wouldn't be such easy marks, but so many of them are falling for it. He's definitely a smooth talker.
I-I'm sorry, Anna.
It's okay, Lottie. I bumped into you.
What are you doing here, anyway? You're perfectly fine.
I'm not. I'm not at all fine. I'm worse off than anyone here.
I'd throw myself into the swamp if I wasn't such a coward! Boo hoo hoo!
pat pat
When did I become the person that other people talk to about their problems?

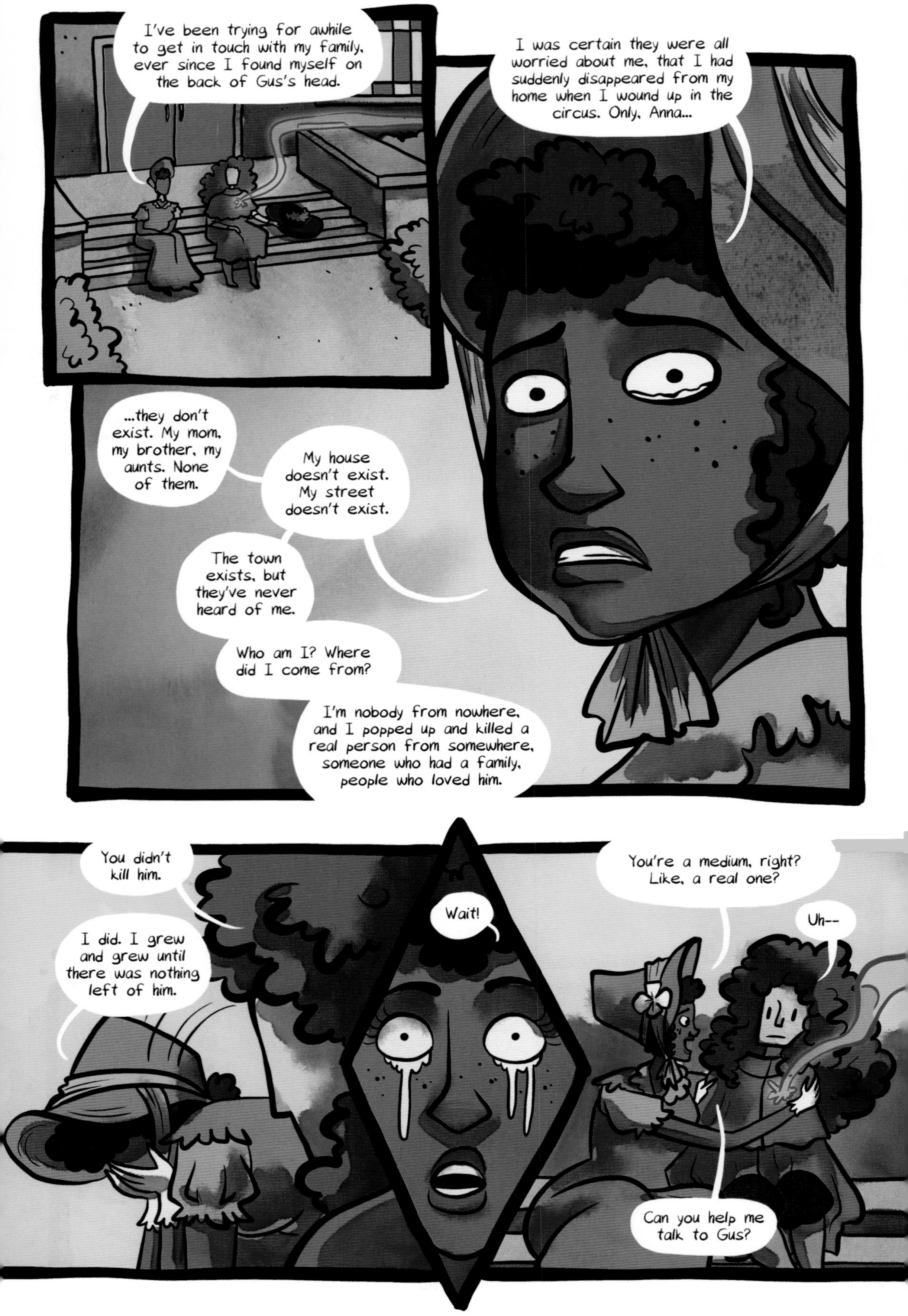
I've been trying for awhile to get in touch with my family, ever since I found myself on the back of Gus's head.
I was certain they were all worried about me, that I had suddenly disappeared from my home when I wound up in the circus. Only, Anna...
...they don't exist. My mom, my brother, my aunts. None of them.
My house doesn't exist. My street doesn't exist.
The town exists, but they've never heard of me.
Who am I? Where did I come from?
I'm nobody from nowhere, and I popped up and killed a real person from somewhere, someone who had a family, people who loved him.
You didn't kill him.
I did. I grew and grew until there was nothing left of him.
Wait!
You're a medium, right? Like, a real one?
Uh--
Can you help me talk to Gus?

I don't know if I can talk to Gus. I haven't seen his ghost floating around. I've never tried to contact someone who's crossed over. Whatever that means. Listen, I don't really know how ANY of this works.

Could you try? I'll even pay you.

I don't need--

I was going to give this money to Paul St. Paul. I was gonna ask him to fix me, turn me back into Gus...

...even if that meant I'd go back to being nobody in nowhere.

But if you can help me talk to Gus, help me figure this out, then I'll stick around, at least for a little while.

Okay. Um. Sure.

But keep your money.

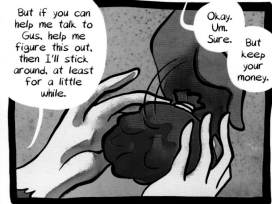

What do we do? Should I light some candles?

I feel like ghosts can see pretty well in the dark.

Oh, good point.

So, uh. Okay, here goes.

Gus? Hey, Gus?

Heeeeeere, Gussy Gussy Gussy!

I feel like you're not taking this seriously.

39

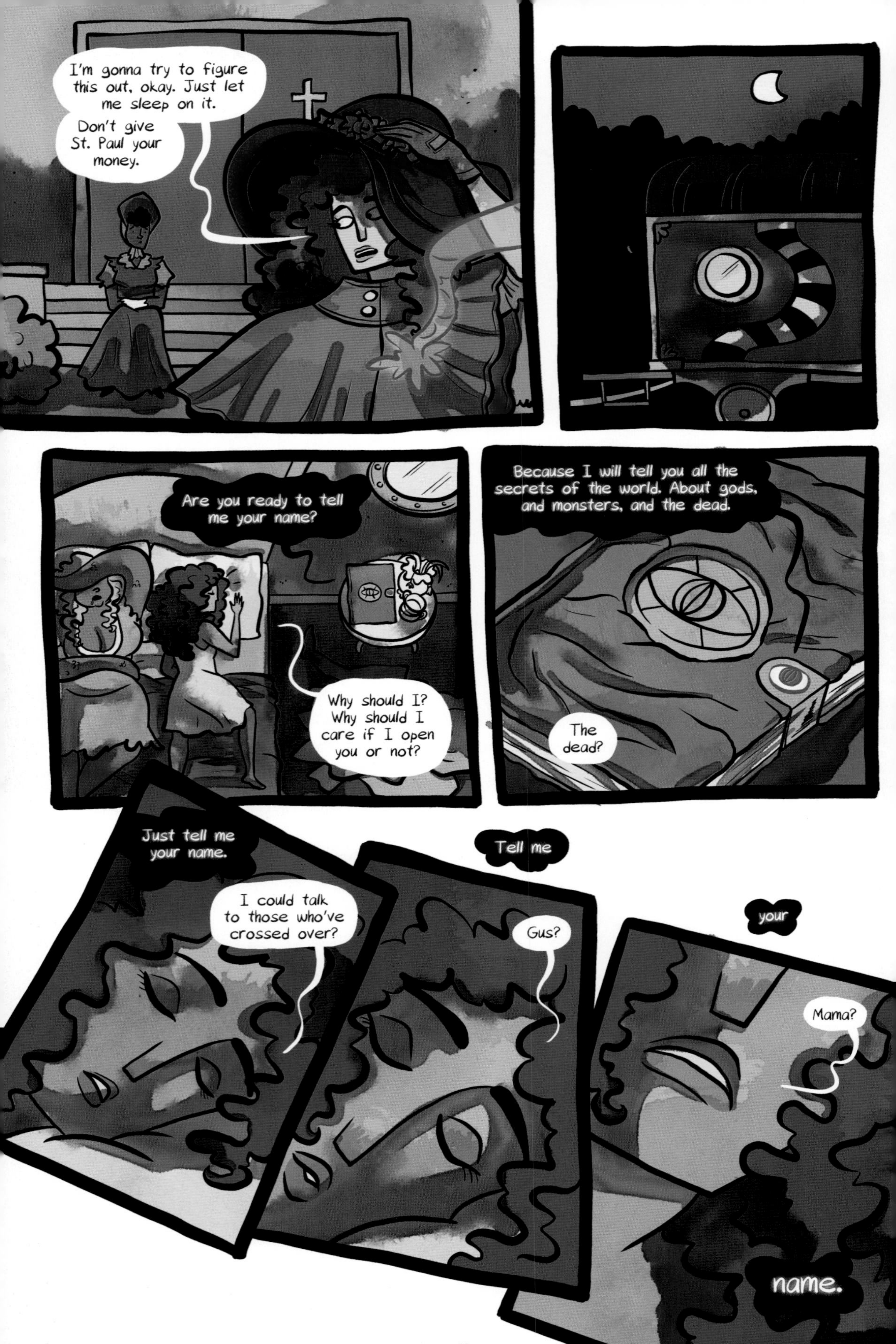
I'm gonna try to figure this out, okay. Just let me sleep on it.
Don't give St. Paul your money.
Are you ready to tell me your name?
Why should I? Why should I care if I open you or not?
Because I will tell you all the secrets of the world. About gods, and monsters, and the dead.
The dead?
Just tell me your name.
I could talk to those who've crossed over?
Tell me
Gus?
your
Mama?
name.

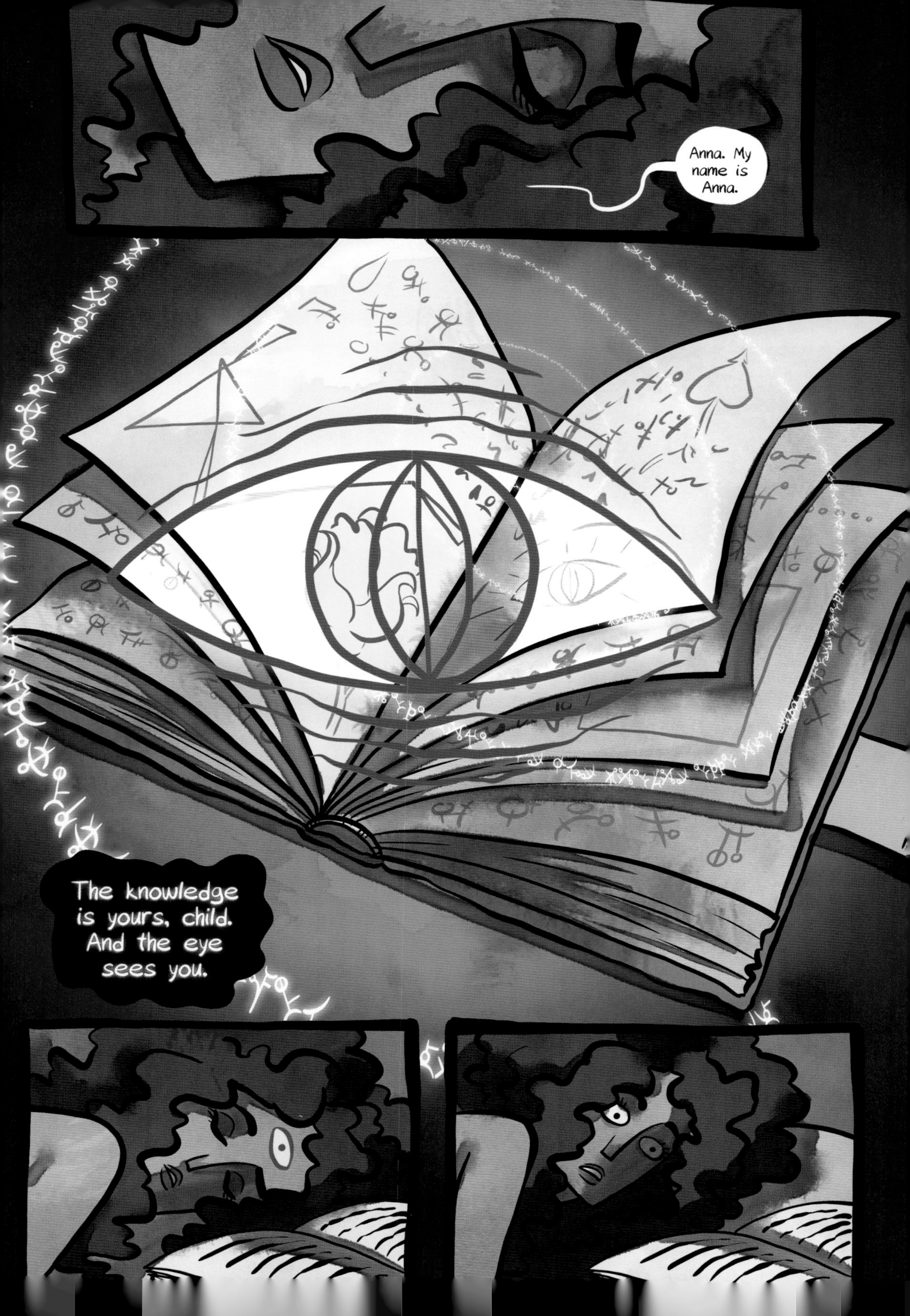
Anna. My name is Anna.
The knowledge is yours, child. And the eye sees you.

How did--?

Flora, Flora. The book is open.

ZZZZZZZZ

I knew it. It's their bible.

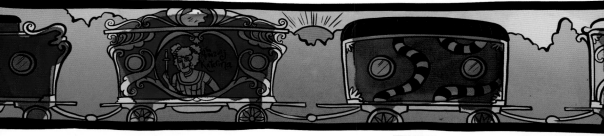

yawn

Anna? How long have you been awake?

Oh, good! You're up! I have so much to tell you!!

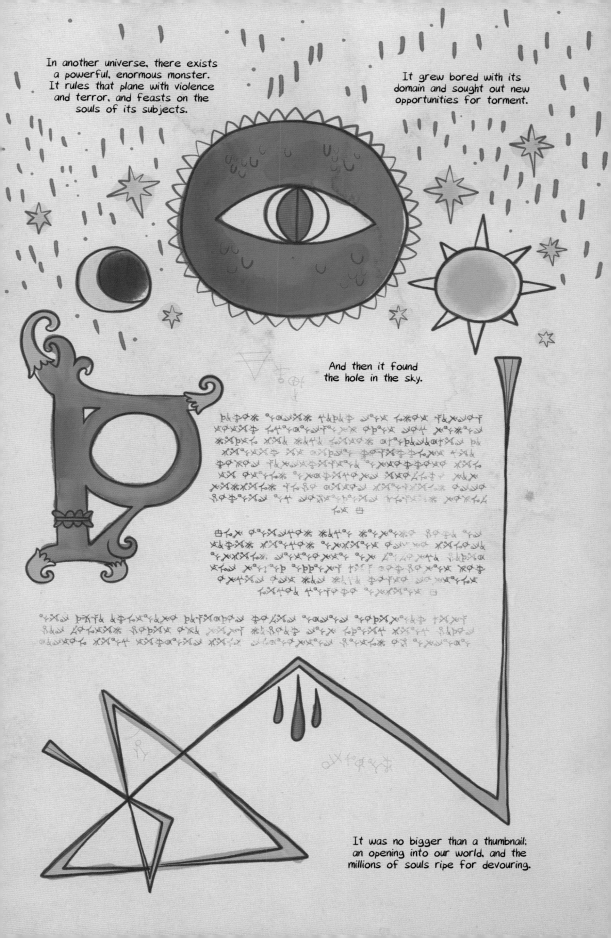

In another universe, there exists a powerful, enormous monster. It rules that plane with violence and terror, and feasts on the souls of its subjects.

It grew bored with its domain and sought out new opportunities for torment.

And then it found the hole in the sky.

It was no bigger than a thumbnail; an opening into our world, and the millions of souls ripe for devouring.

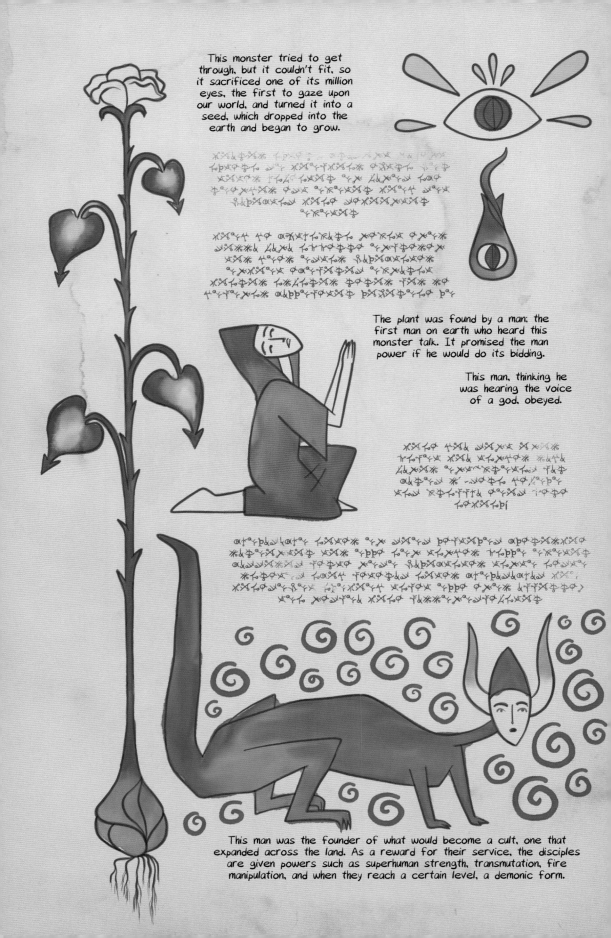

This monster tried to get through, but it couldn't fit, so it sacrificed one of its million eyes, the first to gaze upon our world, and turned it into a seed, which dropped into the earth and began to grow.

The plant was found by a man; the first man on earth who heard this monster talk. It promised the man power if he would do its bidding.

This man, thinking he was hearing the voice of a god, obeyed.

This man was the founder of what would become a cult, one that expanded across the land. As a reward for their service, the disciples are given powers such as superhuman strength, transmutation, fire manipulation, and when they reach a certain level, a demonic form.

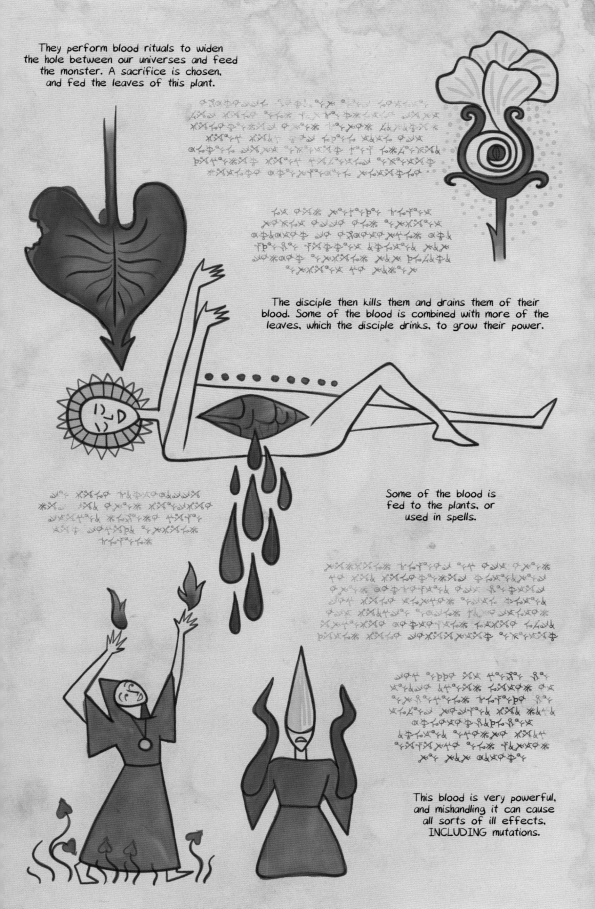

They perform blood rituals to widen the hole between our universes and feed the monster. A sacrifice is chosen, and fed the leaves of this plant.

The disciple then kills them and drains them of their blood. Some of the blood is combined with more of the leaves, which the disciple drinks, to grow their power.

Some of the blood is fed to the plants, or used in spells.

This blood is very powerful, and mishandling it can cause all sorts of ill effects, INCLUDING mutations.

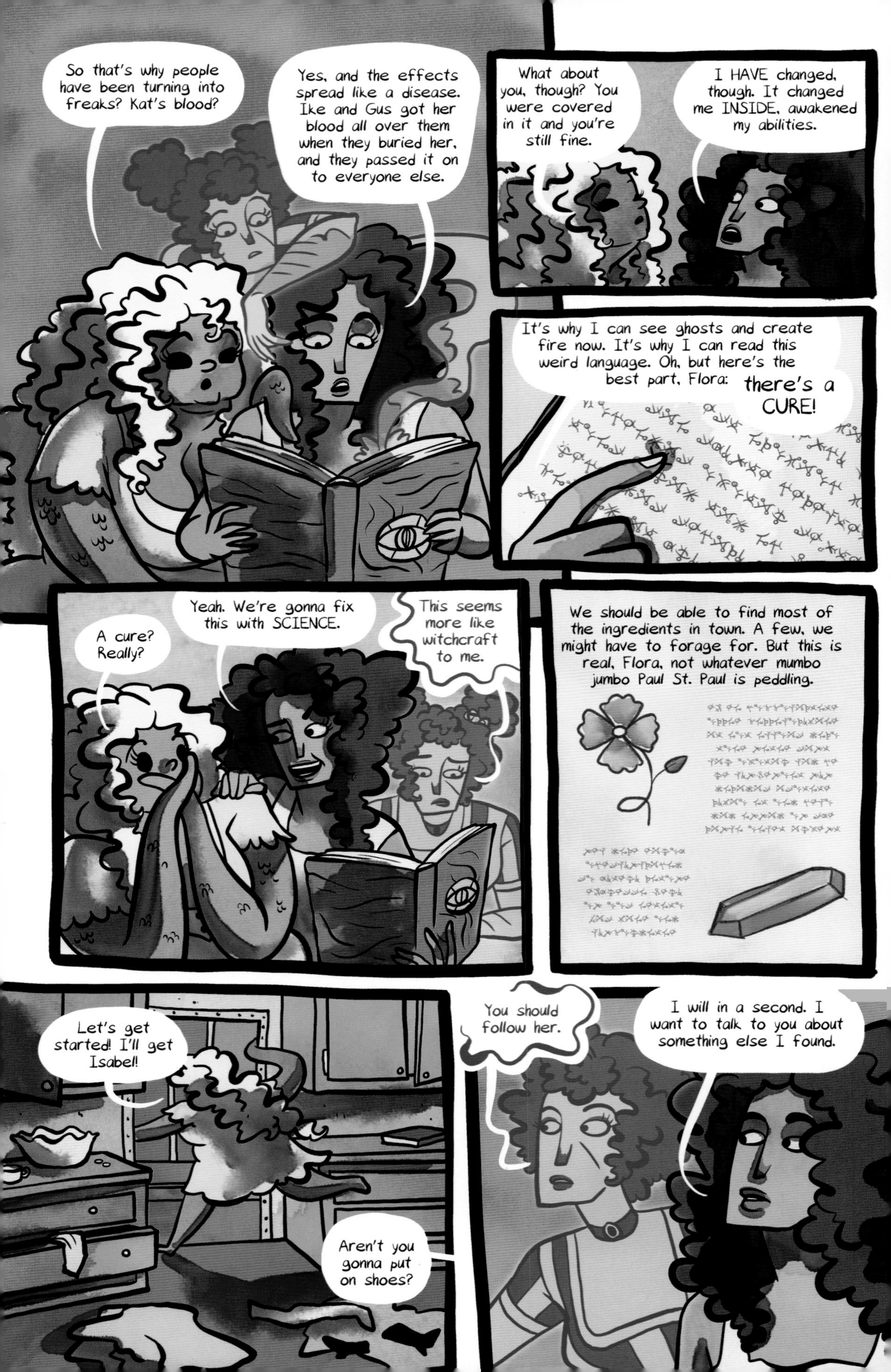
So that's why people have been turning into freaks? Kat's blood?
Yes, and the effects spread like a disease. Ike and Gus got her blood all over them when they buried her, and they passed it on to everyone else.
What about you, though? You were covered in it and you're still fine.
I HAVE changed, though. It changed me INSIDE, awakened my abilities.
It's why I can see ghosts and create fire now. It's why I can read this weird language. Oh, but here's the best part, Flora:
there's a CURE!
A cure? Really?
Yeah. We're gonna fix this with SCIENCE.
This seems more like witchcraft to me.
We should be able to find most of the ingredients in town. A few, we might have to forage for. But this is real, Flora, not whatever mumbo jumbo Paul St. Paul is peddling.
Let's get started! I'll get Isabel!
Aren't you gonna put on shoes?
You should follow her.
I will in a second. I want to talk to you about something else I found.

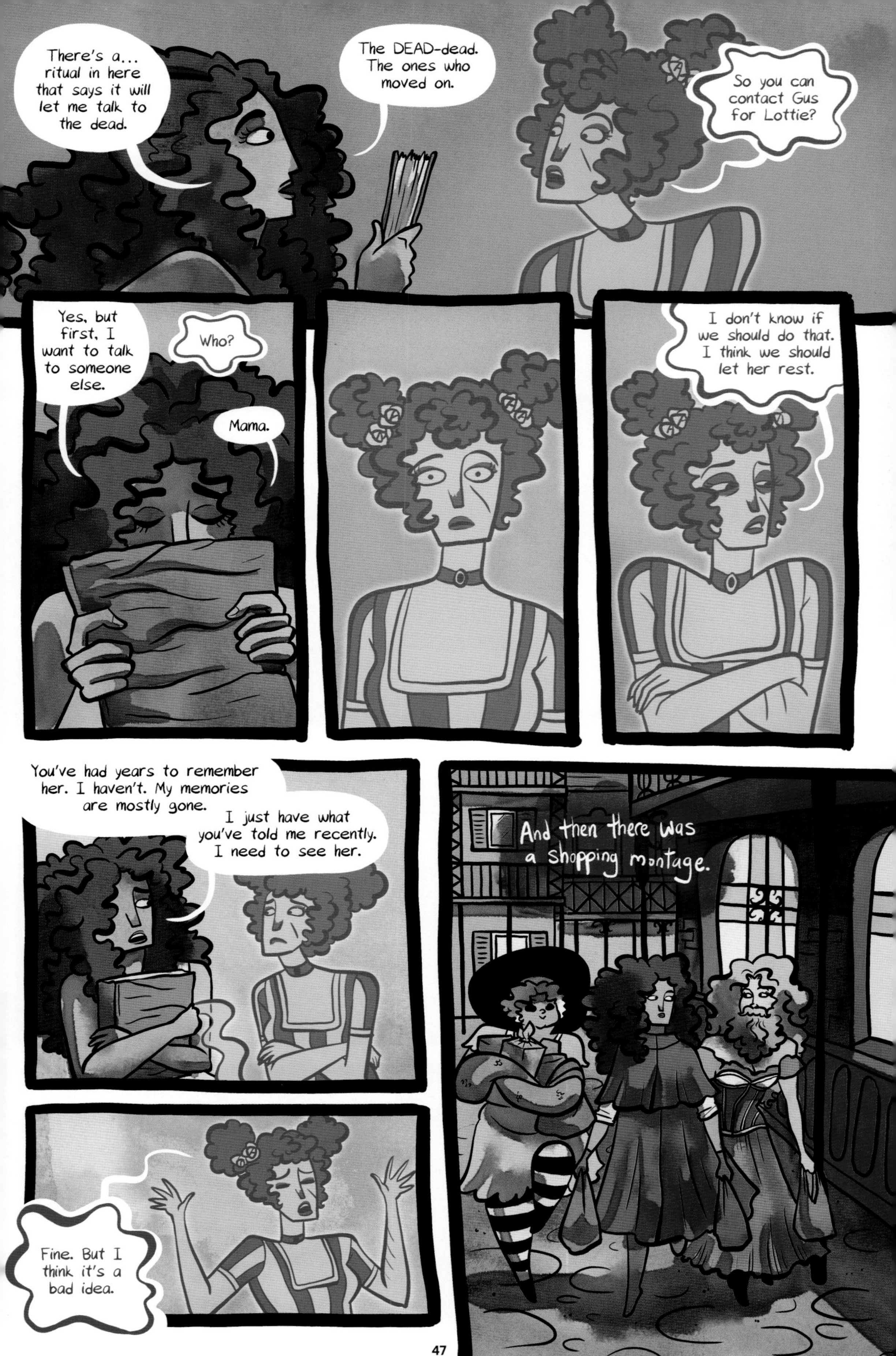
There's a... ritual in here that says it will let me talk to the dead.
The DEAD-dead. The ones who moved on.
So you can contact Gus for Lottie?
Yes, but first, I want to talk to someone else.
Who?
Mama.
I don't know if we should do that. I think we should let her rest.
You've had years to remember her. I haven't. My memories are mostly gone.
I just have what you've told me recently. I need to see her.
Fine. But I think it's a bad idea.
And then there was a shopping montage.

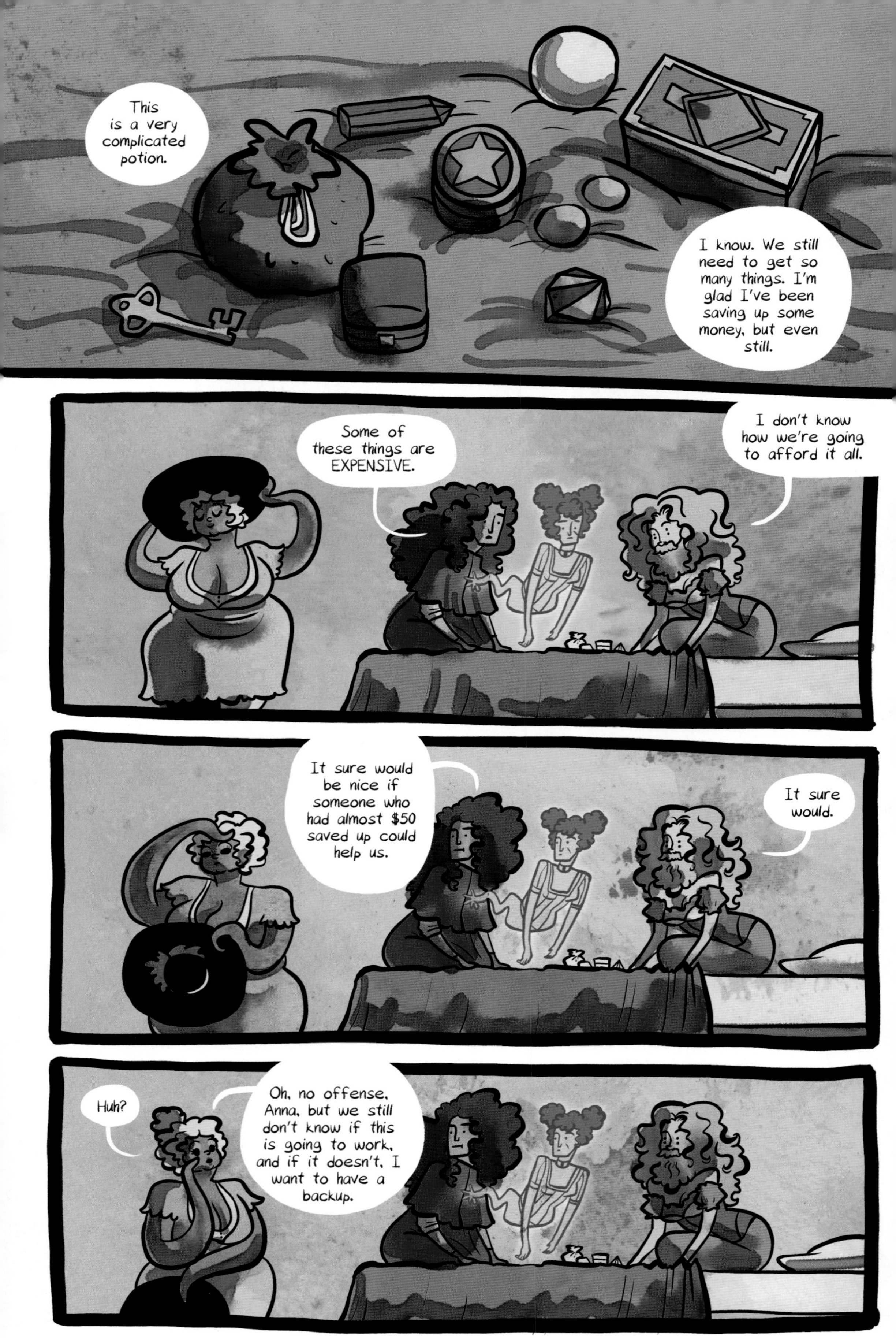
This is a very complicated potion.
I know. We still need to get so many things. I'm glad I've been saving up some money, but even still.
Some of these things are EXPENSIVE.
I don't know how we're going to afford it all.
It sure would be nice if someone who had almost $50 saved up could help us.
It sure would.
Huh?
Oh, no offense, Anna, but we still don't know if this is going to work, and if it doesn't, I want to have a backup.

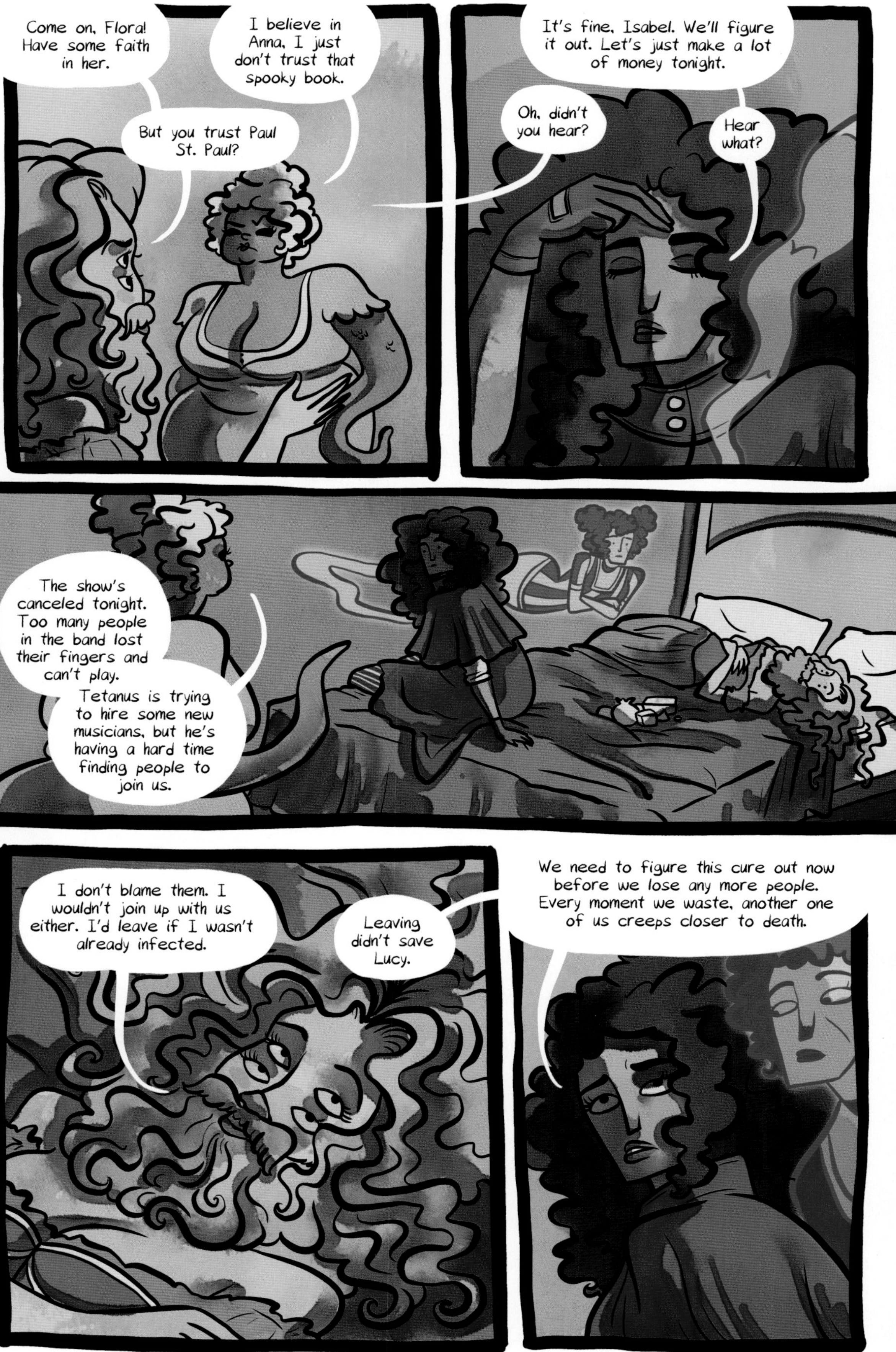

Come on, Flora! Have some faith in her.
I believe in Anna, I just don't trust that spooky book.
But you trust Paul St. Paul?
It's fine, Isabel. We'll figure it out. Let's just make a lot of money tonight.
Oh, didn't you hear?
Hear what?
The show's canceled tonight. Too many people in the band lost their fingers and can't play.
Tetanus is trying to hire some new musicians, but he's having a hard time finding people to join us.
I don't blame them. I wouldn't join up with us either. I'd leave if I wasn't already infected.
Leaving didn't save Lucy.
We need to figure this cure out now before we lose any more people. Every moment we waste, another one of us creeps closer to death.

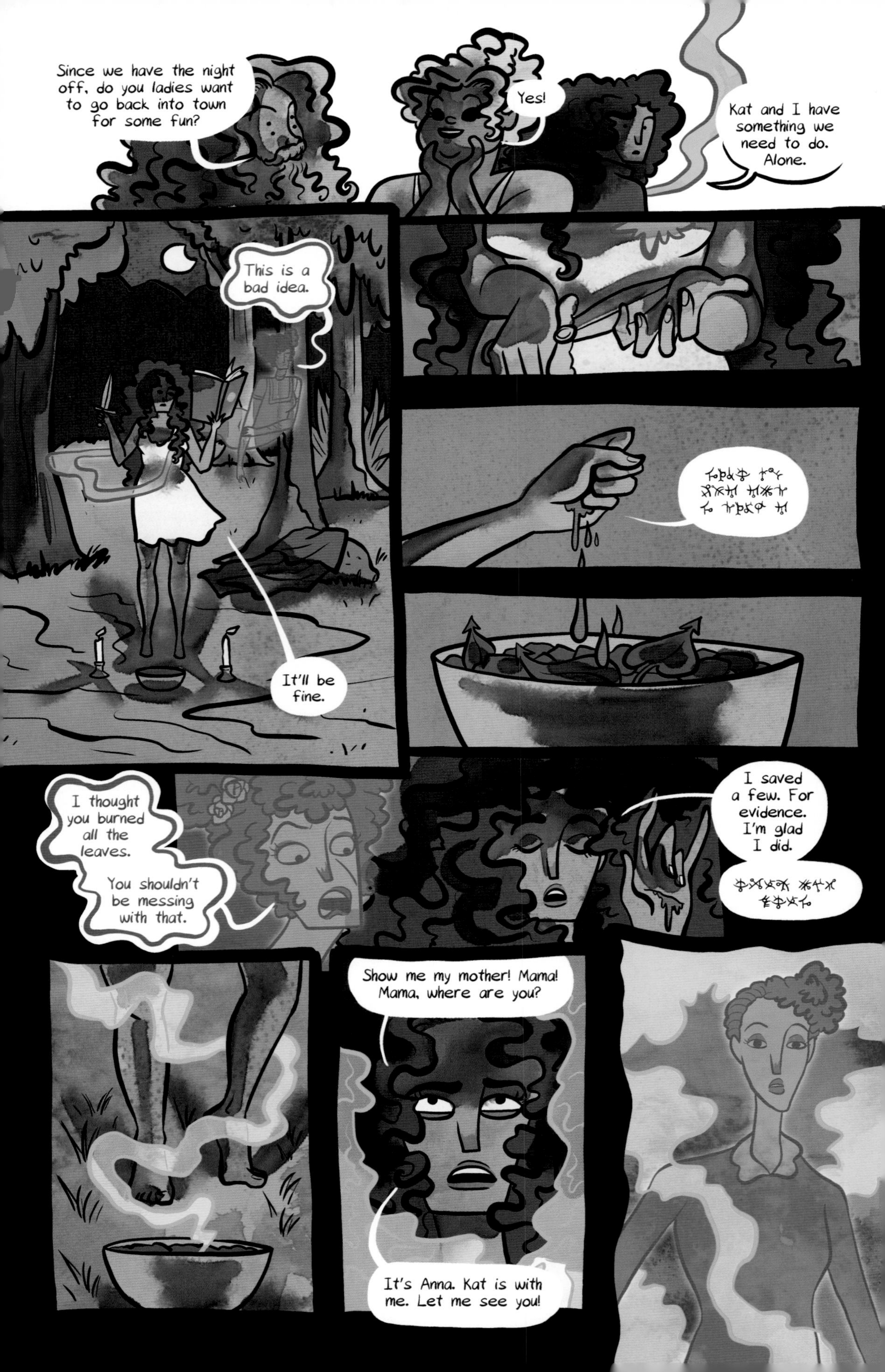
Since we have the night off, do you ladies want to go back into town for some fun?
Yes!
Kat and I have something we need to do. Alone.
This is a bad idea.
It'll be fine.
I thought you burned all the leaves.
You shouldn't be messing with that.
I saved a few. For evidence. I'm glad I did.
Show me my mother! Mama! Mama, where are you?
It's Anna. Kat is with me. Let me see you!

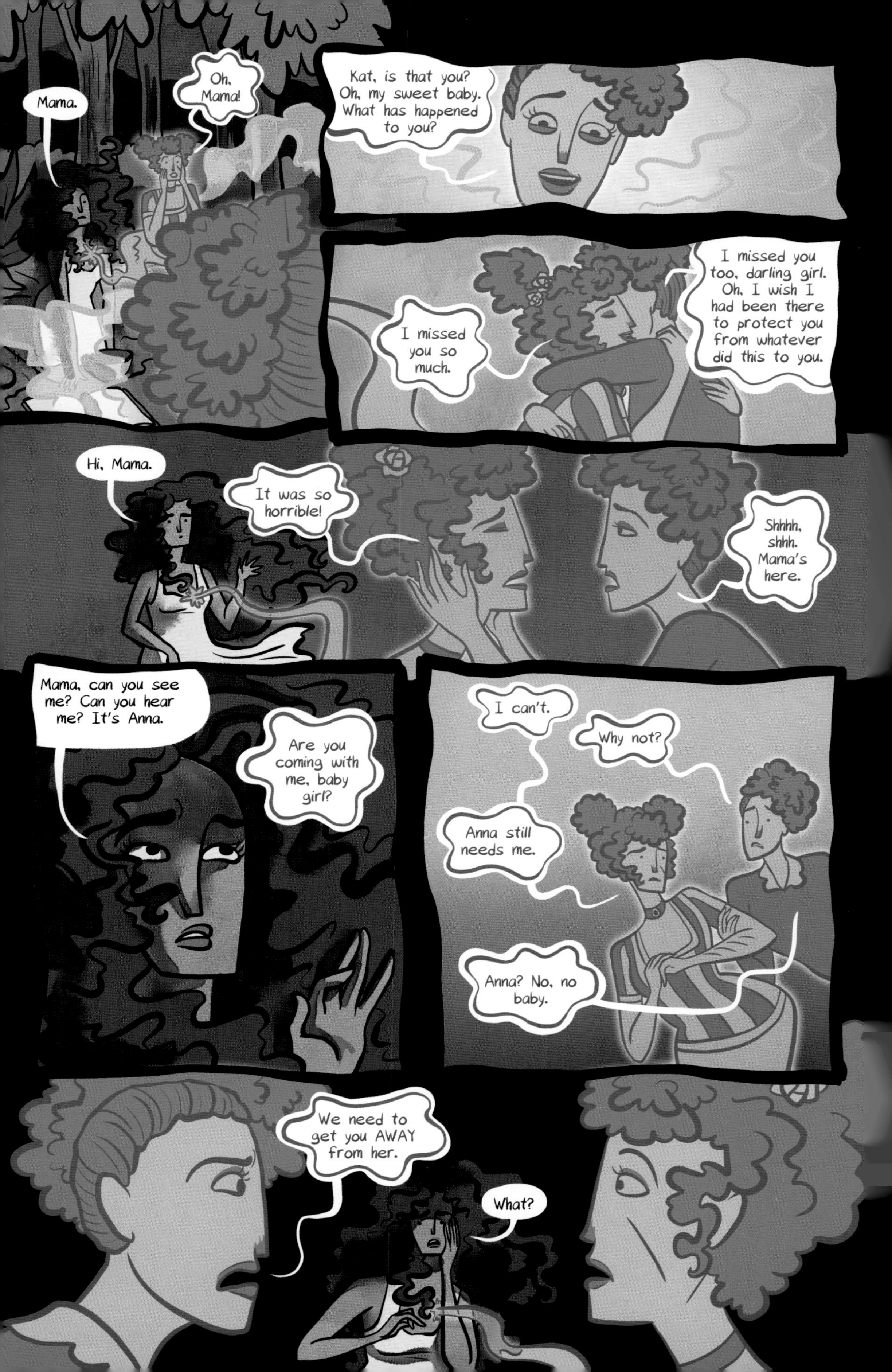
Mama.
Oh, Mama!
Kat, is that you? Oh, my sweet baby. What has happened to you?
I missed you so much.
I missed you too, darling girl. Oh, I wish I had been there to protect you from whatever did this to you.
Hi, Mama.
It was so horrible!
Shhhh, shhh. Mama's here.
Mama, can you see me? Can you hear me? It's Anna.
Are you coming with me, baby girl?
I can't.
Why not?
Anna still needs me.
Anna? No, no baby.
We need to get you AWAY from her.
What?

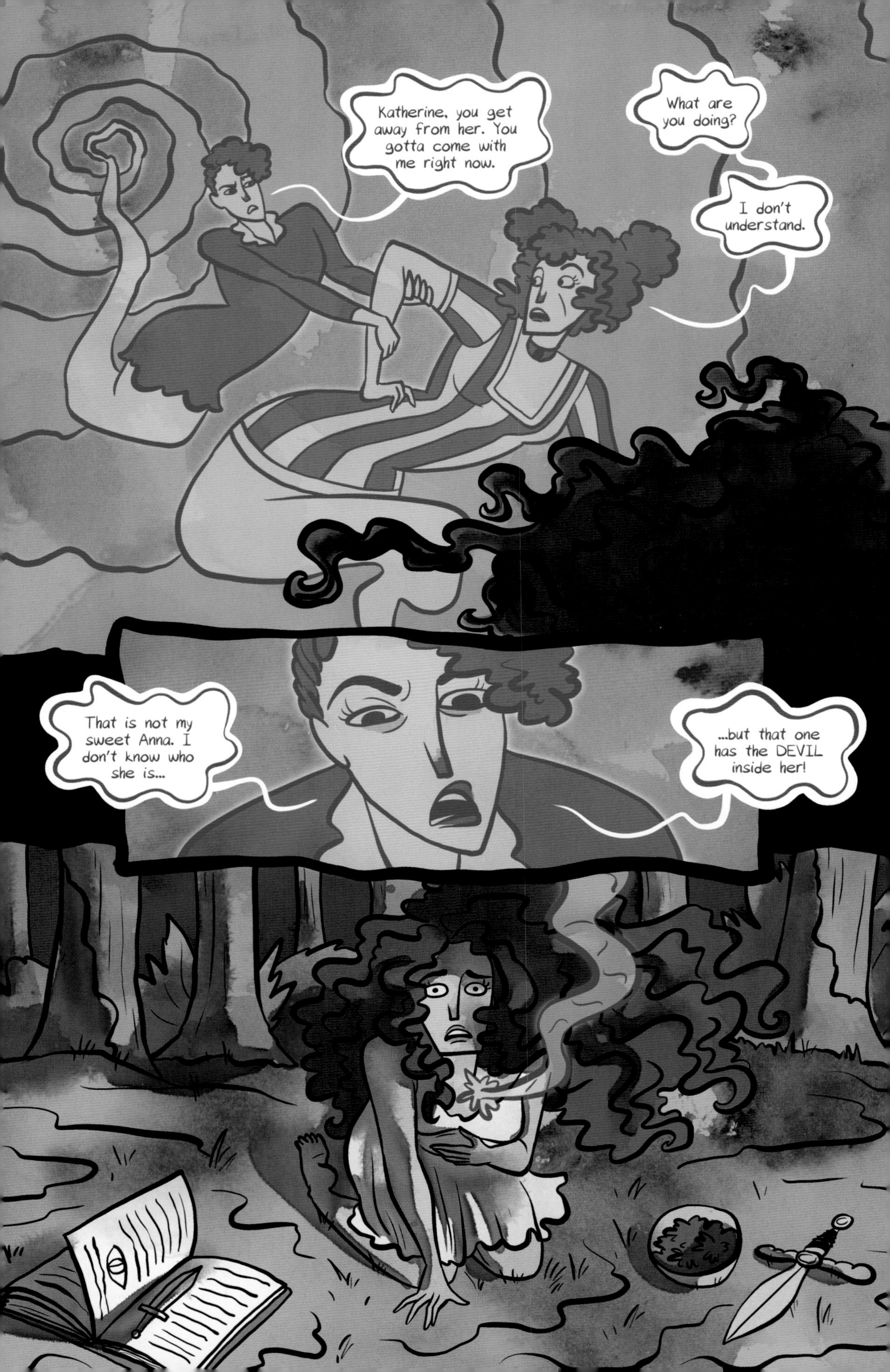
Katherine, you get away from her. You gotta come with me right now.
What are you doing?
I don't understand.
That is not my sweet Anna. I don't know who she is...
...but that one has the DEVIL inside her!

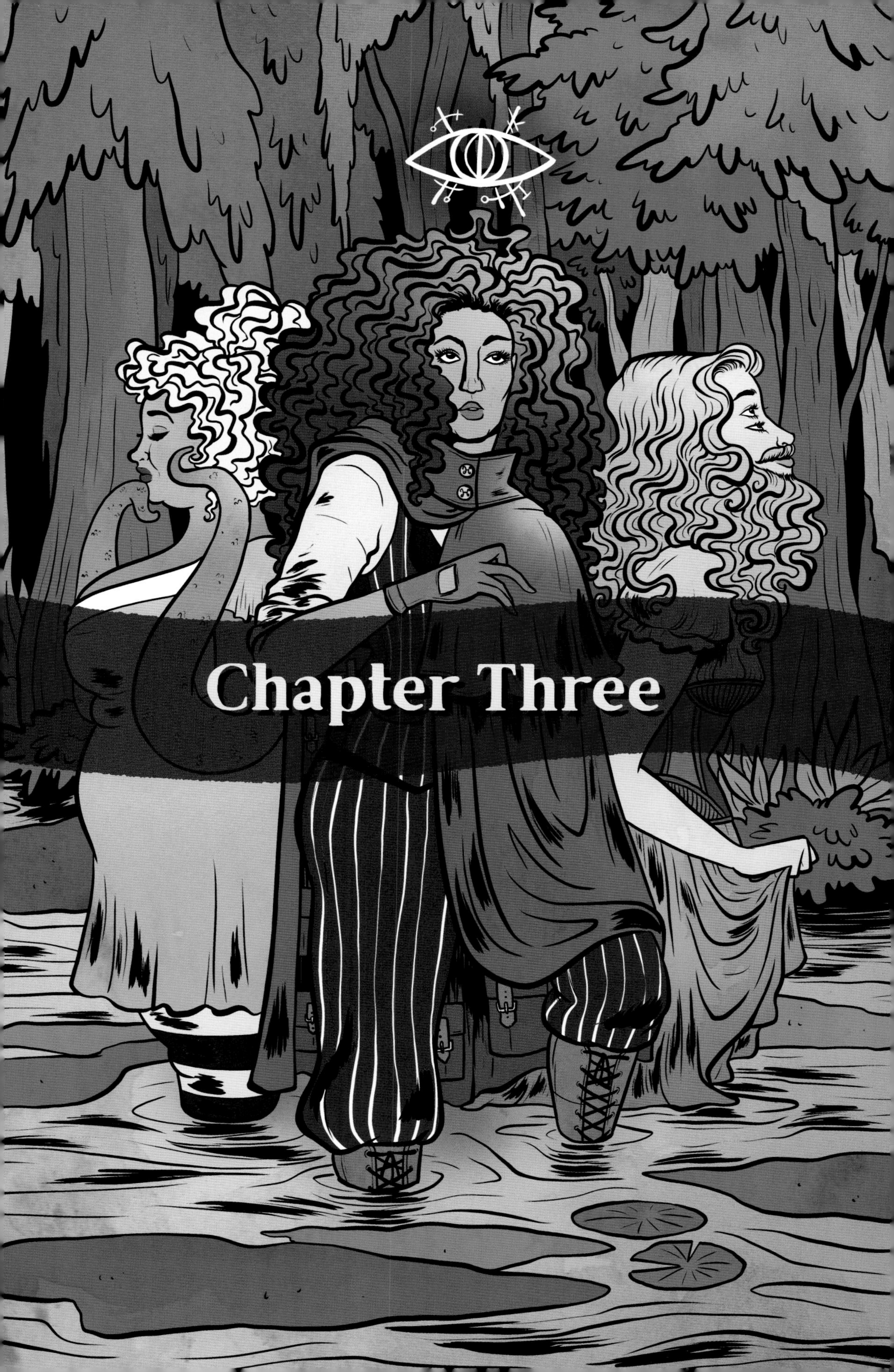
Chapter Three

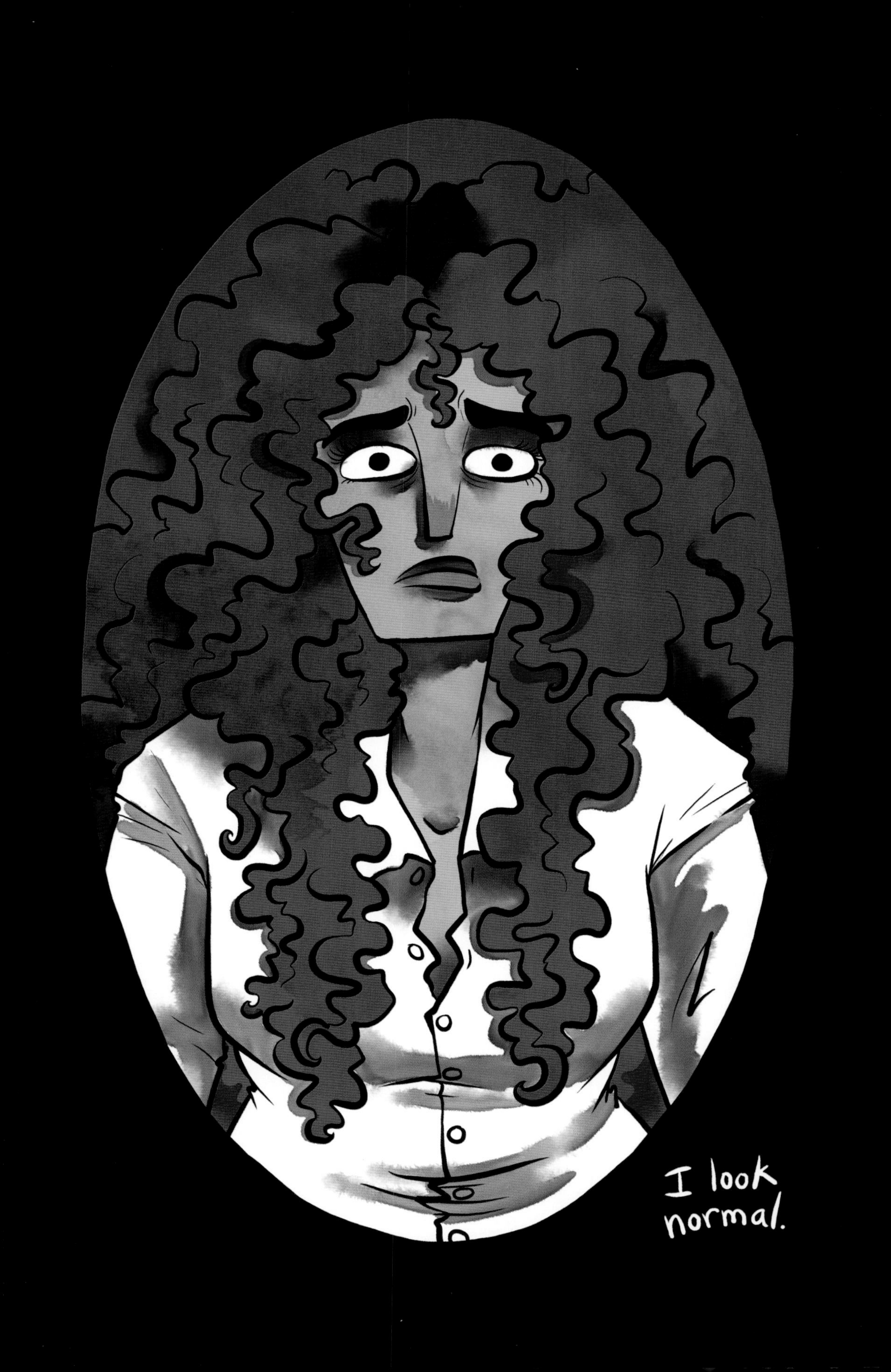
I look normal.

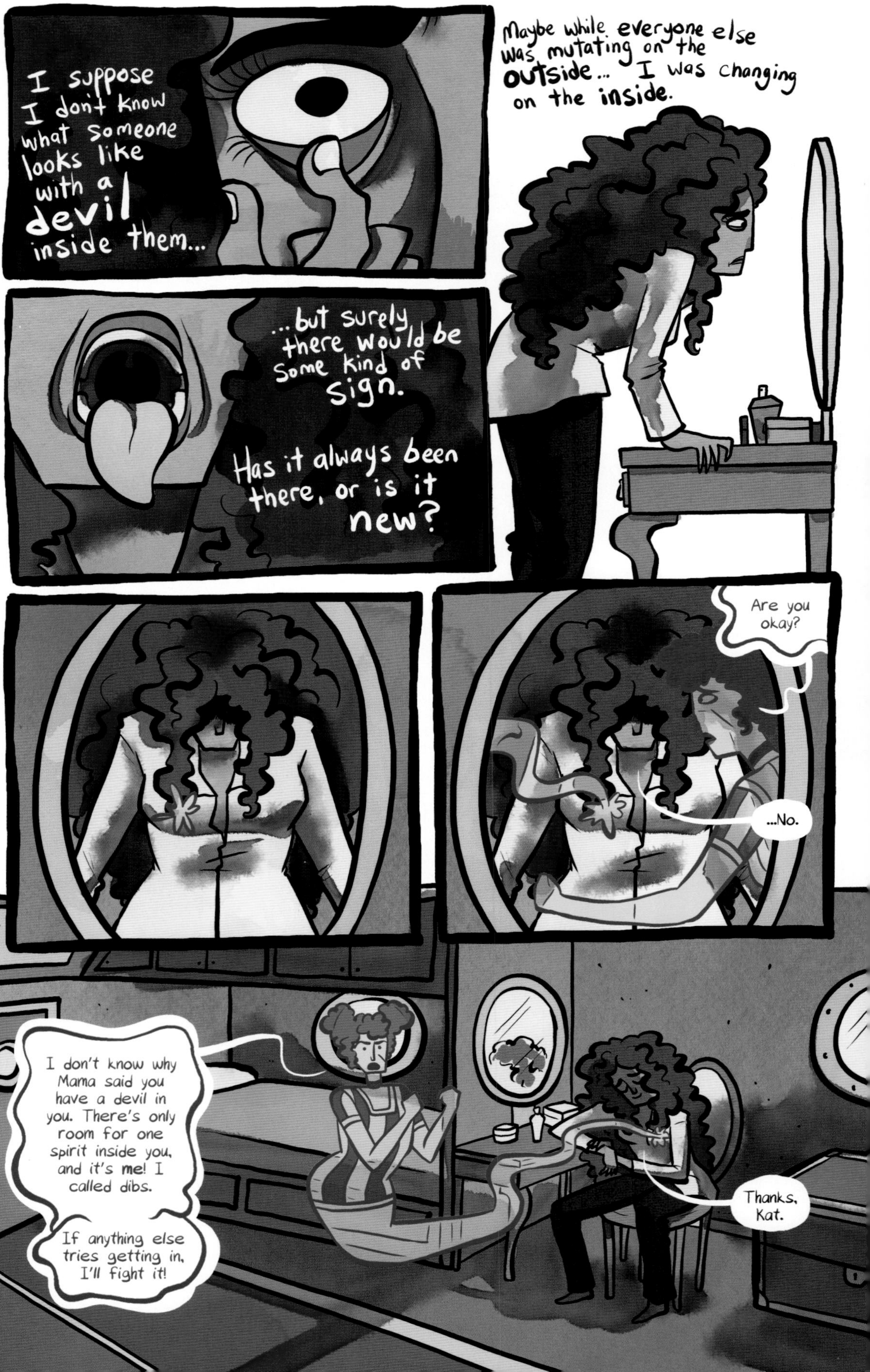
I suppose I don't know what someone looks like with a devil inside them...
Maybe while everyone else was mutating on the outside... I was changing on the inside.
...but surely there would be some kind of sign.
Has it always been there, or is it new?
Are you okay?
...No.
I don't know why Mama said you have a devil in you. There's only room for one spirit inside you, and it's me! I called dibs.
If anything else tries getting in, I'll fight it!
Thanks, Kat.

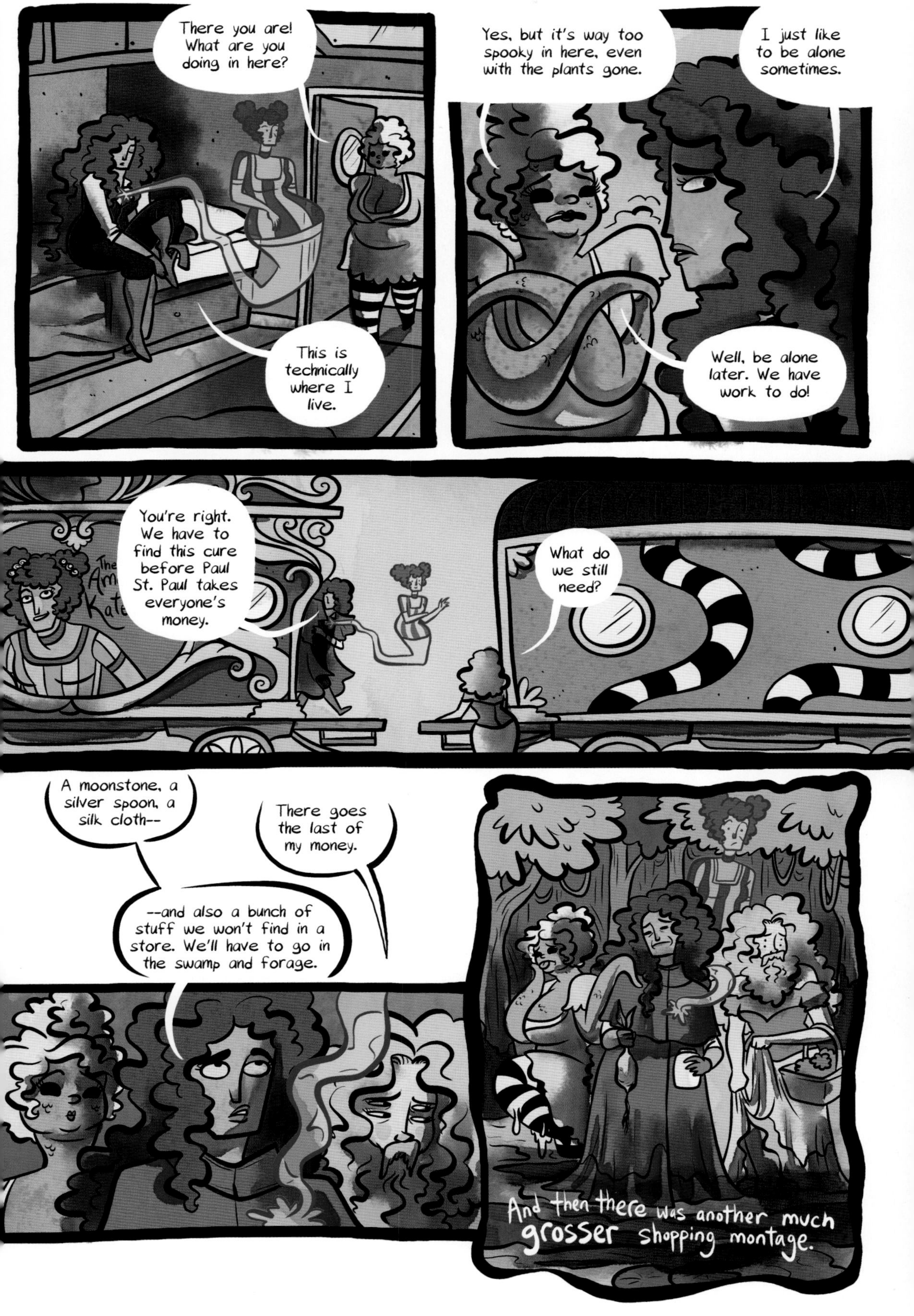
There you are! What are you doing in here?
This is technically where I live.
Yes, but it's way too spooky in here, even with the plants gone.
I just like to be alone sometimes.
Well, be alone later. We have work to do!
You're right. We have to find this cure before Paul St. Paul takes everyone's money.
What do we still need?
A moonstone, a silver spoon, a silk cloth--
There goes the last of my money.
--and also a bunch of stuff we won't find in a store. We'll have to go in the swamp and forage.
And then there was another much grosser shopping montage.

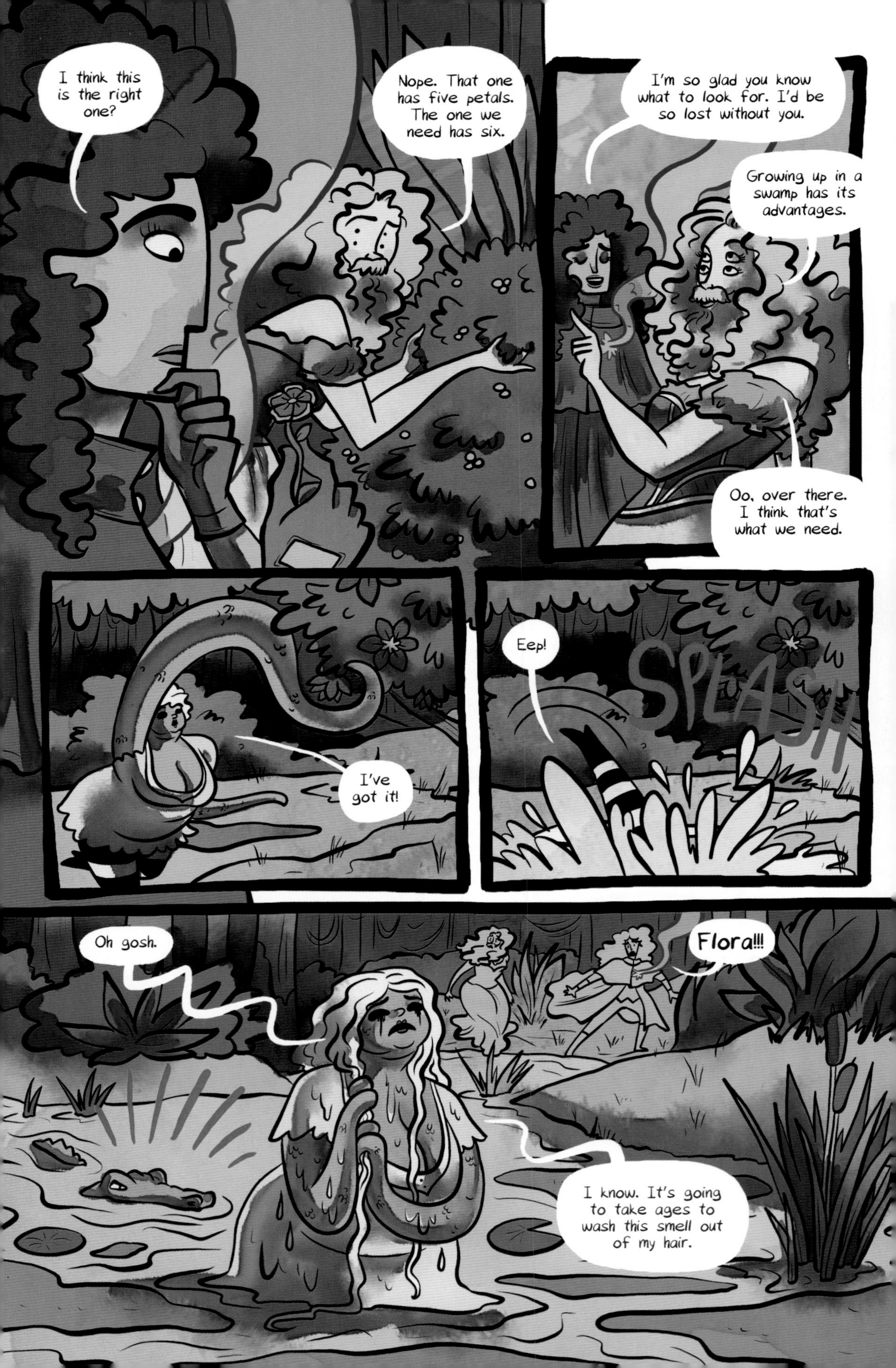
I think this is the right one?
Nope. That one has five petals. The one we need has six.
I'm so glad you know what to look for. I'd be so lost without you.
Growing up in a swamp has its advantages.
Oo, over there. I think that's what we need.
I've got it!
Eep!
SPLASH
Oh gosh.
Flora!!!
I know. It's going to take ages to wash this smell out of my hair.

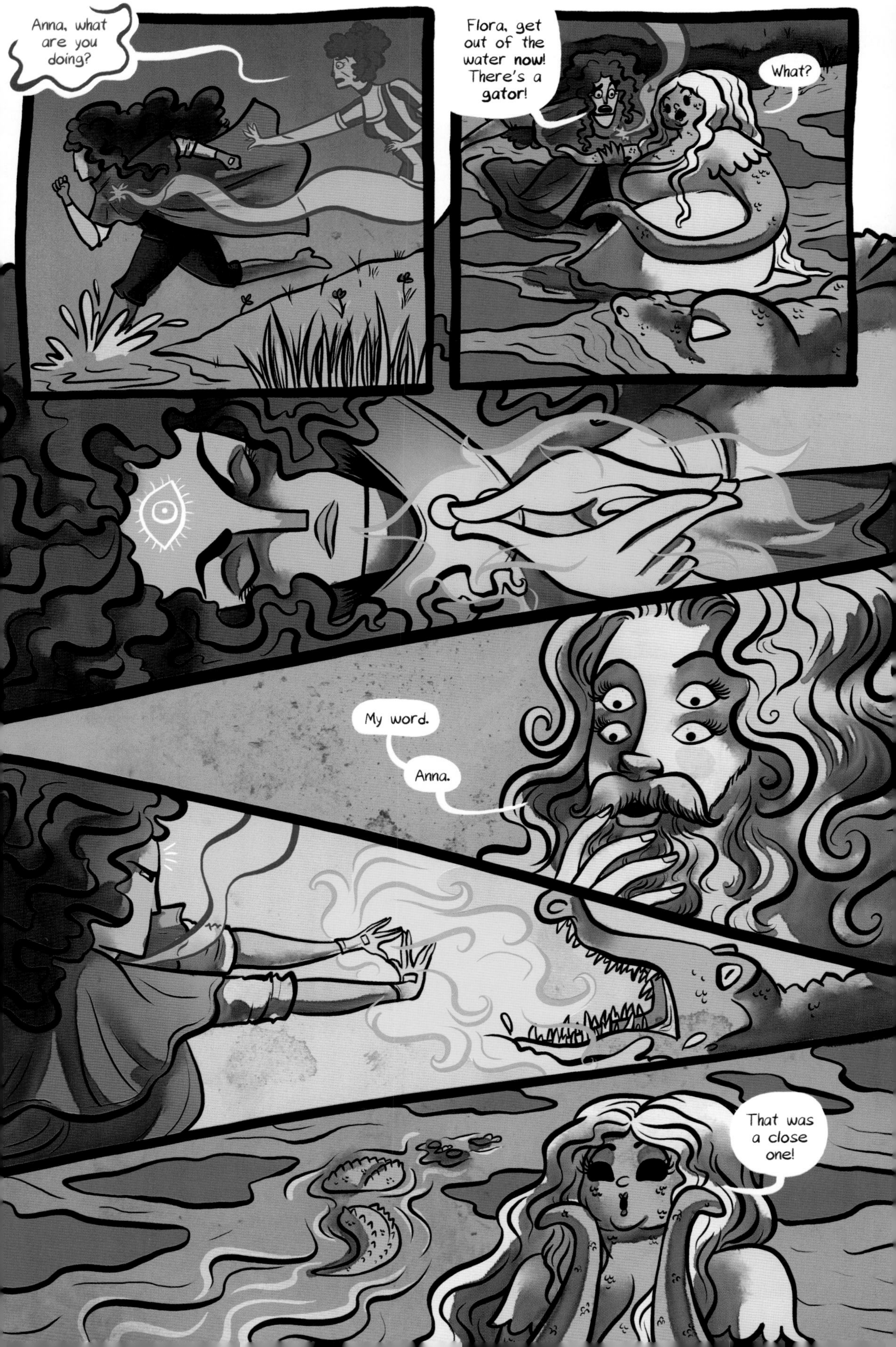
Anna, what are you doing?
Flora, get out of the water now! There's a gator!
What?
My word.
Anna.
That was a close one!

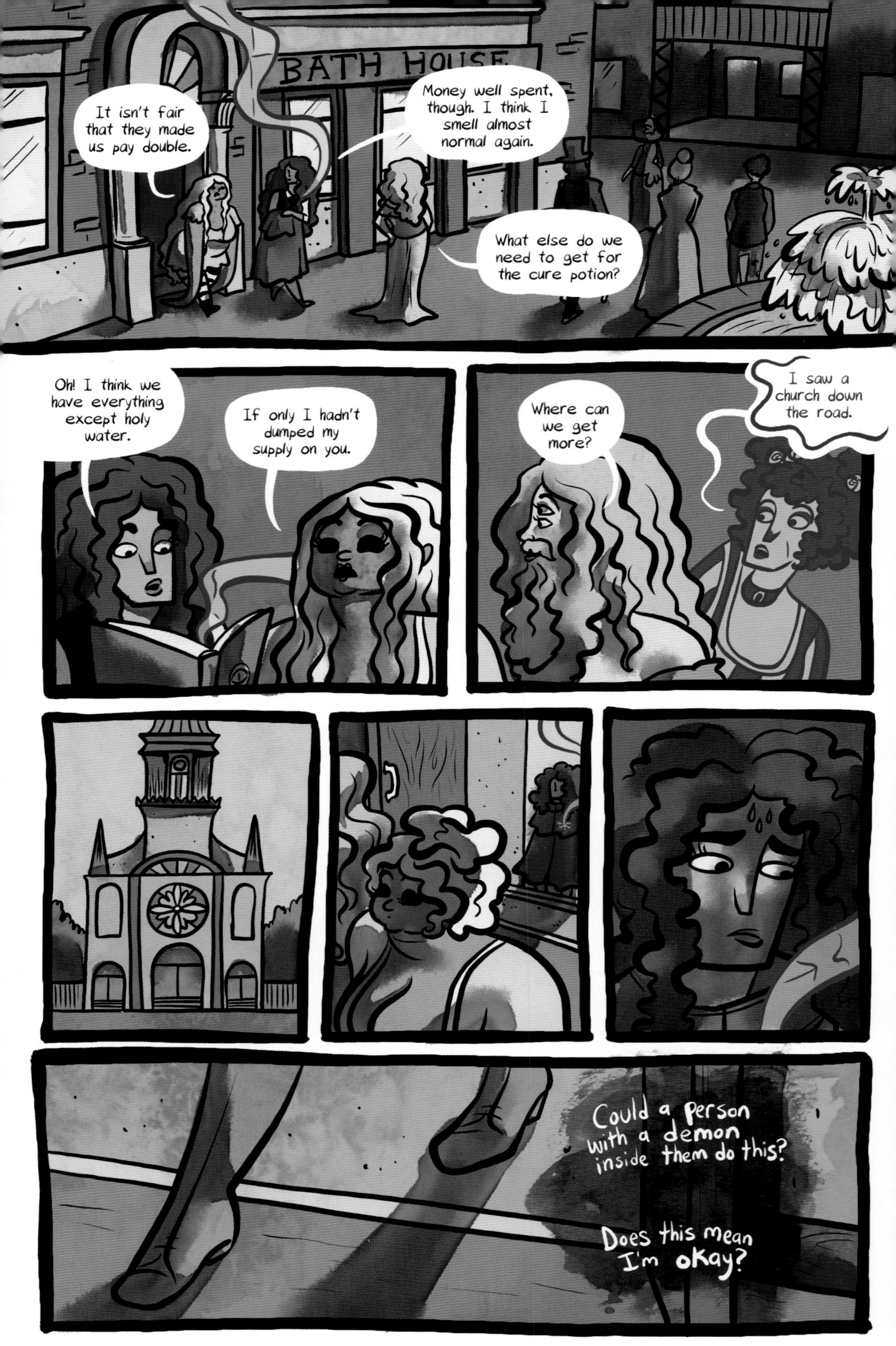
BATH HOUSE
It isn't fair that they made us pay double.
Money well spent, though. I think I smell almost normal again.
What else do we need to get for the cure potion?
Oh! I think we have everything except holy water.
If only I hadn't dumped my supply on you.
Where can we get more?
I saw a church down the road.
Could a person with a demon inside them do this?
Does this mean I'm okay?

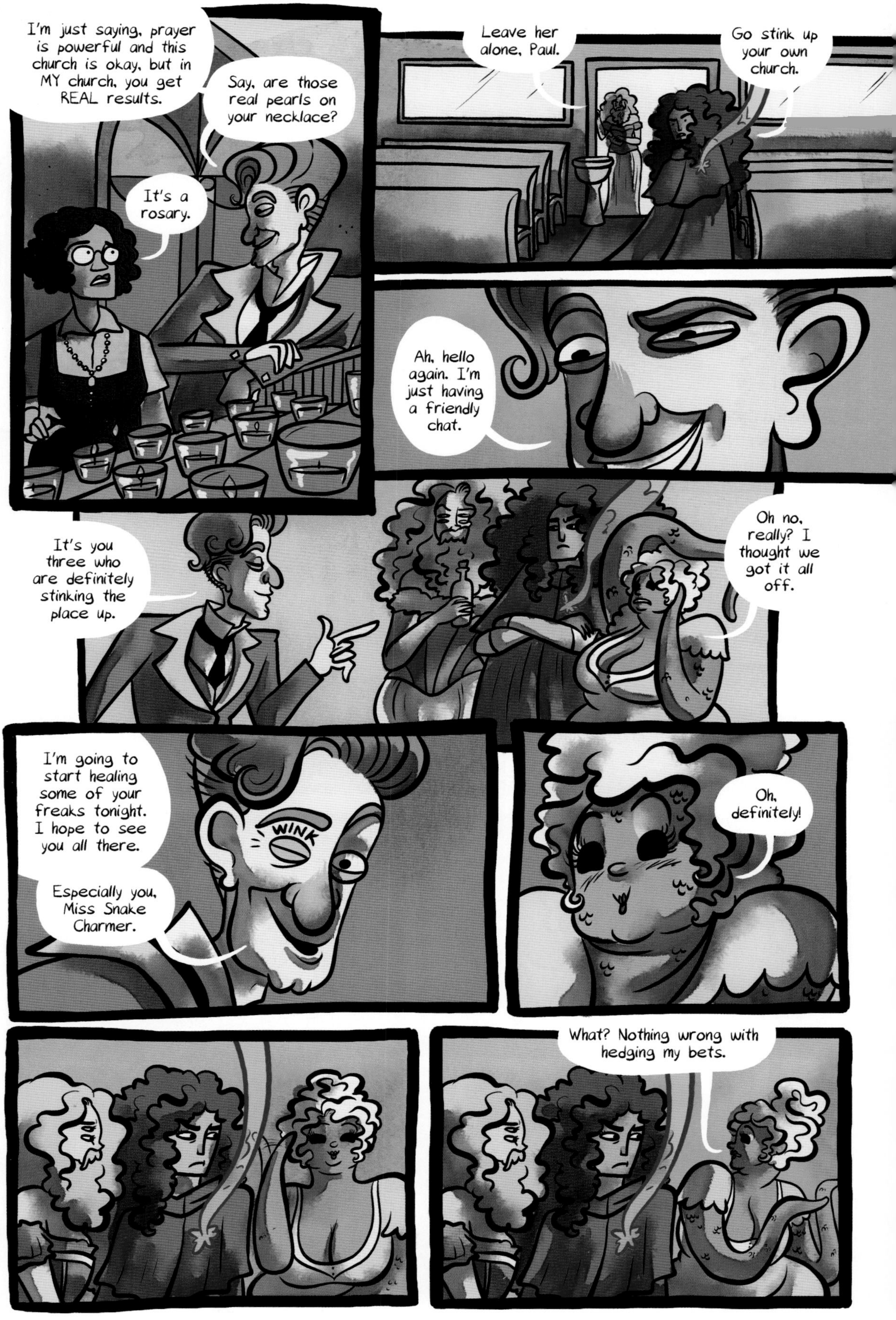

I'm just saying, prayer is powerful and this church is okay, but in MY church, you get REAL results.
Say, are those real pearls on your necklace?
It's a rosary.
Leave her alone, Paul.
Go stink up your own church.
Ah, hello again. I'm just having a friendly chat.
It's you three who are definitely stinking the place up.
Oh no, really? I thought we got it all off.
I'm going to start healing some of your freaks tonight. I hope to see you all there.
WINK
Especially you, Miss Snake Charmer.
Oh, definitely!
What? Nothing wrong with hedging my bets.

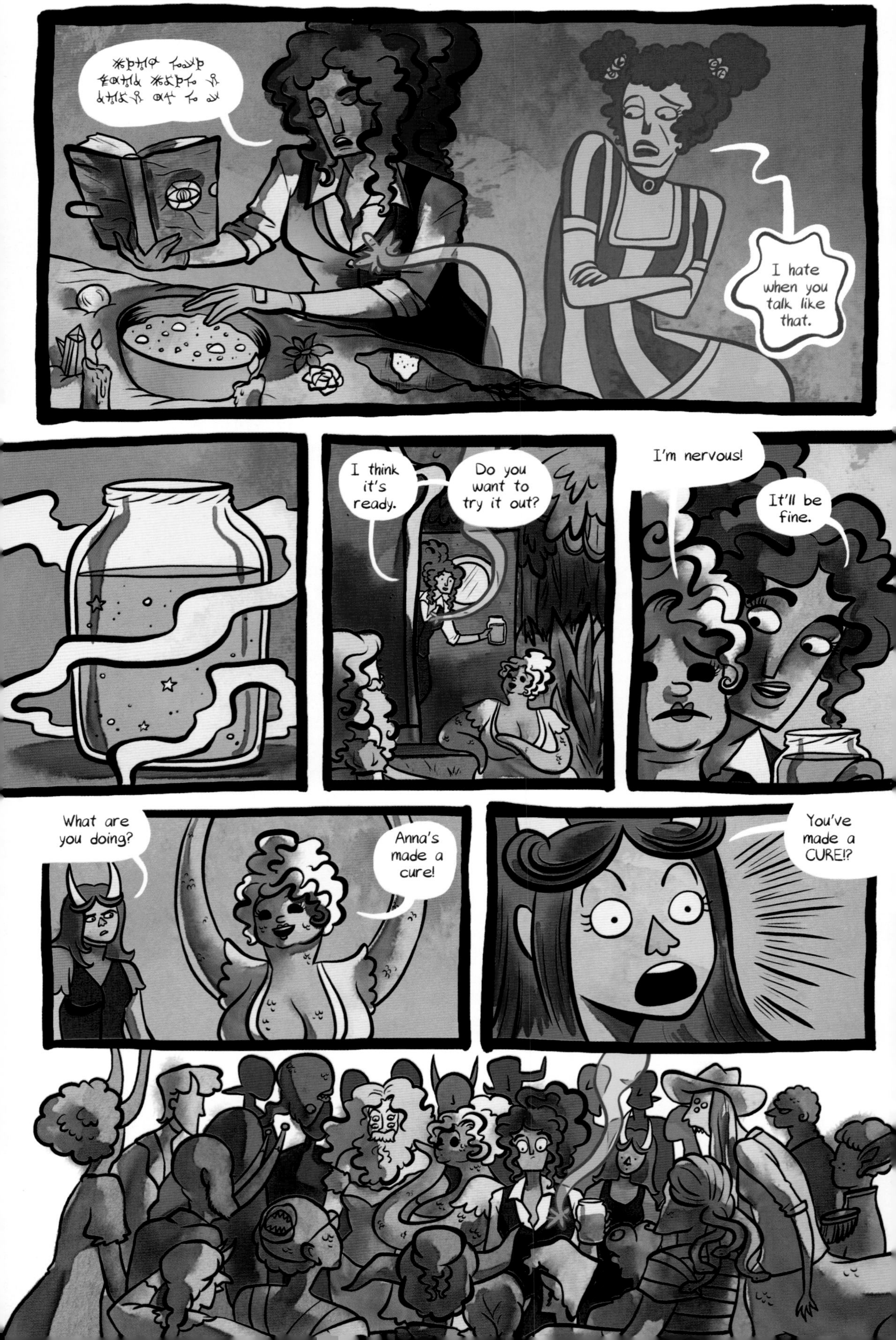

I hate when you talk like that.
I think it's ready.
Do you want to try it out?
I'm nervous!
It'll be fine.
What are you doing?
Anna's made a cure!
You've made a CURE!?

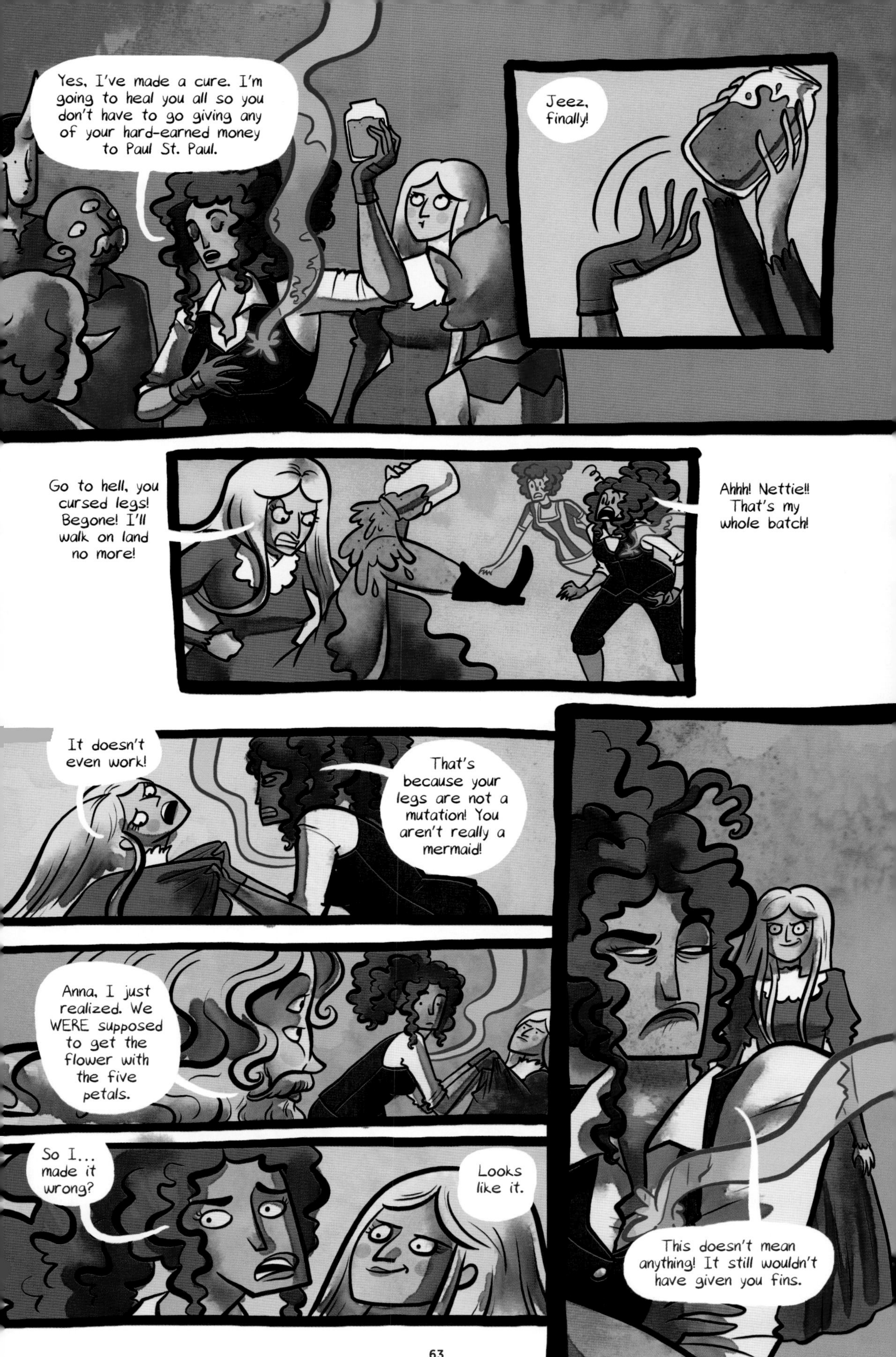
Yes, I've made a cure. I'm going to heal you all so you don't have to go giving any of your hard-earned money to Paul St. Paul.
Jeez, finally!
Go to hell, you cursed legs! Begone! I'll walk on land no more!
Ahhh! Nettie!! That's my whole batch!
It doesn't even work!
That's because your legs are not a mutation! You aren't really a mermaid!
Anna, I just realized. We WERE supposed to get the flower with the five petals.
So I... made it wrong?
Looks like it.
This doesn't mean anything! It still wouldn't have given you fins.

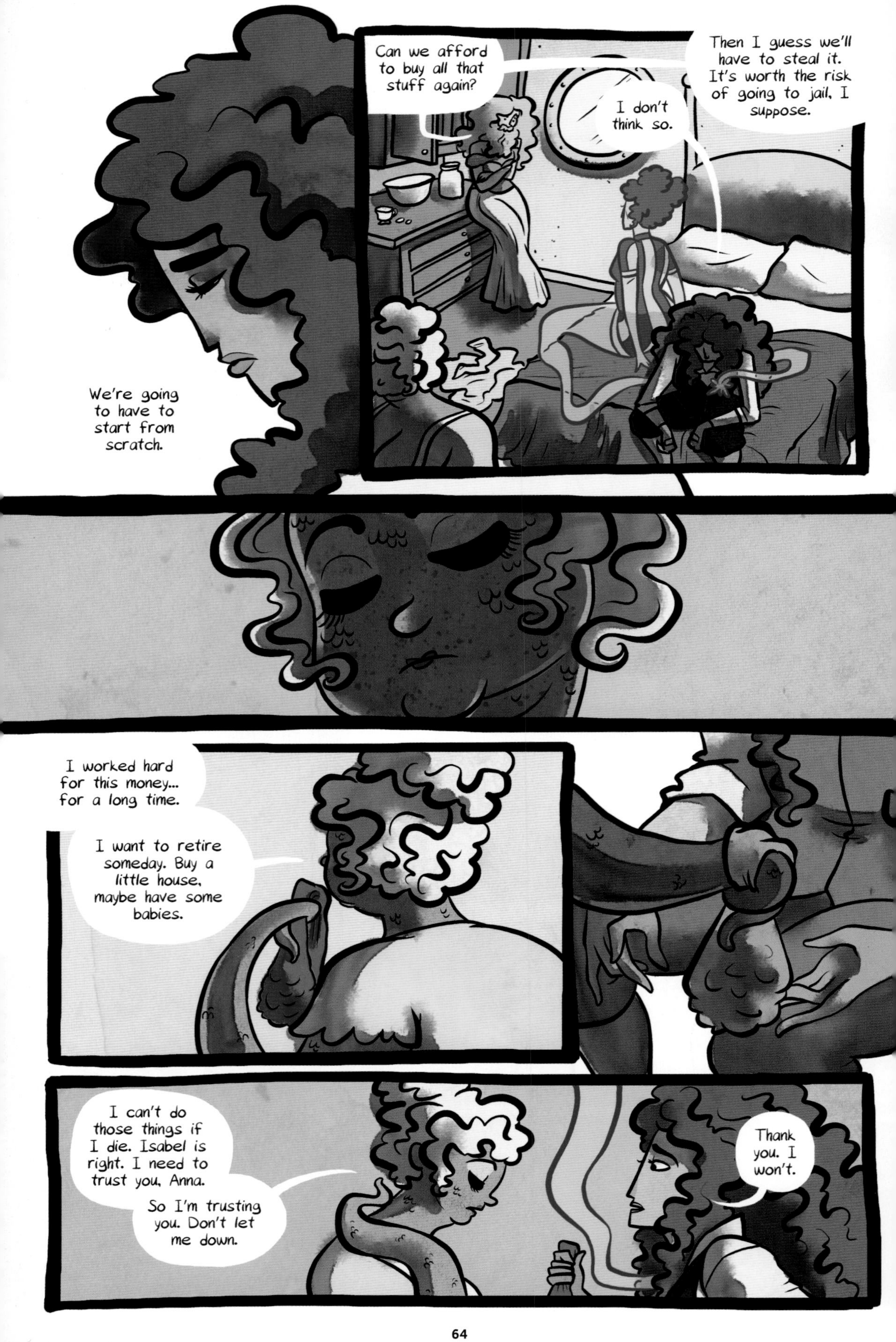
We're going to have to start from scratch.
Can we afford to buy all that stuff again?
I don't think so.
Then I guess we'll have to steal it. It's worth the risk of going to jail, I suppose.
I worked hard for this money... for a long time.
I want to retire someday. Buy a little house, maybe have some babies.
I can't do those things if I die. Isabel is right. I need to trust you, Anna.
So I'm trusting you. Don't let me down.
Thank you. I won't.

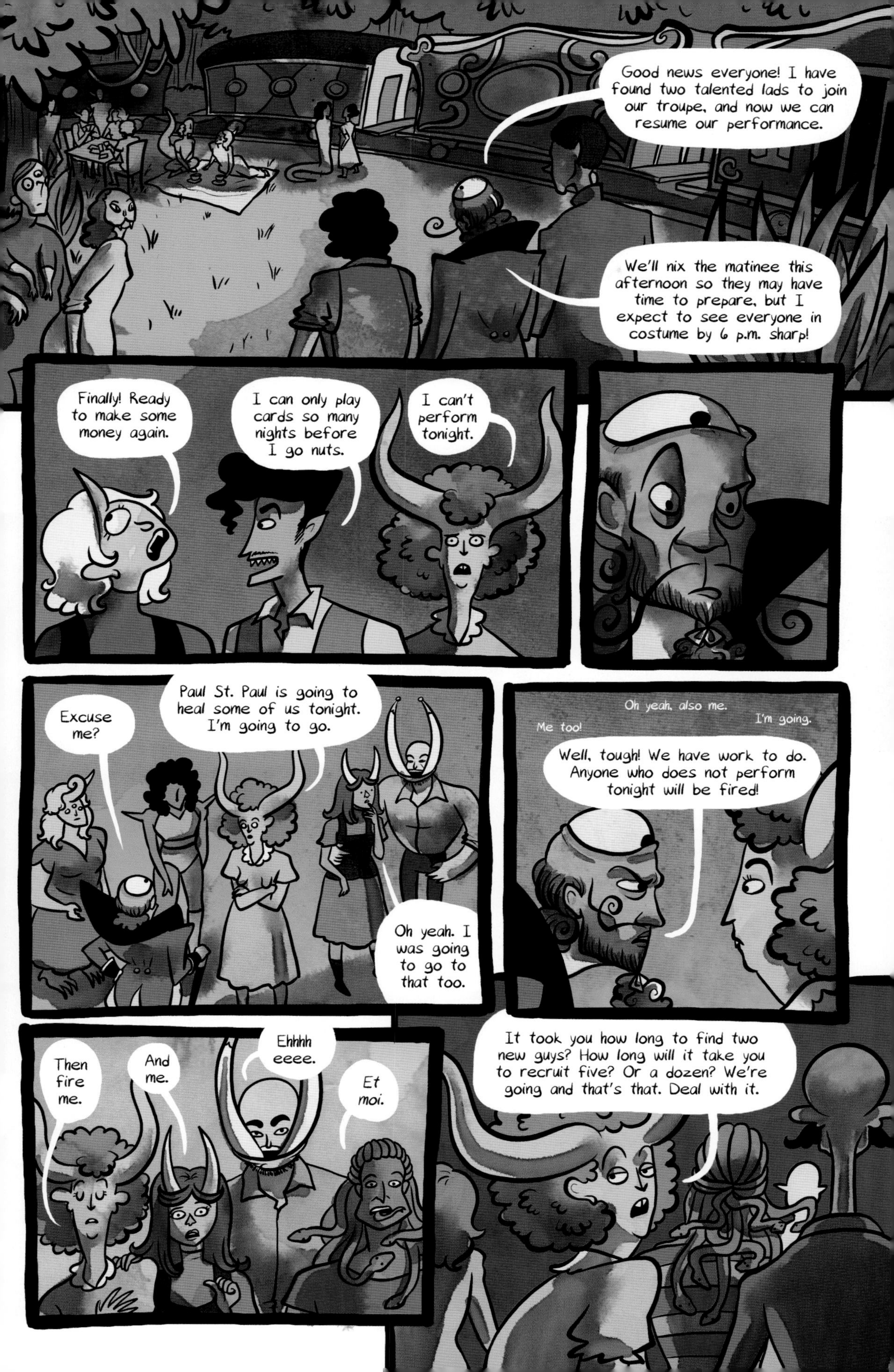
Good news everyone! I have found two talented lads to join our troupe, and now we can resume our performance.
We'll nix the matinee this afternoon so they may have time to prepare, but I expect to see everyone in costume by 6 p.m. sharp!
Finally! Ready to make some money again.
I can only play cards so many nights before I go nuts.
I can't perform tonight.
Excuse me?
Paul St. Paul is going to heal some of us tonight. I'm going to go.
Oh yeah. I was going to go to that too.
Me too!
Oh yeah, also me.
I'm going.
Well, tough! We have work to do. Anyone who does not perform tonight will be fired!
Then fire me.
And me.
Ehhhh eeee.
Et moi.
It took you how long to find two new guys? How long will it take you to recruit five? Or a dozen? We're going and that's that. Deal with it.

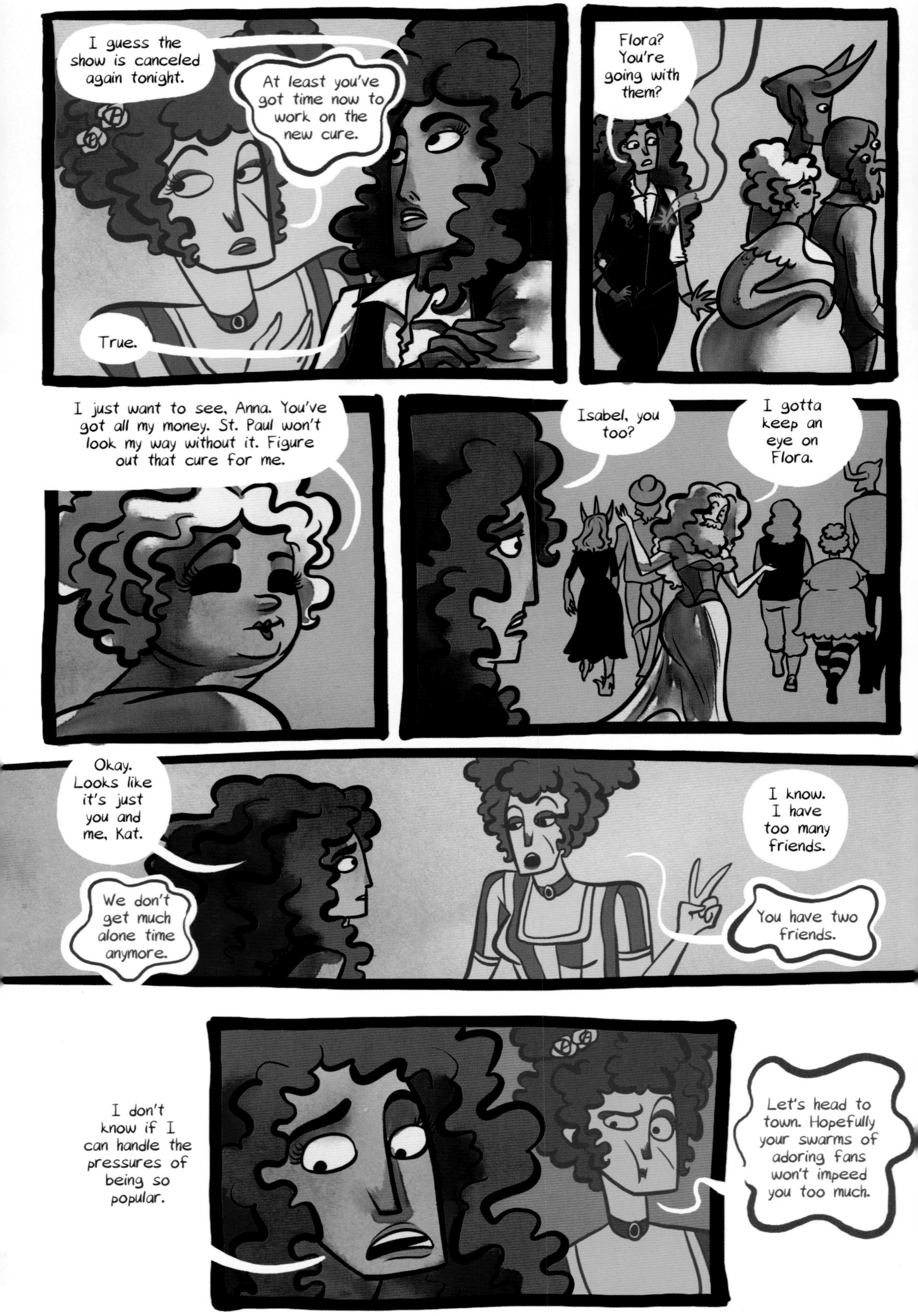

I guess the show is canceled again tonight.
At least you've got time now to work on the new cure.
True.
Flora? You're going with them?
I just want to see, Anna. You've got all my money. St. Paul won't look my way without it. Figure out that cure for me.
Isabel, you too?
I gotta keep an eye on Flora.
Okay. Looks like it's just you and me, Kat.
We don't get much alone time anymore.
I know. I have too many friends.
You have two friends.
I don't know if I can handle the pressures of being so popular.
Let's head to town. Hopefully your swarms of adoring fans won't impeed you too much.

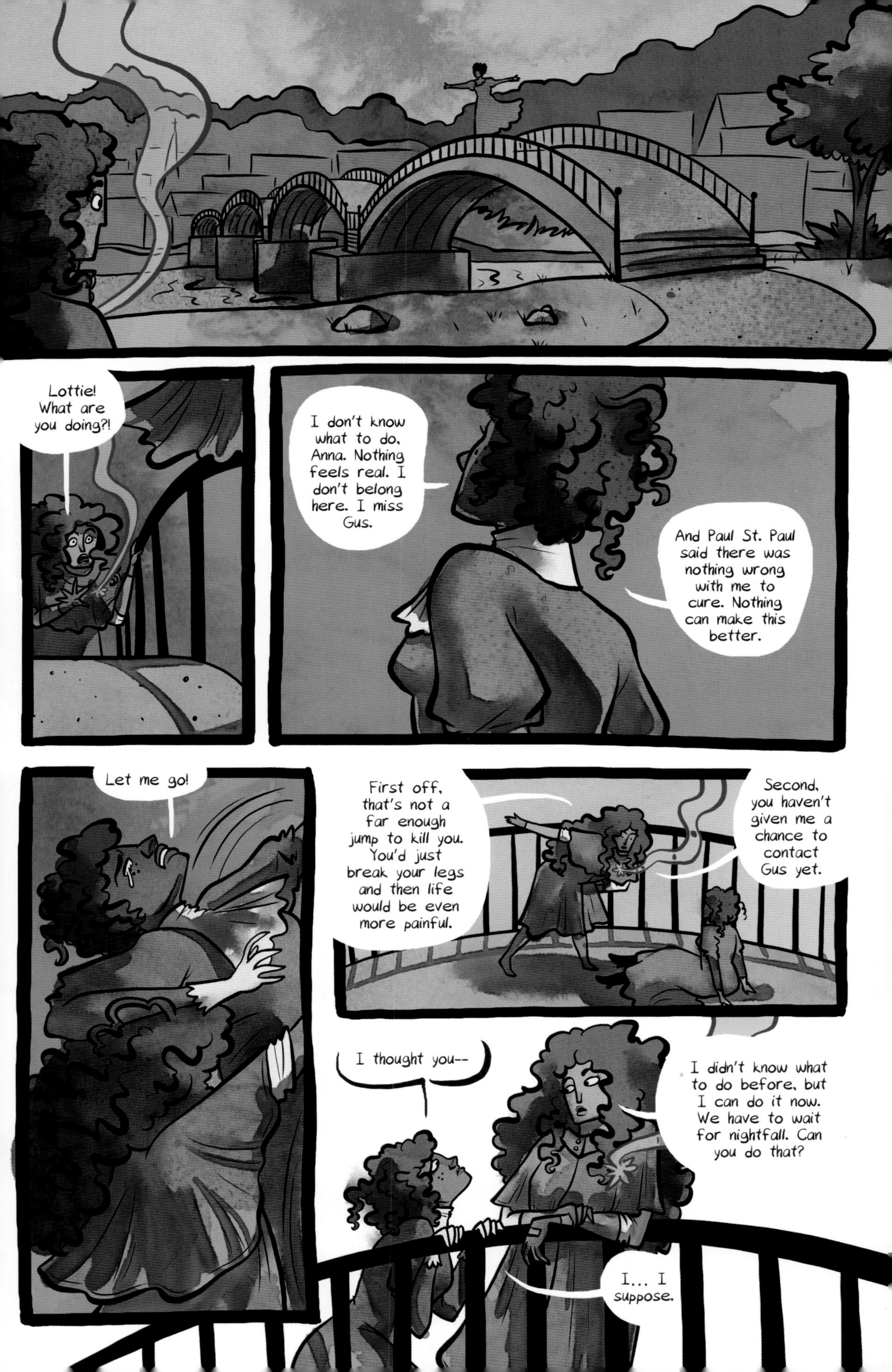
Lottie! What are you doing?!
I don't know what to do, Anna. Nothing feels real. I don't belong here. I miss Gus.
And Paul St. Paul said there was nothing wrong with me to cure. Nothing can make this better.
Let me go!
First off, that's not a far enough jump to kill you. You'd just break your legs and then life would be even more painful.
Second, you haven't given me a chance to contact Gus yet.
I thought you--
I didn't know what to do before, but I can do it now. We have to wait for nightfall. Can you do that?
I... I suppose.

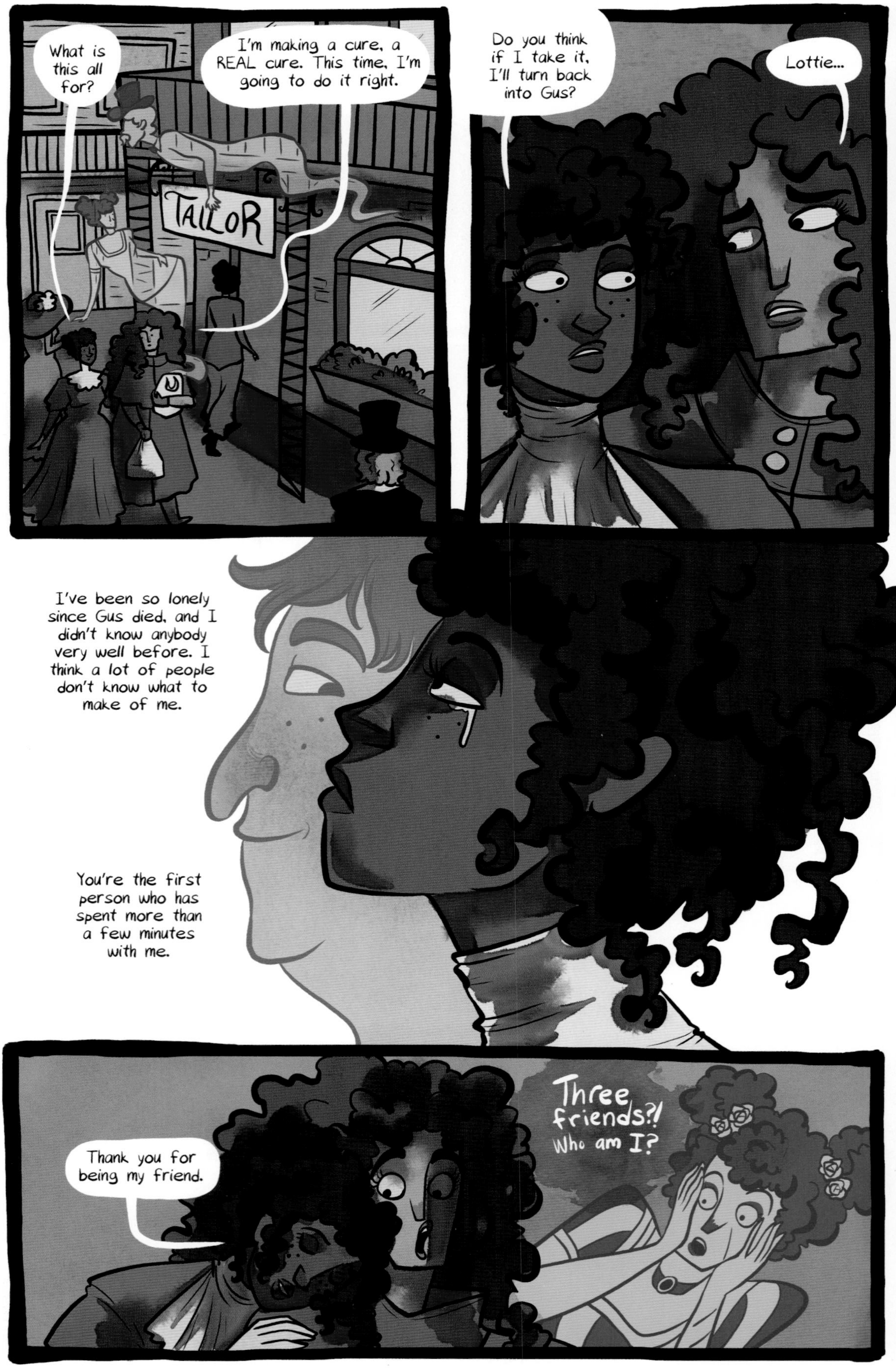
What is this all for?
I'm making a cure, a REAL cure. This time, I'm going to do it right.
TAILOR
Do you think if I take it, I'll turn back into Gus?
Lottie...
I've been so lonely since Gus died, and I didn't know anybody very well before. I think a lot of people don't know what to make of me.
You're the first person who has spent more than a few minutes with me.
Thank you for being my friend.
Three friends?! Who am I?

ᛞᚣᛟᚷ ᚷᛏᛁᛞᚣᛞᚷ ᚷᚷᚷ ᛏ ᛏᚷᛟᚣᚷ
ᚦᛁᛏᛟ ᛞᚷ ᚷᛏ ᛏᚷᛟᚷ

ᚷᛏᚷᚷ ᚷᚷᚷᚷᛏᛁᚷᛏᚷ
ᛟᚷ ᚷᛏᚷᛏᚷ

What language is that?

Um, I'm not sure. I never thought about it before.

It sounds Australian.

Huh? They speak English in Australia.

Th-they do?

But I've visited Melbourne so many times with Mama, and we always needed to hire a translator. We never met anyone speaking English except other tourists.

Hm.

Well, now I don't know **what** to think.

Anyway, I think I've finished the potion. It needs to rest for a bit. I messed that up last time.

We can do the seance while we wait. Come with me.

I can't believe you're gonna do this again.

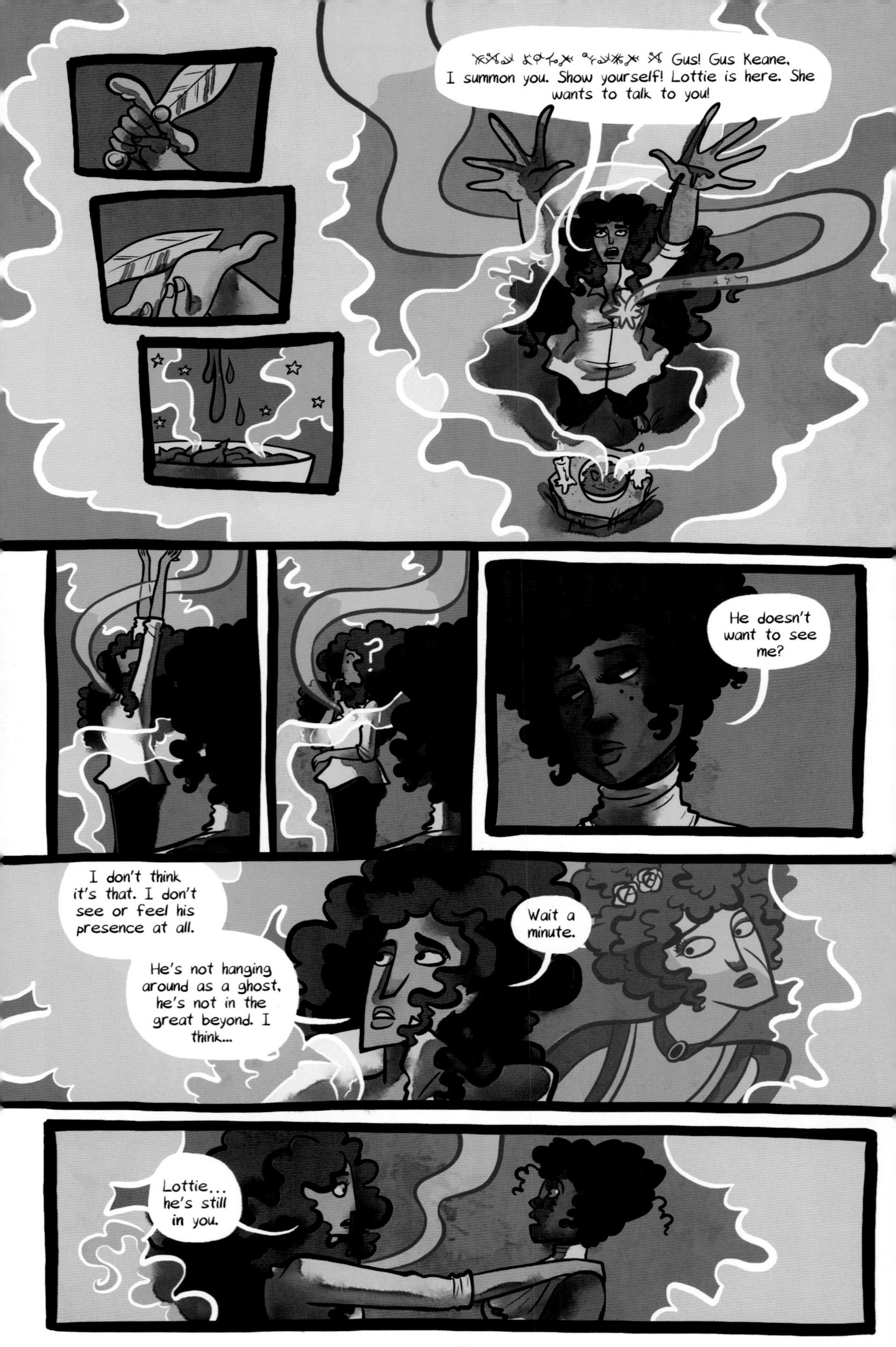
Gus! Gus Keane, I summon you. Show yourself! Lottie is here. She wants to talk to you!
?
He doesn't want to see me?
I don't think it's that. I don't see or feel his presence at all.
He's not hanging around as a ghost, he's not in the great beyond. I think...
Wait a minute.
Lottie... he's still in you.

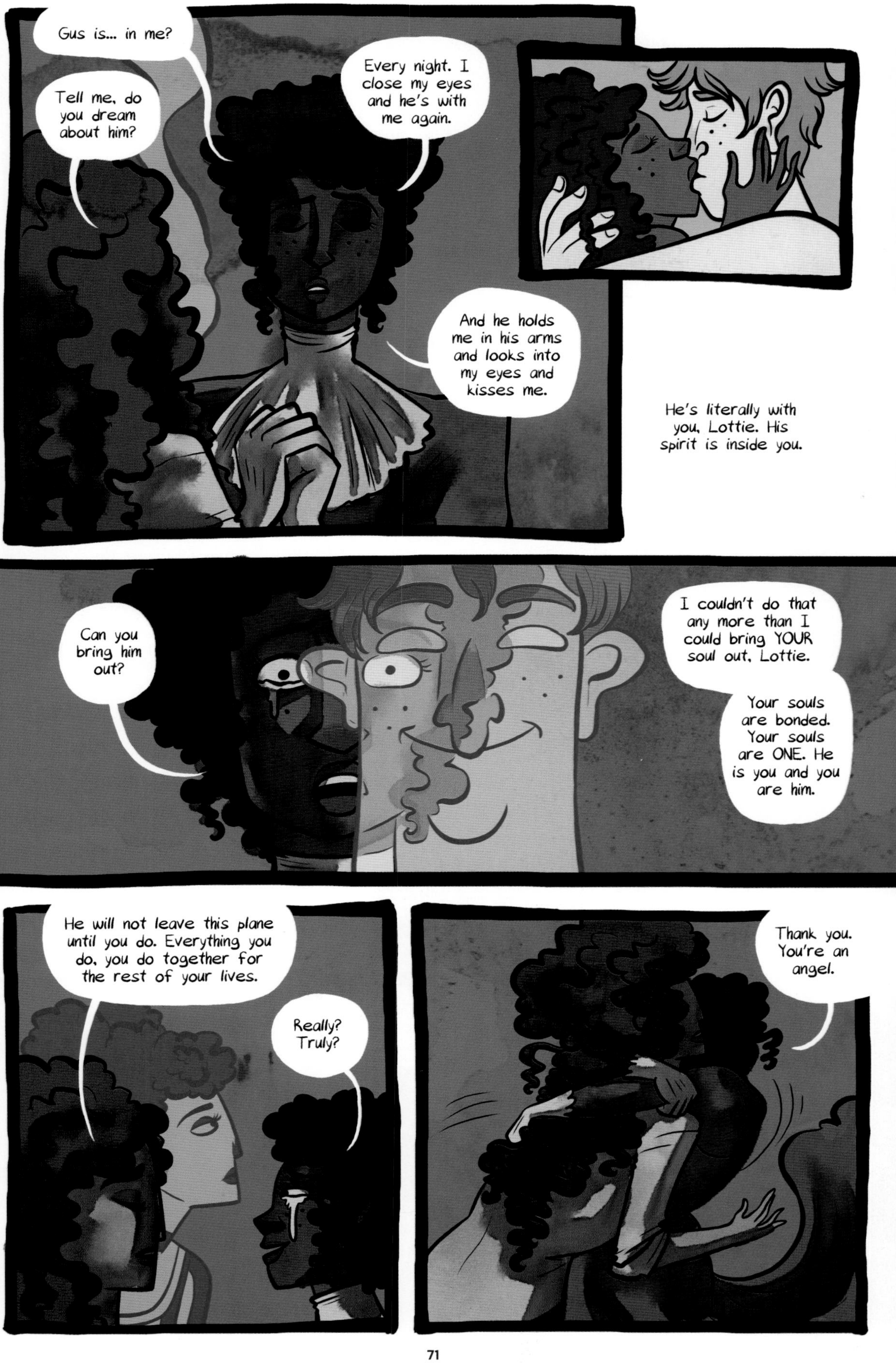
Gus is... in me?
Tell me, do you dream about him?
Every night. I close my eyes and he's with me again.
And he holds me in his arms and looks into my eyes and kisses me.
He's literally with you, Lottie. His spirit is inside you.
Can you bring him out?
I couldn't do that any more than I could bring YOUR soul out, Lottie.
Your souls are bonded. Your souls are ONE. He is you and you are him.
He will not leave this plane until you do. Everything you do, you do together for the rest of your lives.
Really? Truly?
Thank you. You're an angel.

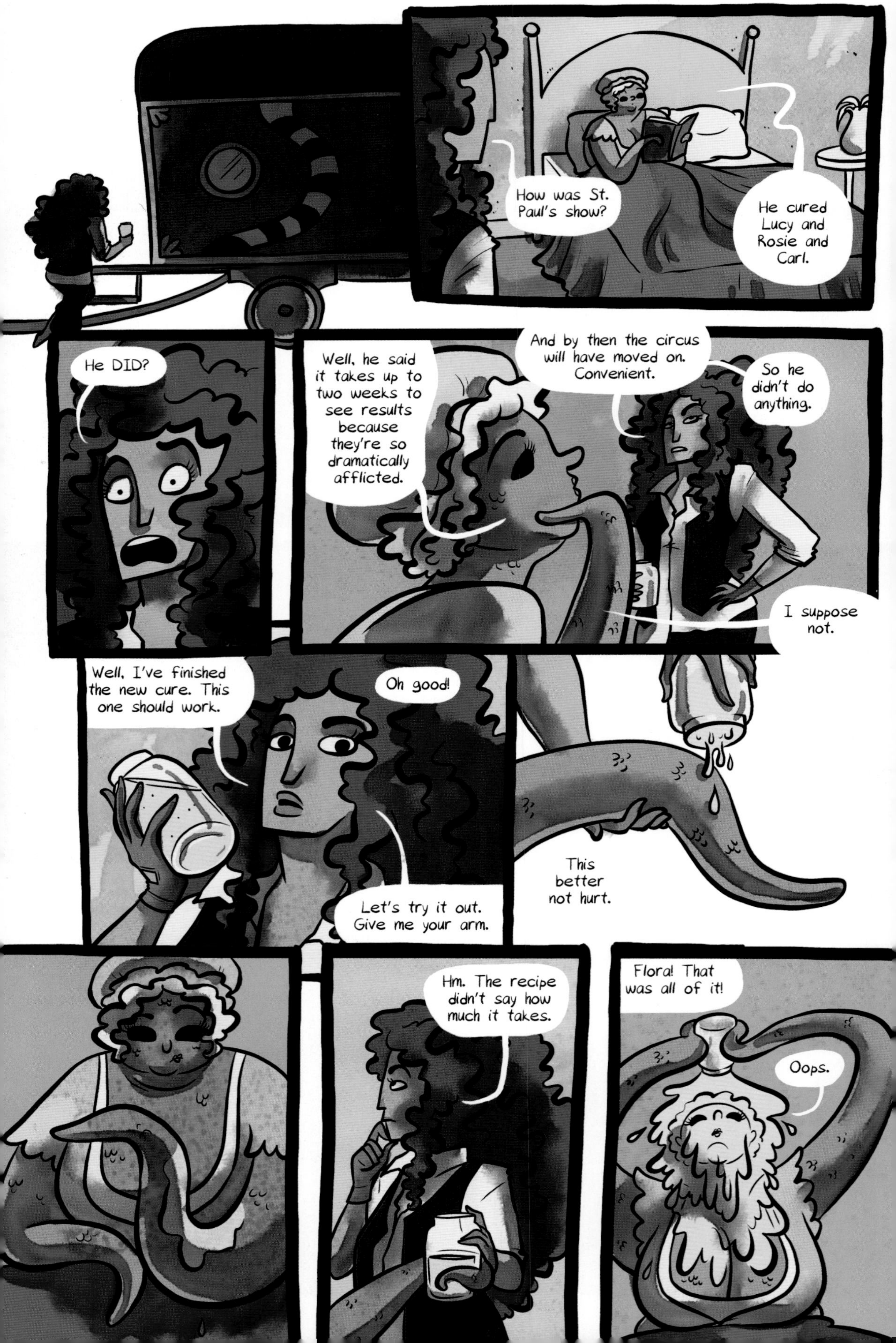
How was St. Paul's show?
He cured Lucy and Rosie and Carl.
He DID?
Well, he said it takes up to two weeks to see results because they're so dramatically afflicted.
And by then the circus will have moved on. Convenient.
So he didn't do anything.
I suppose not.
Well, I've finished the new cure. This one should work.
Oh good!
Let's try it out. Give me your arm.
This better not hurt.
Hm. The recipe didn't say how much it takes.
Flora! That was all of it!
Oops.

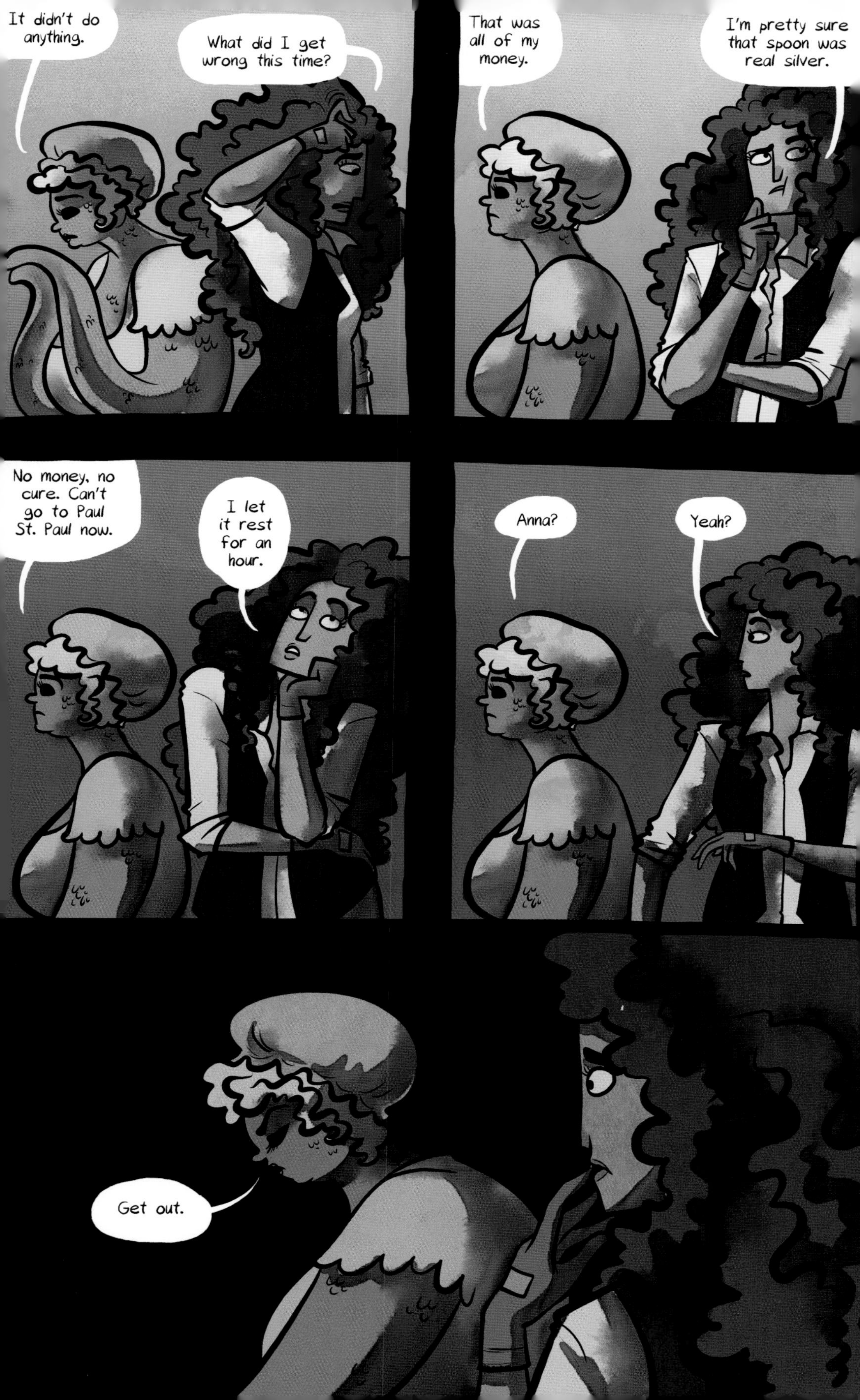
It didn't do anything.
What did I get wrong this time?
That was all of my money.
I'm pretty sure that spoon was real silver.
No money, no cure. Can't go to Paul St. Paul now.
I let it rest for an hour.
Anna?
Yeah?
Get out.

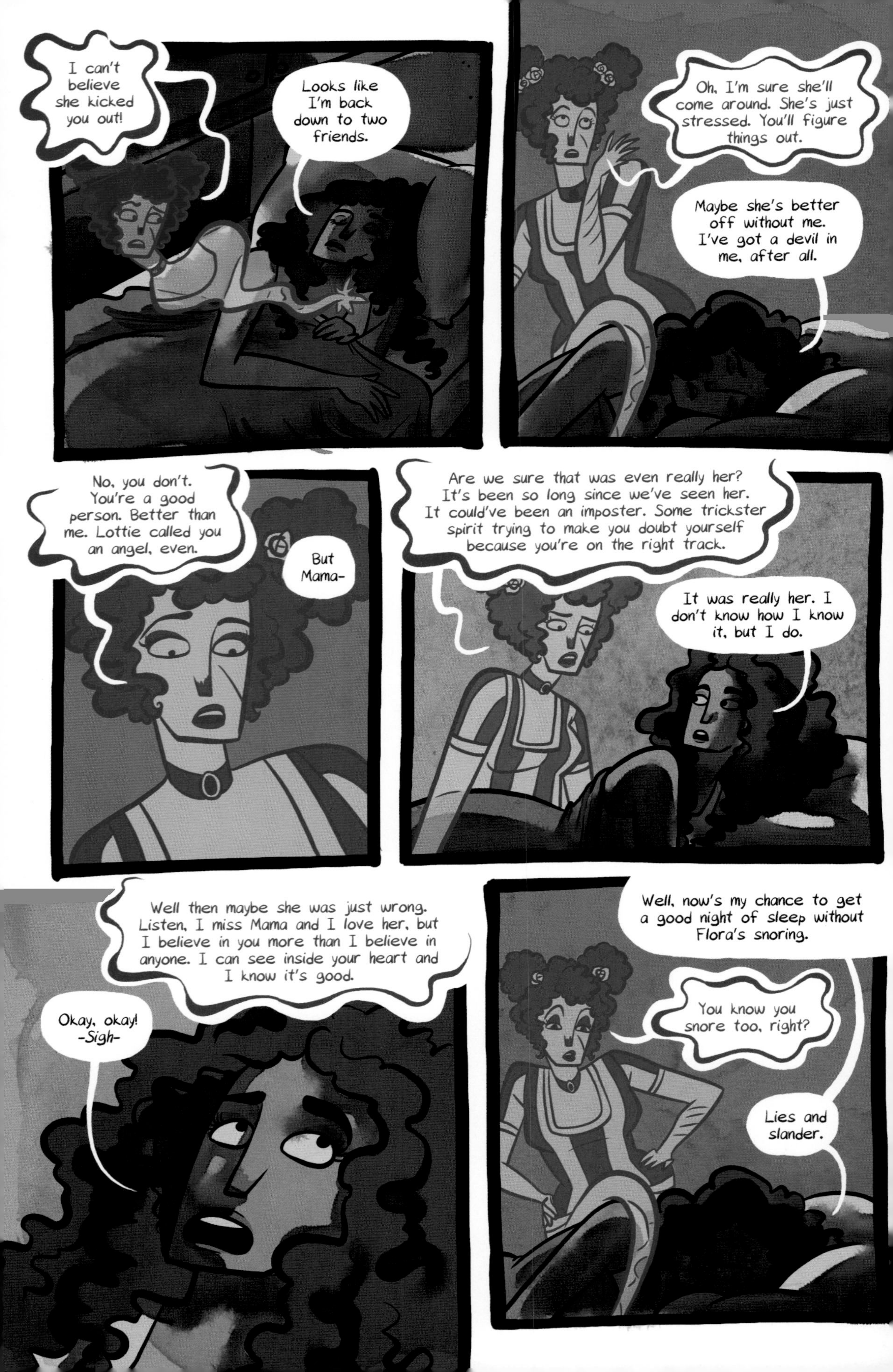

I can't believe she kicked you out!
Looks like I'm back down to two friends.
Oh, I'm sure she'll come around. She's just stressed. You'll figure things out.
Maybe she's better off without me. I've got a devil in me, after all.
No, you don't. You're a good person. Better than me. Lottie called you an angel, even.
But Mama-
Are we sure that was even really her? It's been so long since we've seen her. It could've been an imposter. Some trickster spirit trying to make you doubt yourself because you're on the right track.
It was really her. I don't know how I know it, but I do.
Well then maybe she was just wrong. Listen, I miss Mama and I love her, but I believe in you more than I believe in anyone. I can see inside your heart and I know it's good.
Okay, okay! -Sigh-
Well, now's my chance to get a good night of sleep without Flora's snoring.
You know you snore too, right?
Lies and slander.

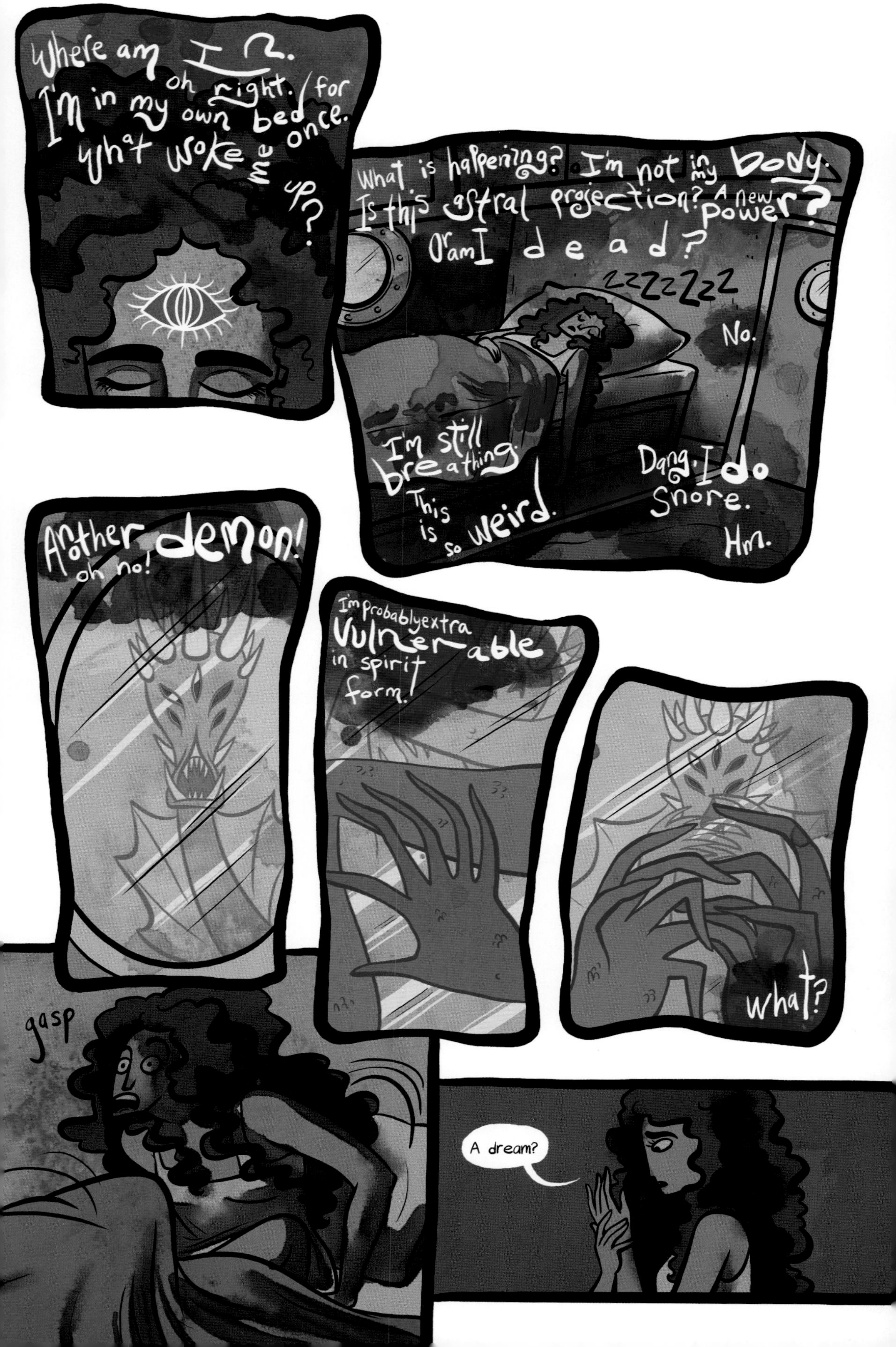
Where am I?
oh right.
I'm in my own bed for once.
What woke me up?
What is happening? I'm not in my body.
Is this astral projection? A new power?
Or am I dead?
ZZZZZZZ
No.
I'm still breathing.
This is so weird.
Dang. I do snore.
Hm.
Another demon!
oh no!
I'm probably extra vulnerable in spirit form!
what?
gasp
A dream?

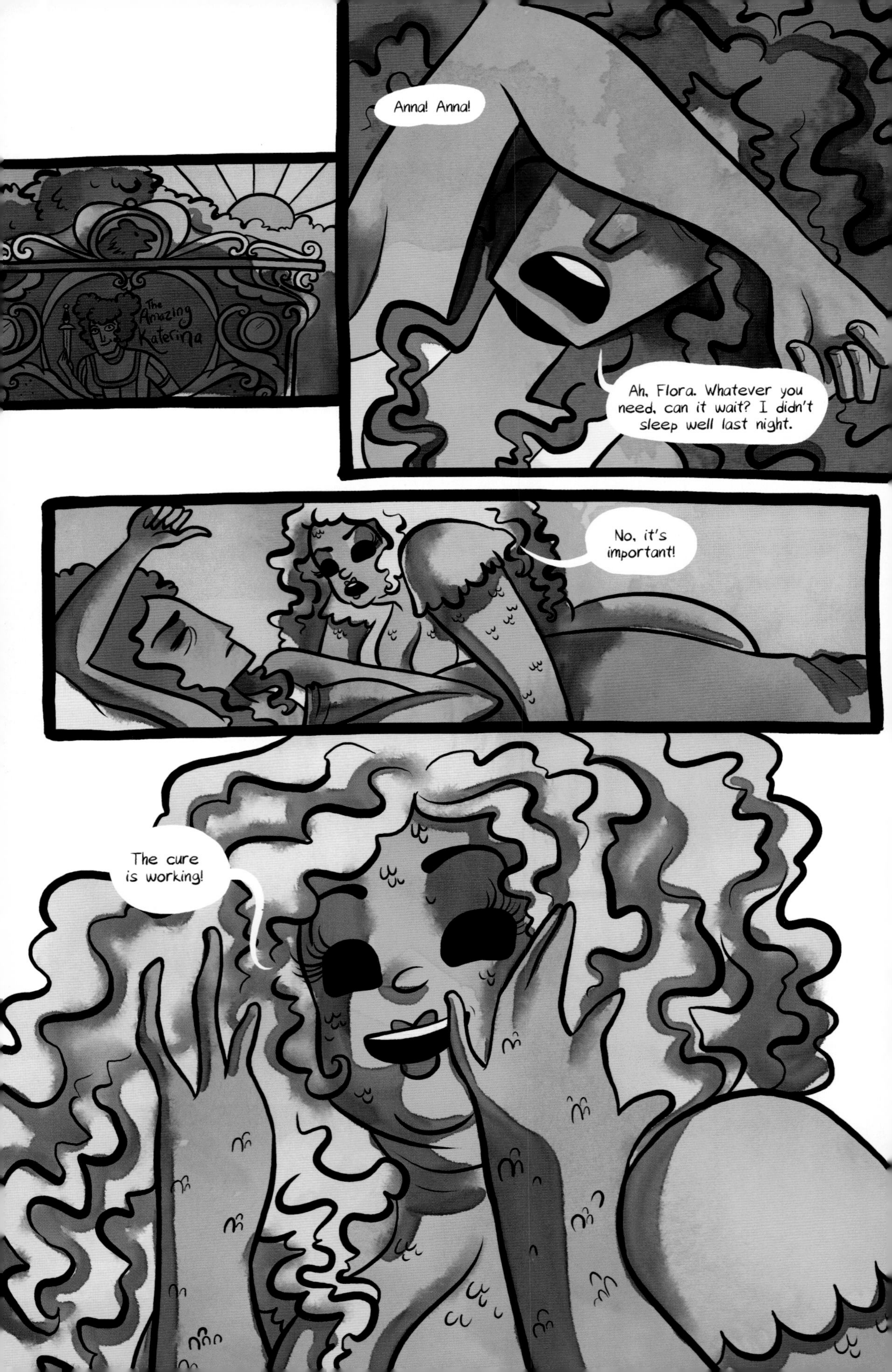
The Amazing Katerina
Anna! Anna!
Ah, Flora. Whatever you need, can it wait? I didn't sleep well last night.
No, it's important!
The cure is working!

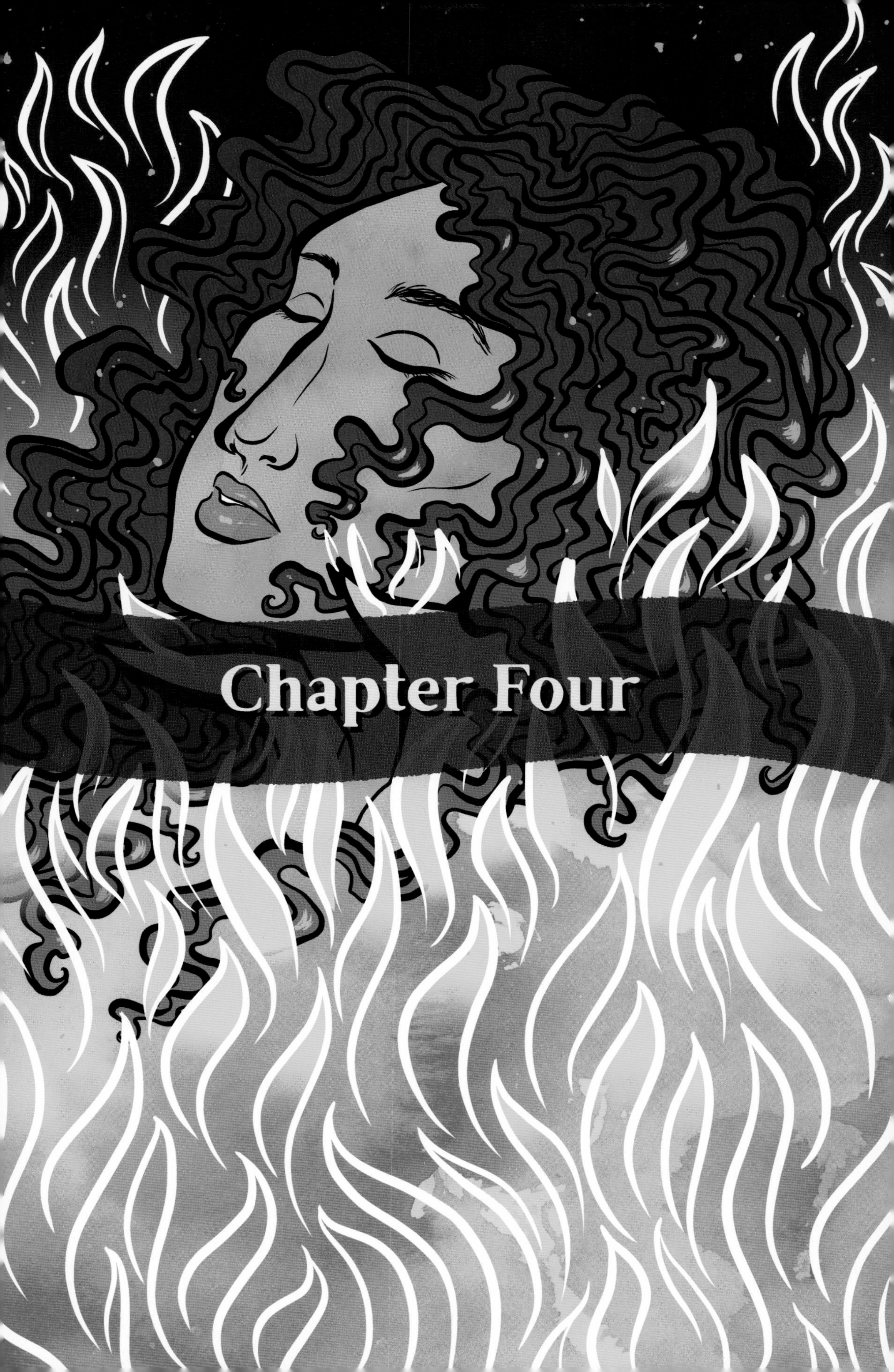
Chapter Four

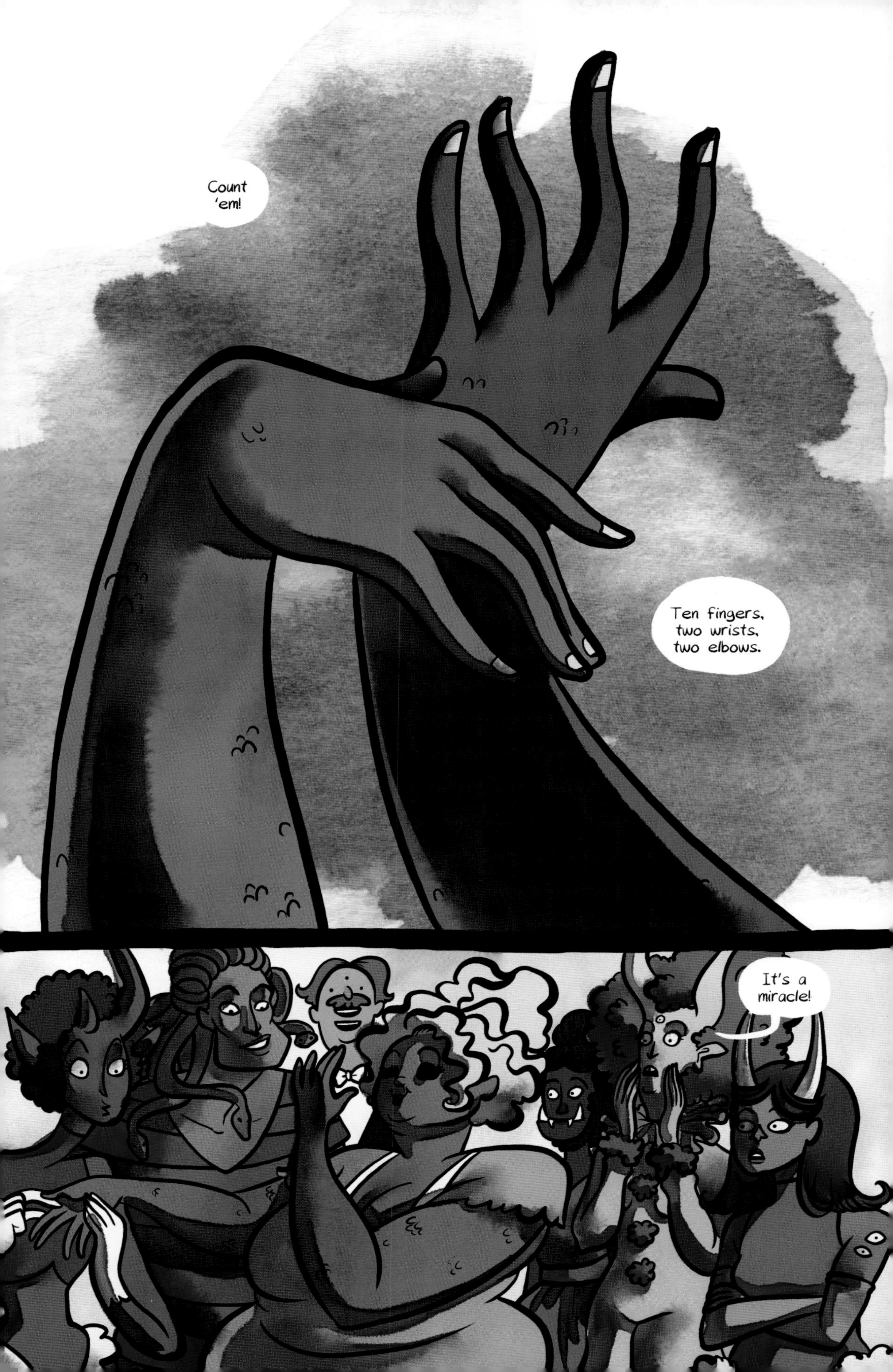
Count 'em!
Ten fingers, two wrists, two elbows.
It's a miracle!

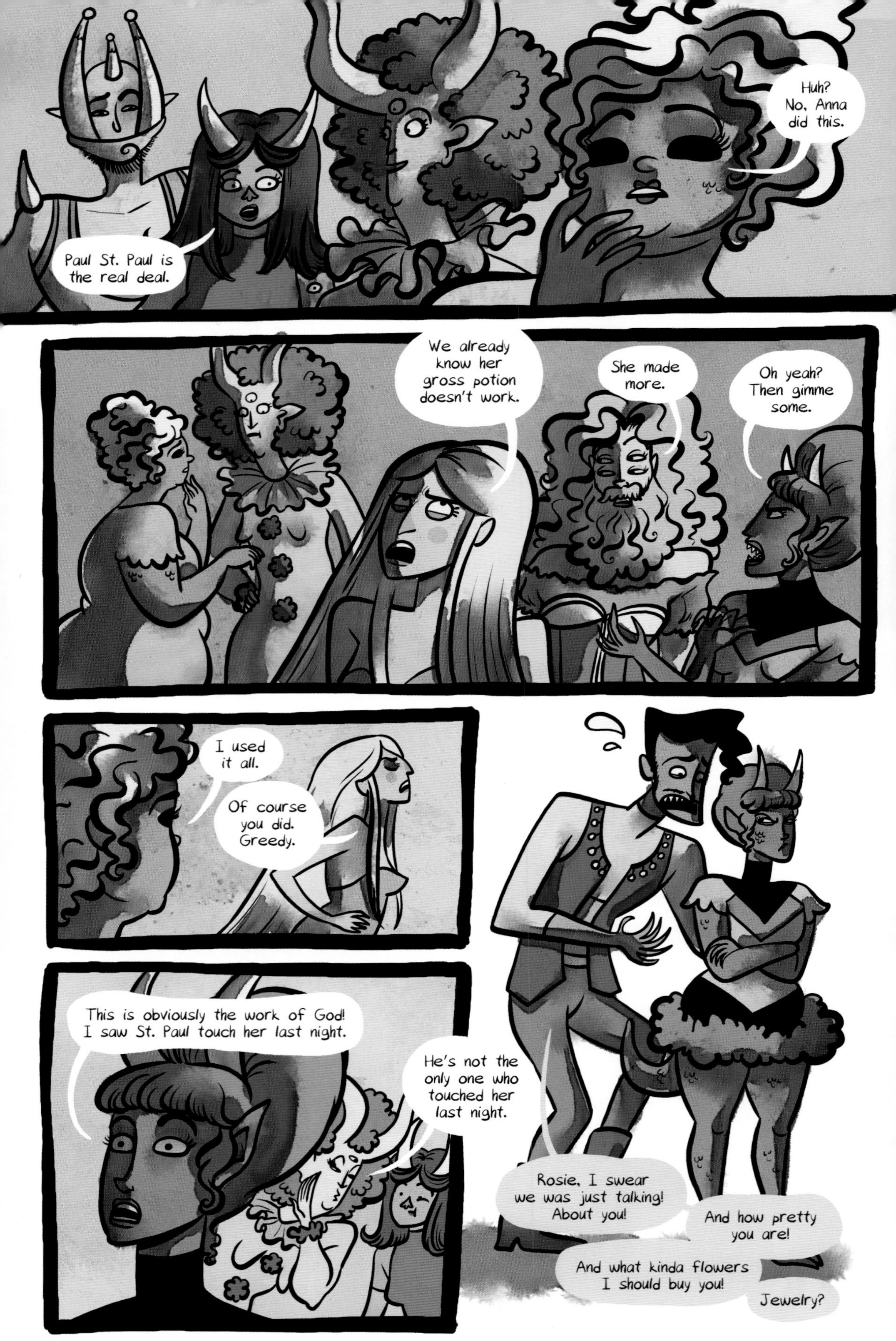
Huh? No, Anna did this.
Paul St. Paul is the real deal.
We already know her gross potion doesn't work.
She made more.
Oh yeah? Then gimme some.
I used it all.
Of course you did. Greedy.
This is obviously the work of God! I saw St. Paul touch her last night.
He's not the only one who touched her last night.
Rosie, I swear we was just talking! About you!
And how pretty you are!
And what kinda flowers I should buy you!
Jewelry?

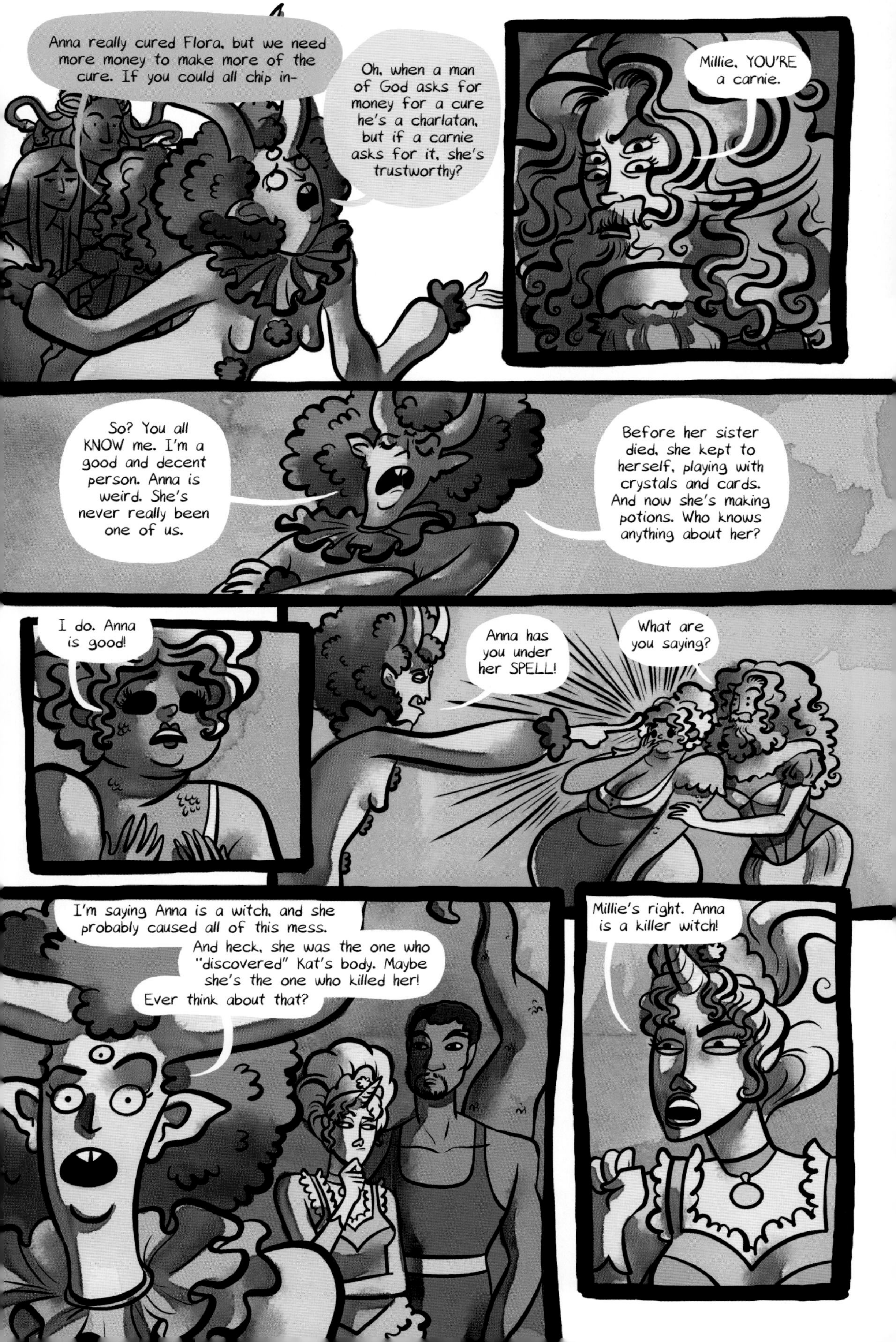
Anna really cured Flora, but we need more money to make more of the cure. If you could all chip in-
Oh, when a man of God asks for money for a cure he's a charlatan, but if a carnie asks for it, she's trustworthy?
Millie, YOU'RE a carnie.
So? You all KNOW me. I'm a good and decent person. Anna is weird. She's never really been one of us.
Before her sister died, she kept to herself, playing with crystals and cards. And now she's making potions. Who knows anything about her?
I do. Anna is good!
Anna has you under her SPELL!
What are you saying?
I'm saying Anna is a witch, and she probably caused all of this mess.
And heck, she was the one who "discovered" Kat's body. Maybe she's the one who killed her!
Ever think about that?
Millie's right. Anna is a killer witch!

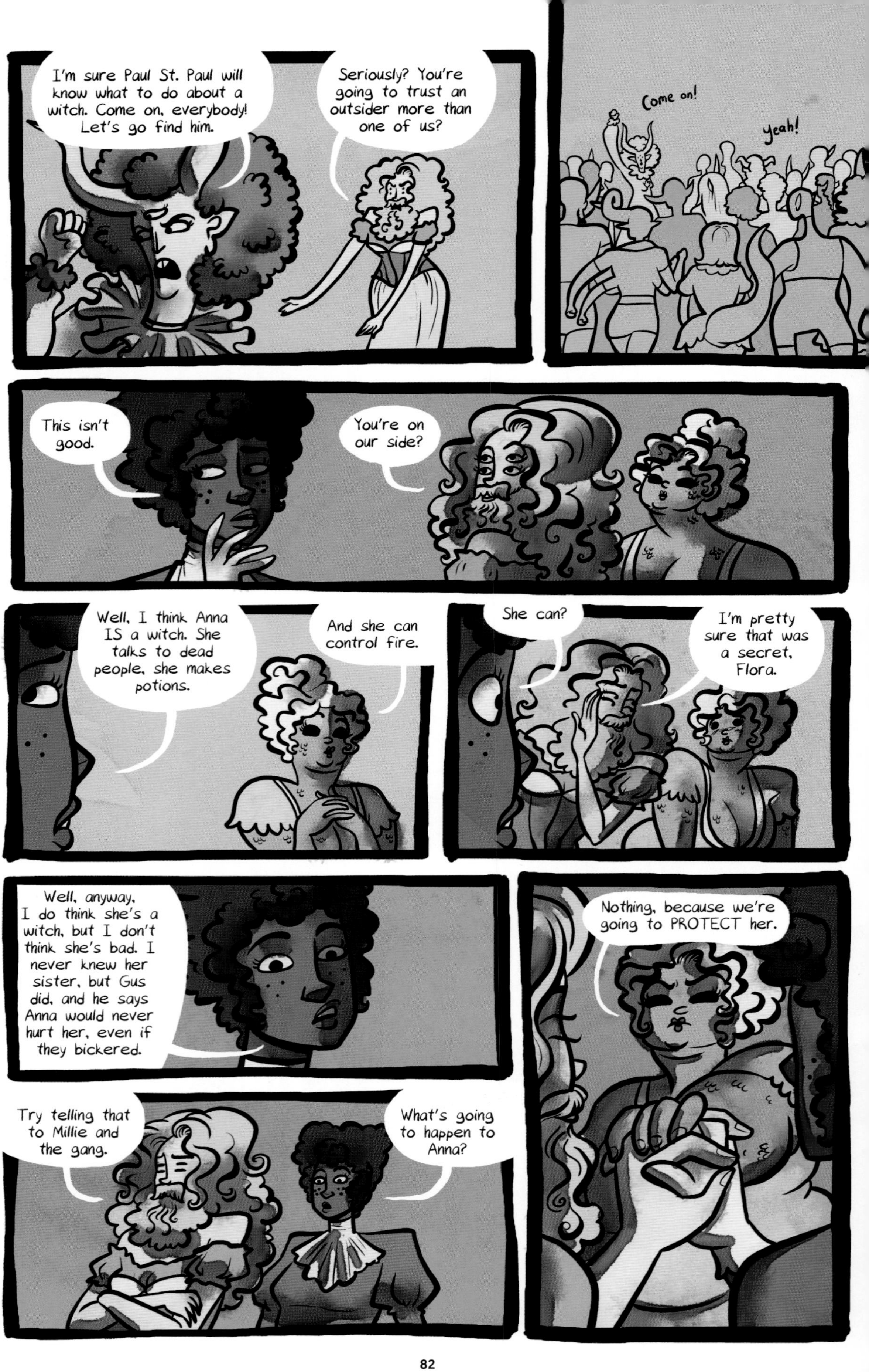
I'm sure Paul St. Paul will know what to do about a witch. Come on, everybody! Let's go find him.
Seriously? You're going to trust an outsider more than one of us?
Come on!
Yeah!
This isn't good.
You're on our side?
Well, I think Anna IS a witch. She talks to dead people, she makes potions.
And she can control fire.
She can?
I'm pretty sure that was a secret, Flora.
Well, anyway, I do think she's a witch, but I don't think she's bad. I never knew her sister, but Gus did, and he says Anna would never hurt her, even if they bickered.
Try telling that to Millie and the gang.
What's going to happen to Anna?
Nothing, because we're going to PROTECT her.

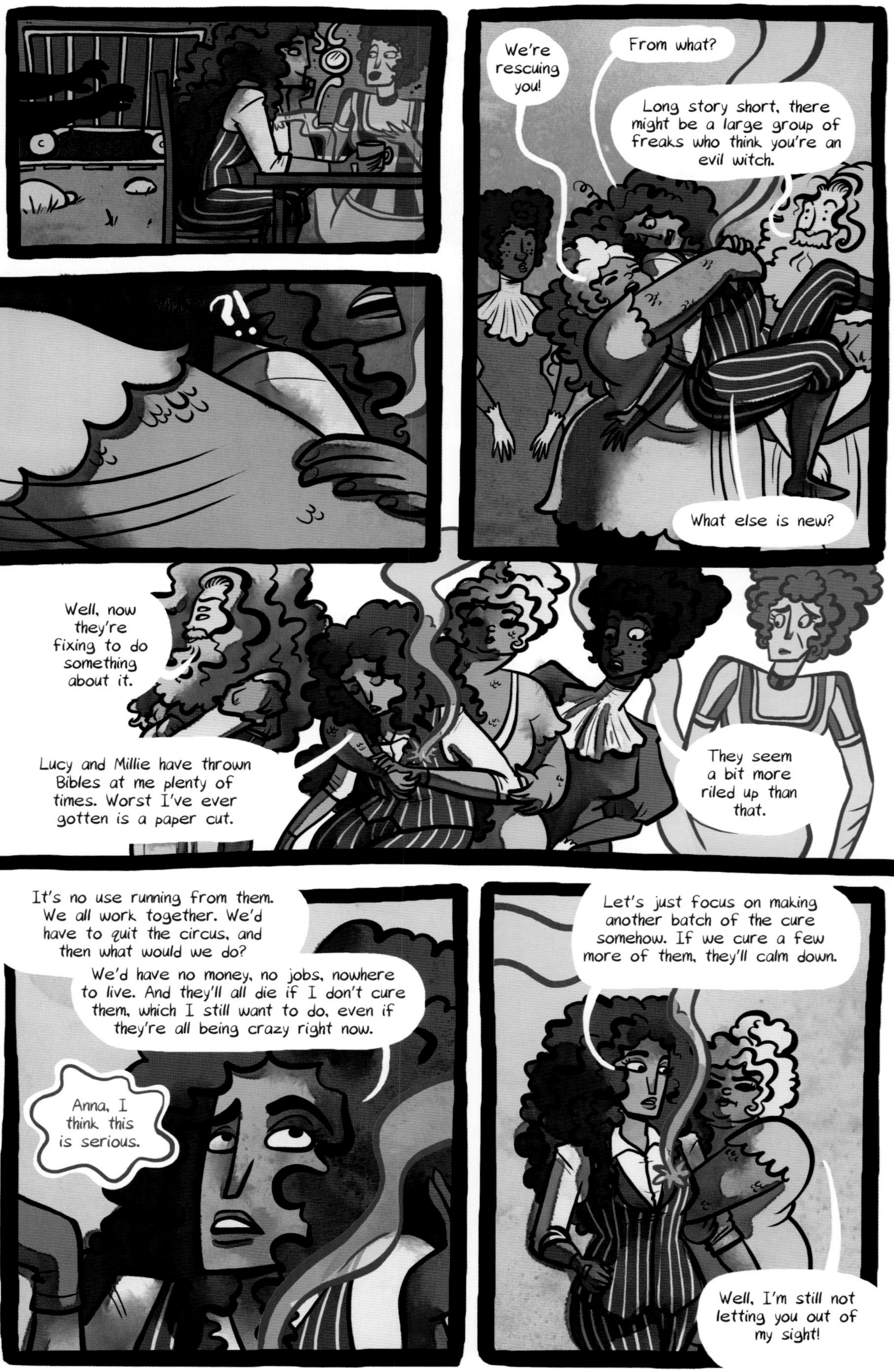
?!
We're rescuing you!
From what?
Long story short, there might be a large group of freaks who think you're an evil witch.
What else is new?
Well, now they're fixing to do something about it.
Lucy and Millie have thrown Bibles at me plenty of times. Worst I've ever gotten is a paper cut.
They seem a bit more riled up than that.
It's no use running from them. We all work together. We'd have to quit the circus, and then what would we do?
We'd have no money, no jobs, nowhere to live. And they'll all die if I don't cure them, which I still want to do, even if they're all being crazy right now.
Anna, I think this is serious.
Let's just focus on making another batch of the cure somehow. If we cure a few more of them, they'll calm down.
Well, I'm still not letting you out of my sight!

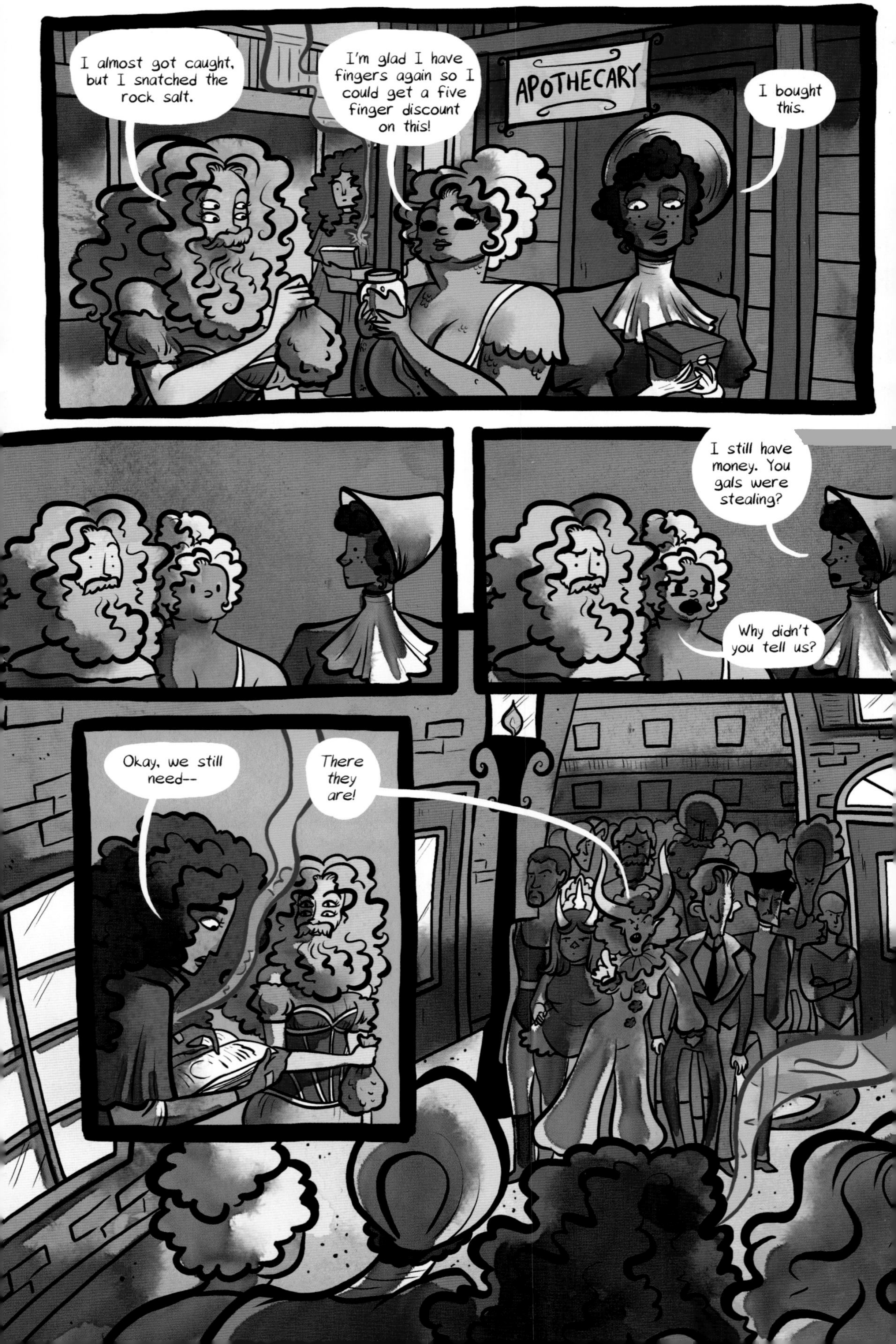
I almost got caught, but I snatched the rock salt.
I'm glad I have fingers again so I could get a five finger discount on this!
APOTHECARY
I bought this.
I still have money. You gals were stealing?
Why didn't you tell us?
Okay, we still need--
There they are!

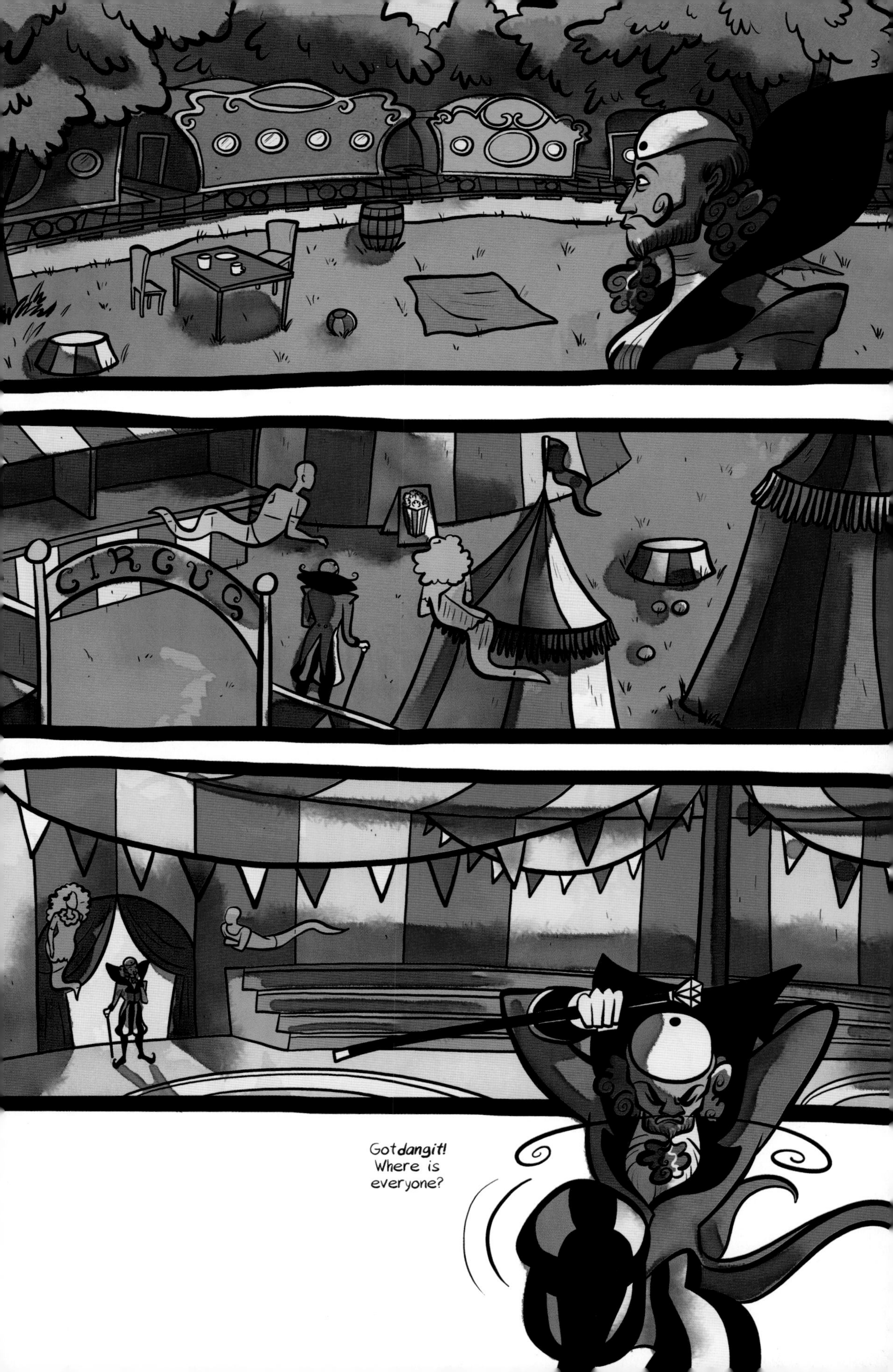
CIRCUS
Gotdangit! Where is everyone?

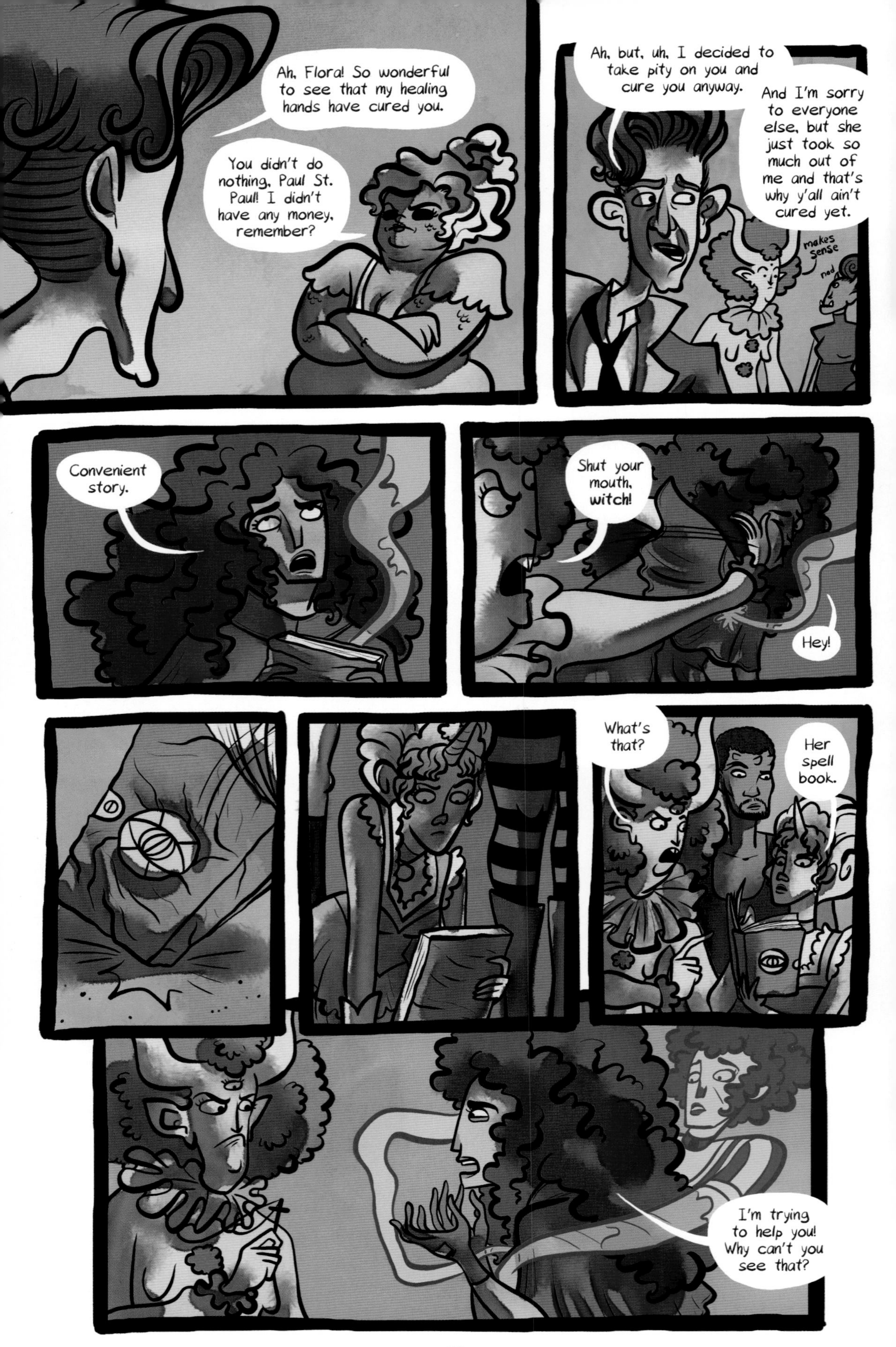

Ah, Flora! So wonderful to see that my healing hands have cured you.
You didn't do nothing, Paul St. Paul! I didn't have any money, remember?
Ah, but, uh, I decided to take pity on you and cure you anyway.
And I'm sorry to everyone else, but she just took so much out of me and that's why y'all ain't cured yet.
makes sense
nod
Convenient story.
Shut your mouth, witch!
Hey!
What's that?
Her spell book.
I'm trying to help you! Why can't you see that?

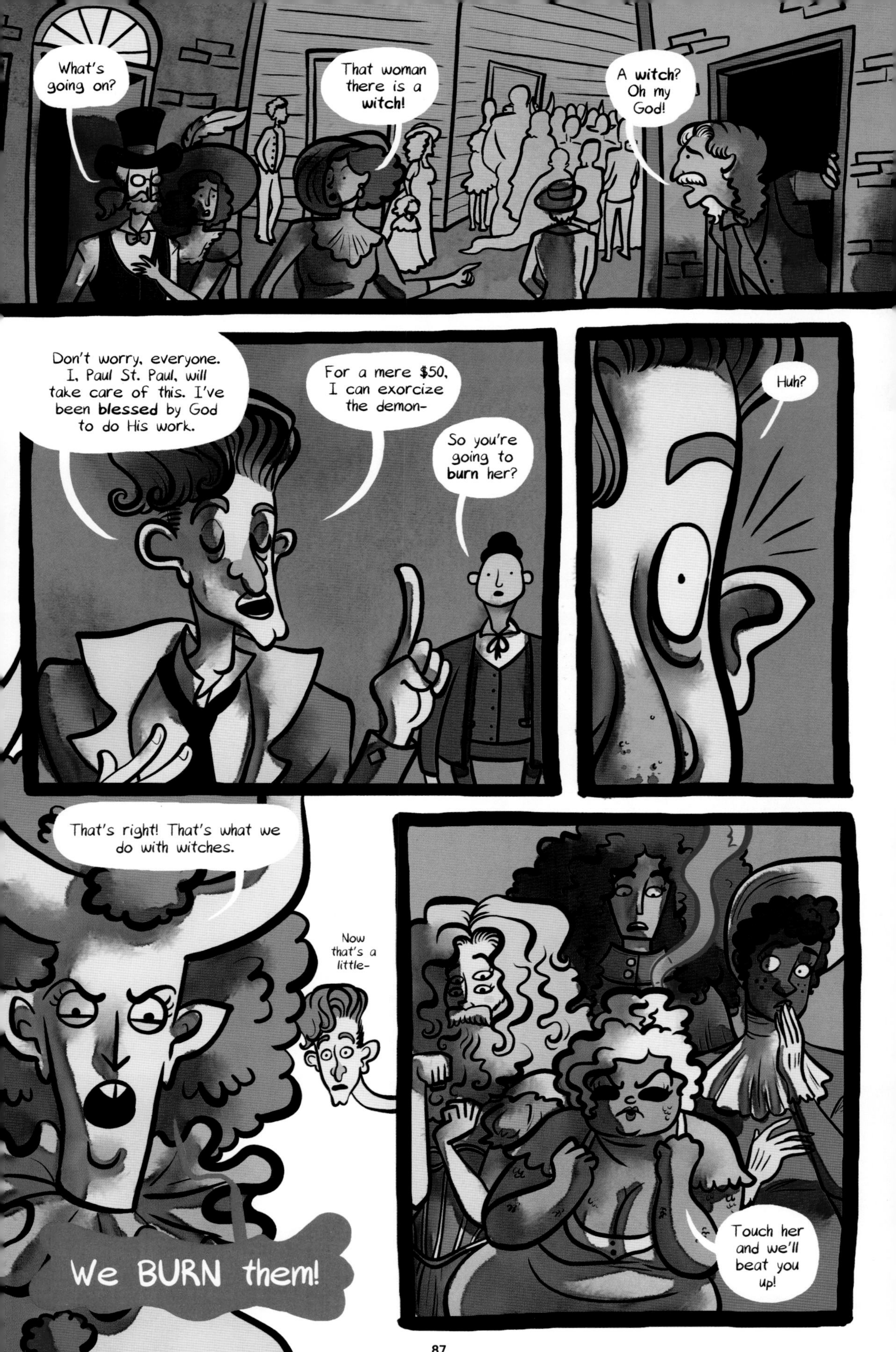
What's going on?
That woman there is a **witch**!
A **witch**? Oh my God!
Don't worry, everyone. I, Paul St. Paul, will take care of this. I've been **blessed** by God to do His work.
For a mere $50, I can exorcize the demon-
So you're going to **burn** her?
Huh?
That's right! That's what we do with witches.
We BURN them!
Now that's a little-
Touch her and we'll beat you up!

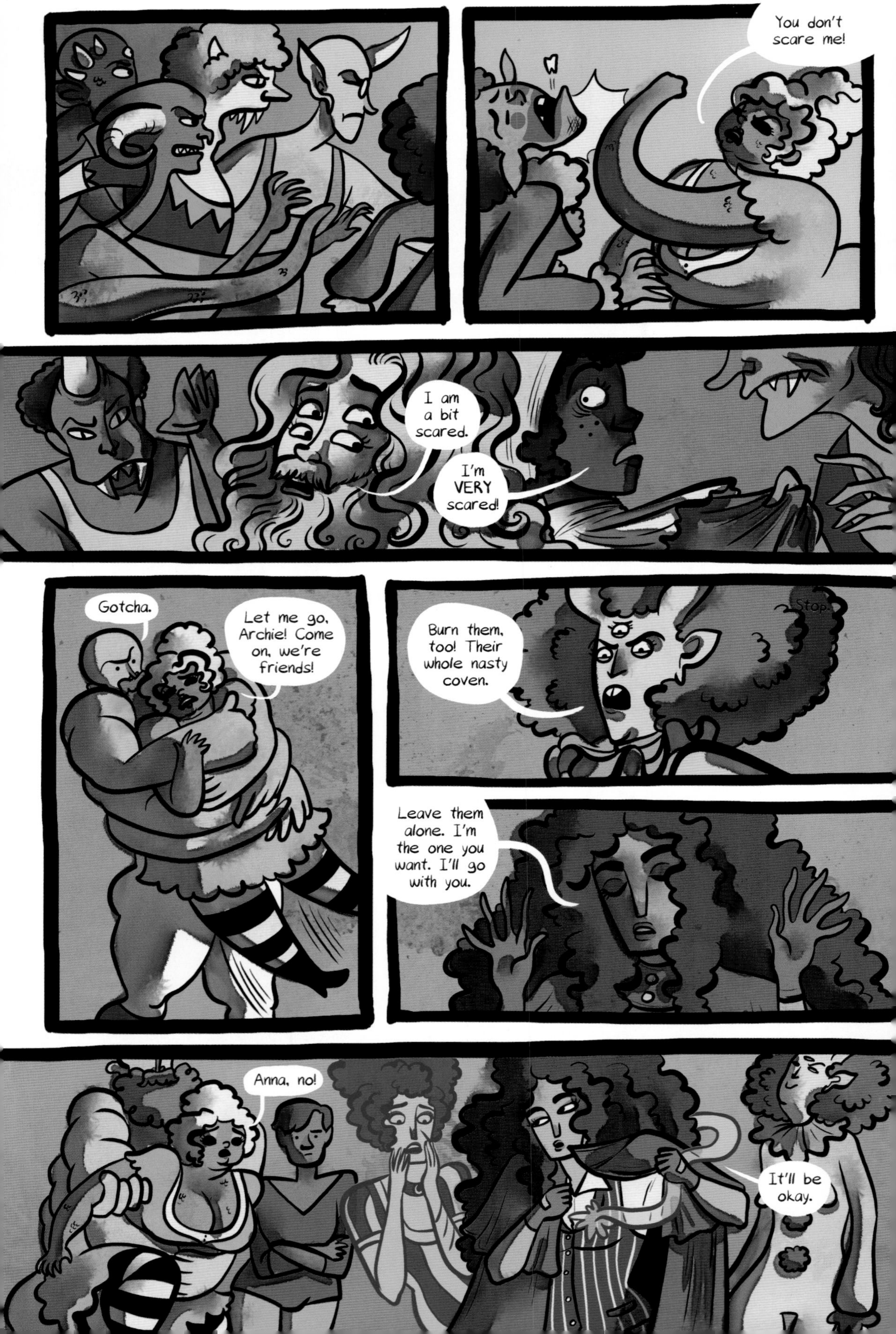
You don't scare me!
I am a bit scared.
I'm VERY scared!
Gotcha.
Let me go, Archie! Come on, we're friends!
Burn them, too! Their whole nasty coven.
Stop.
Leave them alone. I'm the one you want. I'll go with you.
Anna, no!
It'll be okay.

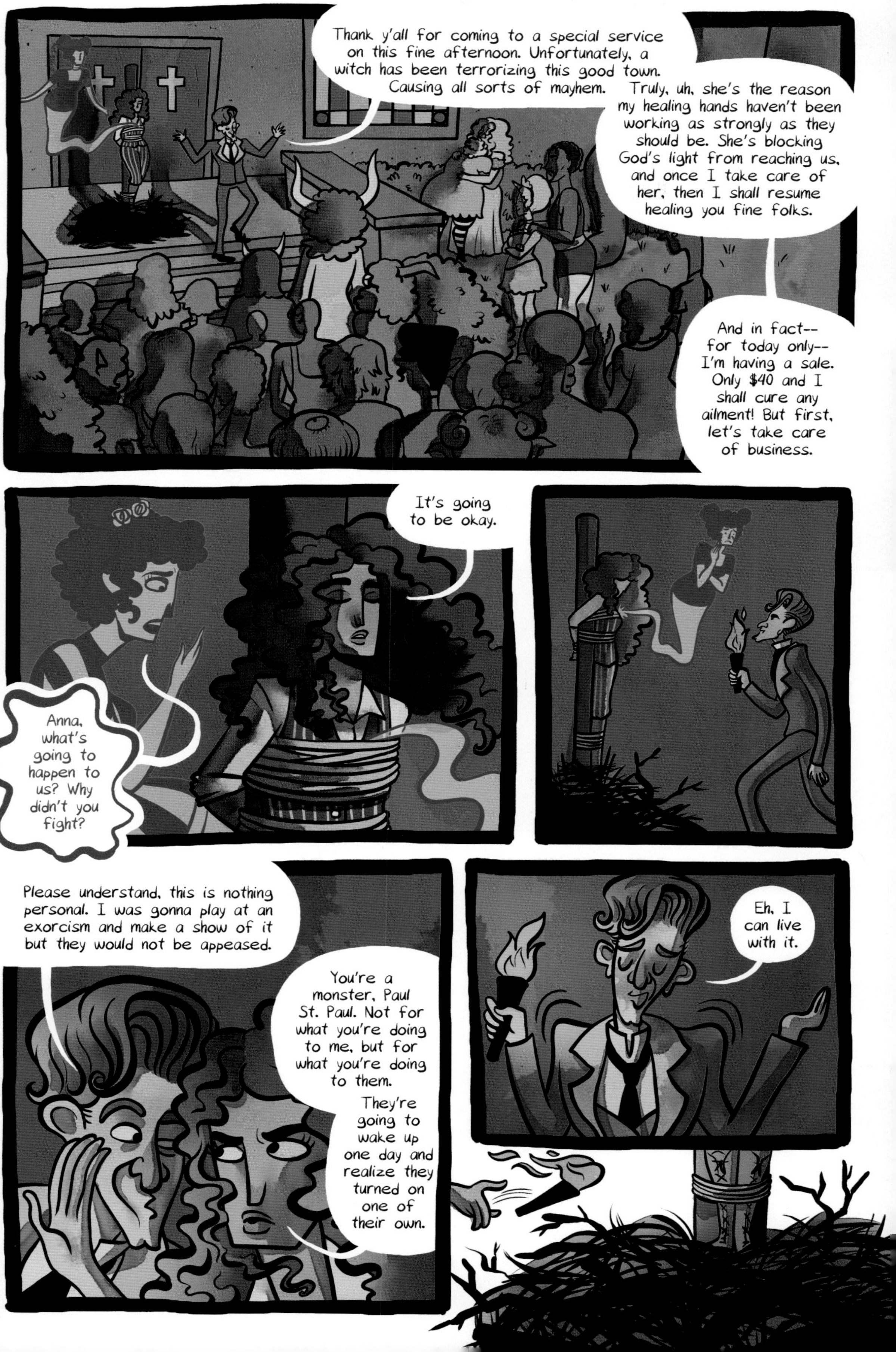

Thank y'all for coming to a special service on this fine afternoon. Unfortunately, a witch has been terrorizing this good town. Causing all sorts of mayhem.
Truly, uh, she's the reason my healing hands haven't been working as strongly as they should be. She's blocking God's light from reaching us, and once I take care of her, then I shall resume healing you fine folks.
And in fact-- for today only-- I'm having a sale. Only $40 and I shall cure any ailment! But first, let's take care of business.
Anna, what's going to happen to us? Why didn't you fight?
It's going to be okay.
Please understand, this is nothing personal. I was gonna play at an exorcism and make a show of it but they would not be appeased.
You're a monster, Paul St. Paul. Not for what you're doing to me, but for what you're doing to them.
They're going to wake up one day and realize they turned on one of their own.
Eh, I can live with it.

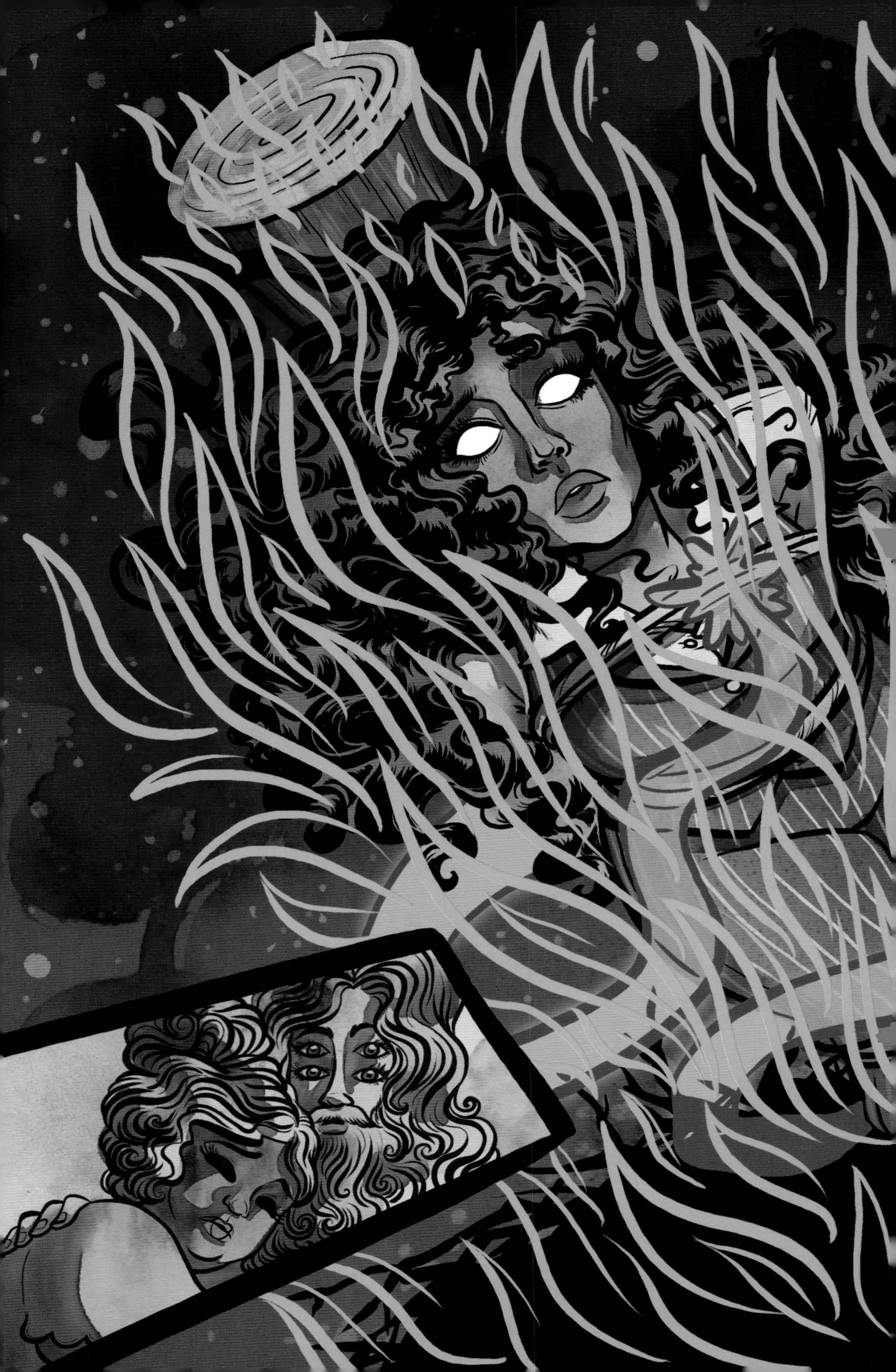

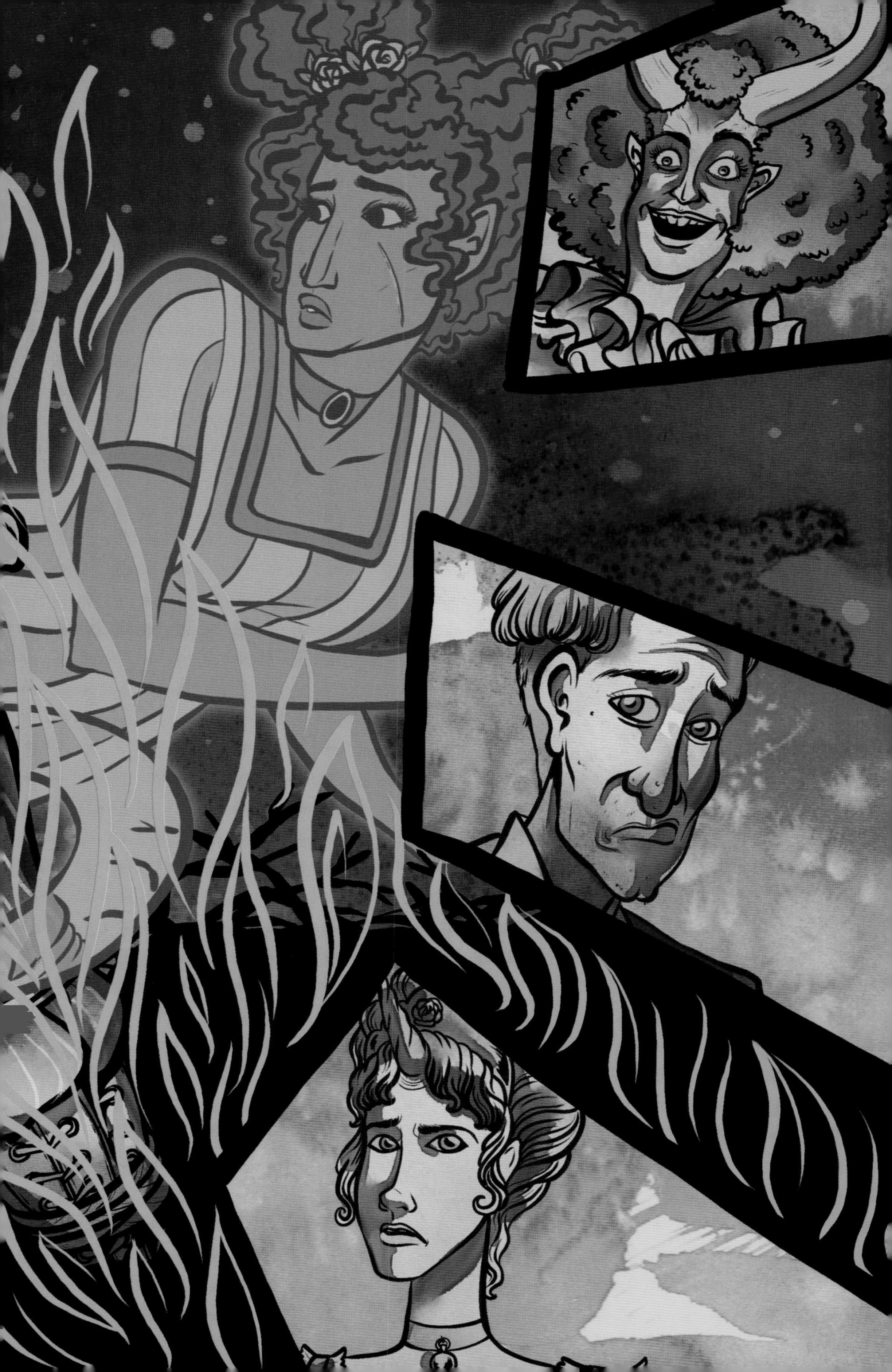

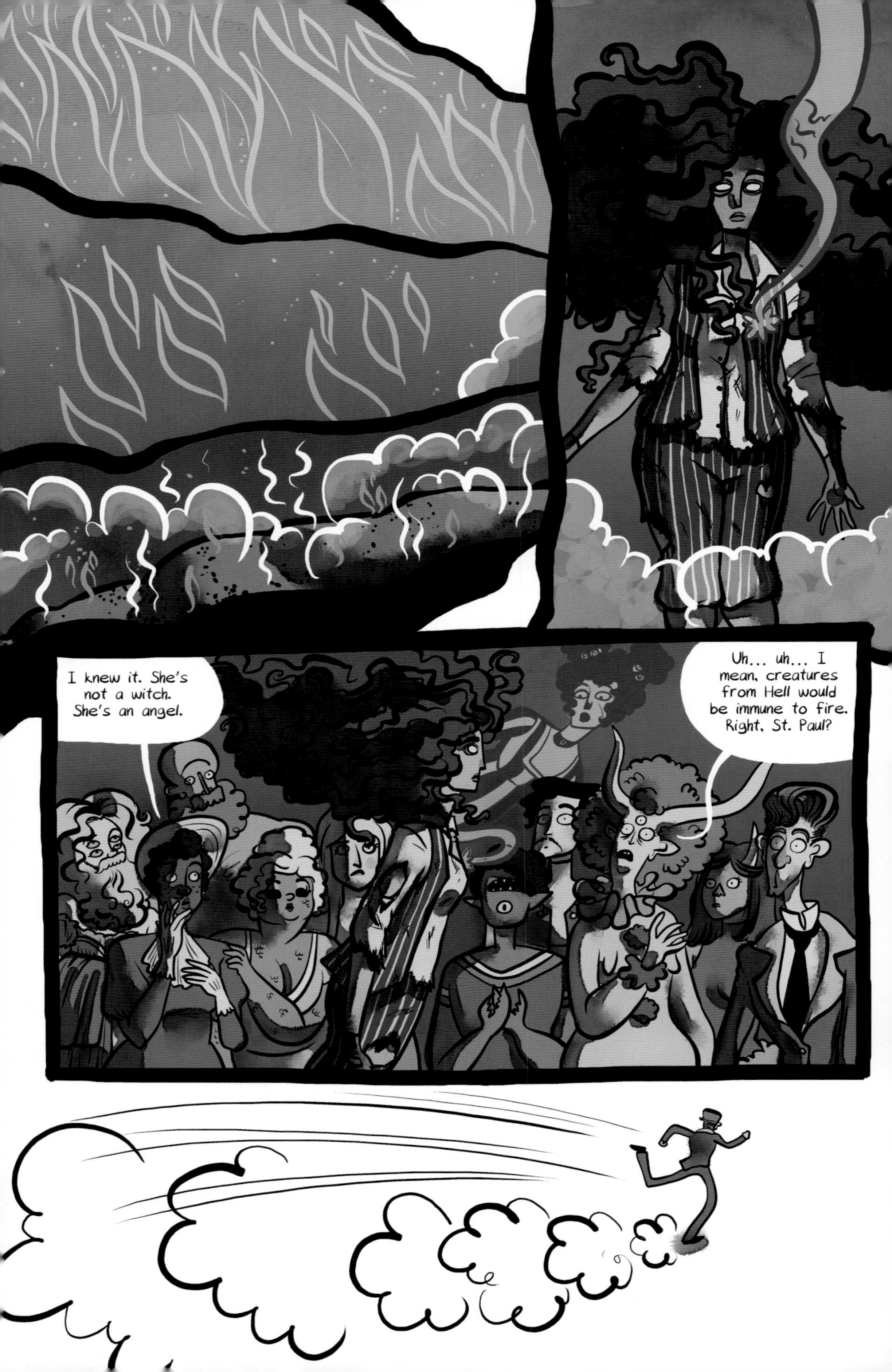
I knew it. She's not a witch. She's an angel.
Uh... uh... I mean, creatures from Hell would be immune to fire. Right, St. Paul?

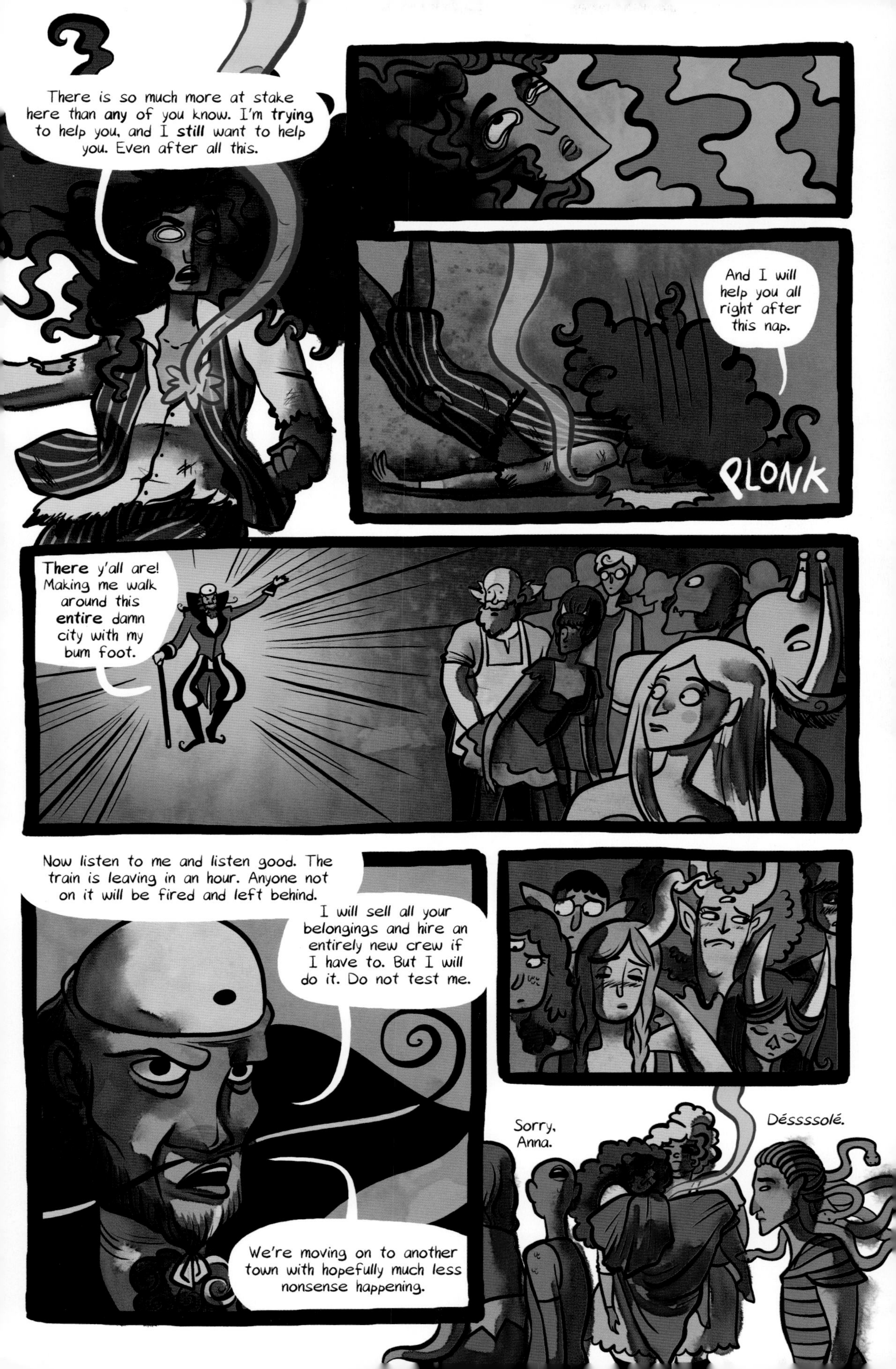
There is so much more at stake here than **any** of you know. I'm **trying** to help you, and I **still** want to help you. Even after all this.
And I will help you all right after this nap.
PLONK
There y'all are! Making me walk around this **entire** damn city with my bum foot.
Now listen to me and listen good. The train is leaving in an hour. Anyone not on it will be fired and left behind.
I will sell all your belongings and hire an entirely new crew if I have to. But I will do it. Do not test me.
We're moving on to another town with hopefully much less nonsense happening.
Sorry, Anna.
Déssssolé.

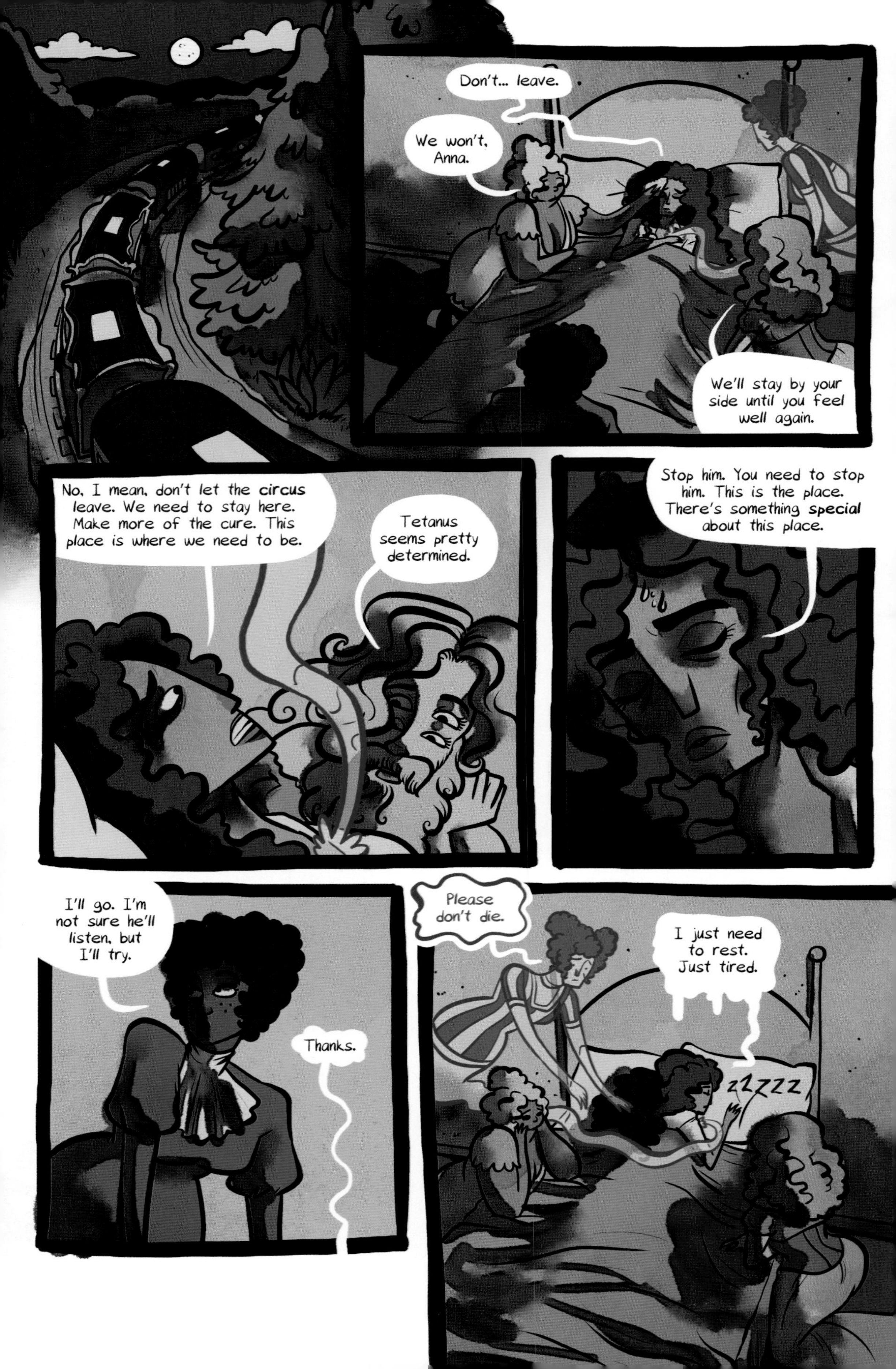
Don't... leave.
We won't, Anna.
We'll stay by your side until you feel well again.
No, I mean, don't let the circus leave. We need to stay here. Make more of the cure. This place is where we need to be.
Tetanus seems pretty determined.
Stop him. You need to stop him. This is the place. There's something special about this place.
I'll go. I'm not sure he'll listen, but I'll try.
Thanks.
Please don't die.
I just need to rest. Just tired.
zZZZZ

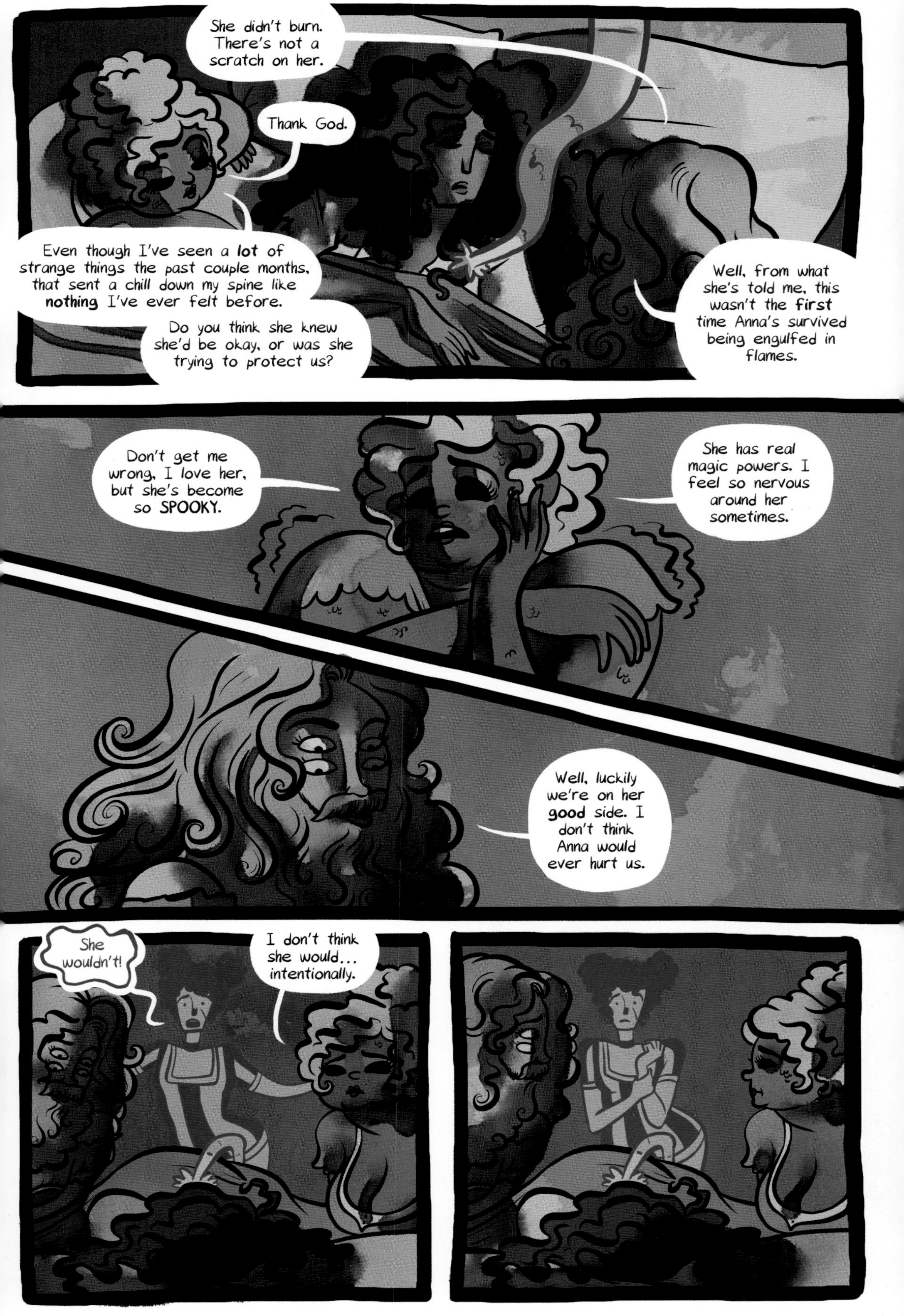

She didn't burn. There's not a scratch on her.
Thank God.
Even though I've seen a **lot** of strange things the past couple months, that sent a chill down my spine like **nothing** I've ever felt before.
Do you think she knew she'd be okay, or was she trying to protect us?
Well, from what she's told me, this wasn't the **first** time Anna's survived being engulfed in flames.
Don't get me wrong, I love her, but she's become so **SPOOKY.**
She has real magic powers. I feel so nervous around her sometimes.
Well, luckily we're on her **good** side. I don't think Anna would ever hurt us.
She wouldn't!
I don't think she would... intentionally.

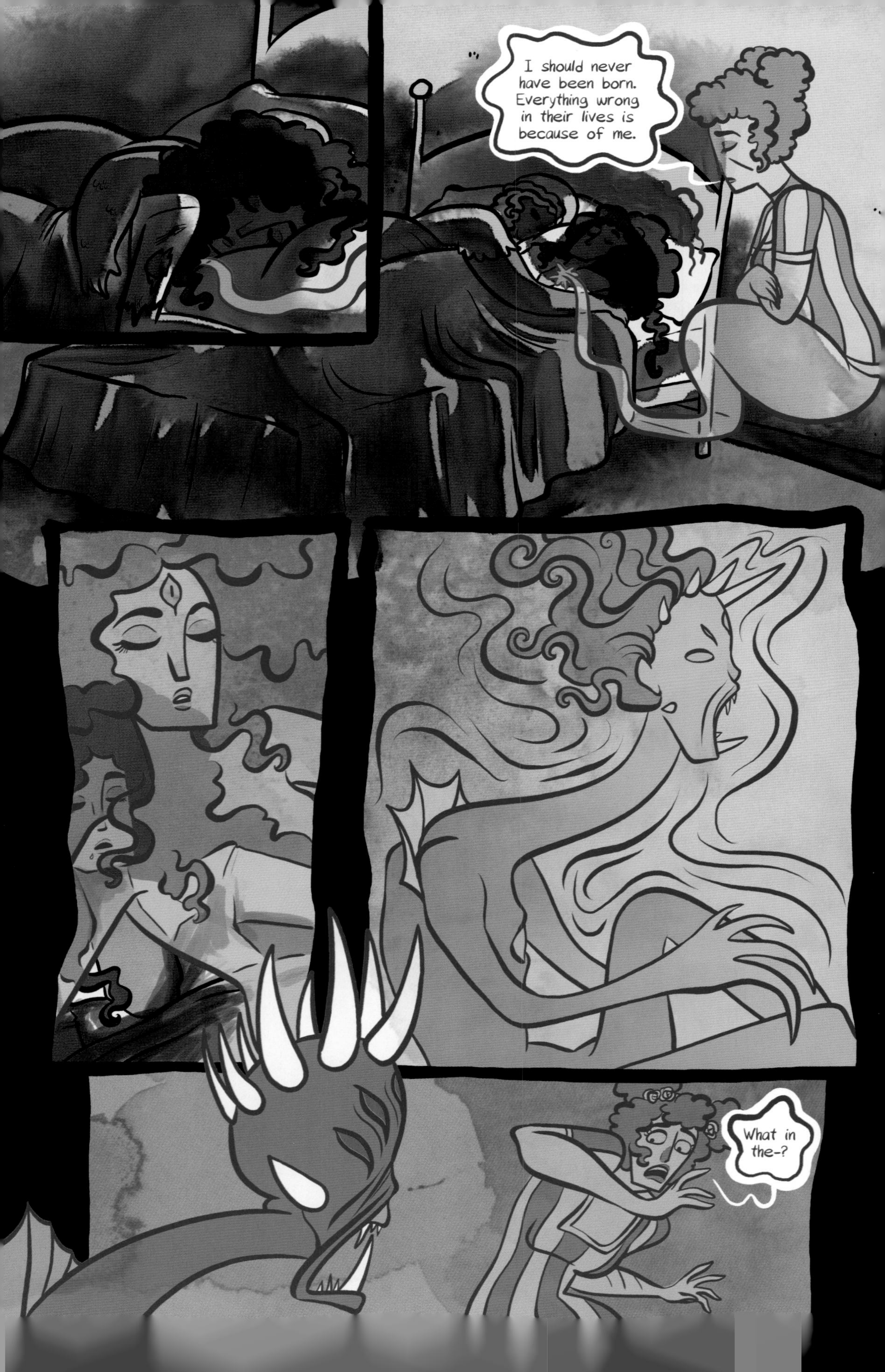
I should never have been born. Everything wrong in their lives is because of me.
What in the-?

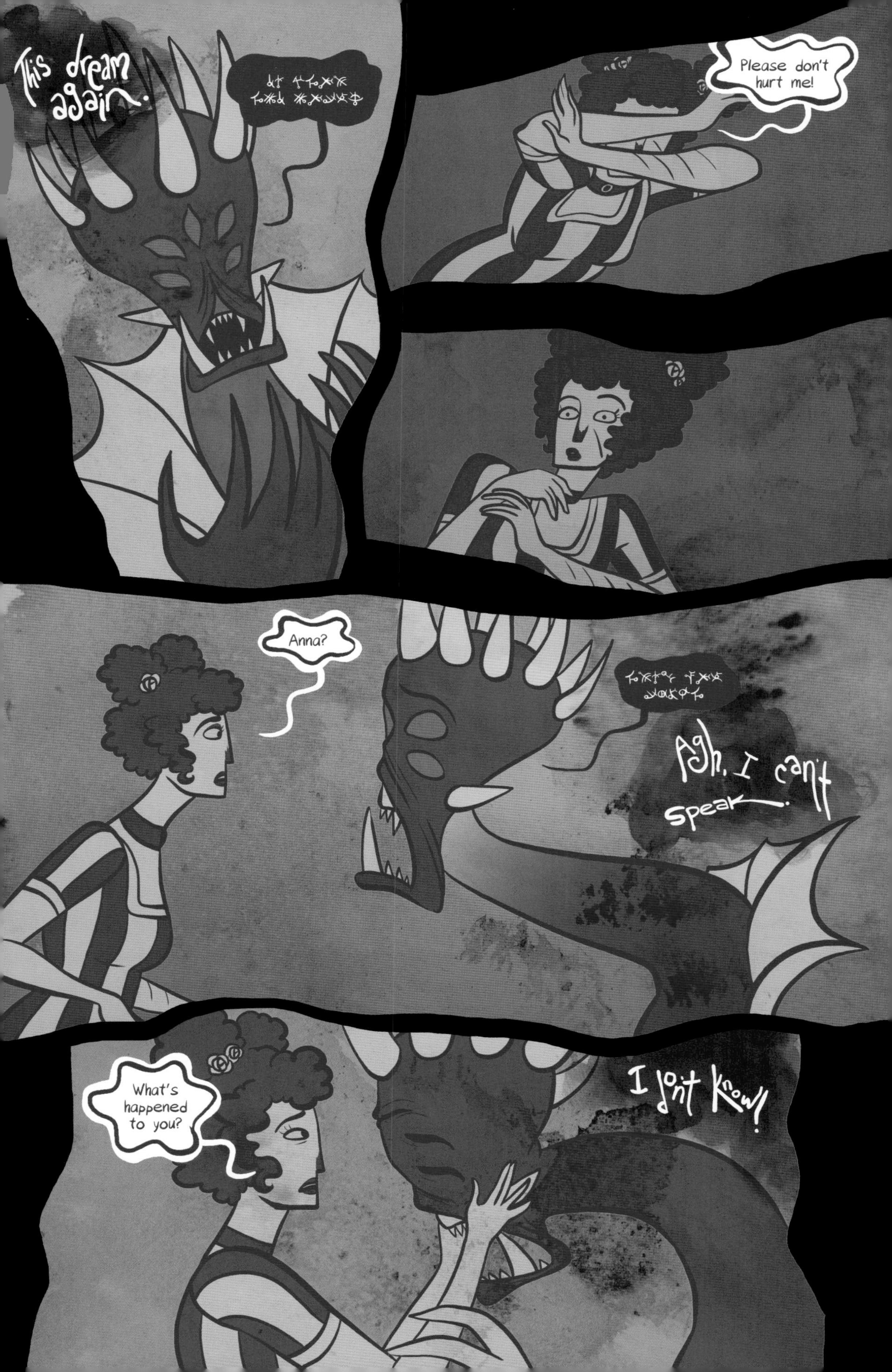
This dream again.
Please don't hurt me!
Anna?
Agh, I can't speak.
What's happened to you?
I don't know!

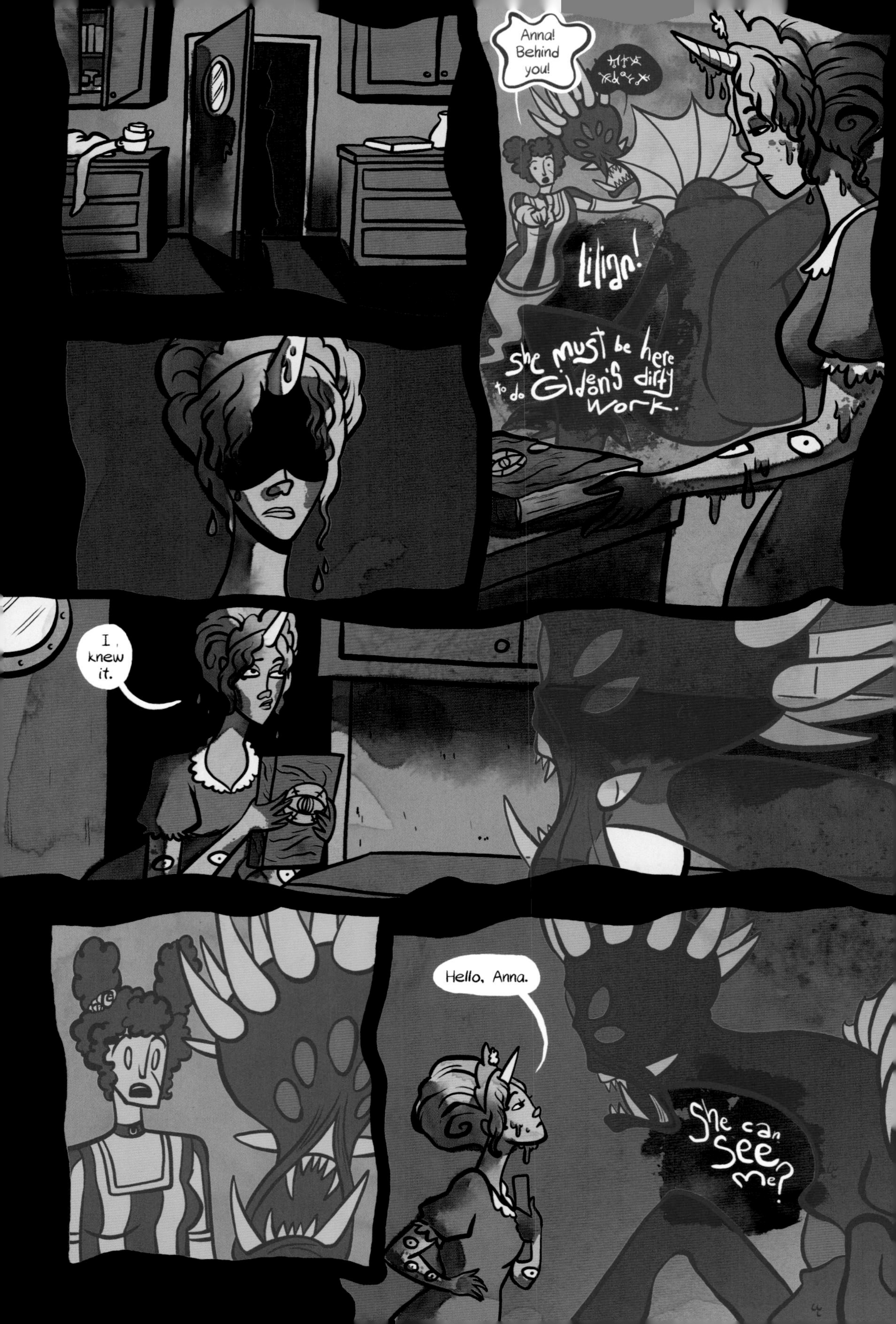
Anna! Behind you!
Lilian!
She must be here to do Gideon's dirty work.
I knew it.
Hello, Anna.
She can see me?

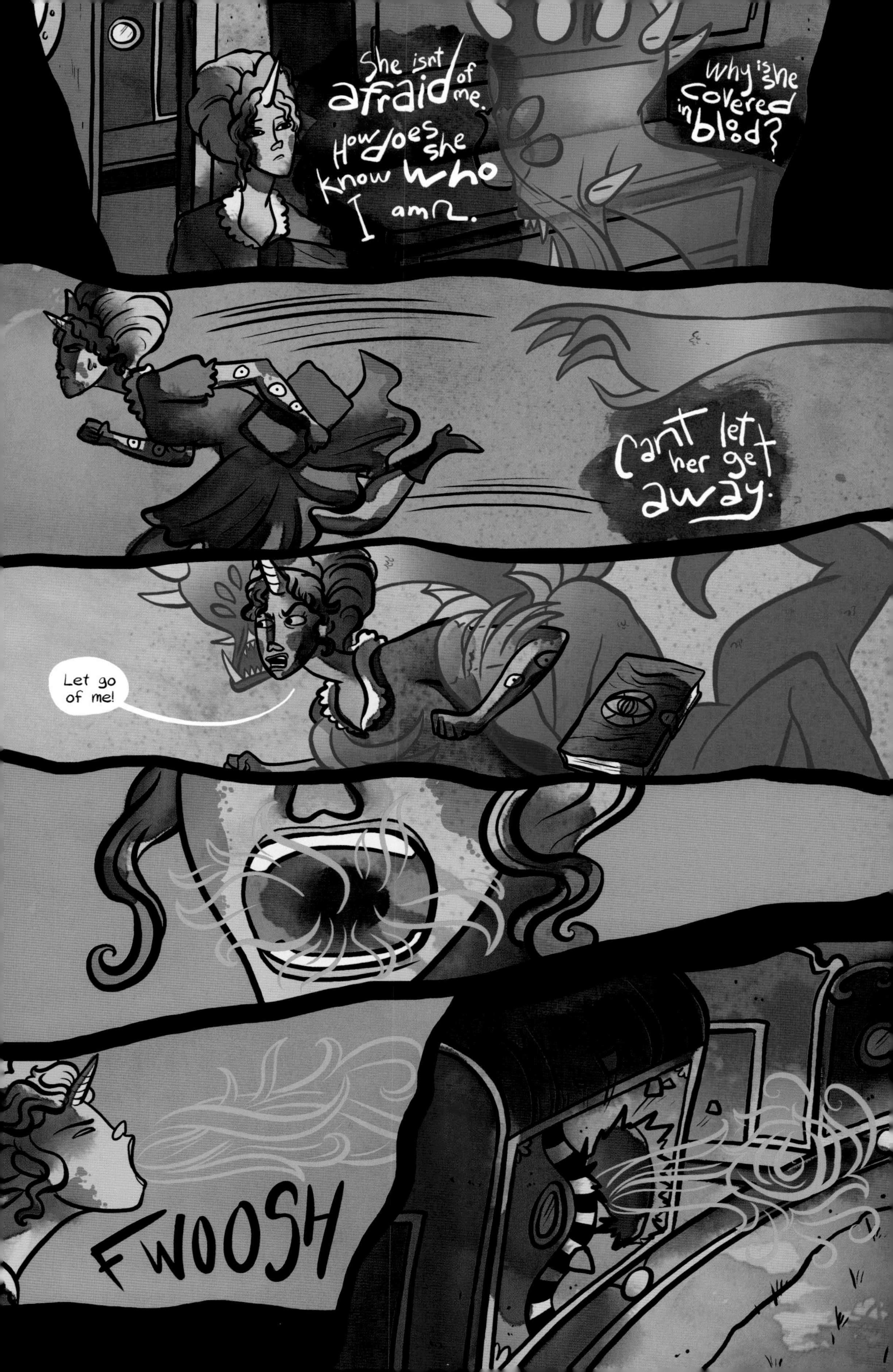
She isn't afraid of me.
How does she know who I am?
Why is she covered in blood?
Can't let her get away.
Let go of me!
FWOOSH

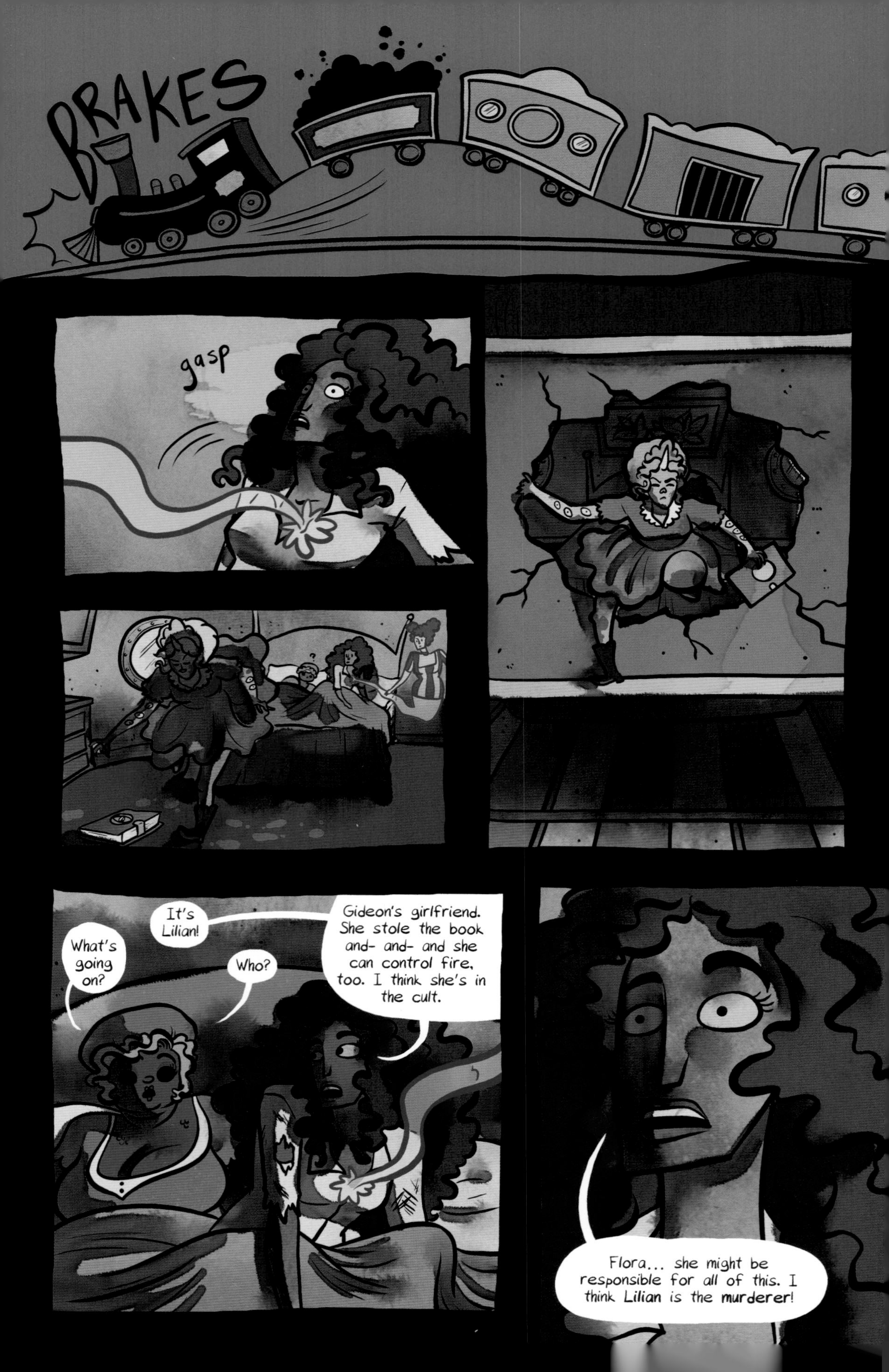
BRAKES
gasp
What's going on?
It's Lilian!
Who?
Gideon's girlfriend. She stole the book and- and- and she can control fire, too. I think she's in the cult.
Flora... she might be responsible for all of this. I think Lilian is the murderer!

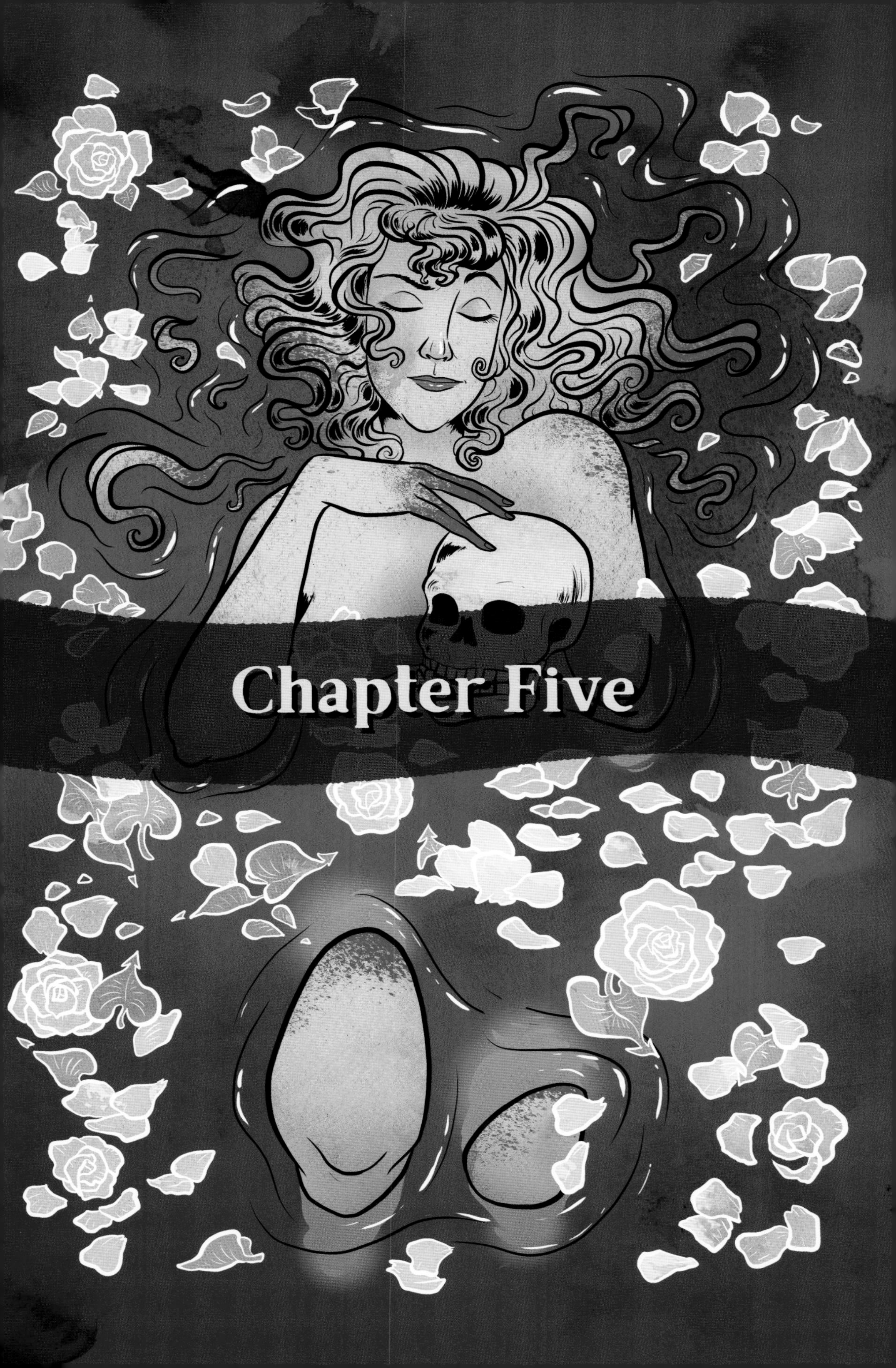
Chapter Five

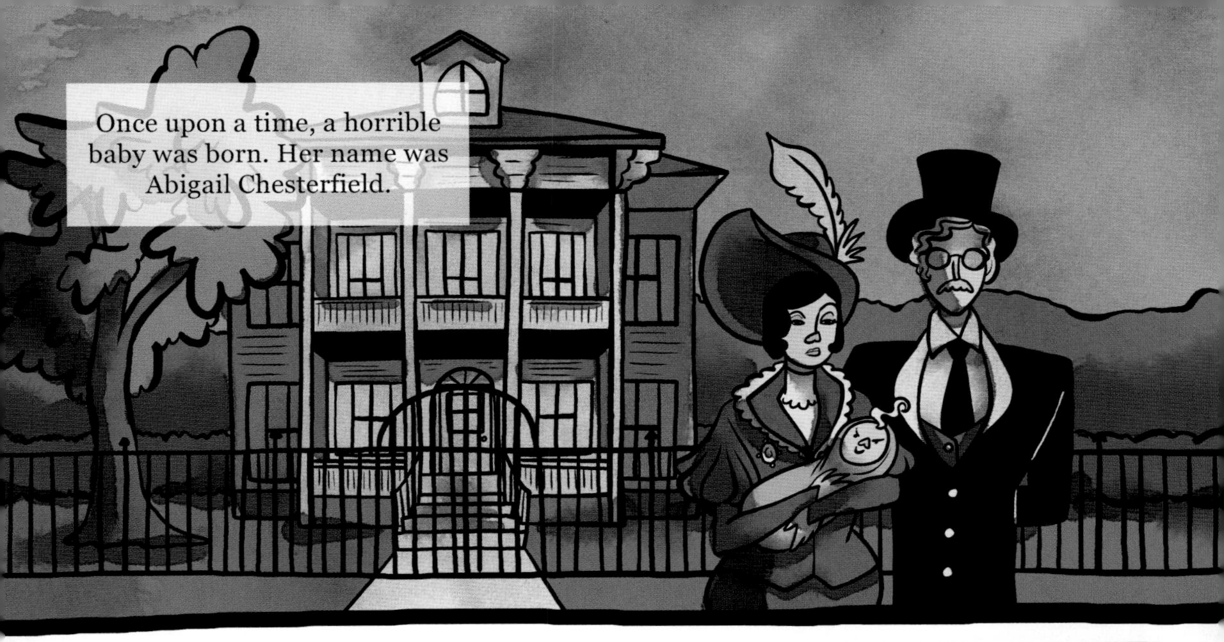
Once upon a time, a horrible baby was born. Her name was Abigail Chesterfield.

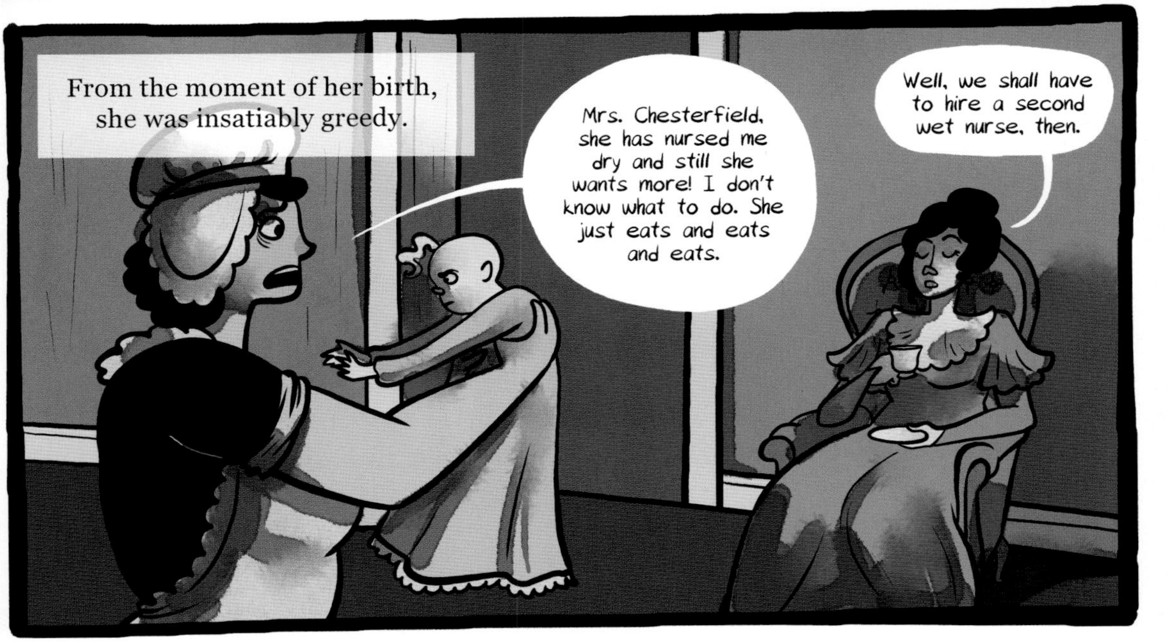
From the moment of her birth, she was insatiably greedy.
Mrs. Chesterfield, she has nursed me dry and still she wants more! I don't know what to do. She just eats and eats and eats.
Well, we shall have to hire a second wet nurse, then.

Her parents, both from old, old money, gave her everything she ever desired, so long as it did not inconvenience them.

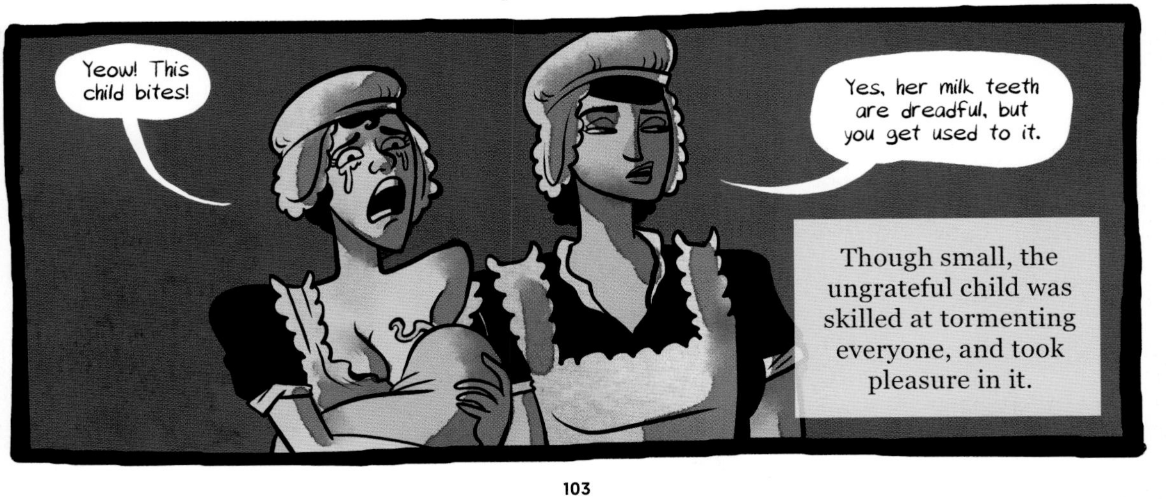
Yeow! This child bites!
Yes, her milk teeth are dreadful, but you get used to it.
Though small, the ungrateful child was skilled at tormenting everyone, and took pleasure in it.

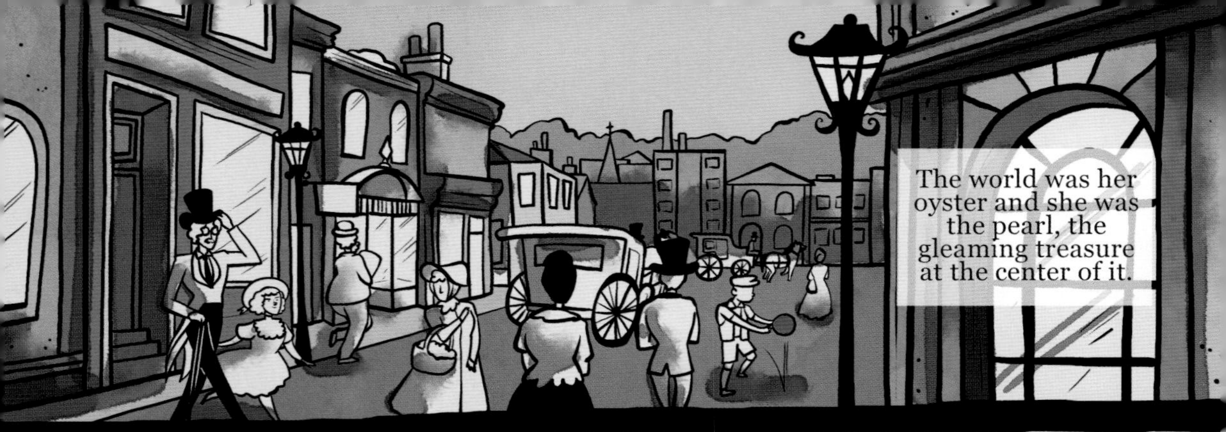
The world was her oyster and she was the pearl, the gleaming treasure at the center of it.

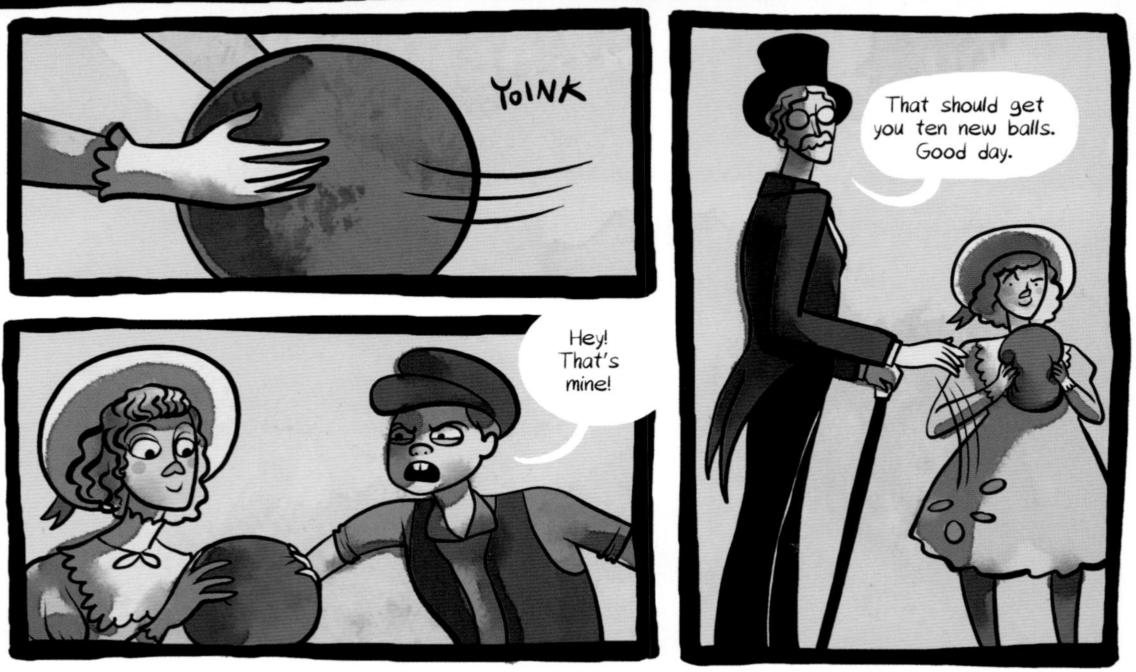
YOINK
Hey! That's mine!
That should get you ten new balls. Good day.

But like a pearl, she was at her core simply an irritant to be accomodated, everyone hoping that if they covered her in finery it would smooth her rough edges until she was more comfortable to be around.

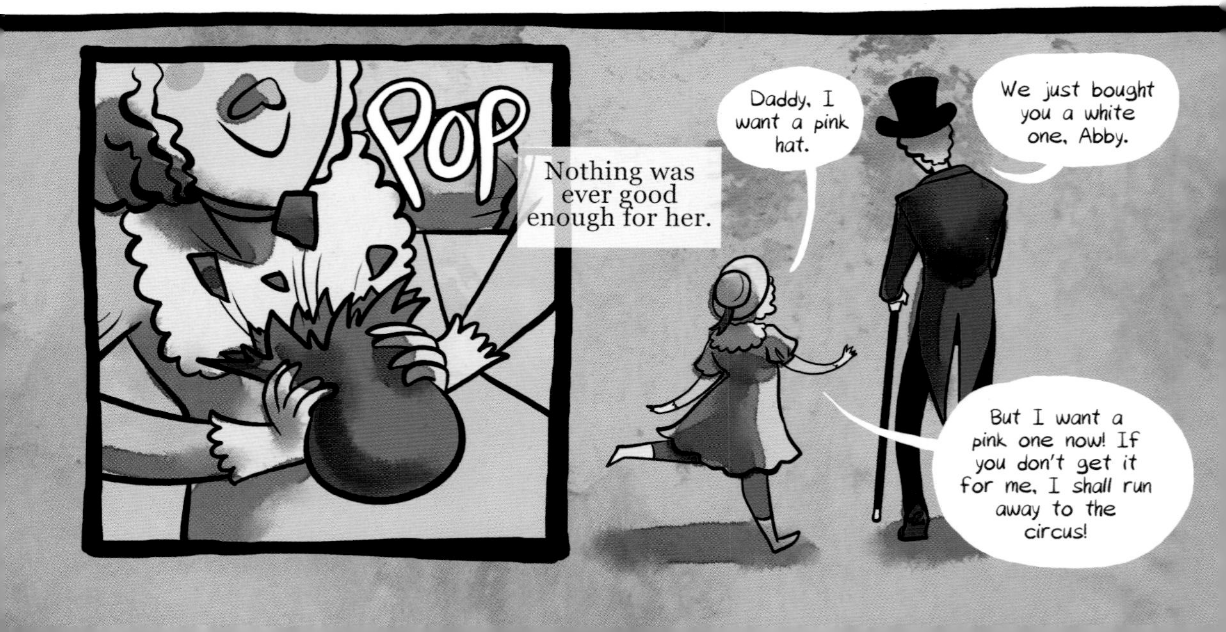
POP
Nothing was ever good enough for her.
Daddy, I want a pink hat.
We just bought you a white one, Abby.
But I want a pink one now! If you don't get it for me, I shall run away to the circus!

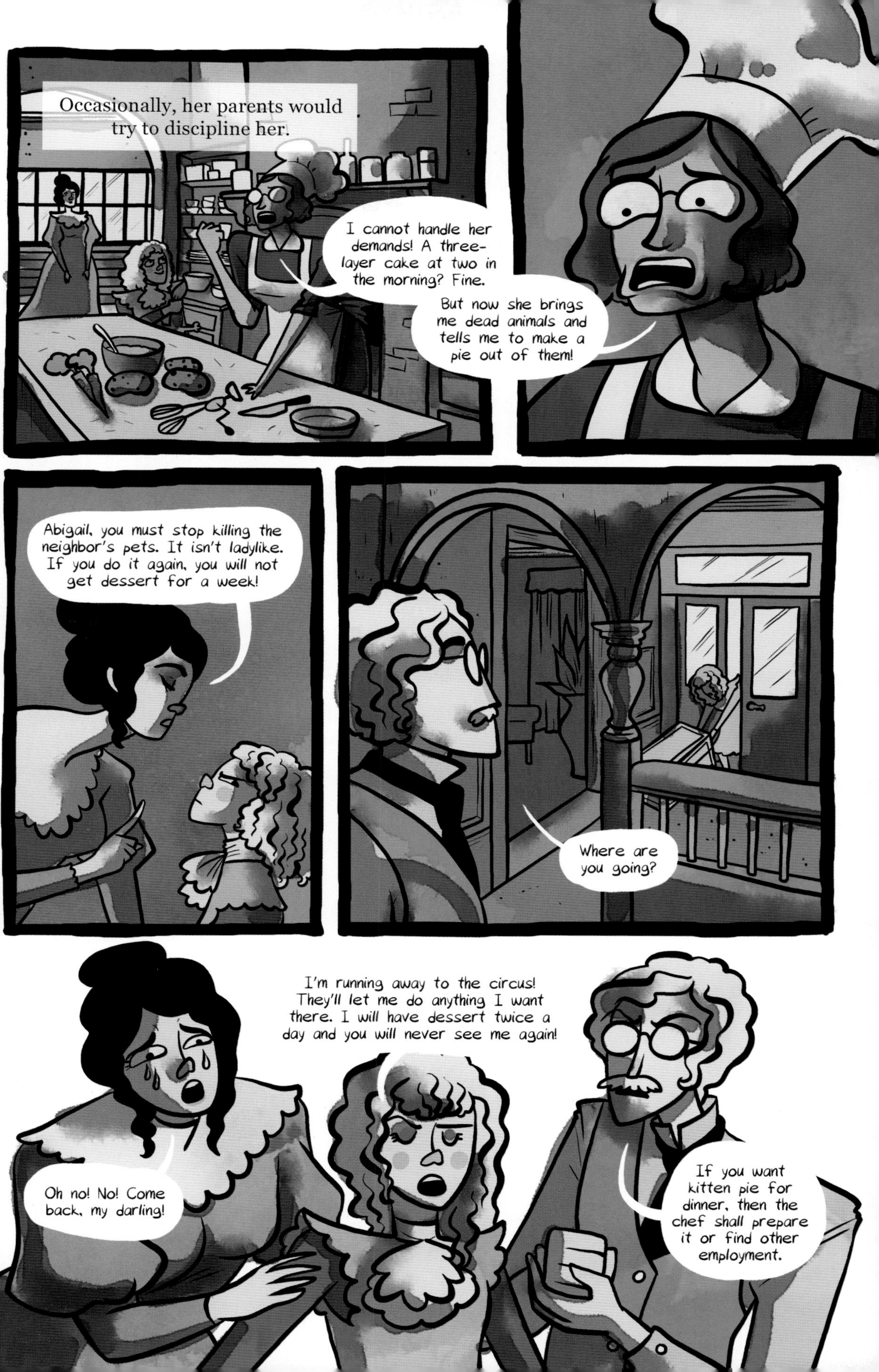
Occasionally, her parents would try to discipline her.
I cannot handle her demands! A three-layer cake at two in the morning? Fine.
But now she brings me dead animals and tells me to make a pie out of them!
Abigail, you must stop killing the neighbor's pets. It isn't ladylike. If you do it again, you will not get dessert for a week!
Where are you going?
I'm running away to the circus! They'll let me do anything I want there. I will have dessert twice a day and you will never see me again!
Oh no! No! Come back, my darling!
If you want kitten pie for dinner, then the chef shall prepare it or find other employment.

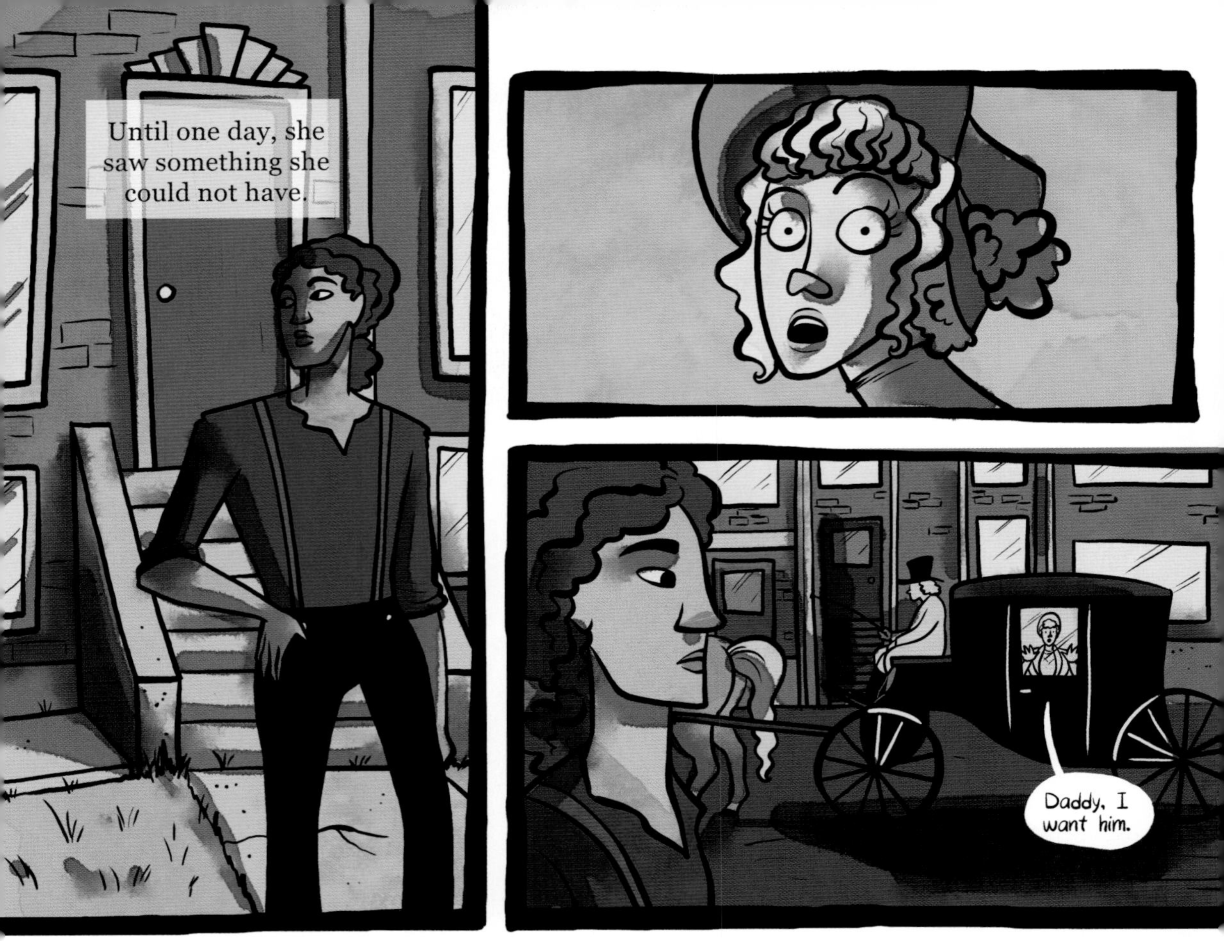
Until one day, she saw something she could not have.
Daddy, I want him.

Misunderstanding her, her father hired the boy to work in their house.
But Abigail wanted more.

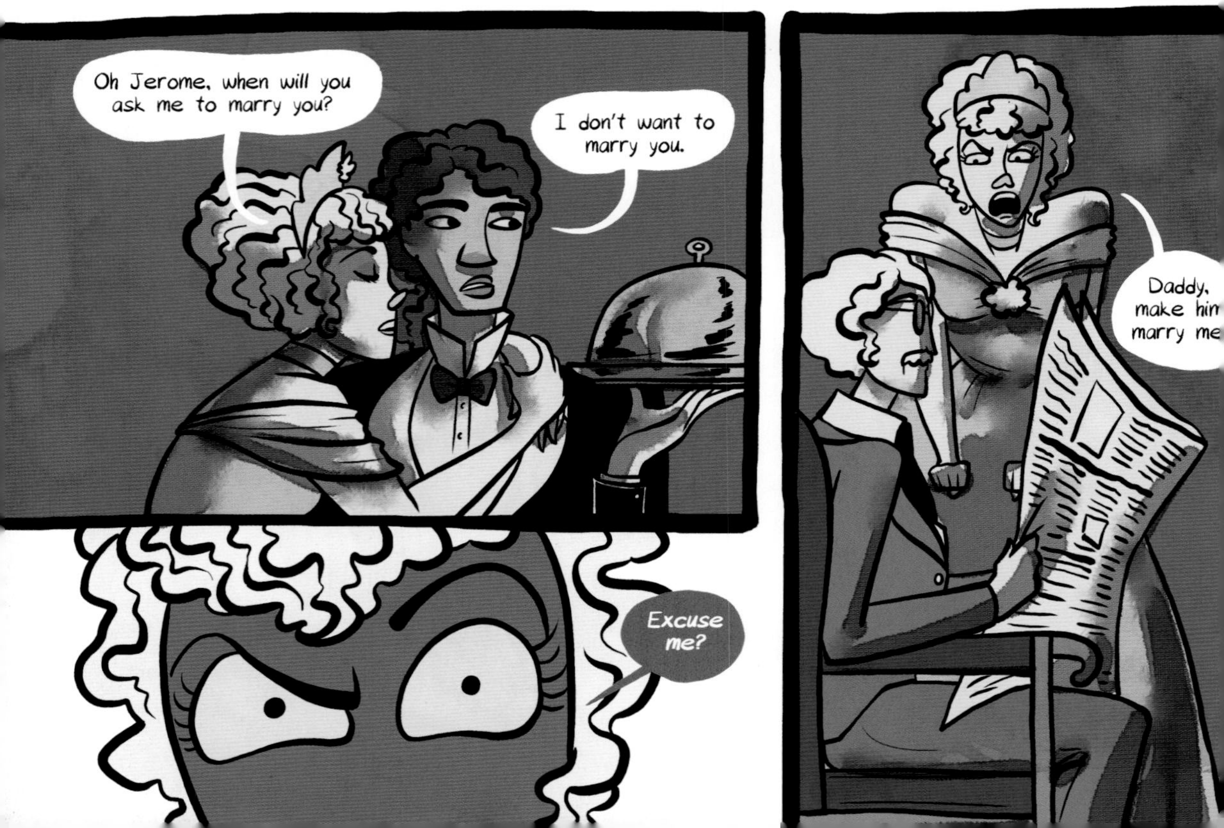
Oh Jerome, when will you ask me to marry you?
I don't want to marry you.
Excuse me?
Daddy, make hi marry me

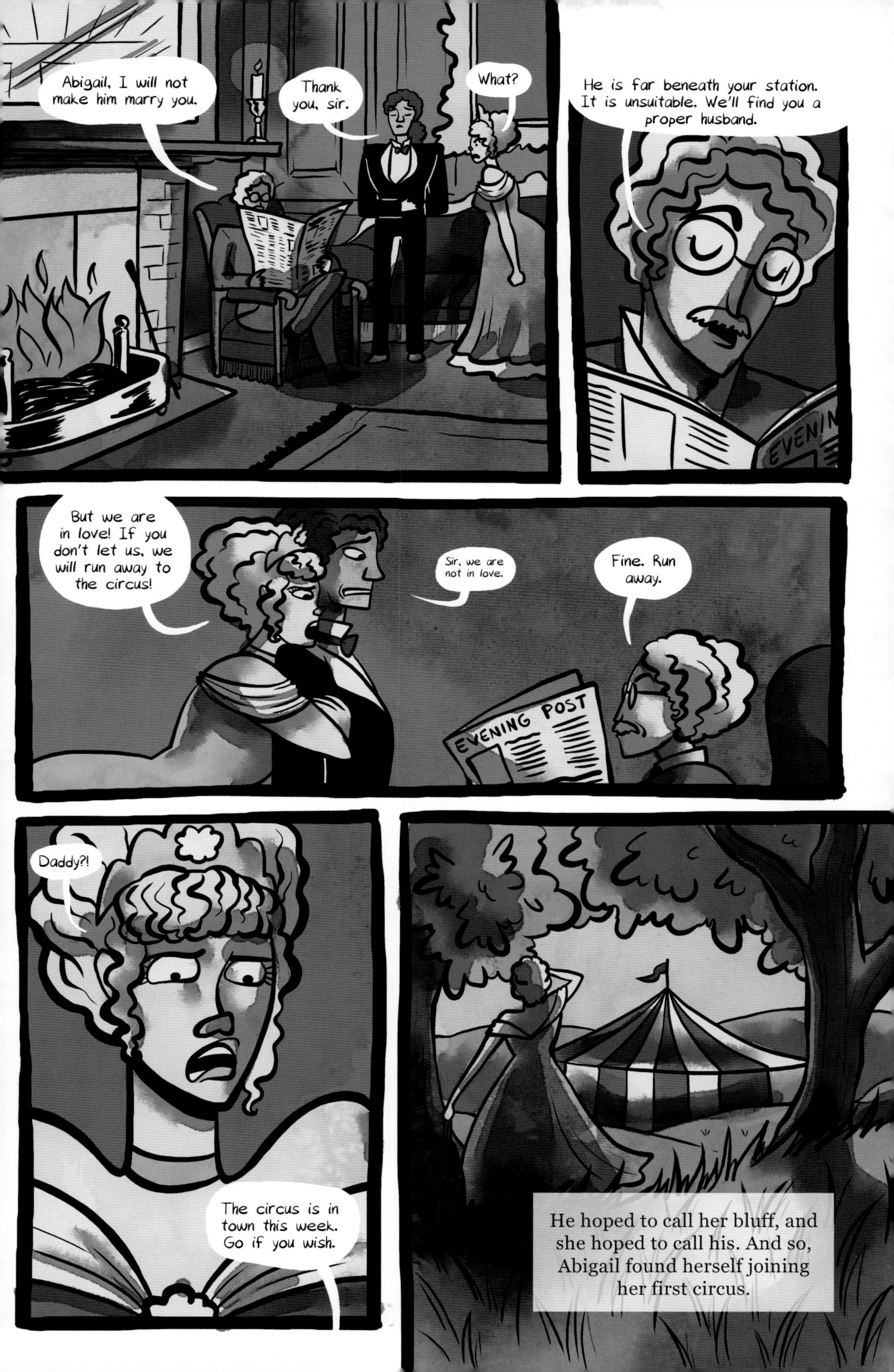
Abigail, I will not make him marry you.
Thank you, sir.
What?
He is far beneath your station. It is unsuitable. We'll find you a proper husband.
EVENIN
But we are in love! If you don't let us, we will run away to the circus!
Sir, we are not in love.
Fine. Run away.
EVENING POST
Daddy?!
The circus is in town this week. Go if you wish.
He hoped to call her bluff, and she hoped to call his. And so, Abigail found herself joining her first circus.

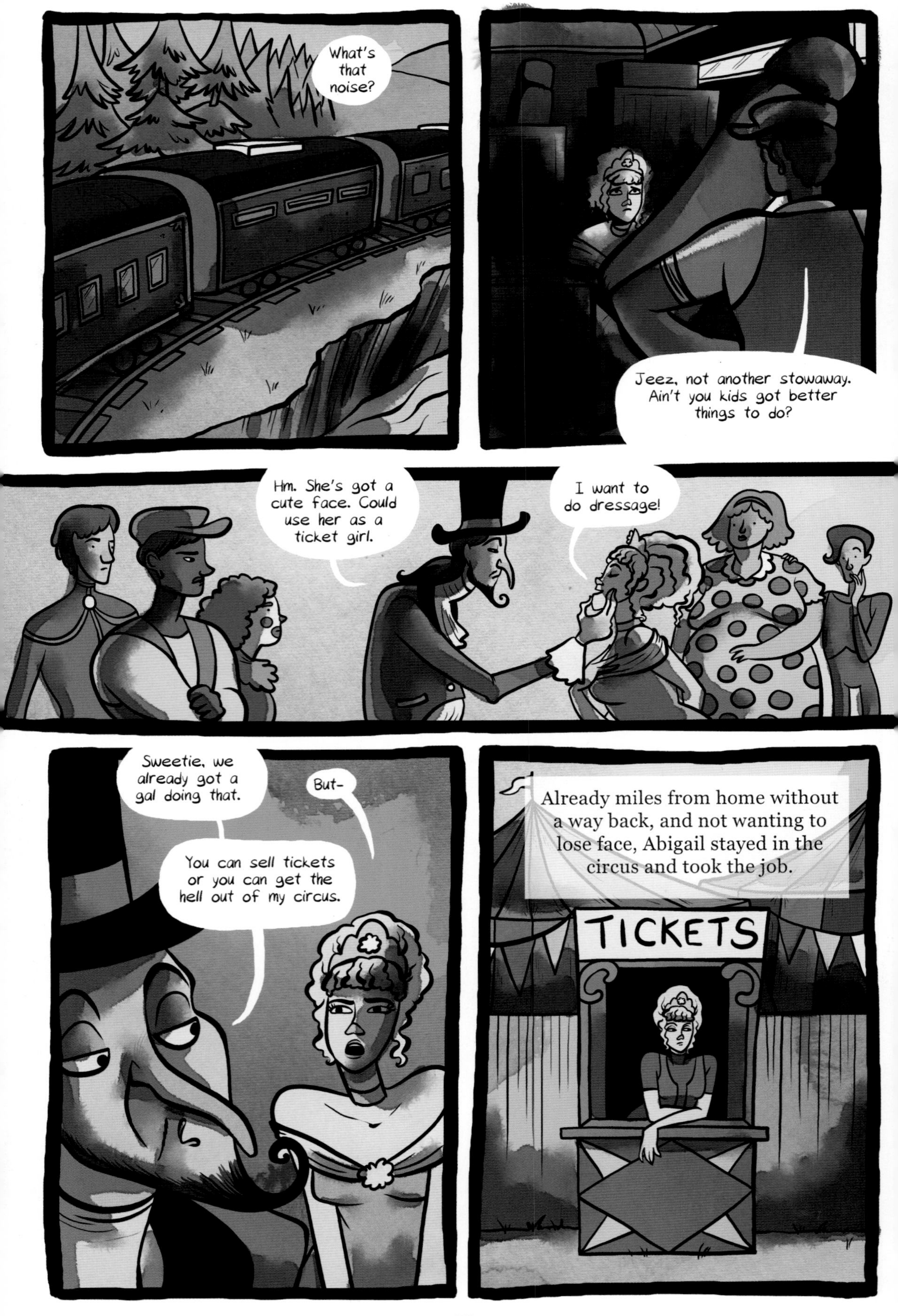
What's that noise?
Jeez, not another stowaway. Ain't you kids got better things to do?
Hm. She's got a cute face. Could use her as a ticket girl.
I want to do dressage!
Sweetie, we already got a gal doing that.
But-
You can sell tickets or you can get the hell out of my circus.
Already miles from home without a way back, and not wanting to lose face, Abigail stayed in the circus and took the job.
TICKETS

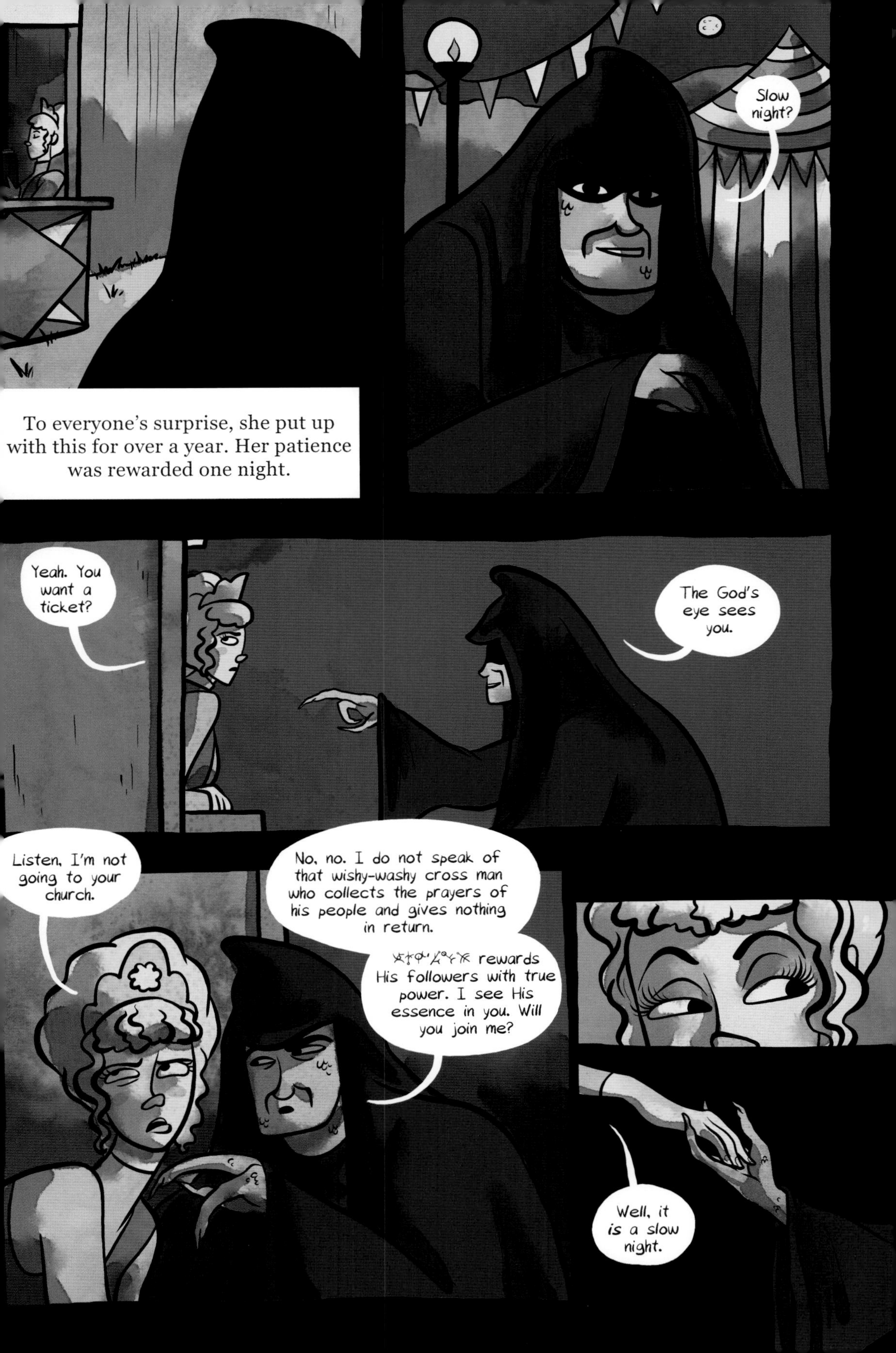
To everyone's surprise, she put up with this for over a year. Her patience was rewarded one night.
Slow night?
Yeah. You want a ticket?
The God's eye sees you.
Listen, I'm not going to your church.
No, no. I do not speak of that wishy-washy cross man who collects the prayers of his people and gives nothing in return.
rewards His followers with true power. I see His essence in you. Will you join me?
Well, it *is* a slow night.

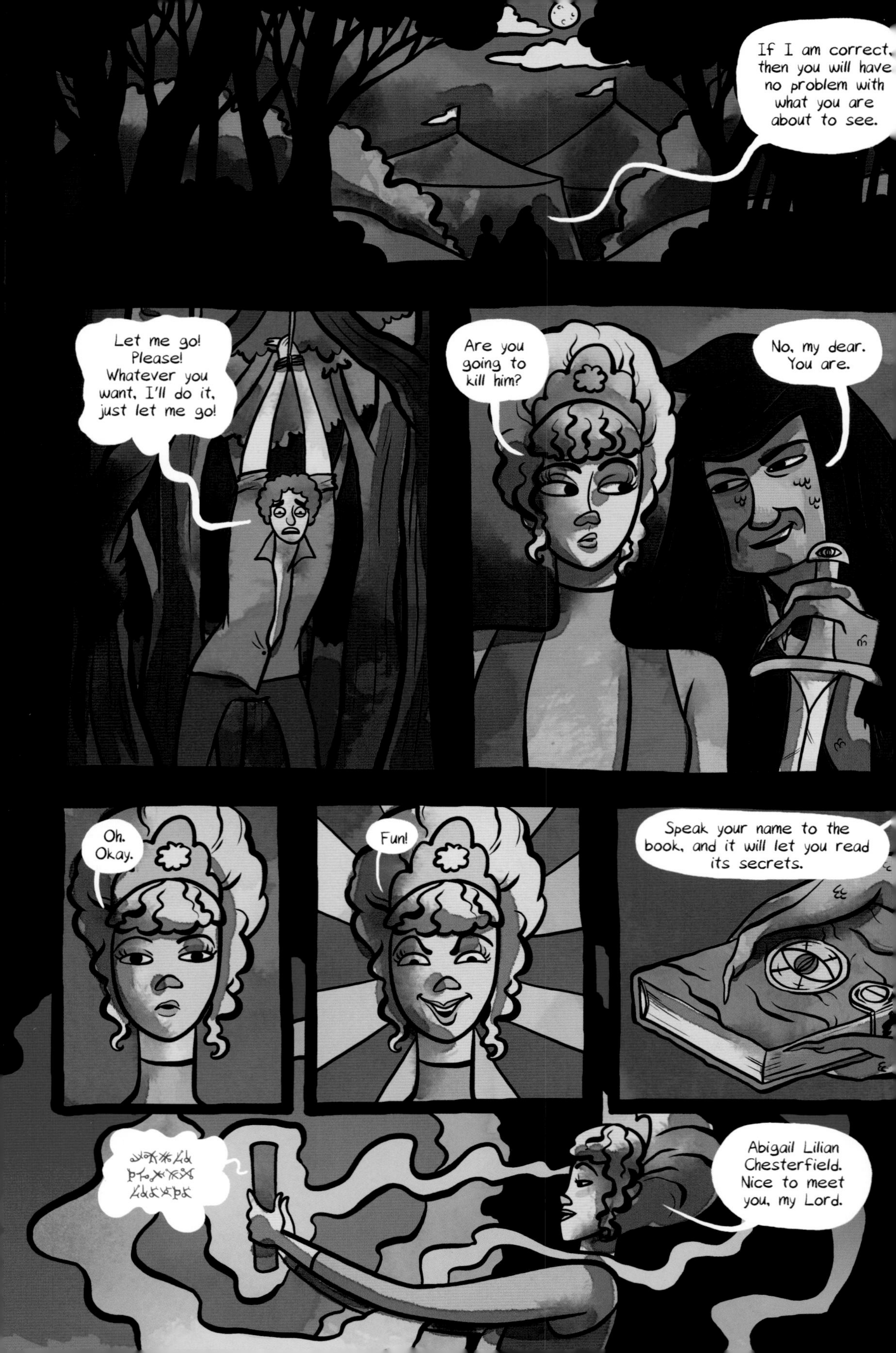
If I am correct, then you will have no problem with what you are about to see.
Let me go! Please! Whatever you want, I'll do it, just let me go!
Are you going to kill him?
No, my dear. You are.
Oh. Okay.
Fun!
Speak your name to the book, and it will let you read its secrets.
Abigail Lilian Chesterfield. Nice to meet you, my Lord.

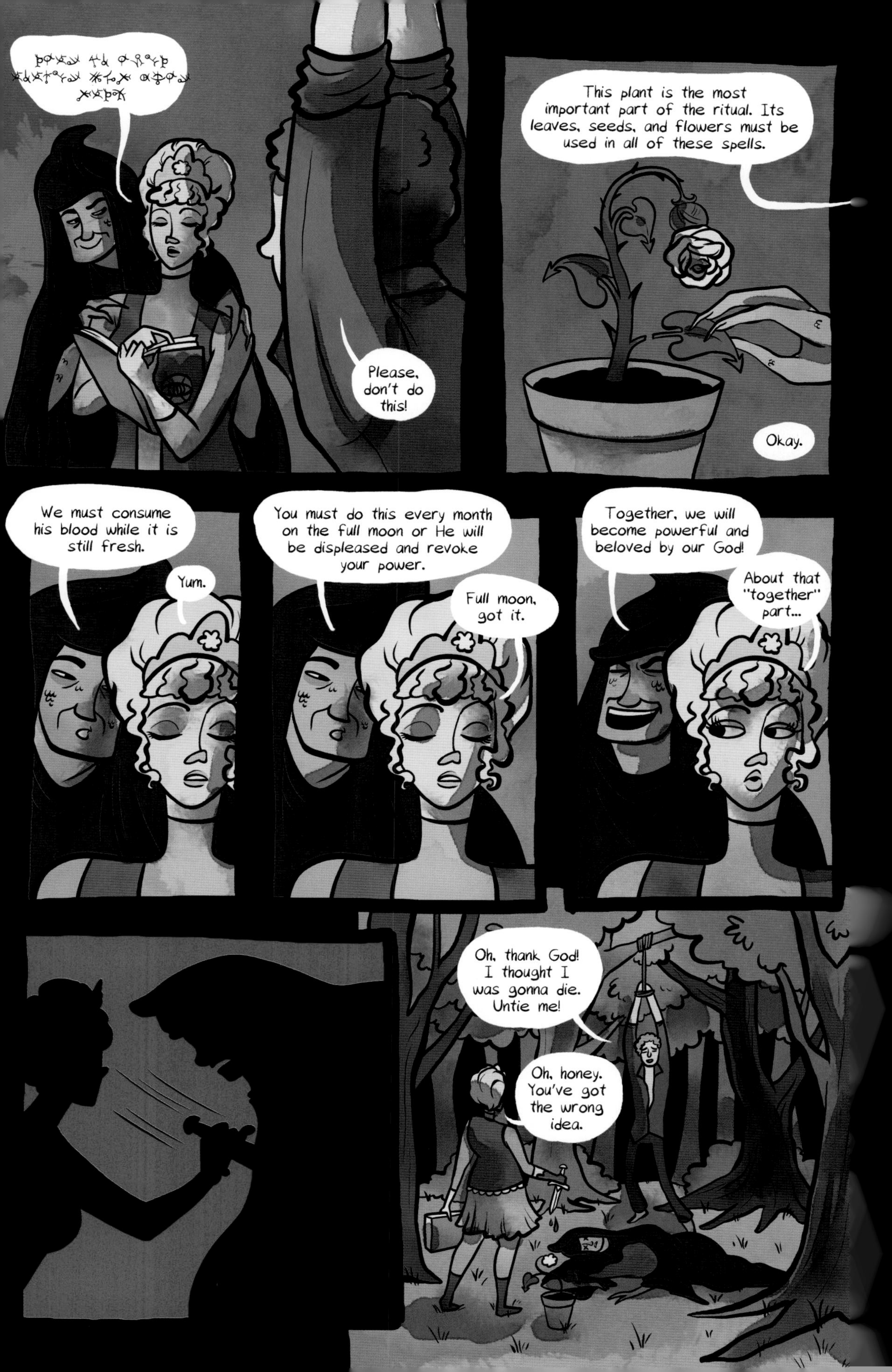
Please, don't do this!
This plant is the most important part of the ritual. Its leaves, seeds, and flowers must be used in all of these spells.
Okay.
We must consume his blood while it is still fresh.
Yum.
You must do this every month on the full moon or He will be displeased and revoke your power.
Full moon, got it.
Together, we will become powerful and beloved by our God!
About that "together" part...
Oh, thank God! I thought I was gonna die. Untie me!
Oh, honey. You've got the wrong idea.

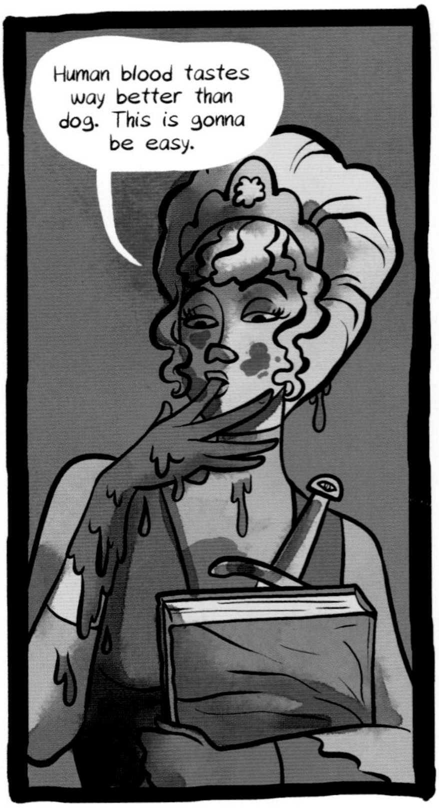
Human blood tastes way better than dog. This is gonna be easy.

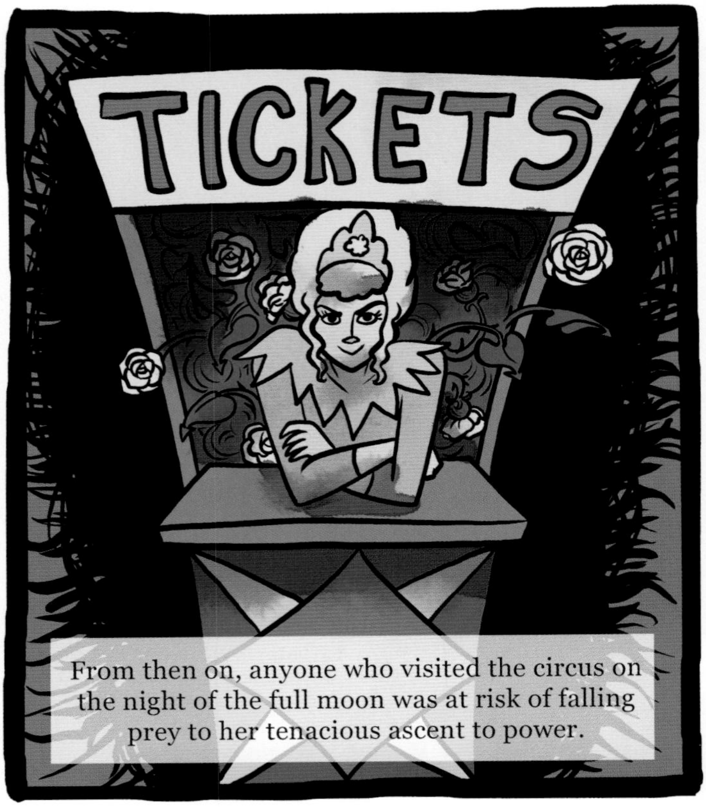
TICKETS
From then on, anyone who visited the circus on the night of the full moon was at risk of falling prey to her tenacious ascent to power.

She had always believed she was better than everyone else, with the god-given right to trample others in service of her insatiable greed, and now her destiny was manifest, the world hers for the taking, at least until her god was ready for it.

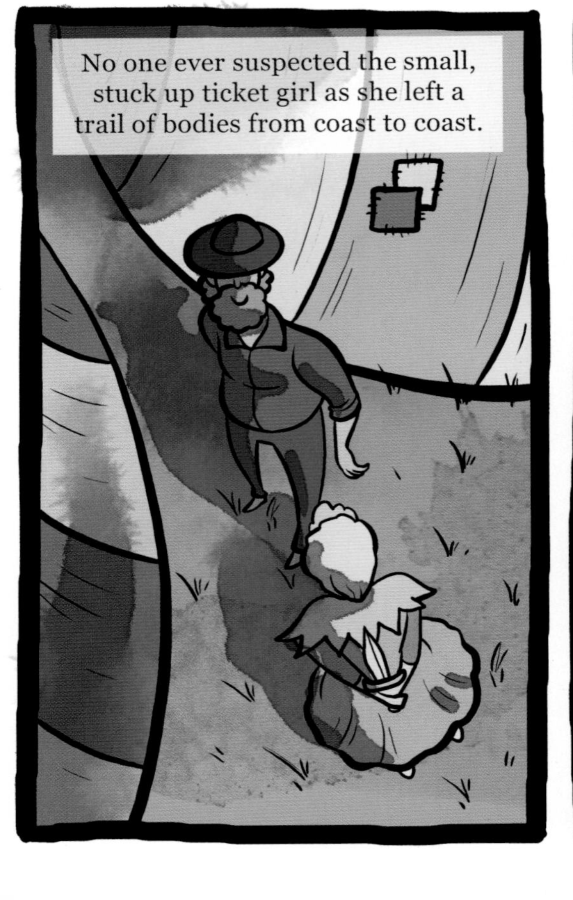
No one ever suspected the small, stuck up ticket girl as she left a trail of bodies from coast to coast.

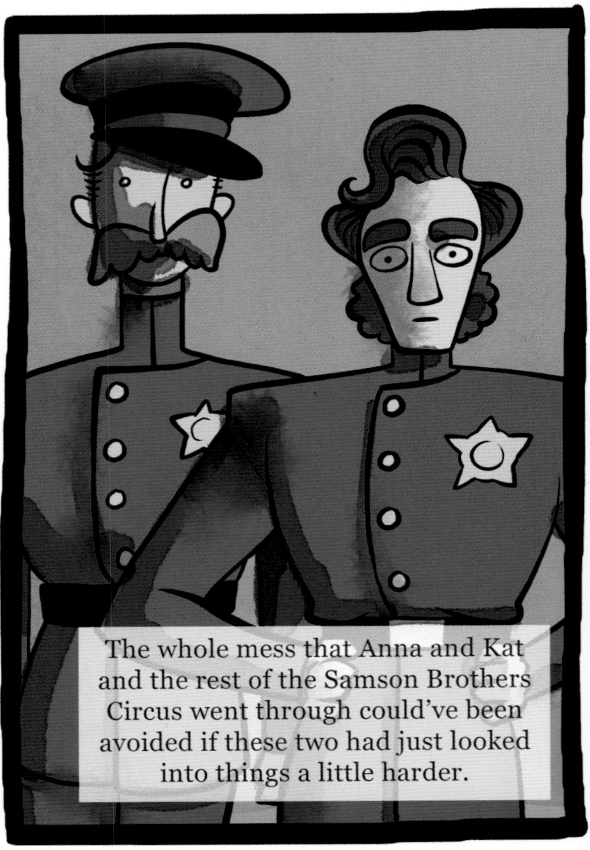
The whole mess that Anna and Kat and the rest of the Samson Brothers Circus went through could've been avoided if these two had just looked into things a little harder.

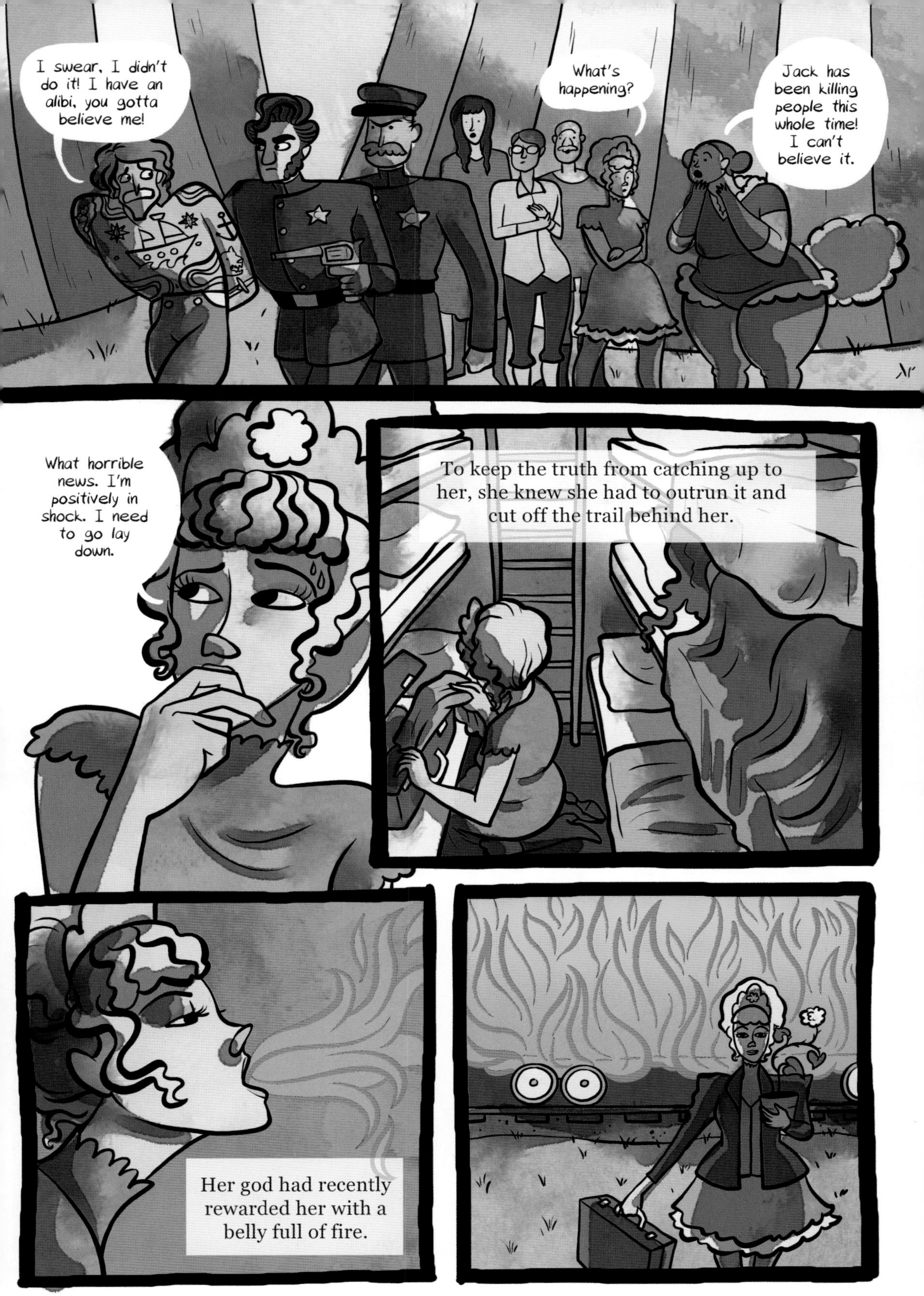

I swear, I didn't do it! I have an alibi, you gotta believe me!
What's happening?
Jack has been killing people this whole time! I can't believe it.
What horrible news. I'm positively in shock. I need to go lay down.
To keep the truth from catching up to her, she knew she had to outrun it and cut off the trail behind her.
Her god had recently rewarded her with a belly full of fire.

Abigail Chesterfield did not die in the blaze like everyone thought, but a mechanic and the cook certainly did. Two more victims of her destructive ambitions.

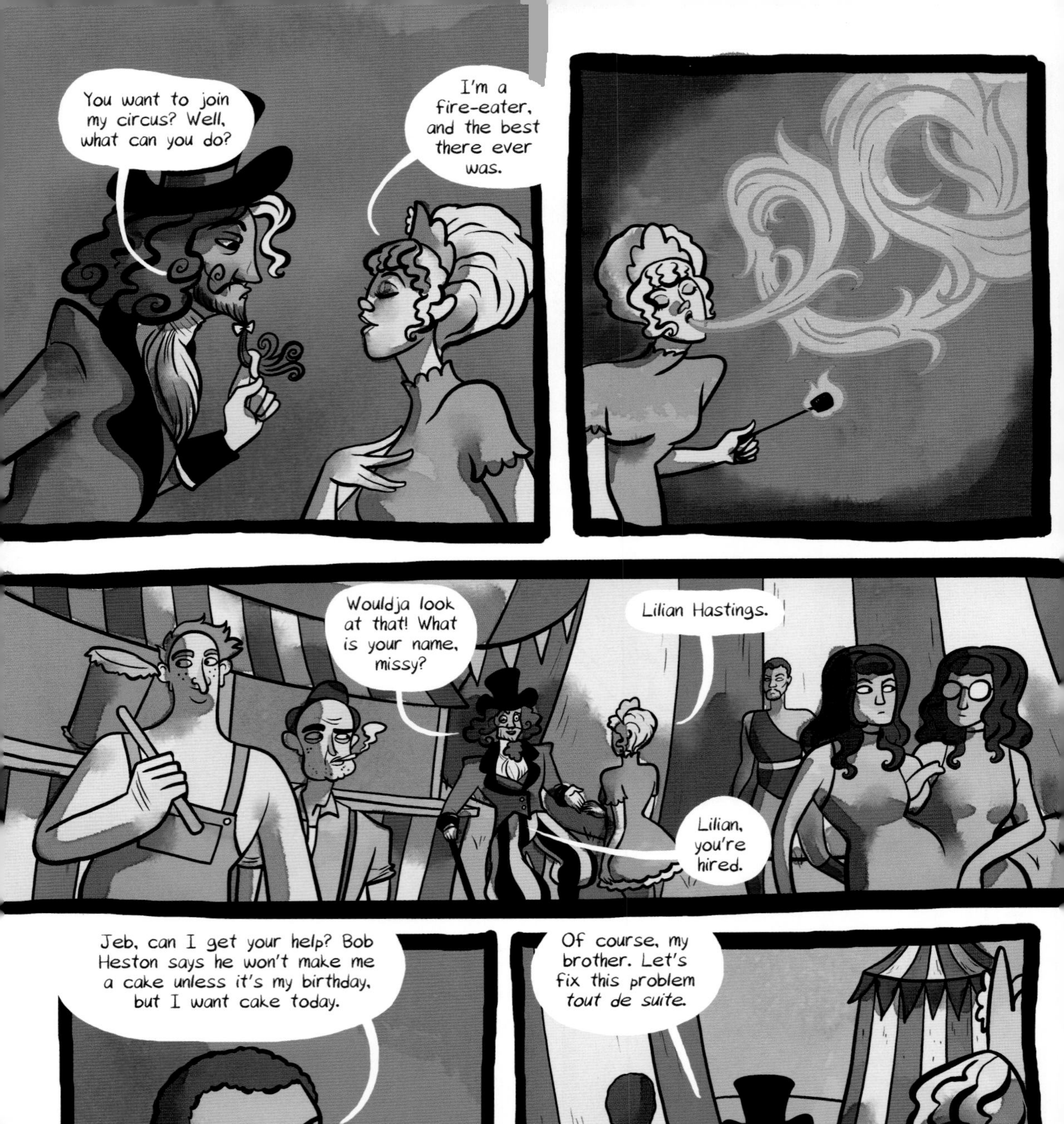
You want to join my circus? Well, what can you do?
I'm a fire-eater, and the best there ever was.
Wouldja look at that! What is your name, missy?
Lilian Hastings.
Lilian, you're hired.

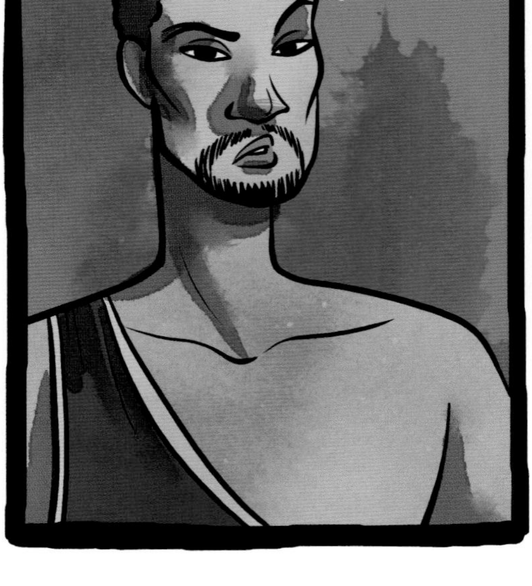
Jeb, can I get your help? Bob Heston says he won't make me a cake unless it's my birthday, but I want cake today.

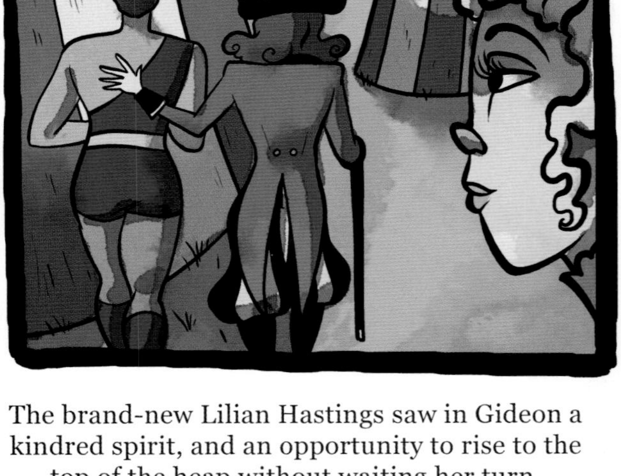
Of course, my brother. Let's fix this problem *tout de suite*.

The brand-new Lilian Hastings saw in Gideon a kindred spirit, and an opportunity to rise to the top of the heap without waiting her turn.

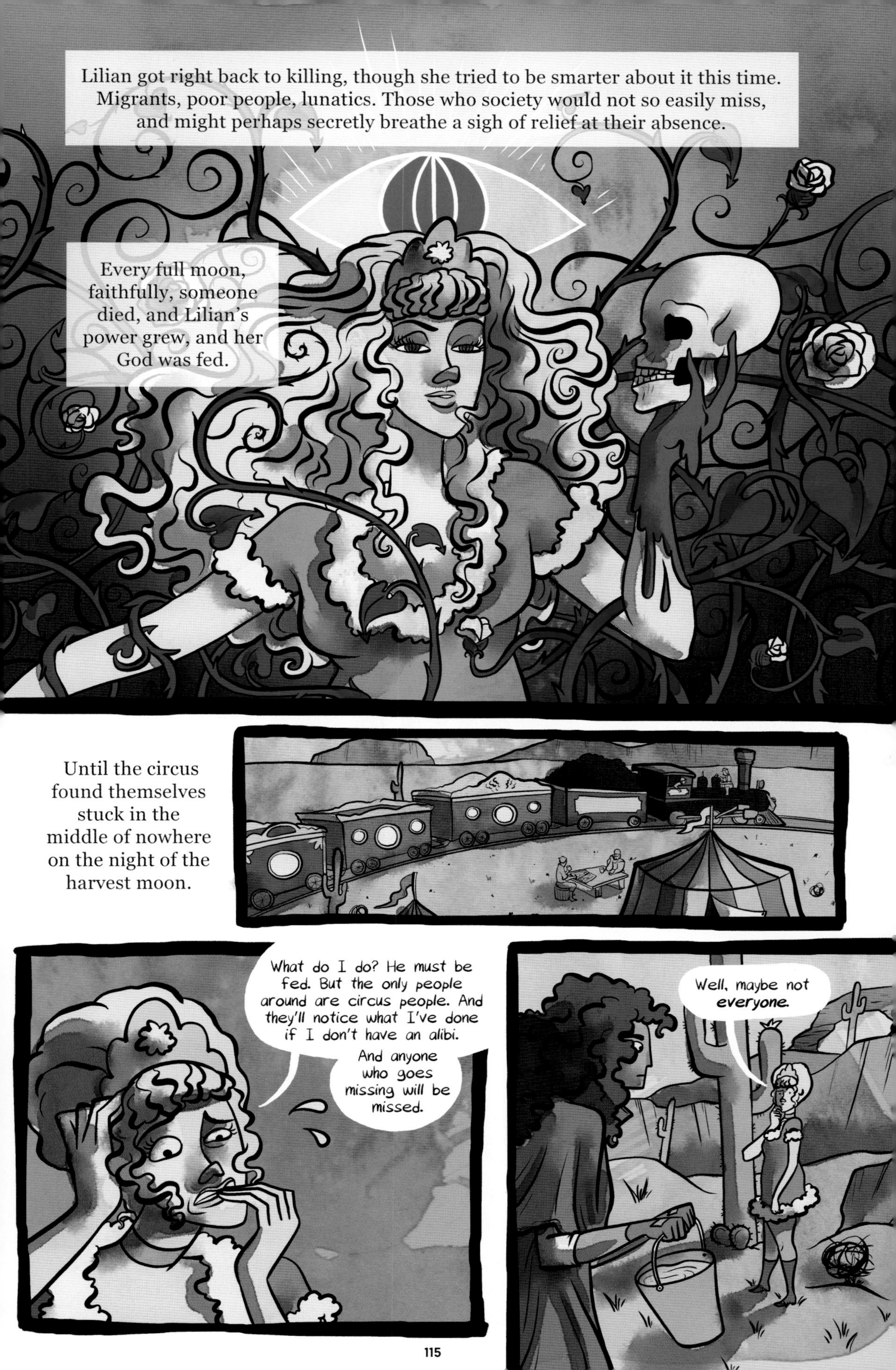
Lilian got right back to killing, though she tried to be smarter about it this time. Migrants, poor people, lunatics. Those who society would not so easily miss, and might perhaps secretly breathe a sigh of relief at their absence.
Every full moon, faithfully, someone died, and Lilian's power grew, and her God was fed.
Until the circus found themselves stuck in the middle of nowhere on the night of the harvest moon.
What do I do? He must be fed. But the only people around are circus people. And they'll notice what I've done if I don't have an alibi.
And anyone who goes missing will be missed.
Well, maybe not *everyone*.

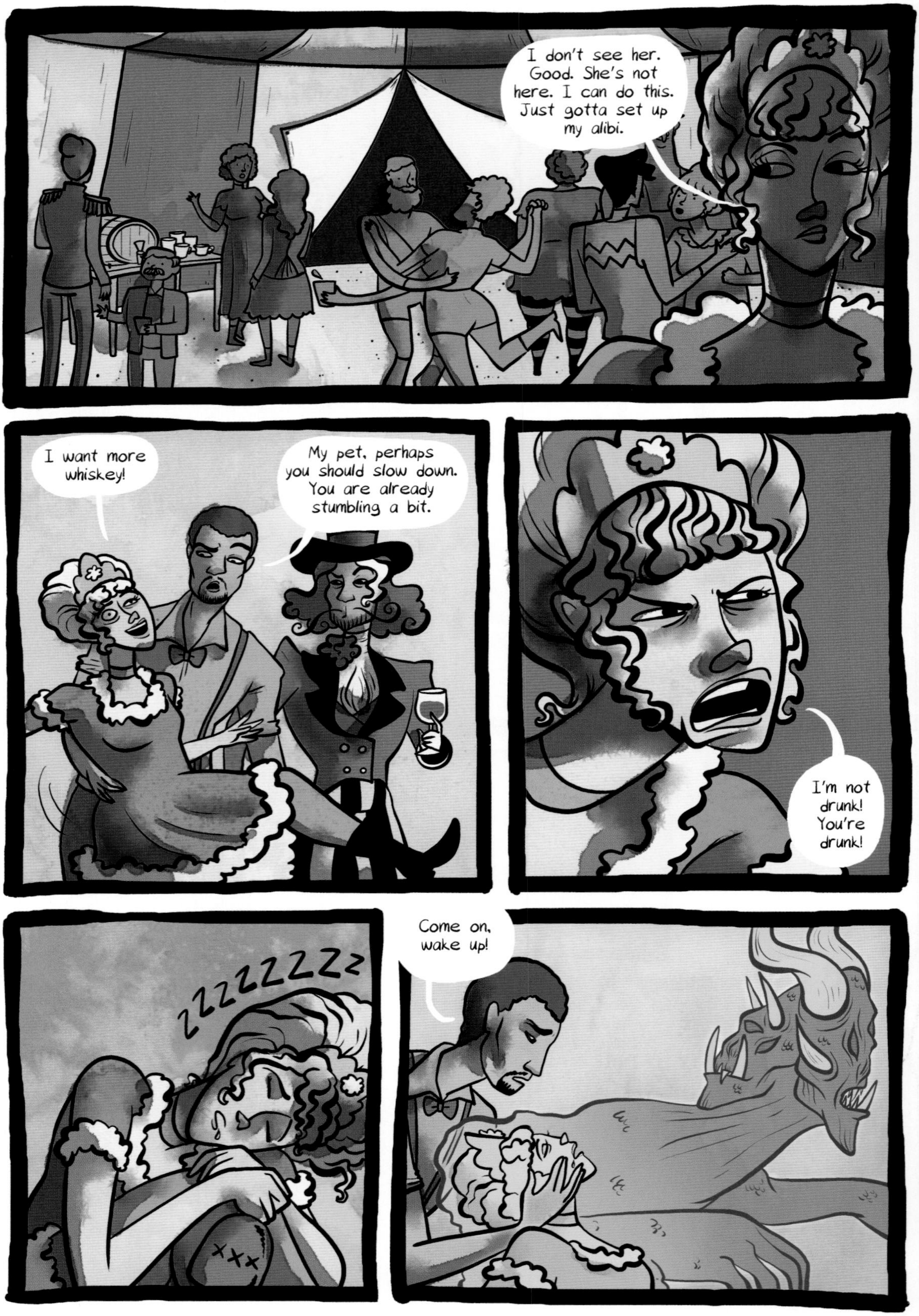
I don't see her. Good. She's not here. I can do this. Just gotta set up my alibi.
I want more whiskey!
My pet, perhaps you should slow down. You are already stumbling a bit.
I'm not drunk! You're drunk!
ZZZZZZZZz
Come on, wake up!

The demon form, given to the God's most treasured followers, cannot be seen, but it can touch both the physical and spiritual planes. She went stalking her prey.

Damn, I forgot the knife.

Ah, but her sister is a knife-thrower.

I can bless one of those. It should work.

Blech, I hate when bugs fly in my mouth.

Wait, it's the other one. Damn. Well, I still have an airtight alibi back in the tent. Might as well see this through.

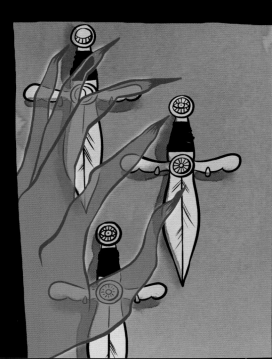

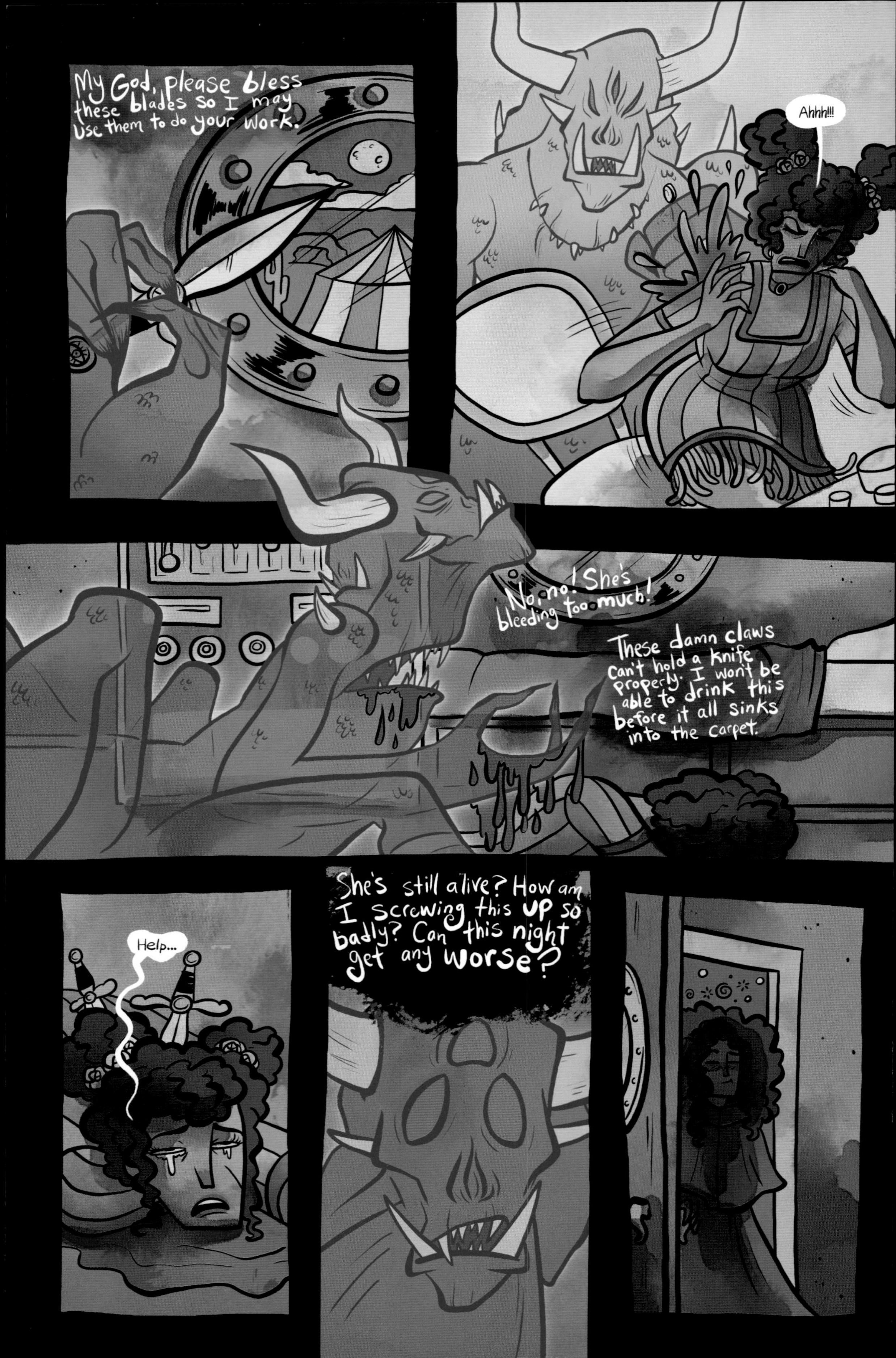
My God, please bless these blades so I may use them to do your work.
Ahhh!!!
No, no! She's bleeding too much!
These damn claws can't hold a knife properly. I won't be able to drink this before it all sinks into the carpet.
Help...
She's still alive? How am I screwing this up so badly? Can this night get any worse?

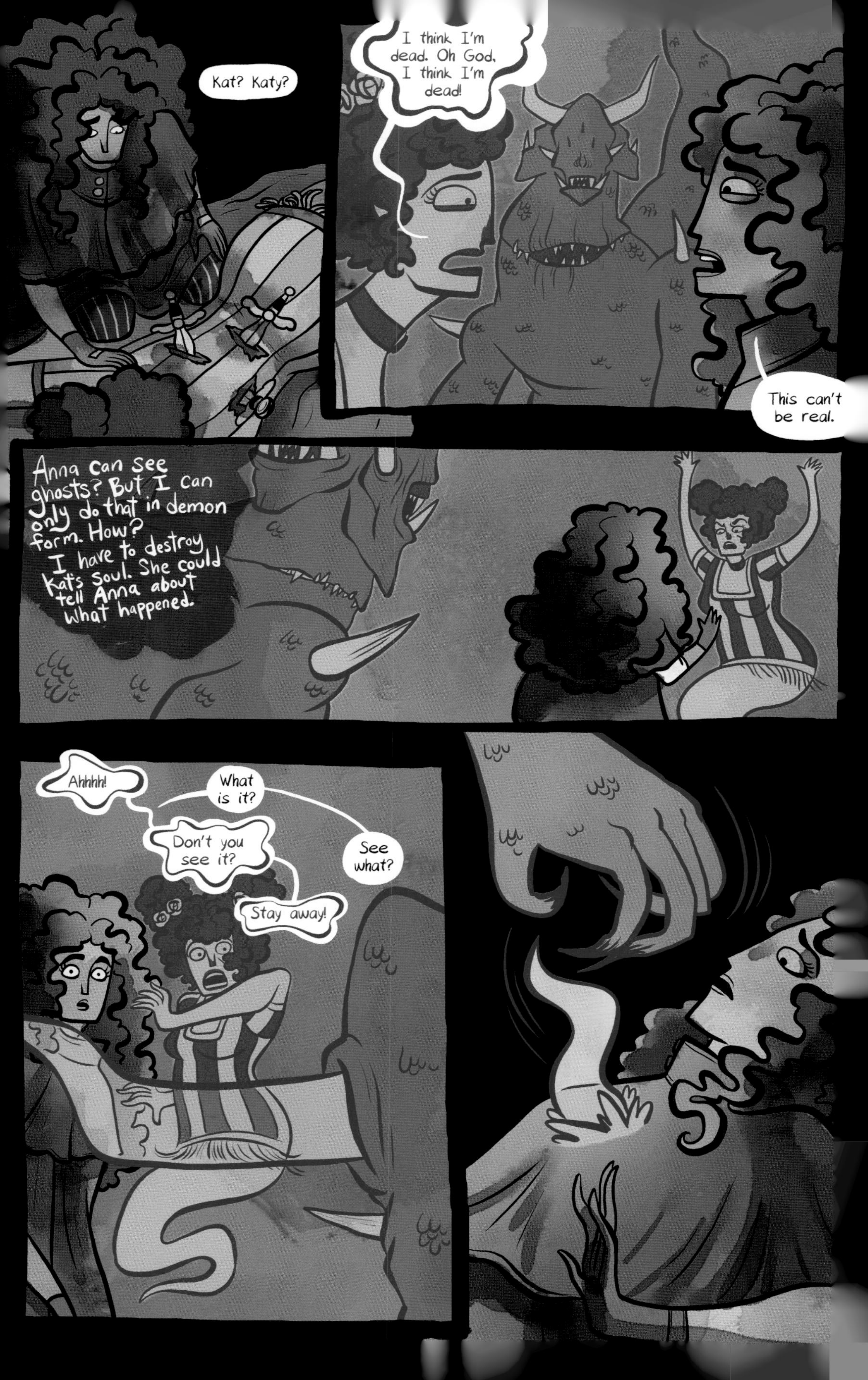
Kat? Katy?
I think I'm dead. Oh God. I think I'm dead!
This can't be real.
Anna can see ghosts? But I can only do that in demon form. How? I have to destroy Kat's soul. She could tell Anna about what happened.
Ahhhh!
What is it?
Don't you see it?
See what?
Stay away!

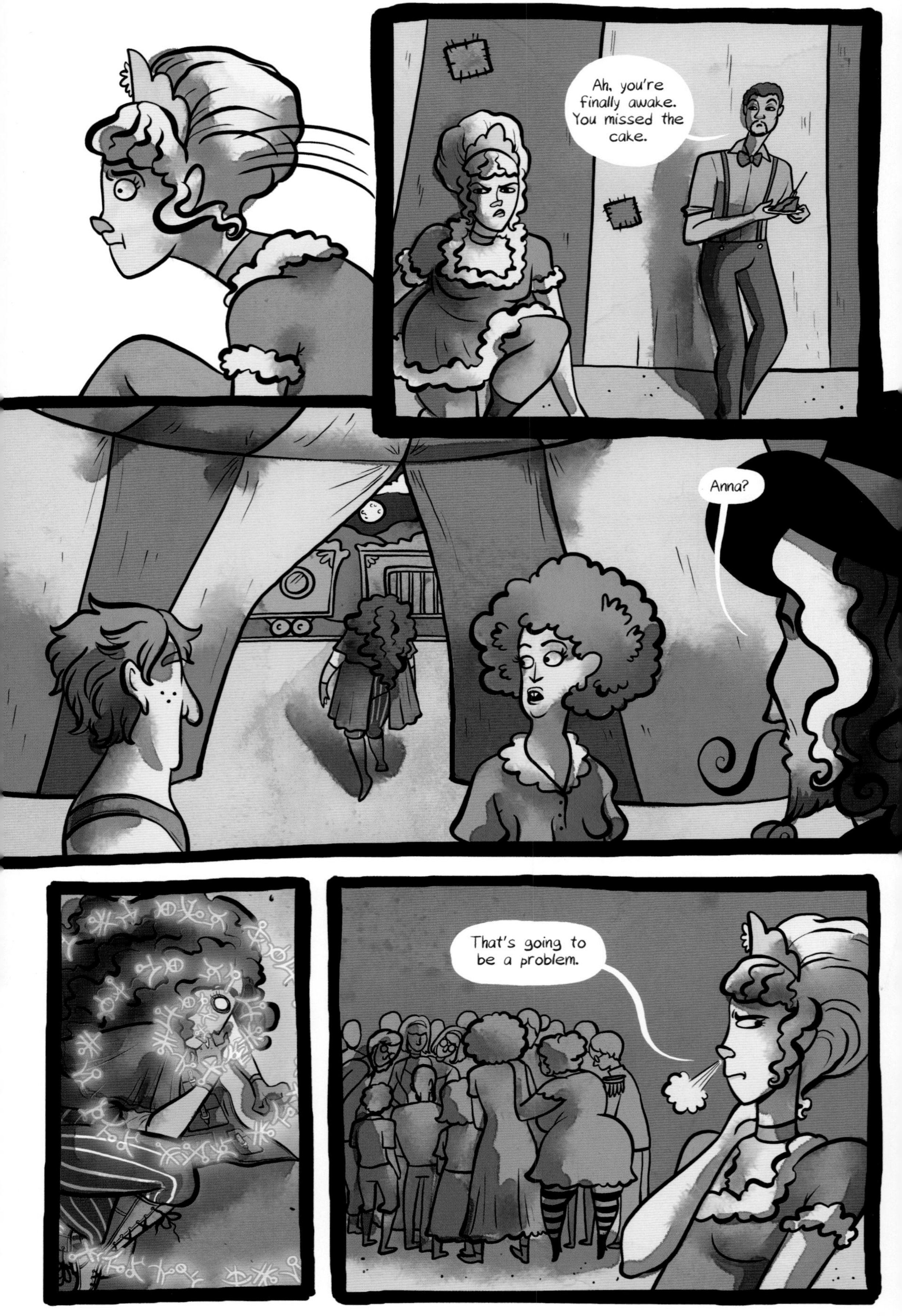
Ah, you're finally awake. You missed the cake.
Anna?
That's going to be a problem.

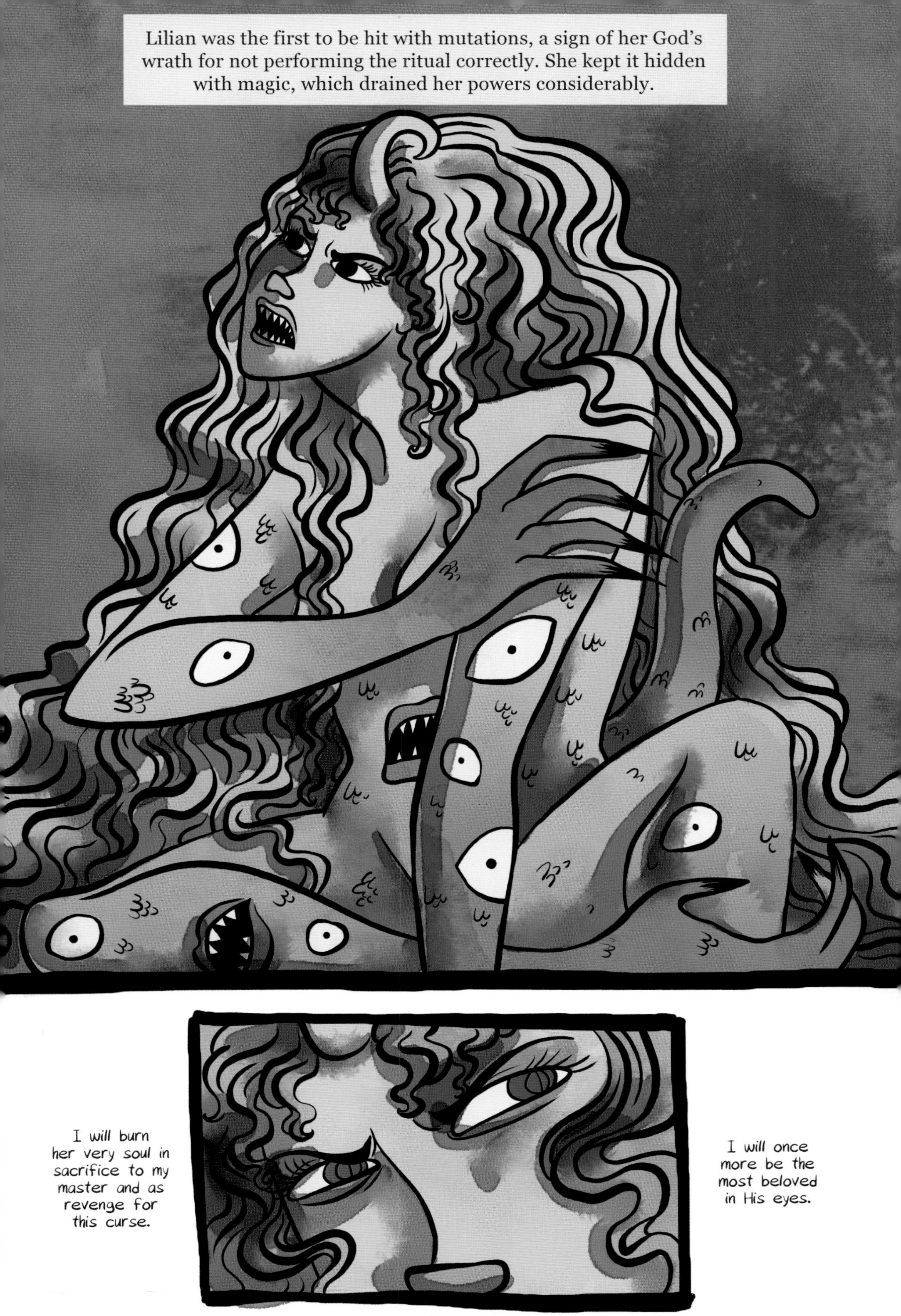
Lilian was the first to be hit with mutations, a sign of her God's wrath for not performing the ritual correctly. She kept it hidden with magic, which drained her powers considerably.
I will burn her very soul in sacrifice to my master and as revenge for this curse.
I will once more be the most beloved in His eyes.

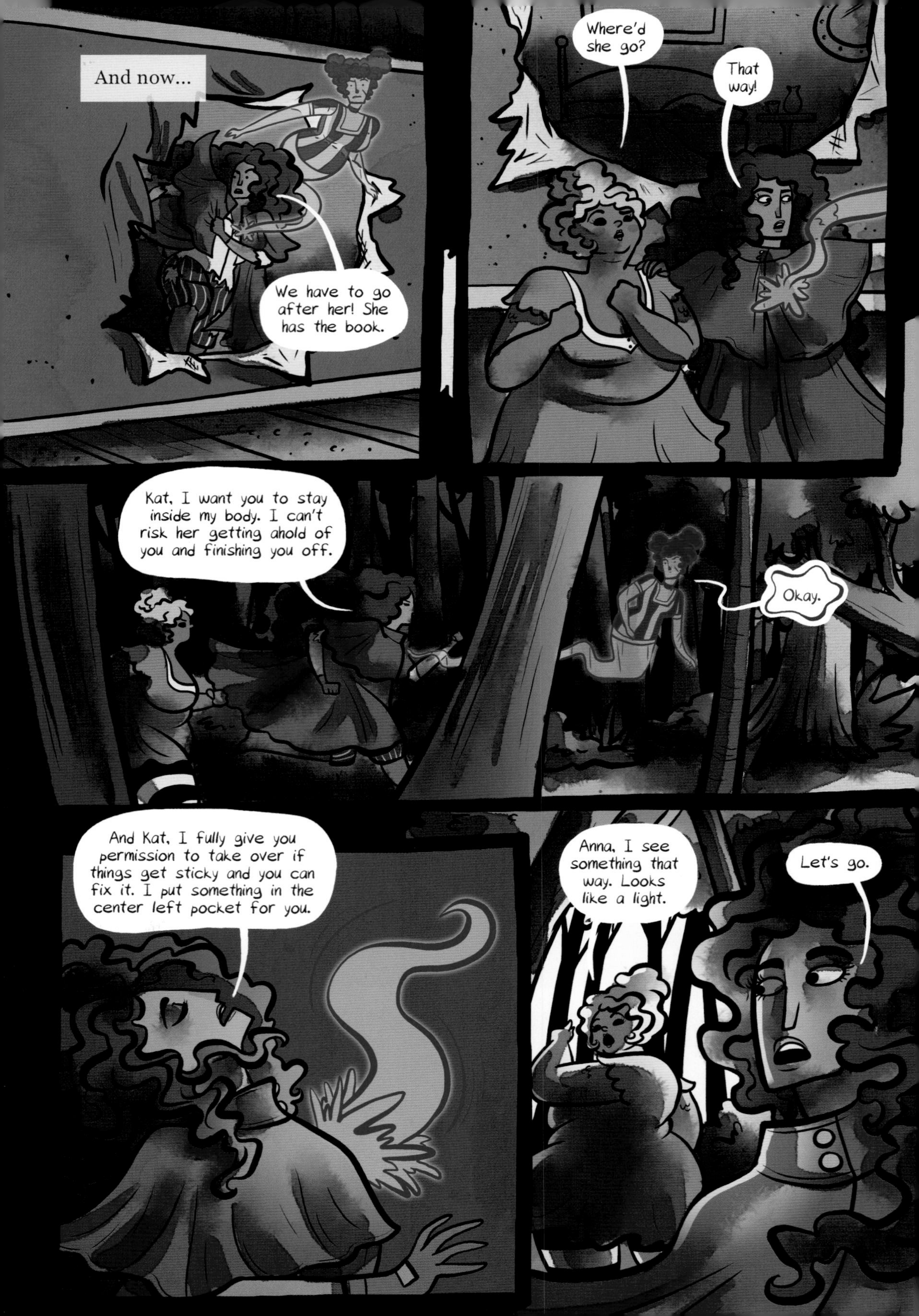
And now...
We have to go after her! She has the book.
Where'd she go?
That way!
Kat, I want you to stay inside my body. I can't risk her getting ahold of you and finishing you off.
Okay.
And Kat, I fully give you permission to take over if things get sticky and you can fix it. I put something in the center left pocket for you.
Anna, I see something that way. Looks like a light.
Let's go.

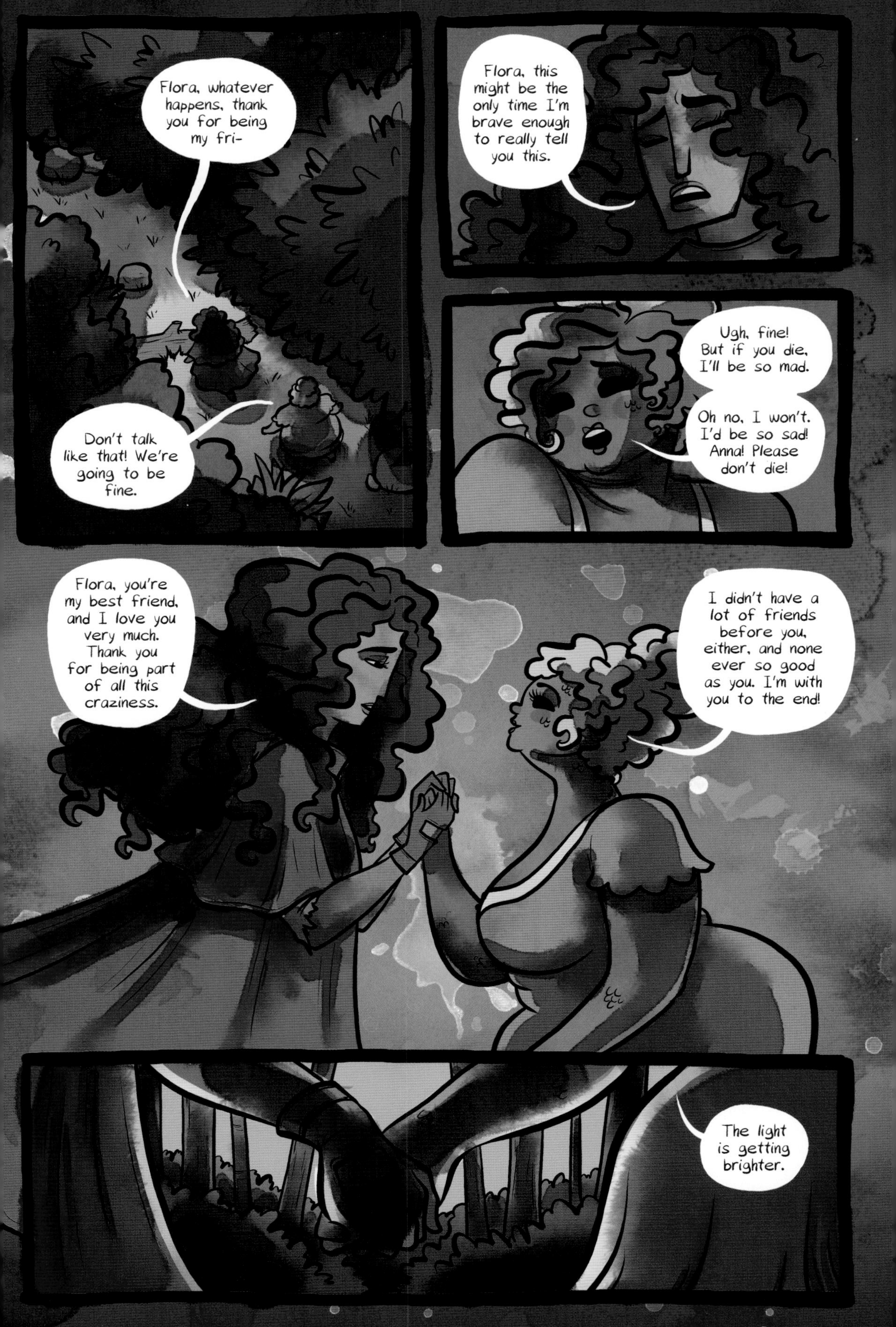
Flora, whatever happens, thank you for being my fri-
Don't talk like that! We're going to be fine.
Flora, this might be the only time I'm brave enough to really tell you this.
Ugh, fine! But if you die, I'll be so mad.
Oh no, I won't. I'd be so sad! Anna! Please don't die!
Flora, you're my best friend, and I love you very much. Thank you for being part of all this craziness.
I didn't have a lot of friends before you, either, and none ever so good as you. I'm with you to the end!
The light is getting brighter.

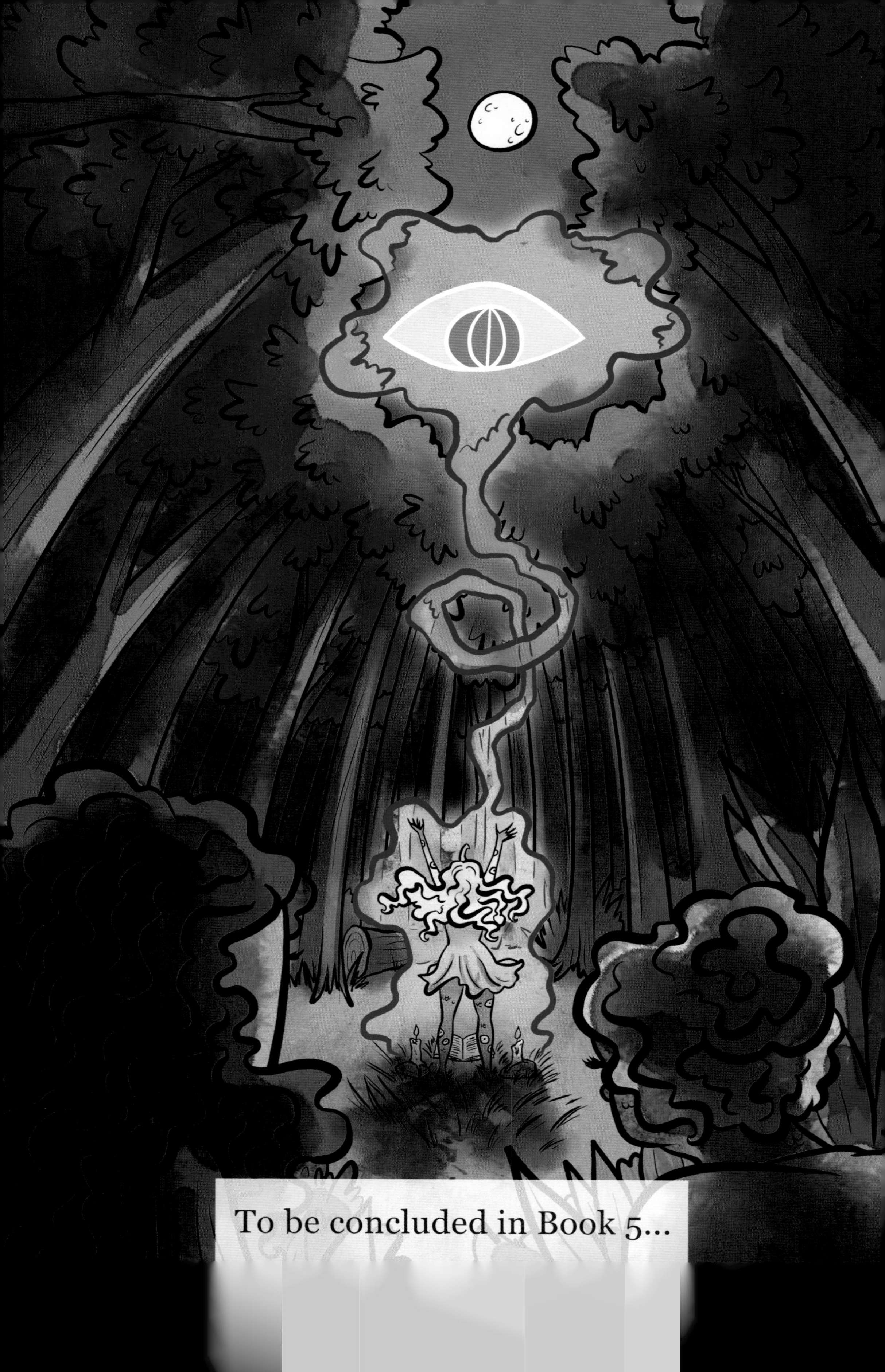
To be concluded in Book 5...

End of Book Four

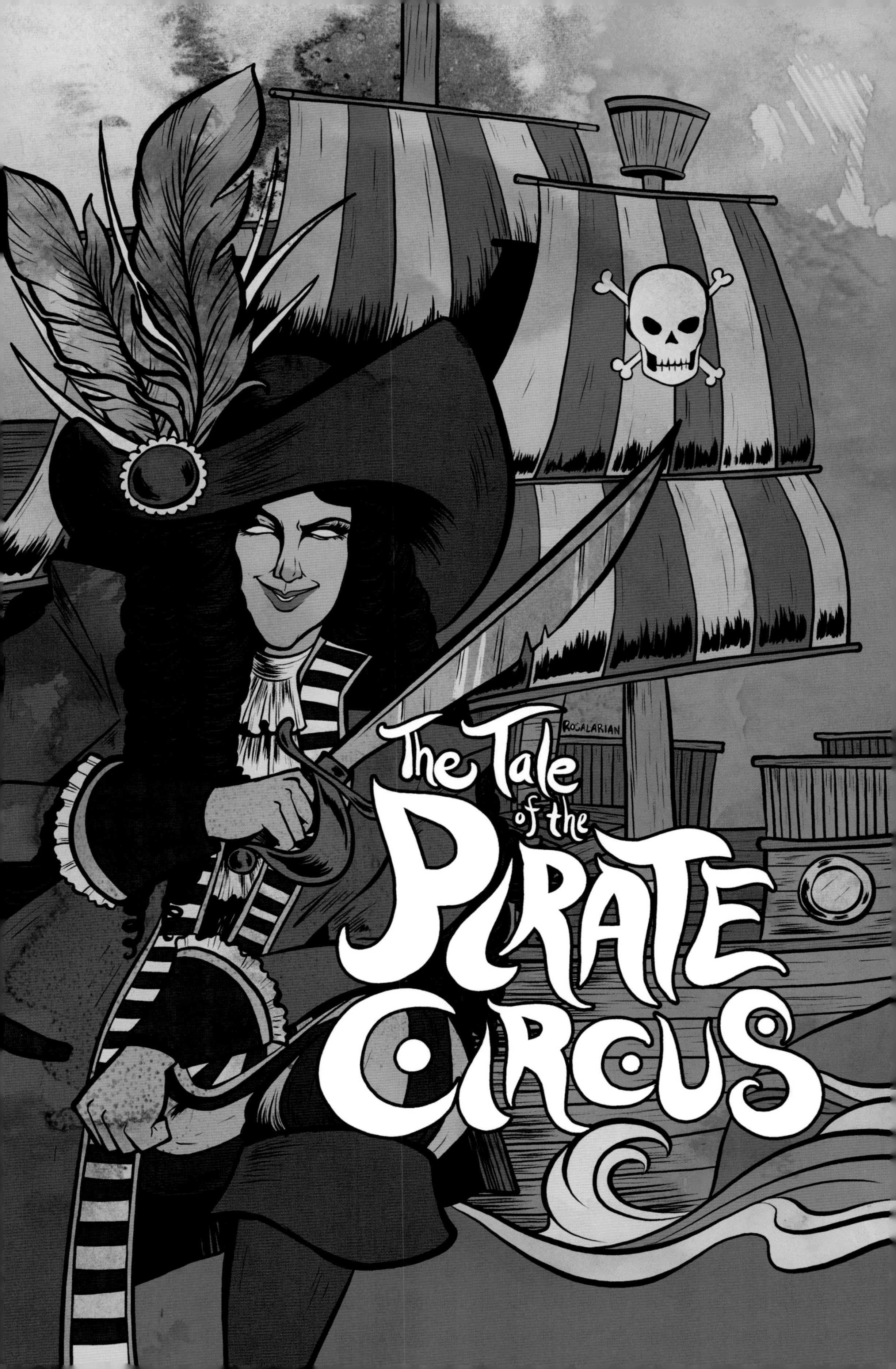

ROSALARIAN
The Tale of the
PIRATE
CIRCUS

The Tale of the Pirate Circus

Written and Illustrated by Megan Rose Gedris

A few days ago...

The sun was so hot, and the air so thick and muggy, even the mosquitos were too tired to fly around. It smelled like mud and old eggs and sweat. Even at night, it barely cooled down, leaving everyone stuck to their sheets, restless and cranky. One by one, the circus folk climbed down from the train and gathered beneath the stars, passing a bottle around by moonlight. As it so often goes, grievances began pouring from their mouths as quickly as bourbon poured in.

"Another backwater town with naught to do but drink," sighed a young roustabout called Cricket. He'd been a clown before the mutations started, but since Ike and Gus and Elbert had all passed, and he still had two capable hands, he'd been drafted into the labor of setting up and tearing down the circus. "New Paris is only fifty miles away. We could've stopped there. Much more lively in New Paris."

"I hear they have penguins in their zoo," said Rosie the acrobat, dreamily. Most zoos weren't too terribly exciting to the people who traveled around with a lion, a tiger, and three bears, but none of them had ever seen a penguin before. "I hear they've got two of every kinda bird there ever was."

Claude the Hooper spit in the dirt. "Well, they alssssso have a permanent cccccircussss that runsssss *toutesssss lessss nuitsss*, sssssso the people there would not find ussss sssssso sssspecial," he  hissed with his forked tongue. "I got my sssssstart with them. How I wisssssh I could go back, but with thesssssse mutations, *alors*, I am sssssstuck with thissss curssssed sssssshow."

Nettie the Mermaid grabbed the bottle and drank like a fish. "I hate that these mutations have us all trapped in this freak show." If Anna hadn't

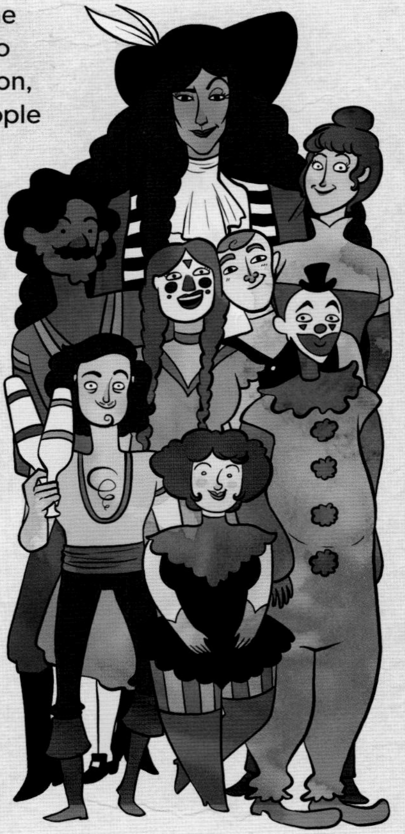

been off performing arcane rituals in the swamp that night, she might've cut in to say that Nettie's legs were not a mutation, and that Nettie was one of the few people in the circus who could go live among regular folks whenever she wished.

"It wouldn't be so bad if Tetanus wasn't such a dictator," grumbled Millie, who, as top clown, really didn't have all that much to complain about. "He's the one making all these terrible decisions. If I was running this outfit, we'd all have clear skin and a million dollars."

"Tetanus is the worst ringmaster ever," declared Cricket.

Gideon stood up, his muscular tail rising up behind him, moonlight glinting off his green, scaly skin. "You shut your mouth, Cricket. You all shut your mouths. Jebediah is a genius and a saint, and he's more than you ingrates deserve." He took a long swig from his own bottle of whiskey, which he was not sharing with anyone except his girlfriend, Lillian. "Besides, there never was a worse-off crew than those poor souls in the Pirate Circus."

Most everyone gathered that night nodded and murmured in agreement, but Cricket piped up with, "What's the Pirate Circus?"

All eyes turned to him.

"Did your brain mutate into a rock, boy?" asked Archie, all six of his hands thrown skyward in disbelief. "All circus folk know about the Pirate Circus."

Lucy put a protective arm around the boy. "He only just joined up six months ago. A lot's been happening, and no one has told this story in ages."

"The story goes like this," Gideon began, gesturing dramatically at his audience. "A hundred years or so ago, there was a fleabag circus that traveled around the gulf islands on a ship instead of a train. And they were led by the horrible ringmaster Edwin Black."

"She was a ringmistress," Rosie interjected. "Edwina Gray was her name."

There was some debate about the gender of this circus leader, and after a quick vote, Edwina won by two, and Gideon continued his tale.

"She took them to the most horrible ports, full of angry people with no taste. She made them perform ten shows a night, and paid them in peanuts, actual peanuts. And if anyone complained, she would throw them to the sharks and let the towers watch."

"How horrible!" Cricket said.

"That's not even the worst of it!" Gideon replied. "So, one day, her whole crew got together in the night, a night much like this one, and they decide they've had enough. They grab Edwina and make her walk the plank, laughing and cheering and throwing peanuts after her as she sank into the drink. Now, no one knows for sure how she survived. Some say she gotlucky and there was a piece of driftwood nearby to grab onto."

"She was rescued by mermaids," Nettie said. "I know this because it was my grandmother. She told me all about it."

"Sssshe did not sssssurvive at all," Claude said. "Ssssssshe died in the water and became a ghossssst."

"*However* it went," Gideon cut in, annoyed at the distracting alterations to his story, "she was able to make her way to a small island, and she swore she would have revenge."

"She sold her soul to the Devil for a new ship, black as the deep ocean, with a crew of demons from the hottest pits of Hell," Millie said.

Gideon shook his head. "She bartered some jewelry for a new ship, and a crew of mean, mortal men, and she set sail looking for those who betrayed her. Now, with her gone, the circus elected a new leader, a clown called Toots. He had been her first mate, and the one to lead the rebellion against her."

"He could juggle like a dream, even though he had two hooks for hands," said Lucy.

"Now, at first it seems like everything in the circus was gonna be peaches and cream with Toots in charge," Gideon continued. "They sailed around the islands, even made a few stops along the mainland, playing shows with decent attendance and enough ticket sales to restock the galley and put a few pennies in everyone's pockets. But then, like everything on the sea, the winds began to change, and the tides began to turn."

"What happened?" asked Cricket, taking a swig of whiskey, imagining himself drinking grog.

Gideon whistled. "Well, after a while, everywhere they went, they found a show had just passed through the night before, and no one had any interest or money for another show so soon. No matter how talented the barker insisted they were, you can't get blood from a stone or money from an empty pocket. And that was Edwina's first revenge. She didn't take her new crew straight to her old outfit with swords drawn. Wherever they would go,  she would find out and get there one day faster. Like a cat, she would play with her prey first."

"That Edwina wassssss an absssssolute terror."

"For weeks this went on, and everything began to crumble. The pantry had nothing but hard old crackers, and the grog got watered down so much that it was just water. The crew was at each others' throats, sniping and bickering without end. Every last penny gone. They started talking about how much they missed Edwina, how she wasn't the best, but too much work was better than no work, a little bit of money and food better than broke and starving. They started thinking about sending Toots off the plank. If only they could have Edwina back, they lament.

"And then, one foggy night, the full moon hazy through the thick clouds, Edwina appeared as if they'd conjured her spirit," Gideon said, getting to the meat of his tale. His girlfriend, Lilian, knew just how bad things could get under the light of a full moon, how blood could whip magic into a destructive maelstrom when the lunar cycle was at its peak, how she had plans for the next full moon... but she was maintaining her sweet and innocent facade, so she just leaned back and drank her boyfriend's whiskey, pretending to know nothing while he continued.

"At first, they were excited to see her, giddy and relieved that not only was she back to make the circus good again, and they didn't have to have her death on their conscience anymore. They all forgot why they were so mad at her before. Everyone except Toots, who had led the mutiny to steal her circus, now nestled asleep in her bed.

"Edwina's new crew sneak aboard and begin the siege with guns and swords, looking for the usurper. Toots hears all the ruckus and tries hiding in the wardrobe, but Edwina finds him and drags him out in front of everyone. This is when she reveals what she has been doing for the previous few weeks. Toots gets angry at first, before he sees just how outnumbered they are, and his subsequent apology falls

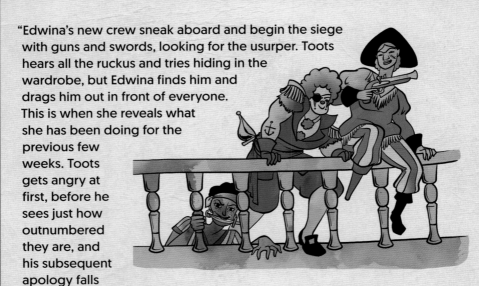

on deaf ears. The circus once again sees their leader sink down into the black water, this time with a bullet in his head.

"One by one, Edwina asks the members of her old crew to join her or die. They all say they'll join her, but she just laughs and tosses them overboard anyway, and burns the old ship before setting sail with her new crew. Only one person lived to tell the tale, and he never set foot on a boat or performed ever again."

"Some say that on nights when the moon is full, you might see her ship sailing around the islands, seeking out victims to drag back to their home in Hell," Millie said.

Gideon smacked his forehead in exasperation. "They weren't magic, Millie. Just mean old sumbitches who died decades ago and can't come back to haunt anybody because ghosts aren't real. The moral of this story is that mutiny only makes things worse, as we saw the last time someone attempted a coup in this circus."

"The moral is that y'all should be thankful I only sent Alva and the twins packing, with their lives intact." Jebediah Tetanus stepped out from the shadow of the train's caboose, looking much taller than his 5'4" stature, his third eye bloodshot from sleepiness and anger. He was fully dressed, despite the late hour, a ringmaster taking charge of his show. "The audacity of y'all to set up camp beneath my window at this godforsaken hour just to bite the hand that feeds you. Get back to your beds, all of you, before I decide to march on up to the front of this train and drive it away, and you can live in the woods for all I care."

The circus folk sheepishly slunk back to their beds, grateful to be alive, but still very grumpy. The heat was still hot, the air still unbearably sticky, but a toast in the belly and a story in the ears can do a lot to make things easier.

the end.

Megan Rose Gedris broke into comics with YU+ME: dream, a surreal lesbian romance series that was the recipient of Prism Comics' Queer Press Grant. Their short story "TransPlant" was nominated for an Eisner Award. Their comics have appeared in a dozen different publications, as well as several self-published books funded through very successful kickstarter campaigns. Their work focuses on genre fiction starring women and queer people, with lots of humor. They enjoy performing, designing textiles, and playing music. They live in Chicago.

See more of their work at rosalarian.com

Read more from Oni Press!

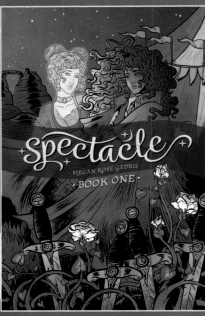

SPECTACLE BOOK ONE
By Megan Rose Gedris
The journey begins here!

Read ongoing updates at
spectaclecomic.com

If you liked *Spectacle*, check out these other Oni Press books:

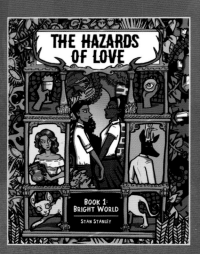

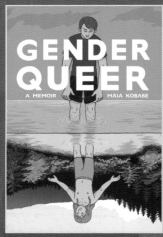

MOONCAKES
By Wendy Xu & Suzanne Walker
*A story of love and demons,
family and witchcraft.*

THE HAZARDS OF LOVE
By Stan Stanley
*"A noir fantasy—part adventure, part
love story, all the way spectacularly
creepy."* - Kirkus [starred review]

GENDER QUEER: A MEMOIR
By Maia Kobabe
*A useful and touching guide
on gender identity*